Titanian Chronicles
~Journey of Destiny~
Book 1

Leisl Kaberry

Cover-Art by Diogo Lando
Illustrated by Kristen Caruana

Acknowledgements

Writing a book, especially your first one, is a long and tiresome process that is bigger than just one person. Therefore I would like to take this opportunity to thank my family and friends who have been on this journey with me, encouraging and inspiring my efforts.

In particular there are a few people who I would like to mention that have given me extra support along the way in varying degrees. First of all I would like to thank my brother-in-law, Graeme for being my reader at the very beginning and giving me the boost of encouragement that I needed to push on. I would also like to thank my nephew Kyle, my first full book reader. It thrilled me to see him connect with the characters and become involved in the plot. Thanks to Melissa Nakaya and my sister-in-law, Tara for giving me great feedback about the book in the stage that it was in. Thank you to Sharon Delaportas who gave me the knowhow to expand the world of Titania and really bring it to life on paper. Thank you to Matthew Goslin who has acted as a story advisor to me over the past year and given me great advice in the realms of fantasy. A special thanks also to Dania Margerison and my mother-in-law Jill who have helped in the editing of the book (which was no small effort) and to L.M.Wilson who not only edited but really pushed me to make this story all that it could be and more. A big THANK YOU Lina Marl who also helped in the editing as well as photographing the pieces of art and to author Frederick Lee Brooke for doing a last minute fine comb for typos and anything else problematic. Thanks to 'my' artist Kristen for her fantastic work on all the art. Being able to take what is in my head and recreate it as an image on paper is a great skill. Finally, thanks to my wonderful sister Sheree who has become my number one fan and confidant, to my Mum and Dad who nurtured my sense of imagination and to my loving and supportive husband, Leonard who has put up with me through this process and constantly pushes me to succeed.

For James, Bethany, Jessi and Coder,
who enrich and enliven my imagination daily.

Prologue

The sound of horse hooves pummelling the hard wet ground resonated against the rock face of the bluff that overlooked a long winding road on the bank's edge of Fraida.

A man dressed all in black with a long scar on the left side of his face rode with great speed and determination. His wavy, shoulder-length blonde hair jetted back behind him as it flew on the breeze under a large rimmed black hat that had a single grey feather sticking out of it.

A little inn, nestled in amongst large leafy red trees overlooking the ocean bank, came into view as he rounded a corner. He pulled hard on the reins, slowing his horse to a trot as he neared the entrance.

Climbing down from his steed and jumping hard onto the muddied ground, he turned around and gave the horse a hard slap on the backside. The horse whinnied and rode away in the direction they had been heading.

The man in black turned around and sauntered up the wooden steps to the front of the rundown inn, then opening the heavy wooden door he walked inside leaving a careless trail of mud as he trod. Choosing one of the many empty round tables to sit at, he took his hat off and placed it on the table then removed his long black coat and slung it over the chair in front of him. Scanning the room for signs of life, he gave a loud impatient cough.

A little balding man in an apron and dark blue shirt appeared from a room just beyond the plain wooden bar.

Journey of Destiny

'Ahhh Master Nagrin, you're here at last, we expected you yesterday... did you run into a little trouble?' the man asked in a joyful manner that made the dark man's skin crawl.

'No trouble, I just had to find myself a horse,' Nagrin mumbled in a low disinterested tone as he took off his heavy black gloves, 'then of course I had to lose some troops on my tail.'

'What was that Master?'

'Never mind,' the man in black said with indifference waving his gloves with importance at the man, 'how are our plans coming together?'

'Good, good... I managed to get you a carriage as requested. Then there are three hooded wagons and a large open wagon that should be big enough for your purposes...'

'Excellent, and the trolls?' Nagrin said with a half smile, sitting down in the wooden chair next to the one holding his coat and kicking his booted feet up onto the table.

'Oh the trolls were no problem, they are eager to help Moorlan in his cause, they fought for his father, you know.'

'Yes,' Nagrin said rubbing his scar absently.

'And I have secured a dozen trolls to go with you in the wagons as henchmen,' the jolly man stated with emphasis.

'Good. You have done well,' Nagrin said, leaning back into his chair. 'What about the purchasing of new establishments?'

The small man looked a little uneasy. 'At this stage we have secured two taverns and an inn. I'm afraid people have been none too interested in selling their establishments.'

'Well I suppose we will just have to start taking the ones we want then,' Nagrin commented then added with a wry smile, 'people do make things hard for themselves.'

'Yes Master.'

Nagrin scanned the room of the tired old inn in thought. The walls needed painting, pictures were hung in a haphazard manner around the room and floorboards were lifting up in places.

'What does a man have to do to be offered a drink?' he said with scorn.

'Yes Master...' the little man said bowing in apology, then clapping his hands together called out toward the bar, 'Sarvina! A drink for our guest.'

A young woman dashed from the room behind the bar holding a round silver tray with a tankard on it. She swept into the room and set the drink down in front of Nagrin. She gave him a shy smile.

3

Nagrin watched her in admiration as she floated around the room. Her golden curls that fell just below her chin and her tall sleek body that glowed in a long flowing blue dress added some colour to the drab furnishings.

The balding man sensing Nagrin's interest attempted to distract his thoughts.

'Who will Moorlan get to work in these establishments when they are set up?'

'Slave girls,' Nagrin said with a little smirk as he took a sip from the tankard of brew, 'the finest girls that I can find, only the best for Lord Moorlan.'

'Of course master, but how do you plan to collect these girls?' he asked. 'I mean, they may be unwilling to go with you.'

'Well of course they will be unwilling. I will be taking them from their homes and families where they are free and have happy lives. No girl in her right mind will want to come but nonetheless I will take whom I please and they will become slaves, owned by Lord Moorlan himself, whether they like it or not... they will have no choice in the matter,' he replied with a sly snarl, '...let them try to make war with me, HA! I would welcome it!'

'So you will search towns then...?'

'And fields, and woodland areas and anywhere else I see fit,' he said eyeing out the young waitress again, '...in fact, I have already found my first prospect.'

The man looked in horror at the girl who was busy wiping tables.

'Master, you can't be meaning Sarvina!' he said, clasping and unclasping his hands as he trembled. 'She is no slave, she is my daughter.'

'How many fathers do you think will plead to me with that same story? Would you have me take pity on all of them?'

'No master but... but she is the only child we have left! Her mother and I lost our other children during the Great War,' the little man said backing up against the wall.

'Are you trying to tell me that the Great War was a mistake on the part of King Ravash?' Nagrin remarked in pointed accusation.

'Oh, no, no, no, no, no, no... nothing like that.'

'Good,' Nagrin nodded taking another mouthful of brew from the clay tankard, 'grab your things girl, you will be coming with me.'

The girl looked to her father in fear, her eyes pleading with him to save her.

The little man seeing his daughter's distress gained some courage and stood up straight pointing his chin out.

'Now, Master I must interject... I have done all that you asked of me, all of it! You promised in return for my obedience that you would leave my property alone and you would let me continue on as before. You cannot take my daughter!'

Nagrin looked at the man with careless nonchalance. Then he seized a small knife that was tucked into a leather holder bound to his thigh and thrust it at the heated little man.

The knife hit between his left side and arm slicing into his dirty blue shirt while securing him to the wall he leaned against. The man shook in fear and the girl let out a silent cry of shock and panic.

Nagrin arose from where he was seated and strode toward the man. Collecting his knife, he swept it up against the man's neck and held it close while he spoke with a hushed voice into his ear.

'This is how it's going to play out... I am going to take your daughter and you are going to go on here in this inn, serving me as I see fit. If you defy me, I will slit your throat here and now, take your daughter AND establishment and leave your wife a widow. What do you say to that little man?'

The man looked up at Nagrin with a pained expression on his face, a single tear falling from his eye.

'Ye..ssss,' the man stammered, fearing the knife at his throat.

Nagrin pulled away from the man and slipped his knife back into the leather pouch. 'Girl, get your stuff together, this is your last chance to save your father.'

The man fell to the floor as his legs gave way beneath him. The girl ran to him with concern and tried to help him up.

'Sarvina, don't you worry about me... just do what Nagrin tells you and you will be fine... you hear me? No one is going to hurt you if you do what you are told,' the man said looking her straight in the eyes, 'now go and get your things.'

The girl looked at her father with sadness and kissed him on the forehead before running out the door.

Nagrin looked at the pathetic man laying on the floor and watched as he raised himself back onto his feet.

'Your daughter doesn't talk much does she? A fine quality in a woman...' he said, drinking the last of the brew left on the table.

'Master, there is something you must know about Sarvina,' the man said with sadness, 'she does not speak, at all.'

Nagrin raised his eyebrows as he put his hands, finger by finger, back into his gloves, 'Like I said... a fine quality.'

'Master... I tell you this because I don't wish for you to misunderstand when you speak to her and she does not reply... it will not be because she is defiant but simply because she can't,' the little man stated, wringing his hands.

'Don't worry, I will take excellent care of her,' Nagrin responded with a laugh as he placed his hat upon his head and picked up his coat. 'Now, how about you show me where these wagons are.'

The little man bowed his head. He did not feel at all confident that Nagrin would look after his daughter. He sighed in defeat and stated with a simple breath, 'This way.'

Chapter

I

Afeclin sat in a wooden rowboat looking out toward the coast of Marrapassa. The woods were thick with untouched trees making it hard to see very far inside.

He was sure he had made it past the elvin borders of Tebelligan without having been seen. He had been careful to leave under the cover of the morning mist so that he would not attract attention from the coast guard high in his tower. He had wanted to keep his leaving a secret. Even though Tebelligan City was built beside the ocean, fishing was left for the farming and fishing communities in the west of Tebelligan. Therefore all boats in the vicinity of the city's coast were treated as suspicious unless prior arrangement with the coast guard was made and Afeclin had made no such arrangement.

He now scanned the coastline in hopes that he might find the little town of his birth. He rowed closer to the shore to make a keener observation.

It should not be far now, he thought to himself as he rowed further on, heaving the paddles through the water with great effort and strain.

The tiny rowboat was just big enough to hold the tall human as he sat with his knees almost to his chest. Afeclin was used to things being a little too small for him. Growing up in an all elf kingdom, things were never quite his size.

Rounding a corner that jutted out from the coast a short distance, he put what little energy he had left into rowing on the still waters.

Once around the corner, he stopped, putting down the wide paddles, to rest for a moment before continuing on.

Hunched over, he let his aching muscles relax as he dropped his head feeling immense fatigue. When he lifted his head again he was surprised and relieved by what he saw.

Just beyond the calm beach were the remnants of a little village nestled in a small valley, which was surrounded by thick vegetation.

Afeclin paddled to the shore with renewed excitement and allowed the boat to slide up on the bank. He jumped out onto the wet sand and pulled the boat further up the beach out of the water.

The afternoon was hot and sunny and the sweat poured from him profusely. Mopping his brow with his shirtsleeve, he began to explore the town.

It was a poor but humble village. Built from the timber cut down from the valley and fortified with the clay found in the ground, the crudely erected cottages were small and boxy.

The little nameless town that was hidden away from the rest of the world was now nothing more than a graveyard.

He wandered around the wide gravel streets that were more an expanse between the houses than designed roads. The place was quiet and lifeless, but not peacefully so. There was not a breeze to be felt in the valley and not a sound to be heard anywhere in the sky or on the ground. The only sounds Afeclin could hear were those he made himself as he shuffled his long black boots through the gravel.

Afeclin undid the lace on the front of his off-white shirt and rolled up his sleeves attempting to cool himself a little.

He felt an intense heat, which was strange, even for time of year. The hot season brought a lot of strong heat and sudden rainstorms, but this place had a different kind of hotness.

It is so hot here, it's as if the fire still rages.

Traipsing from one cottage to the next, Afeclin examined the interior of each house with due respect.

The insides were empty. What little furniture once filled them had been incinerated under extreme heat. The wooden floors had also disappeared leaving a hole through to the ground.

It was sad to see the ashen walls of the black, soot-stained buildings that crumbled with decay and ruin.

While the walls still stood, to some extent due to the clay that had rendered and protected them, the rooves had been completely consumed when the fires raged.

Afeclin stopped still in the middle of the village patting his short chin hair in thought.

It seemed such an out of the way place. It was deep within the Woods of Devan just beyond the border of Tebelligan, hidden away.

Why should anyone attack it? What purpose did it serve?

It didn't make the least bit of sense to him. Whether as a tactical manoeuvre during the war or as some kind of random attack at the end, it seemed nonsensical. The villagers were mere peasants, ignorant of the bloodshed going on around them and weaponless, unable to fight. *Why attack them?*

He closed his eyes trying hard to understand.

When he opened them again, his eyes fell upon a small humble abode on the edge of the village close to a steep incline. There was something unusual about it, something that drew his attention to it.

As he took steps toward the little cottage, he noticed that unlike the other houses, this one did not seem to be burned in its entirety. There was a section in the middle of the house that was completely unaffected by the fire. The walls and even the roof were still intact.

Afeclin walked with nervousness to the entry of the cottage, not sure about how he was going to feel. He held his breath as he passed over the threshold.

The inside of the cottage was somewhat dark compared to the others he had seen. Even though daylight streamed through the missing sections of roof, the undamaged thatched area darkened the cottage significantly.

A section of floor was also still intact and it held the infamous cradle that Afeclin had heard about from his adoptee father, the Elf King of Tebelligan.

A little cradle was the only piece of furniture left in the building.

Afeclin examined the crib closely. The finely carved bed was made of strong bankoi wood and apart from being a little dirty and dusty, the cradle seemed to be in as good of a condition as it ever had been.

So this is where they found me.

Afeclin touched the cradle delicately with one finger.

All of a sudden he fell backward onto the floor as an image of the fire burst into his mind.

He had seen a horrified face that screamed amongst red hot flames.

Afeclin looked with cautiousness around the room. There was nothing there and all was still as before.

He stared at the fine piece of woodwork suspiciously.

It is the crib.

He touched the cradle again with more force and held tight to the sides. This time an image came into his mind and stayed there corrupting his thoughts and hurting his brain. Despite the pain he felt, he did not lift his hands.

He saw a woman's face of ashen white. She was screaming in terror. A man of a tall large stature had his arms wrapped around the hysterical woman trying to pull her away from the blazing fire that was surrounding them. The woman tried in desperation to reach out for something on the other side of the flames and the man was doing all he could to stop her.

Through the thick glass window, many other people could be seen running about and screaming. There were some that tried to run buckets of water from the beach to their house but to no avail. One by one the people outside were hit by burning embers or what looked like fireballs aimed at them and they were killed, smothered to death in murderous flames.

Inside the house the man tried in vain to smash the window with his elbow. The thick glass would not be broken and with his elbow bleeding and torn he started to give in to the smoke that had engulfed the house and was beginning to choke his lungs.

There was a cry from a baby and the woman dashed through the fire to try and get to him. At the same time her long flowing dress was caught by the blaze and she found herself being consumed by the flames. Her long golden tresses were burnt to her scalp. She could do nothing to help her crying son in his crib.

There was a last glance before she burned to death. She had a look of relief on her face as she realised the baby was safe from harm.

No smoke, no burning embers or flames touched the child. He seemed to be protected by an eerie blue energy force that emanated from a rock that had been hung above his cradle.

The man mourned only a brief moment over his lost love. He fell to the floor having been strangled to death by the thick smoke and then he too was devoured by the fire.

Afeclin ripped himself away from the crib, his hands were shaking and his legs felt weak and unstable. He felt the need to sit down and he did so, quavering upon what was left of the timber flooring. Thoughts exploded through his mind as he tried to come to grips with the event he had just witnessed.

My mother died trying to save me.

Tears welled in his eyes. He tried to pull back the emotion he was feeling.

Why? Why destroy such poor innocent people?

The scene kept playing over and over in his head and before long he was crying with convulsions upon the ground.

It doesn't make sense, what kind of people would do such a thing?

The raging fires had killed everyone in that quiet, out of the way village except for one lonely survivor, a baby in a cradle… himself.

They didn't even stand a chance, he whimpered into his long bony hands. *They had nothing of value. They were not any kind of threat and they were out of the way… so why bother with them?*

Afeclin could not get his head around the attack. The more he thought about it the more puzzled he became and before long he was no longer crying but sitting on his knees in the dirt trying to figure it out.

They were hit with balls of fire. What kind of weapon was that?

The only people Afeclin knew that could produce fireballs were wizards. *But could a wizard have done this?* The more he thought it out the more probable it seemed; yet he was still unable to understand why anyone would do such a thing.

He got to his feet, sweeping his fingers through his long, black, sweat-soaked hair.

He was determined more than ever to leave Tebelligan and follow his desire to become a wizard. He knew he had a gift but he had to learn how to use it properly and grow it to its full potential.

I was protected that day. Maybe it was for a special purpose.

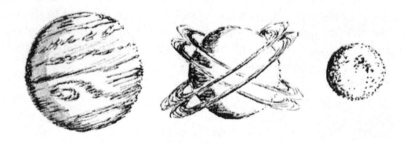

Chapter

II

Two of the three moons of Titania glistened in the night sky. Glendell, the blue moon, which was the closest of the three, looked particularly near this warm summer evening, so near in fact that it felt as if all you needed to do was to sail a boat to the end of the world and you could reach out and touch it. It was a well-known legend that the blue moon of Titania crept closer and closer to the planet's atmosphere and would have an eventual collision, thus being the end of the world. Whilst many people ignored these myths as the ranting of errant fools, the Druids of old had been preparing for it since the dawn of time.

This particular night, Glendell was at her fullest and brightest being that it was the new moon, which signified the coming of the new year. The stars that surrounded her mass twinkled in blues, greens and whites as if worshipping the ancient celestial orb.

The green moon, Astoth could be seen in the distance with its four rings circling it, two circling on one side and two circling on the other, forming an X in the sky. Astoth was said to be the moon of the waters and depending on her positioning in the sky on any given night, and according to the elves, "her mood", it caused the tide to either roll like thunder or be as still and calm as ice.

Sataya, the silver moon and smallest of the three was said to be the place the Gods of Titania dwelt. When she was full and shining with brightness over Tebelligan, it was said the Gods were well pleased but when she was in her last quarter or absent from the night sky, it was said that the Gods were angry and thus absent from Titania.

Wolflang sat at the edge of the water staring into the blue-lit sea, gathering his thoughts. This was his favourite spot. It was under diroriam trees with their large, dark-green feathered leaves and trunks that twisted in and out of each other, such that he was hidden from the path where no one could see him. As an elfling, when he was in trouble, he came to this spot to hide. Now that he was older, Wolflang used it as a place for reflection as he often found peace in the rippling water current and illuminating moons.

On this summer night, crickets chirped in the trees and a light breeze bounced off the water, adding a coolness to the evening that provided a nice relief from the heat of the day.

Wolflang dipped a grimy toe into the blue water and then kicking his leg straight, watched as an arch of water sprang forward, then sprayed back over his body as the wind carried it. Feeling the freshness of the water was exhilarating and he let his legs drop over the rock on which he was seated, into the tranquil water.

Letting his body slump over, Wolflang tugged hard at his pointy ears. He was anxious and frustrated at the important decision he needed to make.

'What to do, what to do?' he muttered out loud as if speaking to his reflection in the water. 'Do I marry Lenna now, settle down and have a few elflings of my own or do I wait a few years, first allowing myself to travel the world and have some adventure?' Wolflang let out a little sigh, *but would she wait?*

It had been the young elf's dream for as long as he could remember to one day travel across Titania and witness how the world beyond Tebelligan's border lived. He had heard stories from his great uncle of magnificent cities that never slept and views from mountains that bring you closer to the Gods. He had heard tales of the lands of snow and ice and delighted in his great uncle's embellishments and fantasies of lands under the ocean and cities in the sky.

It was not in the elves' culture to concern themselves with adventuring beyond their own land, they were a race that found peace in their separation from the outside world. However, journeying beyond the elvin borders was something that Wolflang longed for with all his heart.

Then there was Lenna, a beautiful elf maiden who had also captured his heart. She had been his friend and companion for many years and there was little doubt in Wolflang's mind as to where the relationship was headed. Being wed was the one thing Lenna spoke in length about since their coming of age ceremonies, in which the elves gave an official welcome to the younger folk as full grown, matured people. Being committed to stay in Tebelligan forever though was something that frightened Wolflang.

As Wolflang sighed he bowed his head and his long mousey hair fell forward covering his round, tan face. Bending over the edge he could see his rippled reflection, between his legs, as the moon lit up the water. He shuffled his hair away from his emerald green eyes and cupping the cool water in his small slender hands, he splashed it on his face and behind his neck.

Wolflang heard a splashing sound on the water, a constant drumming that was accompanied by a series of small ripples sweeping into the shore. He looked up and down the coast to see where the sound was coming from. At first he could not see a thing in the darkness beyond the moonlit water. He strained his eyes to follow the sound and as he focused intently on the dark sea a figure materialised out of the shadows.

'Who's there?' Wolflang demanded with an apprehensive swallow.

The drumming sound continued as it came closer and closer.

'Who's there?' Wolflang called again this time with more volume.

'Wolflang it's me,' a voice called out from the small boat that continued to make its way nearer to the shore.

'Afeclin?'

The tall muscular human was the elf's closest friend and confidant. The two had become acquainted at a young age and had remained good friends ever since. As the years had gone on, however, they had seen less and less of each other. Wolflang had taken up a lot of his time with Lenna and Afeclin had spent much of his time studying books of old sorcery and practising his talent for magic.

Afeclin's gift had been something that had bothered the elf and it had formed a slight wedge between them in later years. Wolflang had seen his friend come to be so driven by his ability that he had become somewhat of a recluse, spending most of his time working on and building up his skills. The elf had often encouraged his friend to come out of his sanctuary and spend time with him and Lenna but Afeclin made excuses as to why he just couldn't leave what he was doing.

Afeclin made it to the shore and the two pulled the boat up onto the beach together.

Afeclin looked a mess. His shirt was untucked, undone and soaked in sweat. The sleeves had been rolled up to the tops of his arms and his black pant legs were dirty. His long hair that he kept back in a neat ponytail was now tangled and all over his face. Not only did his

Titanian Chronicles

clothes and hair look unkempt but also Afeclin himself seemed less composed than normal. There was a sadness or despair in his eyes and an overall enervation in his body.

'Where have you been?' Wolflang asked with concern for his friend. 'I have been looking for you all over, nobody has seen you for days.'

Afeclin sat down upon a large grey rock that protruded out of the shallow water.

'I made my way to the village I was found in,' he said as he scooped up handfuls of water and splashed it on his face.

'You did?!' Wolflang exclaimed with surprise. 'Why didn't you tell me you were going to go there? I would have come with you.'

'It was something I needed to do by myself, I needed to see it alone.'

Wolflang hung his head with understanding.

'Did you find it? The place you were found I mean?'

Afeclin nodded, 'Not only that but... I saw it.'

'The blue rock, you mean, that was hung above your crib?'

'No it wasn't there,' said Afeclin trying to find the right words, 'I saw what happened to my people.'

Wolflang was confused. He sat back down upon the rock and tried to follow Afeclin's story.

'What do you mean?'

'When I put my hands upon my crib, a vision flooded my mind. I saw my parents and I saw the fire.'

'You mean the memory returned to you?'

'No, it was different... I could see myself...'

'Well, that's normal. Often when you think back about things that have happened you see yourself in the memory,' suggested Wolflang.

'That is true,' said Afeclin, 'but this was different. I saw in perfect clarity everything that had happened, even things that I could not have seen or noticed as a small child... I watched...' Afeclin stopped. He seemed choked up and unable to continue.

Fighting back the emotion he seemed to be feeling, Afeclin held his head high, '...I watched them burn to death.'

Wolflang felt sad for his friend but didn't know what to say.

'That would be difficult to witness,' he mumbled.

Afeclin nodded, 'The whole thing got me thinking though and I now more than ever need to leave Tebelligan.'

'You are still planning to seek out the wizard Zall... Zall...'

'Zallucien.'

'Yes. Are you going to seek him out to teach you?'

15

'Yes, I feel I must,' answered Afeclin with more clarity, 'he is the only one I know of that can teach me what I need to learn. I have come as far as I can on my own.'

'You are still determined to become a wizard then.'

Afeclin nodded. 'Somehow it is in me and I know now it is something I must do.'

In the distance they could hear the sound of celebrating in the nearby centre square.

The elves of Tebelligan rejoiced in celebrating the new moon. Being a superstitious race they believed it good tidings to be able to start the year anew. Celebrations would last for days and nights without end during which time the elves drank, sang and made merry until it was over. Following the festivities there was a peace throughout the city as everyone returned home to sleep.

It was common for young elves not to see the rest of their family, as they would often keep company with their friends for the duration.

This year's new moon signified the start of the rest of their lives. Each decision they made now was vital and a stepping-stone to their future.

'Well I envy you. I wish it would be that easy for me to follow my dreams.'

'Your dreams… you are not referring to Lenna?'

'I do love Lenna but there is a big part of me that longs to leave this place and travel for a time before I settle down with a family,' said Wolflang with anguish, 'is that so wrong?'

Afeclin appeared to be annoyed as he stroked the hair on his chin.

'It is not wrong to follow your dreams,' he said with frown, his voice almost bitter but controlled, 'but do not forget there is an elf maiden who has her heart set on being wed to you and it would be unfair on her if you do not discuss with her what you want to do.'

Wolflang hung his head in shame, 'It's just not that easy… she constantly talks about our future together and I just don't want to let her down… although I know that I must eventually.'

Afeclin shook his head, 'I think you are crazy.'

'What do you mean by that?'

'I mean, I would choose Lenna over adventuring out of Tebelligan,' he bit.

Wolflang stared at Afeclin in confusion. The human looked bedraggled and tired. He did not appear to be himself. Wolflang let out a laugh.

'No you wouldn't, she's an elf… it would be strange.'

Afeclin bowed his head with a despondent nod.

'I meant if I were you… of course.'

16

All of a sudden they were interrupted by a loud crack in the distance followed by the sky lit with an array of colour. The New Moon sky display exploded to life over the water and the two friends sat in quiet together watching the spectacle while behind them, just inside the city gates, screams of joy and wonderment could be heard from the celebrating elves.

Small silver metal balls that were attached to each other were propelled high into the night sky. As they spun about and dropped they would hit and explode on impact. The gas that was released from the silver balls changed colour as it came into contact with the planet's atmosphere and caused patterns to splash and paint the firmament with contrast against the large new moon that glowed alongside the exhibition.

When the last explosive spheroid had burst, Afeclin let out a sigh and stood up. 'It is just my opinion of course but I think you have all that you could ever want or need right here. The world outside of Tebelligan is strange and foreign to us and neither of us really know what dangers exist out there. We have been so sheltered by our kingdom that we have no idea whether there is a war on or not. We have no idea who we can trust and we do not know what the people out there think of us elves... well you.'

Afeclin had lived all his life with the elves that in some ways, he was one. He had never met another human before and the only way he knew how to live was the elvin way. It was not all that strange that he thought of himself as one. Perhaps not so ridiculous that he would consider an elf for a bride after all.

'I've made my decision, Afeclin,' said Wolflang with conviction, 'I understand what you are saying... perhaps I don't see what I have right in front of me... but I also don't think I will ever appreciate it until I leave Tebelligan and find out for myself.'

Afeclin nodded his head.

'I will accompany you to find your wizard. You could use a good bowman at your side. My dear friend I will see you safely to your destination and then I will continue on to Rengal. It is the one city I have always longed to visit.'

Wolflang was very good with the elvish bow and arrow and had become quite the hunter, like his father.

'Well, if that is what you want, I guess it would be nice to have company on this journey.'

'When will we leave?' Wolflang asked, finding it difficult to conceal his excitement.

'The day after tomorrow, when everyone has returned to their home. This way there will be less fuss. Only our families need know of our departure.'

'And of course Lenna,' Wolflang frowned then added in jest, 'perhaps I could write her a letter?'

'Yeah, that would assure her of feeling the least pain,' said Afeclin with a wry smile.

The two began to walk back to the main streets of the city where all the noise and excitement was coming from. This would be their last new moon celebrated here among their friends for a while, perhaps forever for Afeclin, so they decided to enjoy it.

When they reached the main street, Lenna came running up to them, her long crimson red hair flowing behind her. She was a very beautiful looking elf with big dark brown eyes, long eyelashes and skinny lips that supported a stunning smile. She was wearing an ox hide skirt that dropped just below her knees and a short top that matched with tassels covering her naked belly, which accentuated her slim figure.

The men watched her in admiration.

'Don't say a word about this... please,' Wolflang whispered to his friend before Lenna was close enough to hear.

Before Afeclin could reply, Lenna had bounded into them, greeting both of them with a big warm hug.

'Where have you two been? I've been looking everywhere for you! Did you see the sky show? I think it was better than last year, don't you?' she paused as if noticing Afeclin for the first time. 'What in Titania happened to you?'

'Oh nothing really,' he answered combing his fingers through his knotted hair, 'it's a new look. What do you think?'

Lenna looked the human up and down with a sly smile, 'Oh do be serious Afeclin, you look as if you were shipwrecked.'

She giggled as she gave him a teasing shove to his chest, 'Come on, the banquet is just beginning. We have to hurry if we want to sit at our favourite table by the fire.'

It was obvious to the men that she had already had a little elvish brew and although she wasn't quite drunk her tan cheeks were flushed and she talked so fast she barely had time to take a breath.

'You two go ahead,' said Afeclin, 'I'm going to join my father this year.'

'Spoil sport,' Lenna teased as she put her skinny arm through Wolflang's and pulled him towards the banquet tables.

'I'll see you later!' yelled Wolflang when they were some distance from Afeclin.

The two managed to reach their favourite spot by the fire just in time. Another happy couple had been edging their way towards the table but Lenna sat down first and declared in a loud voice the seat to be hers.

'How much have you had to drink, Lenna?'

'Ooh Wolfy, only a couple, I swear.' She took a deep breath then continued, 'Actually I think I'm just overly excited. The end of the year, the celebrations, but this new moon is the beginning of the rest of our lives together.'

She pulled herself closer to him and put her soft cheek on his shoulder as she sighed a deep, harmonious happy sigh.

Wolflang grabbed a chalice off the table and gulped down a mouthful of the thick brew. His heart was racing. *How can I tell her of my plans when she sits there happily planning out our future together?*

Wolflang watched Lenna as her face lit up with excitement over the endless possibilities they faced together.

Tomorrow, he thought to himself, *tomorrow I will break the news to her and possibly break her heart while I'm at it but as for tonight we will be merry.*

ॐ ॐ ॐ

Afeclin wandered through the crowded street lost in his own thoughts.

As he passed people, several elves nodded to him with respect while others paid little to no attention to him at all. Other races had not been allowed into Tebelligan since the human war so Afeclin was every bit a standout in the crowd. However, seeing the lanky human was not unusual to the elves.

Afeclin had never had any problem with the elves of Tebelligan. While his differences were obvious, he had been treated with respect by the elvin people and rather than seen as odd he was celebrated as special. This of course had a lot to do with the fact that his father was a king whom the elves revered.

The only elves who had ever given him trouble were the King's sons Alga and Garrad. The two brothers had always been envious of their father's undying affection for Afeclin and despised him for it. Therefore whenever their father was out of earshot, they teased and tormented Afeclin and refused to accept the human as kin.

Afeclin had never been willing to use his magical powers for practical jokes. He was much too serious about his craft. When it came to his elder brothers however, it was a different story. Alga and Garrad were so awful to him that he found himself unable to resist the temptation. He was able to play nasty tricks on them without them ever knowing that he was the culprit and therefore there was never any risk of further repercussions.

There was one time, after Afeclin's face had broken out in pimply blotches, that Garrad had teased him with unremitting candour. His father, Endorf had told him that it was just a growing up part of being human. Afeclin, upset as he was by his skin, concocted a spell, a potion that he managed to sneak into Garrad's tea. Within hours Garrad's own face had developed a serious case of elvish warts, the sort that grew big and round and had tiny hairs that rose out of them. They were awful looking and Garrad was horrified and embarrassed by them but he never mentioned another word about Afeclin's blotches after that. It also made Afeclin feel better about his own skin condition.

Another time Alga pushed Afeclin hard into a wall knowing full well that the taller human would not react. What Alga did not realise was that Afeclin *did* retaliate. He managed to cast a spell that caused Alga to walk into invisible walls. It created a lot of amusement and stir, as he looked very foolish when he would crash into what seemed like nothing at all. It drove Alga insane for the rest of that day.

While Endorf had tried to discourage Afeclin from using his magic to play practical jokes, he was understanding of Afeclin's plight and appreciated the fact that the young human did not do anything of genuine terror or with permanent effects. He instructed Afeclin that revenge did not bring about peace. In his simplicity the young human had explained that it was not so much revenge as it was teaching them a lesson.

His greatest power against his brothers was that they knew nothing about it. Afeclin had kept his magical ability a secret to all but a handful of his closest friends at the request of Endorf. As the King had said, 'You are already different enough as it is. Let's not give anyone a reason to fear you.'

He appreciated Endorf's concern for him and loved the King as a real father. Endorf had given Afeclin all the rights and privileges afforded to royalty and treated him every bit like one of his sons. As the only father he had ever known, Afeclin felt a sincere belonging to the King even if they did not look anything alike.

Since it was uncommon for elves to leave the kingdom, Afeclin was unsure whether Endorf would understand his need to visit the place of his birth. Therefore he had slipped away in the middle of the night during the first evening of the New Moon celebrations. Now he needed to explain to his father that he was going to leave Tebelligan for a long time, maybe even forever.

Seeing the town of his birth had hit him hard and had brought certain realisations to him.

There were also many thoughts and feelings he wished to express to his father, things he had never considered before but were now in the forefront of his mind. There were concerns that he had about the safety of Tebelligan after seeing the devastation of his birth town.

His father was a loving king. Afeclin knew that. He had done all that he could to prevent his people from ever having to fight in a war again, perhaps to the detriment of the elves who were untrained or out of practise in their fighting skills.

Tonight he hoped to have the opportunity to express himself to his father and while he knew that Endorf had always listened to him, this time he hoped for understanding.

Afeclin found his father at the royal table. He was drinking, laughing and enjoying the celebrations.

The table was filled with a wondrous array of foods. Roasted meats, cheeses of all kinds, cakes and treats, always made it an enticing spread. The smell that wafted through the air was spicy and delicious. One could almost taste the food without putting their lips to it. Elvish cooking was one thing he knew he would always miss and was sure there could not be anything as good in the rest of the world.

Endorf looked up rather surprised to see Afeclin standing beside him and greeted him in his cheerful manner.

'Ahh my son,' his merry voice boomed, 'are you going to join me this year?'

'Yes father, have you room for me?'

'But of course,' he said as he stood up and hollered at the people next to him, 'move on down and make room for my son, he is dining with us this year!'

Although Endorf wore kingly robes of deep purple velvet with golden trimmings that made him glow with wealth he was a humble king and was happy to sit and associate with any of the more commonplace elves. He trusted and loved them all as his friends and acted as one of them when occasion permitted.

Endorf's thinning hair was grey and his round old face was weathered, sporting a few whiskers here and there. He had a kind and wise smile that spoke volumes of his education and experience.

'What is with this look Afeclin, you are not your usual refined self? Is there anything wrong?' Endorf asked with concern.

'Father, I wish to speak to you after the feast,' whispered Afeclin, 'it is important.'

'Of course Afeclin,' he answered with affection 'we will sneak off after the New Moon's toast.'

Afeclin sat motionless at the royal table for a while watching the elvin folk eating and drinking and having a merry time as they did every new moon.

The main street square was alive with activity. Where market stalls once stood as the main centre for trade, large tables, littered with food, were now scattered about. This took up half the square. A dozen elves or more surrounded each table on long plank benches. In the centre of all the tables, a large fire was lit warming those that sat at the tables closest to it.

The royal table had a slight elevation above the rest and stood at the very edge of the circle in front of the city hall. From here Afeclin could see Wolflang and Lenna through the flickering flames of the fire. Lenna's face glowed from the heat and her red hair shone in the moonlight. She looked as sweet as buttermilk, and how happy she seemed. His heart raged in anger. *She wants Wolflang and he is just going to leave her... how I wish she wanted me.* Wolflang's words flooding back to him, all of a sudden, made him reconsider with bitterness. *But then I am human... it would be deemed strange.*

He had been in love with the radiant elf maiden from the very first time he had laid eyes on her as a child. They had been inseparable until a certain elf had burst into their lives and changed everything. Lenna did not take long to fall for the heroic Wolflang. While the three friends spent much of their childhood together, as they got older Afeclin had felt more and more like a third wheel and kept more to himself. He took his time up with more useful activities like practicing his craft.

Afeclin pushed his jealousy away and turned his attention to the other half of the centre square that was cluttered with elves dancing the elvish jig around a band who were playing music on a platform in the middle of the crowd. A couple of fiddlers stamped their feet in a merry jig. Their fingers lithely sped along the neck of their instruments drawing well crafted bows across the strings with great speed and skill. A young elf, holding a long wooden instrument with many pieces of flat metal attached to its arms, banged and shook the wood, creating a clattering of sound as another elf, playing a tuneful tin whistle, danced and excited the crowd.

On either side of the street, large stone buildings stood peering down on them. With long sloping clay tile rooves and arched windows in the stone, the buildings were old but well maintained. Circular windows were features under the eaves where the roof met at right angles. Sculpted patterns and carvings of great craftsmanship surrounded the windows in various designs, presenting Tebelligan nature. In the darkness they looked dull and a little eerie but in the light of day they were cheerful, boasting various coloured rooves, doors and carvings that beautified the city.

Both sides of the square and the streets beyond them were symmetrical. Therefore whatever building was built in one corner of the city square, the same design down to the last detail was built in all four corners, giving the city its very attractive, even look.

The palace, which stood on top of a small mountain, to the north of the centre square, loomed down upon the city like a monstrous vulture. The palace was the oldest building in the kingdom, and the only one that did not have a twin on the opposite side to keep the city perfectly symmetrical. Kings of old had discussed building another palace but considered it impractical.

The palace was in essence a large tower, which sprang forth into the sky from the centre of a hexagonal building with large arched entryways on each side.

Built of stone by master craftsmen, it had been rendered in clay which had patterns sculpted around windows and door frames, some of which stuck out as if growing out of the wall. These patterns again depicted the nature found in and around Tebelligan. Elongated stained glass windows wrapped around the main tower on the lower level and above these, plain arched windows wound around the building to the highest peak. At the very top of the palace tower stood a large brass bell which was used in ceremony and cases of threat.

Afeclin turned his attention back to the centre square. At each end of the square there was an old stone bridge. Beyond the bridge on the west side, the cobble street became a wide dirt road and followed on throughout Tebelligan passing many farms and villages. In due course it led to the small fishing towns on the country's coast.

Beyond the bridge on the east, the street became a less used smaller dirt track that led through the bankoi and tall traffita trees, out of the elvin kingdom and into the rest of the world.

Afeclin held his breath a moment and stared into the dark woods beyond the east bridge. Soon he would find himself riding that road, leaving the kingdom he grew up in at long last and entering a world he knew very little about.

'Afeclin, you're not eating! Is not the food at my table good enough for you?'

Endorf's booming voice made Afeclin jump, startling him from his thoughts.

Picking up a chalice of brew he toasted his father in silence. His father reciprocating the honour, smiled.

Wolflang sat looking into the dancing flames of the fire only half listening to Lenna.

She had spoken on and on about their future together, barely stopping for a breath. By now it was almost the new day and Endorf was just about to give his traditional speech for the New Year's Moon.

'My friends!' he spoke up in a loud voice beckoning for the band to stop playing, 'How happy it makes me to sit here and watch you all having a wonderful time. Why it reminds me of the momentous celebrations we had just after the human war. What wondrous times we live in and how great our blessings from the fair Goddess whose radiance shines bright over all Tebelligan on this night of nights.

We are at peace with our neighbouring countrymen; no matter what wars they may be fighting between each other we can find comfort in the fact that we will never again fight with or against them.

My youngest son, Afeclin who has chosen to sit with me, this his coming of age year, has honoured me. What a fine man he has become, I can't say that I have ever been prouder of any of my sons than I have of my human son.'

As Endorf spoke, Wolflang watched Afeclin's two older brothers sitting with their wives at their own tables. How angry and jealous they seemed at the moment.

Alga beat his fist on the table and cursed whilst Garrad's dark eyes stared with fierce resentment at Afeclin. Garrad then leant backward to the table behind and whispered something to his brother.

'So my friends, the time draws near the hour, let us raise our glasses and toast the new year in!' Endorf said beginning to count down. '10... 9... 8...'

As Endorf lifted his glass the crowd joined in whilst high above them an enormous crimson red balloon floated up into the sky.

'7... 6... 5... 4... 3... 2...' the crowd chanted.

'ONE!'

At that moment a loud bang was heard in the sky as an arrow pierced the balloon. Bits of silver paper and glitter-covered leaves fell upon them as if in slow motion, twinkling as they did so in the light of the moons.

The crowd swayed and sang elvish songs of times gone by and the road ahead.

As Wolflang sang he saw Afeclin and Endorf leave their table and disappear through the crowd. Seeing his friend leaving to discuss their plans with the King sent a surge of excitement running through his body. *It is really going to happen, we are really going to leave.*

As his eyes were returning to Lenna he spotted a man in the crowd still seated, glaring straight at him. The man's hooded face as far as Wolflang could tell was oddly human. Wolflang pulled Lenna to him and kissed her soft cheek.

'I'll be back in a moment,' he whispered into her ear.

Lenna nodded.

'Any longer than a moment and I'll come looking for you,' she giggled.

Wolflang began making his way to the hooded stranger being careful not to take his eyes off him. The man sat still, keeping his eyes fixed on Wolflang. *Who is this man and what is he doing here? Surely he hasn't been invited.* Wolflang was determined to find out, since the man seemed to be taking a keen interest in him. Just as he came to the stranger's table a couple of drunken elves collided into him.

'Sorry 'bout that,' the shorter one slurred.

'My fault,' Wolflang said to them in a dismissive manner, taking his eyes away from the stranger for the briefest moment.

When he looked back again he was surprised to see that the man had disappeared. All that was left behind was the chalice he had been drinking from. Wolflang picked up the empty vessel and looked around. There were elves on every side of him and the crowd was thick. He had no idea which way the man had gone.

'Did you see a man in a hood just now?' he asked a young elf now seated in the spot the stranger had been.

The elf lifted his head toward Wolflang with a strange expression on his face.

'Nobody wears hoods at this time of the year.'

'That is true,' said Wolflang, 'so you would notice if somebody was, yes?'

'Sure,' answered the boy, 'but nobody was, why would they? Are you drunk?'

Wolflang grew frustrated with the boy and replied with sharpness.

'No I'm not! There was a hooded man sitting right here just a moment ago. Are you sure you didn't see him?'

'I don't know what you're on about,' the young elf said in irritation, 'I've been sitting here the whole time 'cept when I stood up to sing but I would definitely notice a hooded man sitting next to me. In fact I would notice if there had been anybody sitting next to me, but there wasn't. You're either drunk or seeing things.'

The boy turned his attention toward the pretty elf maiden sitting on the other side of him.

Wolflang felt bewildered. He didn't feel drunk at all. *Was I seeing things?* He did think it strange that a human man could be sitting amongst them and nobody notice.

Two little arms wrapping themselves around him from behind interrupted his thoughts.

'I found you,' squealed Lenna squeezing him tight. 'What happened to coming back in a moment?'

Wolflang loosened Lenna's grip then turned around to face her.

'From our table, did you happen to notice a strange-looking man wearing a hood?'

Lenna thought for a moment, then giggled.

'Oh Wolfy, nobody wears a hood at this time of the year.'

Chapter

III

Endorf placed his wrinkled hand on Afeclin's shoulder.

'Shall we?' he asked with a grin.

Afeclin arose from the table his heart pounding. He could not believe just how nervous he was about speaking to his father.

Endorf opened the front door to the city hall and they entered the dark room.

As Afeclin was closing the door behind him, his father took down a lantern that was hanging on a hook in one corner. He lit it and then walked in silence to the end of the large room where there was another door. Afeclin hurried along after the smaller man.

Through this door there was a small passageway with many doors to other smaller rooms. These were closed but Afeclin was well acquainted with them. He had often been stuck there as a child waiting for his father to get out of a meeting and he had explored all the rooms to keep himself occupied, all of them except the door at the end of the corridor which had always been kept locked. He had figured it was just a storage cupboard or something like that since he had never seen anyone open it.

His father trotted straight past the other rooms and headed for the unused door. He retrieved a small key from a hidden pocket in his velvet robe, unlocked and walked through the mysterious door. He then turned around and beckoned for Afeclin to follow.

The young human obeyed with curiosity.

Behind the door, there was neither a cupboard nor a room but rather a dark, dank stairwell.

They crept down the stairs being careful not to miscalculate any steps. Soon they had reached the bottom. From what Afeclin could see, which wasn't very far, they appeared to be in some kind of secret passageway under the city.

There was a damp smell that was acrid, perhaps from animals that had found their way down into the dark and failed to find their way out again. It made breathing very difficult at first. Afeclin attempted to breathe through his mouth until he could adjust to the smell.

With the lantern's help they could see a couple of feet ahead of them. From what Afeclin could make out in the dark, cobwebs with large, hairy red spiders hung about all over the stone walls. Many webs made a messy spread from one wall to the other. In some instances he found he had to duck under the thick web to get through. Not being fond of any spider, Afeclin kept a careful, weary eye upon any he could see and cringed when he walked through any webs he hadn't seen.

Endorf, on the other hand being much smaller in stature than Afeclin, was able to stroll along, unaffected by the webs.

The two walked on without speaking and Afeclin began to grow anxious. Feeling like the passageway would go on forever, he was about to break the silence and ask his father where they were headed when they came to a dead end.

Endorf swept his hands over the rough stone as if looking for something.

'I know there is a latch here somewhere,' he muttered to himself.

All of a sudden there was a thud and the whole wall turned counterclockwise revealing a nice looking, well-lit room. Afeclin rubbed his eyes in the brightness of the lights while his father pushed the wall back into place.

Looking back at the wall he would never have guessed there was a well-concealed passageway behind it.

'Come on, we are only halfway there,' Endorf said marching out of the room and into another corridor.

'Father, where…?' Afeclin began but his father hushed him.

It wasn't until they were halfway down the long, dimly lit corridor that Afeclin realised where they were. The architecture of the rooms with the unique paintings hanging on the walls was very similar to the design of his own room in the palace. The candlelit chandelier in the centre of the hall, the granite finish on the walls and the opulent furniture spread about were characteristic of the palace design. From this he deduced that they must have been in one of the lower, underground levels of the palace where he had been forbidden to go.

They reached a lift and with the press of a button the doors opened and in they stepped, sitting down upon a finely carved wooden bench.

The lift itself was very old. On the walls and ceiling a mural had been painted depicting an imaginary city in the sky and dragons of many colours flying around it. Afeclin had always found this picture very interesting and relaxing to look at whilst ascending to the upper levels of the palace.

The ancient lift was powered by magic and was the only one in the kingdom. An elvin wizard named Orin who had been aiding the king of that time in the preparations for war, designed it for the palace many moon years ago. Orin had found it an exhausting task and a waste of valuable time each day to climb the hundreds of stairs to the King's chambers at the top of the palace. Therefore he designed a small compartment that was capable of lifting its occupants to any of the higher levels of the palace through a long shaft, in order to save time and energy. Whatever magical power he had used at that time did not seem to expire, so the old lift was still well used many moon years later.

'It took you awhile to figure out where we were,' Endorf said with a grin.

'I have not been to the lower levels of the palace, father,' Afeclin answered with respect, 'you forbade it.'

'Yes, well… unfortunately it's hard enough to get adults to keep secrets let alone energetic young boys,' Endorf responded with affection. 'As it is, the only elves that know about its existence are those that work in the below levels, keeping things clean, tidy and prepared, a couple of my most trustworthy officials who have been sworn to secrecy and now you.'

'Prepared for what? I do not understand. What is the secret? I mean apart from the passageway, it all seems like a bunch of unused rooms below the palace.'

'That is exactly what they are, a bunch of unused rooms below the palace,' he repeated, 'however they serve a purpose of vital importance.'

'How so? A hideaway?' Afeclin jeered.

'Somewhat yes,' Endorf smiled at Afeclin's confusion, 'you see, the lower three levels of the palace were built beneath the ground in the mountain, two are made up of suites like the one you saw just now and the third is a food storage and eating facility. If by chance we are ever attacked by outside forces, there is enough room for all the elves in the city to hide for years on end if need be until it is safe to return to the topside through the secret passageway we have just come from. The city could be flattened to a pile of dust and we would not be discovered by the enemy.'

Endorf had a proud grin on his face.

'So you do think that such an attack is possible?'

Endorf's smile fell from his lips as he turned to Afeclin with a grave look.

'I have done what I can to give the other races of Titania no reason to bother with us, but I am not such an old fool to think that others will not prize our land and want it for themselves. I fear that such a day is imminent. I feel very strongly that it is more of a question of when, than if.'

'I understand... I have been wondering about that myself, about protecting the elves from such an attack,' Afeclin began, trying to find the right words to say, 'my concern is... is it enough? I mean, what if they are found and invaded by an onslaught? The elves have not the skills anymore to protect themselves.'

Endorf looked quite surprised by Afeclin's comments but he gave a little laugh.

'Afeclin, you do worry. You always did. They will not be found beneath the ruins of the city. They will be well hidden from danger.'

'But father, why should the city fall at all? If the elves were taught to protect themselves, only the women and children need go into hiding until it is over,' Afeclin dared, 'the city could be protected too.'

The King nodded with kind understanding, 'I appreciate your sentiments Afeclin, this is our home... nobody wants to see it destroyed... but a kingdom we can rebuild... lives we cannot.' Endorf hung his head. 'War is not a pretty thing Afeclin. In the human war we lost a lot of good men and at the same time took many lives of beings... who were in any circumstance other than war, probably decent hardworking people with families.'

Afeclin could see the love Endorf had for his people and could accept his reasoning, but still he had his doubts.

The old King could sense it.

'What is the problem Afeclin, you do not seem yourself today... the way you look, this sudden concern for our people, what is going on?'

The lift jolted to a stop. They were on the top floor of the palace, just above the guard's room and below the bell tower, his father's suite.

The doors of the lift swung open into a medium size sitting room surrounded by large windows. Afeclin wandered over to a window that overlooked the city. He could see the party on the street beyond many buildings and the large bonfire lighting up the night sky.

'Shall we sit here?'

'Here is fine,' said Afeclin smirking, 'in fact the city hall would have done the job too.'

'Not as comfortable,' Endorf jeered and then added, 'and we would certainly not have had such a good view.'

Afeclin could not help but laugh. They had come a long way for a bit of comfort and a view.

Endorf added as if reading his thoughts, 'We have all night after all.'

True, it isn't like the celebrations are going anywhere in a hurry.

'Wine?'

'Thank you,' Afeclin replied heaving a sigh.

Endorf poured them both wine from a long, clay amphora that had been resting on a stand nearby and then sat down upon the comfortable lounge adjacent to the one in which Afeclin was sitting.

'Now tell me what this is about son,' Endorf demanded with a soft voice and concerned look.

Taking a large mouthful of wine Afeclin swished it around in his mouth as he searched for the words he wanted to say.

'I have been beyond the borders of Tebelligan...' he began.

The old King sat still, frowning a little but waiting in patience for Afeclin to explain himself.

'I needed to see it father, where I came from... where I was found.'

'I see,' was the short reply that Afeclin found difficult to read.

He continued. 'I cannot explain how, for I do not quite know myself but I saw a vision of the attack and my own parents dying before me.'

'Oh Afeclin,' the King looked solemn, 'that I could have kept you from witnessing such a thing.'

'I needed to see it for myself father. I needed to learn for myself the truth,' he sorrowed. 'It was painful but it helped me to see things more clearly.'

'How so?'

'I need to leave Tebelligan. I have toyed with the idea for a long time now but there was so much keeping me here. After seeing what happened to my family, I now know what I must do,' he said with soft conviction.

Endorf nodded his head with a heavy heart, 'And what is that?'

'You know that for as long as I can remember, I have had this ability or power. I have studied what I can with the books that were left by that old mage, Orin… but… I now must find a wizard to teach me what I cannot learn on my own,' Afeclin responded without emotion. 'I have read much about the wizard Zallucien. I wish to travel to Lawry Castle and petition him to take me on as an apprentice.'

Endorf's face looked very grim but there was no hint of shock or surprise.

'I knew this day would come sooner or later,' said Endorf with a slight smile, 'I always felt that you were destined for something greater than this little kingdom could give you.'

'Father I worried that you would not understand.'

'You are a part of us and our culture because you came to us at such an early age. However your soul and instincts are human. If I were to take a baby leopard and raise him with a flock of sheep he would become like the sheep. He would be placid, maybe timid, would stay with the flock and perhaps eat grass but eventually he would feel the call of the wild and desire to wander away from the flock in pursuit of something more. It is only nature Afeclin, and there is no point trying to deny it,' Endorf said in a profound manner.

'Yes, perhaps that is a part of it,' said Afeclin with thought.

'Probably more than you realise,' said Endorf, scratching his whiskers. 'Humans are wanderers after all, much more so than elves who are content to stay in the one place forever.'

Afeclin sighed as he thought of Wolflang, 'Well not all of them.'

'No, not all of them… I assume you are referring to your friend.'

'Yes… he plans to travel with me, how did you know?' asked Afeclin surprised at the King's awareness.

'Your friend Wolflang is unsettled here,' Endorf chuckled and then went on, 'he is adventurous… like his great uncle, a trait that is not often seen in elves. I could not imagine him settling down in Tebelligan any time soon… if at all.'

Afeclin sat in silent fuming. He felt like a raging fire was burning inside of him. He felt angry at Wolflang and sad for Lenna.

'You are unhappy with his decision? You do not want his company on your journey... or perhaps this is about Lenna,' the old King probed.

Afeclin looked up at Endorf, shocked by his insight. He shifted in his seat.

'Come now Afeclin, I have watched over you your whole life. You think I do not know when my own son is in love with someone?' Endorf teased.

Afeclin did not know what to say. He had never told anyone of his feelings for Lenna.

'Is it that obvious?' he questioned with concern.

'Only to someone who knows you as well as I do,' Endorf said with a compassionate smile. 'It is why you started keeping more to yourself and taking your time up with your craft, is it not?'

'She would never have felt the same for me,' said Afeclin more to himself then his father.

'You never gave her that chance,' Endorf said with force and then softened, 'however, I do think you have done the right thing. You need to explore your roots before you can even consider settling down here with a wife. Once that is out of your system, come back and you never know, Lenna could be still available then.'

'I would have done anything to be with her... even given up my hope of becoming a wizard. Wolflang has her and he will just throw her away!' he erupted, surprising himself with his own outburst. Then he added with softness, 'Lenna is one of the reasons I originally wanted to leave, but I do not want to leave her and break her heart by taking Wolflang with me.'

Endorf's wise old face looked sympathetic. Arising from where he was seated, he walked over and sat down next to Afeclin and put a comforting hand on his back.

'I know how you feel my son but life isn't always fair. We just have to play the hand we were dealt as best we can.' He let out a deep sigh and had for a moment a faraway look.

Afeclin stared at the King in wonderment. It was a rare occurrence to see Endorf lost in his own thoughts. He pondered what the old man could have been thinking about. *Perhaps his queen?*

Endorf's wife, Sazamel had died in mysterious circumstances during the war, well before Afeclin had been found and brought to Tebelligan. Many of the King's confidants had thought that Afeclin filled the void that the aging King had felt after the loss of his love, but Endorf himself never spoke of such things, never of her. While there were still reminders of her about the palace, like paintings of her in various long and colourful traditional elvish gowns, he would not speak of her. It was too painful. Whatever had happened to Sazamel during the war was a mystery and one that only the King and a select few knew.

'I bet Wolflang is wishing right now he was in your position.' The old man continued as if he hadn't missed a beat. 'It can't be easy for him to tell Lenna of his plans and I think he will find it difficult to leave his father alone, but I imagine he feels he is making the right decision.'

Afeclin felt overcome with shame. Instead of supporting his friend's decision he had made an unfair judgement, after all it was not Wolflang's fault that Lenna's love for him was stronger than his was for her. Nor was it Wolflang's fault that Lenna was not in Love with Afeclin. *I guess you can't help who you fall in love with.* He felt that with fervour. After a pause he let out a deep sigh and said, 'And so we will leave.'

'I am very proud of you and if your human parents were alive today I am sure they would be too. You are a very honourable young man and I do believe you could become a great wizard if that is what you truly desire. My advice to you is this… never lose sight of who you are and make the work you do always be for a good purpose.' Endorf then arose and beckoned for Afeclin to follow. 'Come with me.'

They went into his father's study, which was through two tall doors nearest to them and opposite the large windows. The study itself was lined from floor to ceiling with shelves full of books. In the middle of the room was a large solid wood desk with nothing but a small glass lamp on top of it and an uncomfortable looking chair matching the table resting behind it. To the right of them was a soft velvet easy chair with a footstool in front and to the side of it a little glass table. Endorf adored reading and would pick up a book whenever he had a spare moment or two, so he had dedicated his study to reading. There was a large library on one of the lower levels of the palace but it was opened to everyone and the King found it too distracting.

Endorf sat down behind his desk and opened one of the drawers. He then proceeded to pull out all that was inside. There were papers and notepads, an old pair of reading glasses, a large inkpot and a couple of quills. When it was empty he thumbed the bottom of the drawer and pulled it out revealing a long narrow hole carved into the wood.

Afeclin watched with interest, as the old man placed his fingers into the hollow and produced a small, blue, pear shaped rock. It was about the length of the King's hand and at his very touch it had an intense glow.

Afeclin took a deep steady breath, 'Is that it father? Is that the rock that was found above my crib?' He whispered as if the rock were so delicate that a mere voice would shatter it.

'Yes,' Endorf whispered back seeming lost in the beauty of the rock, 'it is a mysterious thing, is it not?'

'I thought it had been left in the ruins?' Afeclin inquired, now finding his voice.

'Originally I had only heard of it, my men had been skeptical about touching it and had left it behind, where it hung, as you say, within the ruins. It was many years later that I awoke one morning from a peaceful slumber in my chamber bed to find it hanging above my own head. Of course I called for my guards, but as I did so I heard a soft, small voice inside my head telling me not to be afraid. So when my guards came I sent them away, lying that I'd had a nightmare,' Endorf paused a moment looking again at the rock in his hand before continuing. 'That same voice then told me to safeguard this rock until such time as was right for you to receive it. It was very strange. I had never heard that voice before nor have I ever again, therefore I know with certainty that it was not my own thoughts in my head but instead someone talking to my mind.'

'I know what you mean father. I have read that most wizards have the ability to send thoughts or messages to a person's mind. That way they are kept completely secret, nobody can intercept the message.'

'A wizard sent me the message?' Endorf pondered.

'Well, it is possible.' Afeclin paused gathering his thoughts, 'I really felt after being in the ruins that I was saved for a purpose, perhaps I am destined to become a wizard.'

Endorf's face was troubled at this suggestion. 'You were either saved for a divine purpose or it was somebody's will. Be careful. After all it may have been an evil sorcerer sending me that message and dictating your future.'

'Yes father.'

Endorf handed the glowing rock to his son with a trembling hand.

For the first time in his life that he could remember, Afeclin felt strong and confident holding the blue rock, as if he were invincible.

Afeclin could feel a transformation taking place within him. He felt as if his boyhood hopes and dreams were fading into nothing and in replacement he was becoming a man. Confidence and a sense of self-worth replaced his immaturity and anguish.

Afeclin was quiet and thoughtful for a while. His mind went back to the past day's activity. He was still bothered by Endorf's plan for the safety of his people.

'How will you know when you are going to be attacked? How will the elves have enough warning to gather in the great hall of the palace, to be taken into the lower levels before the attack?'

Endorf looked taken back.

'We are back to this again?' he asked with a sigh. 'You know the way it works if an attack is imminent. We will receive word from the border, we will have plenty of time to gather before they make it through Taybie Woods.'

'But father,' Afeclin said with reverence, bowing his head with a troubled sniff, 'I made it out of Tebelligan and then back again without anyone ever knowing.'

Chapter

IV

The early morning sun shimmered as it peered over the tall trees of the Taybie Woods to the east of Tebelligan. At this time of the year the sun rose early in the morning and set late in the evening, making for rather long days.

Wolflang sat watching the now almost burnt out bonfire in front of him. Lenna had dozed off in his arms hours earlier and he had spent the time considering the preparations he needed to make so that he and Afeclin could leave the following day.

The noisy cobblestone square, teeming with partygoers the night before, had now become busy with elves cleaning up the mess left behind. Others had returned home to prepare for their journey to Payden's Pool.

Payden's Pool was a large farm several hours west on the main road and the location of the afternoon's festivities. For many years

Payden had welcomed the elves of Tebelligan onto his land for the first day of the New Moon, being the prime location for swimming and general relaxation.

'Come on you two get moving,' a chubby little lady yelled at them, awakening Lenna from her dreams, 'unless of course you would like to help us clean up!'

'No thank you,' Wolflang replied hastening to his feet and helping Lenna to hers, 'we'll get moving out of your way.'

'Typical, you young elves are all alike, always willing to make a mess but never willing to clean up afterwards,' the lady snarled in complaint.

'I don't like her,' Lenna sulked when they were out of earshot, 'she's evidence of what becomes of elf maidens who don't take the opportunity to be wed when they can. They become fat, crabby and mean.'

'Who? Eldina? Why she's harmless,' Wolflang said with an uneasy laugh. Then he added, feeling the need to protect the idea of not being wed, 'that's... just the way she is, I bet she would be the same even if she were married. She's a real nice lady... once you get to know her.'

'I don't think so,' Lenna sniffed. 'I think she's lonely and just like any unmarried spinster, she goes around making everybody else pay for her misfortune.'

Wolflang laughed again, *poor Eldina*. Through her hard nature there was a kind and sensitive woman inside, though it was rare that anyone saw it. She was unattractive as the years had not been kind to her. Her once rich golden hair was greying and her face was wrinkled and weathered. In her youth she was said to have been stunning and many elves had proposed to her but she had been in love with one particular elf by the name of Ferguston.

Eldina had a fiery temper and Ferguston was stubborn, which had been a bad combination from the start. The lovers often fought but always managed to make up with each other afterwards. As the story was told around Tebelligan, Ferguston had forged a beautiful necklace out of pure gold that he had found in a cave off the coast of Tebelligan. The necklace took him weeks to perfect, finishing it with a priceless diamond that had cost him all that he had including some of the unused gold. Ferguston presented it to Eldina as a symbol of his love for her with a proposal of marriage, whilst on a small boat on the ocean for added romance. Eldina was horrified, and knowing he was not at all a wealthy man, accused him of stealing the necklace and of being a liar. She did not believe for a moment that he had made the striking piece of jewellery or that he had miraculously struck gold. To make matters worse she feared that he would be in much trouble if found with it, so she threw his handmade masterpiece into the water. Ferguston, who had cuts and burns on his hands as proof of the blood, sweat and tears that had gone into the magnificent gift, could not bring himself to forgive Eldina for her mistrust and although the elf maiden begged, he would have nothing more to do with her.

Eldina never overcame her lost love and for that reason never married.

That would not happen to Lenna. If she is still unmarried when I return to Tebelligan, I will most certainly marry her. She will never end up a lonely old spinster like Eldina. Wolflang thought to himself. *There is nothing to feel guilty about.*

'Is there anything you need to do before we leave for Payden's Pool?' Wolflang asked, trying to change the subject.

'Umm no... ' Lenna thought for a moment, 'although I should like to change clothes, I feel icky.'

'Okay then, how about I meet you back here on the hour?' suggested Wolflang.

'Ooh,' Lenna moaned with disappointment, 'did you not want to come with me?'

'There are some things that I need to do.'

'Like what? Perhaps we can do them together.'

'Nothing exciting,' Wolflang said trying to come up with a plausible excuse that she wouldn't feel the need to be a part of. He then looked down and saw an ugly mark on the front of his shirt. 'Like... I need to change my shirt, I spilt brew down the front of it last night.'

Lenna looked at his shirt and sighed, 'You're right, you really do need to change that shirt. I'll meet you back here on the hour.' And with that said, she kissed him on the cheek and ran off in the direction of her family cottage.

Wolflang stood for a moment watching her, relieved that he had been able to get rid of her with such ease. His shirt was the last thing on his mind, in fact he didn't care at all about the stain. *It's lucky that Lenna cares about such things or I never would have been able to get away.*

🐾 🐾 🐾

Lenna strolled along the small dirt path that led to her cottage. The sun shone through the diroriam trees that bent and twisted between each other along both sides of the track. Above her the higher branches of the trees had twisted with the diroriams on the opposing side of the path, creating a ceiling of dark green foliage with small yellow flowers that would rain tiny petals whenever the wind blew.

Lenna had always enjoyed the walk from the centre square to her home. At this time of the year the flowers were sweet and fragrant and the smell lingered on her as if she had been doused in perfume. The trees provided perfect shade from the heat of the sun and bright red butterflies danced around her head.

As she walked Lenna stumbled over loose rocks on the track. *Goodness, I must have had more to drink last night than I thought!*

Reflecting on the evening's activities, her mind played over her excited conversations with Wolflang about their future. The strange thing was that when she tried to remember Wolflang's reaction and response to the prospect of marriage, he seemed to be blank and less than interested.

Did I just imagine that or was he really indifferent?

The more she thought about it, the more it bothered her.

Lenna had grown up in the perfect elvin home. Her father, Fynn, an elect on the high council, afforded their family much respect in Tebelligan. Her mother, Jebinna, had spent most of her time rearing Lenna and her younger sister Matia. While in her spare time, Jebinna had grown various herbs and plants that she prepared into remedies that on occasion treated the local elves' illnesses.

Lenna had adored spending time with her mother in her herb garden. She enjoyed the aromas that came to life as Jebinna cooked the herbs in her concoctions. Her mother had taught her much about the wonder of herbs and what they could do.

Lenna had also watched Jebinna do all that she could to be a good mother and wife. She took care of her family and took great pride in it. Lenna wanted so much to be like her mother but apart from that, it was all she knew. *One grows up, gets married and has elflings... that is how it works... what else is there?*

Despite the fact that Lenna had been well educated by her mother in home duties and herbal remedies, she was far from the feminine elf maiden one expected her to be. Having spent her childhood with Wolflang and Afeclin she had learnt much in the way of fighting and hunting. Lenna had spent many hours with Wolflang and his father hunting wild pigs in the woods. She had mastered the art of the bow and arrow with great deft and dexterity and was close to being as good as Wolflang. She had learned to sword fight at a young age with Afeclin who had been tutored by Endorf's best instructors. Of course once Afeclin discovered that his gifts lay in other areas, he lost interest in the use of the sword. Lenna on the other hand continued to learn and to practice. She enjoyed the feeling of strength and power that it gave her wielding the sword, especially in game play against Wolflang, who was strong but not skilled enough to beat her.

Lenna giggled as she envisioned the countless times she had forced Wolflang to the ground at sword point. "Perhaps you should stick to the bow and arrow," she would laugh.

She sighed.

She couldn't imagine her life any other way or with anyone other than Wolflang. Afeclin had been her closest friend since they were very young but she did not feel for him the way she felt for Wolflang. She loved Afeclin with all her heart, but it was a different kind of love, a love that was reserved for kin. *He's like a brother*, she determined with logic. Apart from not being in love with the tall human, she considered it impractical to have feelings for a human man. She was an elf, marrying outside her race would be a strange and uncommon practice. Besides which, Afeclin had made it clear that soon after the New Moon celebrations he would be leaving Tebelligan to seek out his destiny. They had talked in length about it only a few nights prior. She would miss him a great deal but she understood his desire and recognised she had no right to stand in his way.

Any way she looked at it, it made much more sense to marry Wolflang.

Distracted by her thoughts she miscalculated a step, tripped and fell flat on her face. The disgruntled elf maiden lifted her head gingerly and blew her long red locks away from her eyes.

Ow that hurt, she thought, as she lay flat on the road feeling pitiful.

She lifted an arm and rubbed the dirt off her face before making a move to stand. It was then that she happened to notice a strange glow from the corner of her eye.

What is that? she wondered placing an ear to the ground and straining to look in the direction the light had come from.

In a small nook at the base of two diroriam trees, the peculiar glowing radiated from within.

Lenna crept closer on her stomach. Keeping her cheek to the ground, she tried to get a better look. There was something with an odd shape trapped between the trees.

Lenna was curious but could not make out what it was. She wanted to reach in and pull it out. She pushed a slender finger in and felt its hard surface but thought better of grabbing it and pulled her finger out hastily. *What if it's something dangerous?*

She sat up and began to dust herself off. From a sitting position the strange glow could not be seen at all.

How odd.

She began to stand but just as she was getting onto her feet she heard a whispering, a strange hush that called her name and spoke in a language that she could not understand. Lenna fell to her knees, listening intently.

The sound seemed to be coming from the hidden nook. Lenna lay down on the ground again and stared into the alcove. *What is that?* Curiosity getting the better of her, she pushed her hand into the hole and using two fingers worked the object out. No sooner did she have it in her hand, the unusual item went cold and stopped glowing, there were no more whisperings, just a spiral-looking seashell with intricate carvings on the surface.

Lenna studied the carvings with interest. They had the look of ancient script fashioned over the exterior of the unique pearl-textured shell, which was delicate and very beautiful. There was something mystical about it, as if it was enchanted with ancient magic.

Magic was something that she knew little about. She had always enjoyed seeing Afeclin doing his magical tricks but she had no real understanding of the power involved to do it. As far as Lenna was concerned it was a special gift to be able to use magic, something that she had not been blessed with. This was despite the fact that the Great Orin, the only known elvin wizard, was her great, great grand elf-father on her father's side. Whatever gifts and powers Orin possessed had not been passed on through the generations and so Lenna and her ancestors were very ordinary elves. Lenna had never known him herself but there had been many marvellous stories that had been passed down through the generations about the Great Orin and Lenna had delighted in hearing them.

'I must show this to Afeclin,' she said to herself studying the beautiful object as she turned it over in her slender fingers, '…after the celebrations are over.'

🐚 🐚 🐚

Wolflang's childhood home was a small three-room log cottage on the water's edge just north of the city. His mother, Karalee, who had died from illness when Wolflang was only a young elfling, had decorated the cottage with her own taste and style.

There were colourful coverings on each window that she had spent many a late hour sewing. Tapestries hung on walls representing past ancestry and fine painted porcelain plates decorated the mantelpiece. It was a quaint, feminine-looking abode but warm and homey. Although Wolflang's mother had died many years earlier, both he and his father, Bargran had kept the place just as she would have so that her presence could always be felt within the things that she had touched.

It was this time of celebrating each year that affected his father most of all.

Karalee had loved the New Moon celebrations and would fly about the house like an excited elfling in anticipation of it.

Wolflang found his father sitting in an old wooden rocking chair by a large window, smoking his joba leaf pipe and reading his mother's journals.

'Will you be coming to Payden's Pool today, father?' asked Wolflang.

'Ahh, no son, I'd much rather sit here with me old faithful,' he answered tapping his pipe.

Wolflang's head sunk. He had hoped he might be able to speak with his father that afternoon and tell him of his plans to leave.

'Yew wanted to speak to me about something, son?' asked Bargran in his raspy voice that had a western Tebelligan drawl.

Wolflang looked back. His father's weathered face was expressionless and his long, dark, greying hair knotted with wildness down his shoulders. In his right ear a big silver tribal ring, symbolic of the hunting order he belonged to, glistened in the sun that burst through the glass.

'Yes father I wanted to tell you...' Wolflang started, struggling to find the words he needed to say. He took a deep breath, summoning all his courage, 'I wanted you to know that I... that is Afeclin and I have decided to leave Tebelligan early tomorrow morning and venture throughout Titania seeking out our destinies.'

Bargran's expressionless face appeared to plummet to the floor. Then followed an awful silence that seemed to last forever.

'I see...' When Bargran spoke it was with a sadness in his voice that penetrated the very soul of Wolflang.

'Father... I...'

'No, no... there is no need to explain, it's just that... yew are all I have left in this miserable city,' Bargran said in his solemn manner, 'me own father died in the war, me ma died of a broken heart soon after, ya dear mother died of illness and her wealthy parents blamed me saying it was due to the poorer life we led... I just feel like I am losing me only son too.'

Wolflang had quite expected his father to react in such a way. On any other day, Bargran was a fun-loving man who loved to entertain and enjoy a good joke but there were certain holidays and anniversaries that took their toll on the older man. They would remind him so much of Karalee that he would go into a depression where his outward demeanour would change. At times he was snarly, other times, despondent and there were times when he was impossible to live with. Wolflang felt sad for his father but he knew Bargran could be much worse.

'Father, this wasn't an easy decision to make and I will miss you... but would you have me stay purely for your sake?'

Bargran's body slumped. He closed his eyes and shook his head as Wolflang noticed a single tear roll down the old man's cheek.

'No, I don't want that, certainly not.'

Bargran held himself upright in the chair with pride.

Wolflang watched as Bargran puffed on his pipe, lost in his own thoughts.

After what felt like an eternity, Bargran's face lifted and he spoke, 'My son, I am so very proud of ya. Ya defiantly have me blood running through ya veins! Yew have the adventurer's spirit for sure, just as I did before I met ya ma. Yew're right of course, yew should follow ya dreams, I guess I'm just envious. Why, if it weren't for me dodgy leg, I'd be inclined to come wit' ya.'

Wolflang was surprised by his father's sudden change in enthusiasm. Bargran's eyes were now wide with excitement, a look he had seldom seen since his mother's death.

Wolflang let out a breath, 'Will you be okay without me?'

'At first I thought to meself, me wife is gone, now I lose me son too, but then I remembered how much I longed to leave this place when I was y'age. Although I will miss ya company, I see that now I can live those adventures that I dreamed of all those years back, through yew.' Bargran paused to relight his pipe. 'Will ya write to me and tell me all ya adventures?'

'I would love to, but I'm not sure how you would receive mail from outside of Tebelligan.'

'Oh there is an old mail system in existence... of course there has been no need for it in recent years but it still works. Once ya letter reaches the Tebelligan border, it would be passed on to the guards there and brought into the city.'

'Well then, of course I will write father,' Wolflang said feeling much love and appreciation for the older man.

'And ya gal, what of her?' Bargran questioned, his mood much more temperate than before.

'I have yet to tell her. I think she will not take the news very well. She has already made plans for our future,' said Wolflang looking down to the floor.

'Wolflang, if ya love for her is not enough to make ya stay, maybe it was never meant to be in the first place.'

'Do you ever regret the decisions you made?' Wolflang asked.

'Never! The love I had for ya ma exceeded that of leaving Tebelligan. Had I 'ave gone, I would have regretted leaving 'er. I couldn't imagine a world without her and the world beyond Tebelligan would 'ave been worthless to me.'

Wolflang let out a sigh.

'I just don't feel that strongly for Lenna.'

'Then yew're definitely making the right decision. But don't put off telling 'er, that will only hurt 'er more. Yew don't want 'er to feel like she's the last to know.'

'I will tell her today.'

Chapter
V

Afeclin arrived at the city wall after a long night's discussion with Endorf. He had found himself arguing the point against many of his father's opinions and plans for his people. Endorf, always the patient king had listened and had agreed to evaluate some of their strategies with the town council after the New Moon celebrations.

He found Lenna sitting on a rock just outside the city wall. With her skinny arms folded and her lips in a pout, she kicked her feet against the rock with impatience, watching handfuls of elves boarding the wagon.

Lenna looked attractive in her short, green, stitched top with beaded leather straps that wound around her middle. She wore a pair of tan pants that cut off at her shapely calves and pieces of flat leather on her feet that were held together by leather straps that wound around her ankles with beads threaded on the top of each foot. Sections of her rich red hair were braided and littered with little yellow diroriam petals.

'Is everything alright Lenna?' Afeclin asked as he approached her, wondering whether Wolflang had perhaps spoken to her about leaving.

Lenna startled, almost falling backwards. 'Oh Afeclin, you frightened me,' she said frowning with a hand on her chest, 'do you not know that it is impolite to sneak up on somebody!'

'Sneak up?' he teased. 'You should have seen me coming.'

'Well I do not have eyes in the back of my head now, do I?' she replied with an indignant air.

'Where has your intuition gone Little Peep?' Afeclin said sitting down upon the rock next to her.

'Do not call me that Afeclin, you know I loathe it.'

Little Peep had been a childhood taunt of Afeclin's. He had started using it on Lenna after an incident involving peepinco berries that to this day she had not been able to live down.

Lenna had been forced each year to help her grand elf mother in making and preparing peepinco wine. Thousands of peepinco berries that had been picked by the farmhands, including Wolflang and Afeclin that day, were tossed into a large round barrel. Then the elvin women were required to dance around on top of the berries and pummel them into juice with their bare feet. It was a family tradition that took place on the first day of the summer solstice, the longest day of the year. Lenna had always hated it. She was forced to wear a large traditional dress that was heavy with the many layers of fabric in the skirt. The colourful layers represented the colours found in Tebelligan nature with greens and golds and blues and reds. The short white embroidered lace layered sleeves and thick-ribboned belt that was tied into a large bow gave her the look of an elven raggy doll.

She had never been any good at the peepinco dance and she didn't like the feeling of the black peepinco berries squelching between her toes as she trod. The squashed berries were also very slippery and Lenna had to be careful not to lose her footing and fall.

She had been doing well, keeping her balance when both Afeclin and Wolflang had arrived back from the fields with a fresh box of berries to add to the mix. Once they saw Lenna in the complete traditional ensemble they burst into laughter. Upsetting the fiery elf maiden, she lost her concentration and slipped, plunging into the squishy berry mess. When she had stood up she was covered from head to toe in the black berry juice. The two young boys had found it hysterical and roared on the ground with laughter. Afeclin had, from then on referred to Lenna as a 'Little Peepinco Berry' or 'Little Peep' for short.

'I know you love it,' taunted Afeclin.

Lenna crossed her arms, stuck her chin out and huffed. This meant that he was right but she was not going to admit it.

After pretending got too much for her she turned back to him and asked, 'What happened to that shipwrecked look from last night?'

Afeclin combed his fingers over his slicked hair that was now tied up into a neat ponytail that sat at the nape of his neck.

'Oh that was a one night only deal,' he jeered.

'What a shame… it was such a good look for you, so disorderly and relaxed.'

She giggled.

'I thought you weren't impressed by that look.'

'I was just surprised by it, that's all,' she said, her eyes wide and sparkling in the sunshine. 'Are you really going to be leaving us Afeclin?'

Afeclin looked her in the eyes and nodded, 'I need to. I can no further study my craft here and there is nothing else for me in Tebelligan.'

'I am here,' she stated putting a tan arm through his, 'I mean Wolflang and I are here.'

'Yes, well…' Afeclin began, not knowing quite what to say. *Evidently he has not told her yet.*

'I know what you are thinking, everything will change once we wed, but it does not need to, I will always love you. What would I do without my Magicman?' she purred, putting a soft cheek on his arm.

Love. She uses that word so carelessly, he mused, almost with bitterness.

'Oh I am sure that you have things you want to do in your life that do not involve either me nor Wolflang.'

'Oh, I am not sure yet, perhaps I will more fully learn the art of herbs from my mother and heal people, I already know a little… wait a minute,' she said sitting up straight all of a sudden, 'what did you mean by that? What did you mean without you or Wolflang?'

'I did not mean anything more than the fact that you always need to have your own interests… as well,' said Afeclin wishing he could take back the words he had just said.

'No… what did you mean by that? You meant something else, I have known you long enough to know your little word games when I hear them,' Lenna challenged with concern. 'Has Wolflang said something to you? He has been acting very strange lately. I am not sure if it is just my imagination or if he really is less than interested in being wed.'

48

'Lenna, if you feel that way, perhaps you should talk to Wolflang about it, I mean maybe he is not ready to settle down yet,' Afeclin said, hoping he was not making things worse.

Lenna's big brown eyes searched Afeclin for signs of truth, 'So he did say something! Is that it... he does not want to be wed just yet?'

'Lenna... I...'

Just then, he noticed Wolflang walking up the road to the city gate.

'You took long enough,' Lenna wailed when she saw him. 'We've already missed the first wagon.'

'I'm sorry, I was speaking with my father,' he said, adding, 'you know how he is at this time of the year.'

'Oh, yes of course,' Lenna said biting her bottom lip with guilt. 'How was he?'

'The usual.'

Lenna shook her head, 'That poor lonely man...'

Afeclin mouthed the words, 'You have not told her?' when Lenna's back was turned.

Wolflang responded with a shake of his head and when Lenna had turned back to face Afeclin, added in silence, 'I will today.'

In their youth Afeclin and Wolflang had learnt to read each other's lips quite well, this was the way they had kept secrets from Lenna. She often knew what was going on and it had driven her crazy. This time Lenna did not catch on to what they were doing.

'Well... come on you two, I don't want to miss this next one,' she said pulling the two towards the horse drawn wagon waiting across from them that was now quite full of elves ready to make the journey out to Payden's Pool.

🐿 🐿 🐿

The journey to Payden's Pool was long and slow but not tiresome. The wagonload of elves kept it alive with songs and jokes with what was left of their voices from the night before. The wagon itself was long and narrow with big bails of hay in the middle to seat the elves. Ahead and behind them they could see other wagons full of elves laughing, singing and enjoying themselves. Each wagon carried about fifty elves, young and old with four horses straining to pull their load.

Once the wagons were past the wooded area surrounding the city, the land became flat and treeless. Horses and llamas, grazing in the sunshine, dotted the landscape. Haywood birds with their long curved beaks and scarlet plumage danced on the breeze with each other, as if they too celebrated the new moon.

The dirt road for the most part had been well maintained in this part of the country, however the odd hole or rock in the path sent the elves bounding in the hay as the wagon's wheel struck it.

After journeying for some time along the rickety road, the wagons passed by a farm with a large orchard and beautiful berry trees. Lenna slunk in her seat trying to conceal herself between Wolflang and Afeclin.

'Hey Lenna, isn't that your family's farm where you make Peepinco Wine?' asked one young elf with a cheeky grin.

'You know it is Bartenu,' Lenna said with a growl.

'I seem to remember someone falling into the berries and coming out looking like one,' an elf maiden with long blonde hair giggled, giving a wink to Lenna.

'Really? It must have been such a long time ago, I barely remember.'

'Of course you do,' retorted another elf with a laugh, 'it was you Lenna, as if you would forget such a thing.'

'I was doing the dance that day with Lenna, she was so awkward as she tried to hold up her long skirts and dance the peepinco jig with some level of agility and style,' said Nieegra, a cousin to the fiery elf.

'Yeah, and I was a farm hand that day, I saw her feet go up over her head. It was hilarious,' laughed Bartenu inciting others to join in on the joke.

Lenna sat scowling, she hated this part of the journey every year, when the other elves would feel inclined to remind her about her clumsiness.

Wolflang and Afeclin sat in silence trying not to laugh themselves, they knew better than to join in.

'Cheer up, Lenna,' said Wolflang with a smile, 'it could be worse… at least they seem to have forgotten when…'

'Don't say it Wolfy, the last thing we want is someone overhearing and having another thing to mock me about,' she said putting a hurried finger to his lips.

They reached Payden's Pool at high noon, the hottest part of the day. Many were hungry from the journey and flocked to the large paddock, laying out blankets to sit on in the shade of the enormous bragabell trees that had leaves the size of watermelons, and fat potbelly trunks like large bells.

In the centre of the paddock was a dam that many elves were already swimming and frolicking in. The water shimmered in the sunlight and was refreshing to look at as the day had become hot and humid and there was not a single cloud in the sky.

'The sweat is just pouring off me,' Lenna moaned as she climbed down out of the wagon.

'Well then we shall find some shade and cool down.'

'No, I am headed straight for that water, I'll race you.'

Without bothering to wait for a reply, Lenna took off at a steady pace, running down the slight incline towards the calm pool. Wolflang and Afeclin watched after her a moment as if contemplating whether or not to follow.

'You coming?' asked Wolflang breaking the short silence.

'Sure am.'

Afeclin started running at top speed after Lenna.

'Hey!' shouted Wolflang bolting after the two.

Afeclin, having such long legs, had no trouble catching up to Lenna. Overtaking her, he dived into the revitalising water. Wolflang and Lenna plunged into the water at the same time, splashing each other and laughing.

After lunch Afeclin decided to doze for a while in the cool shade whilst Lenna and Wolflang took a ride in an old wooden boat.

Having food now in his belly, Wolflang felt languorous and found it wearying to row the boat and pay attention to Lenna at the same time.

'Isn't this romantic Wolfy?' she purred.

'Hmmm?'

'Oh you look very sleepy you poor thing,' she said with sympathy, 'perhaps you could stop rowing and let us drift for a while.'

They were now out in the middle of the dam and well away from anyone swimming, so Wolflang pulled the oars in and let the boat drift.

Now would be the last opportunity he would have to talk to her before Afeclin and himself left the following morning. Wolflang plucked up every bit of courage he had left in him.

'There's something I need to talk to you about, something important...'

'I know what you're going to say.'

Wolflang's heart stopped for a moment. *She knows? Did Afeclin say something? Maybe this will be easier than I thought.*

'I watched you last night and you seemed very distant,' Lenna continued. 'I was all excited about our future together and you did not act very interested. That bothered me, at first but then I realised I was rushing things for you. I'm sure you want to work, save some money and perhaps purchase some land before we even consider getting married. I can help too, I was thinking of learning the healing art of herbs from mother. We just need to sort ourselves out first. We have plenty of time... the rest of our lives in fact.'

Wolflang held his breath and tugged at his ears. He felt sick.

Bringing his thoughts together Wolflang stammered, 'Lenna, that certainly is a p..part of what I wanted to talk to you about... you see... how do I put this?'

'Wolfy we're sinking!'

Wolflang looked down at his feet and sure enough water was seeping into the boat. Cupping his hands he tried to scoop the water out but it was all in vain. Before long they were up to their necks in water and the boat had sunk to the bottom of the dam. Lenna gave a heartfelt laugh as they swam to the nearest bank. Wolflang didn't find it half as amusing.

Dripping wet, Lenna had laughed so hard that now her side ached as she pulled herself up onto the wall of the bank. Wolflang, who had been just behind her, pulled himself up and gave Lenna a big hug. He sorrowed as he felt her wet body against his.

'Just know that I love you,' he whispered into her ear, 'no matter what happens.'

'What are you trying to say?' she asked, with sudden concern.

By now Wolflang had lost all of his energy, the swim had drained the last of it. Instead, he kissed her hard and strong on the lips, like he had never kissed her before.

❦ ❦ ❦

By the time they arrived back in the city, it was dark. The three moons shone and there was a pleasant, cool breeze, which was a nice change to the afternoon's heat. Lenna had lain in Wolflang's lap and slept for the entire journey home. She roused when the wagon came to a stop.

After helping her down from the wagon, Afeclin grabbed the sleepy elf maiden and held her close. 'I will miss you when I leave, Little Peep.'

'And I you, Magicman,' she responded with a drowsy nod, standing on her toes to embrace the lanky human.

'Come on Lenna, I'll take you home,' said Wolflang yawning, then added to Afeclin, 'I'll be over early in the morning.'

Afeclin nodded and mouthed the words 'good luck' as he walked away.

Wolflang had not been very talkative for the journey home. He had been contemplating how he was going to break the news to Lenna. He wanted the truth to be out in the open but it had never seemed the right time to tell her. He had been wrestling inside with the secret he kept from her... a secret that would change her life. Yet whenever he tried to tell her, words had failed him.

Wolflang took hold of Lenna and walked her home. When they got there he took her to her room in the tiny cottage.

The room may have been small but it was feminine and reminded him of his mother. Embroidered window furnishings hung above a small bed that had a large feather pillow and patchwork blanket.

The room had sparse decorations, a small plant here and there, some wooden ornaments on the window sill and a large oil painting of a wooded grove hung on the wall. Opposite the small bed sat a wooden desk and chair. Papers covered the desk top, many of which had sketches of people on them. Wolflang smiled at one that depicted himself holding his bow and arrow poised and ready to strike. *She's quite the artist.* He chuckled.

Helping her into her bed, he pulled up the blankets. Lenna was still so tired that she fell back to sleep as soon as her head hit the soft downy pillow.

Wolflang pushed back his mousey hair and sighed, 'I will miss you.'

He then spotted a long green feather quill lying on top of the old wooden desk. Although he had only joked the day before with Afeclin about writing her a letter, at this moment it seemed like his only option.

My dearest Lenna, he wrote:

It pains me for you to find out this way but I find myself left with no option. I hope you will find it within yourself to be understanding and in time forgive me for not delivering this news personally.
As much as I love you… and truly I do, I have a great yearning and desire to explore the world before I settle for a family. I want to live and explore the land beyond our elvin home of Tebelligan and see what this world has to offer.
I know you don't share my enthusiasm and excitement for the world beyond our borders but I ask for your patience. I will of course return one day and on that day it will be you whom I will be excited to see and if you have not yet wed, I would hope that you would marry me. However I am not asking for you to wait, I realise that would be an unreasonable request.
In the meantime I will write to you as often as I can. Remember my love for you is strong and will endure far beyond the borders of this land.
I remain yours truly,

Wolflang.

He wiped the quill clean of ink with an old piece of rag that was lying on the floor near the desk. Placing the quill back where he had found it, he picked up the letter and re-read it. Wolflang felt sad that she should find out this way. It was not his intention to cause her pain and he imagined that it would hurt her more to find out he had left without saying a proper farewell.

Wolflang placed the letter back on the desk where Lenna would be able to see it when she awoke. Eyeing another sketch, which had been strewn on the table, he picked it up and admired it. It was a self-portrait and the perfect likeness of Lenna, her eyes that sparkled, her slender lips that held a knowing smirk and her hair that fell around her face in waves. Wolflang folded the picture and tucked it inside his shirt. He was just about to leave the small room when he glanced once again at her beautiful face. The blue moon's light streamed into the room adding a soft glow to her cheeks, giving her a peaceful, angelic look as she slept. Wolflang tried to comb his fingers through her long crimson tresses but found it difficult as her hair was thick and matted after all the swimming earlier that day.

A soft breeze blew in through the open window causing Lenna to stir. Wolflang, not wanting to be there if she awoke, crept out of the room in silence.

Wolflang plodded home, feeling as if it were the last time he would ever see Lenna. His head was bowed and his long tangled hair fell over his face. He wondered whether he was sadder for Lenna or for himself.

Wolflang's body ached as it longed for sleep and he cringed at the thought of the early start they had the following day. He would have to be up at dawn so he could prepare for his journey. Then his heart started to race with anticipation. There were only hours before he would leave this place and his adventures could begin.

Chapter

VI

Afeclin awoke the following morning as soon as the sun peaked over the trees allowing sunlight to pour into his room. He climbed out of his bed, stretching his arms as he thought about what he needed to do in order to leave. His stomach grumbled with hunger.

'Food,' he muttered to himself.

After a hearty breakfast of bacon, eggs and crusty bread, which the palace cook had prepared for him, he got to work.

Organising a large garboa cloth bag, he decided what he would need to take.

After much deliberation he managed to fill the bag: a couple of wizardry journals, a notebook, an ancient-looking map covering the Land of Marrapassa, a silver water flask and some food and monetary provisions were among the items that he packed. Then he slung the long strap of the bag over his head and left shoulder, testing the weight. The bag felt a little heavy but he knew the garboa cloth was strong as it was made from coarse goat hair.

Once he had all that he needed, he pulled back the covers on his bed and let his hand search under the thick mattress for a small hole. Reaching one slender finger into the hole, he drew out the stunning blue rock that his father had given to him. Looking into the deep blue crystal he could see his reflection. Afeclin pondered its beauty for a moment before tying the leather holding the rock around his neck and slipping it down his shirt to sit against his chest. The glowing rock felt warm against his skin and was somewhat energising.

The last thing he needed to do after he had picked up his thick velvet cloak from the winter cloakroom was to say goodbye once and for all to his father.

Afeclin went to his King's grand suite with the expectation that Endorf would still be there, sound asleep. Instead he found the bedclothes pulled up and his father nowhere to be seen. Then he took the lift down to the first floor in order to meet with Wolflang as they had planned. He sorrowed that he may not be able to say goodbye to his elvin father before he left.

Wolflang had been waiting for him when he stepped out of the ancient lift.

'Good morning Afeclin,' Wolflang said in good spirits.

'Yes, it is a great morning, the weather is perfect for travelling,' answered Afeclin. 'Are you ready to leave then?'

'I don't think I could get any more ready,' he replied with a yawn, 'apart from being tired I feel quite good.'

'Do you have all that you need?'

'Yes, I believe so,' Wolflang said looking to the gear he was carrying.

Around his waist was an old leather pouch that wasn't quite as big as the bag Afeclin was carrying but it was large enough for the elf's needs. Over his head and left shoulder he carried a large bow and on his back, attached to straps crossed over his chest, was a long leather quiver that carried around ten to fifteen good size arrows. Just like Afeclin he held his own cloak in his arms, not knowing quite where to store the bulky item.

'Have you said goodbye to King Endorf?'

'No, I did not know where he was,' said Afeclin with sadness. 'Have you said goodbye to your father?'

'Yes, he wished me well after giving me his old hunting water-sack to use,' Wolflang answered pointing at the grey boar skin bottle that hung from his belt.

They walked out of the doors of the grand hall and into the palace courtyard. 'How did you go with Lenna?'

'Not bad I guess,' said Wolflang hanging his head and refusing to look Afeclin in the eyes, as if trying to avoid the question. 'I think it will take some time for her to get over it.'

'That is to be expected,' Afeclin said. 'I hope you said farewell for me.'

Afeclin felt sad that he had not been able to tell her in person that he was departing that morning but he had not wanted to get in the way of Wolflang telling her of his plans.

'Well… I…' Wolflang began to respond when he was interrupted by the sound of horses hooves clopping against the stone in the courtyard. The two turned to see Endorf himself rounding the corner of the building leading two healthy horses.

'Father, what are you doing here?' asked Afeclin embracing Endorf.

'I have a going away gift for you both,' said Endorf handing the reins of an attractive black stallion with a white muzzle to Afeclin. Then handing the reins of a slightly smaller chestnut mare to Wolflang he added with pride, 'These are the finest young horses I have and I want you to take care of them because as you look after them, they will in return take care of you.'

'Thank you father, I did not expect…' started Afeclin feeling a little choked up.

'Nonsense. What were you going to do, walk all the way around Titania?' Endorf laughed.

Afeclin embraced his father once more.

'Thank you for all that you have done for me, I will miss you.'

'Just be careful my son, the world is a very different place,' he warned.

'I will write and let you know how I am doing,' said Afeclin climbing up onto the great stallion. Wolflang followed suit, thanking the King as he did so.

'You watch out for my son,' said Endorf, his weathered eyes narrowing in seriousness, 'I hear you are quite a natural with the bow and arrow. You keep Afeclin from harm and if you ever wish to come home to us I will give you a top job as one of my personal guards.'

'Thank you your highness,' said Wolflang with respect, quite overcome by the King's offer.

'May the Goddess light your paths and bless you always,' Endorf prayed with tears welling in his eyes.

Afeclin took one last look at the palace. As he did so he thought he saw his brother, Alga peering out one of the higher windows. The face disappeared before he could be sure of whom he was seeing. With that they walked their horses down the cobblestone streets towards the eastern bridge. After each had looked back at the fine city for the last time, they passed under the bridge, gave their horses a good firm kick and galloped away through the trees, heading east along the old forgotten road to leave Tebelligan, the only place they had ever known.

Wolflang and Afeclin galloped non-stop through Taybie Woods for a good part of the morning. Tall traffita trees with their elongated willowy white trunks and long slender leaves that draped from the top of their stem, loomed down upon them as they rode, giving them partial shade from the early morning sun. Birds flew in and out of trees, some screeching and some singing their dawn songs. Every now and then a low flying bat would pass over their heads causing them to duck out of the way. Gaandi forest mice, with their large round ears and short stubby tails, scampered in and out of the grass and across the track making narrow escapes from being trampled by the pounding hooves.

The old forgotten road, once a well travelled stone track out of Tebelligan, was now covered in long grass and moss. Nowadays the track was only used for the odd communication from the outside world, otherwise it was forbidden for any other race to set foot inside the Taybie Woods.

An hour before the sun reached high noon they decided to let the horses walk for a while, allowing them to cool down.

Although both Wolflang and Afeclin were good riders, the riding was very tiring. Soon after the horses had begun to walk, Wolflang began to get sleepy. First he started to yawn, then he found it difficult to keep his eyes open and before long he was nodding in and out of sleep as the horse walked on. He began to dream about Lenna. *She sleeps at peace in her bed when all of a sudden she awakes and sees the note on the wooden desk. She reads the note once and then as if having trouble comprehending what is said, she reads it again...*

A loud whirring sound dashed by Wolflang's ear causing him to startle awake, lose his balance and fall off his horse. As he fell he rolled amongst the long grass. Grasping his bow and collecting an arrow from the leather quiver as he rolled, Wolflang made it back onto his feet with bow and arrow in hand, poised and ready to shoot. This manoeuvre was one that his father had taught him when he first started to learn the fine art. "Sometimes ya enemy will take ya by surprise," Bargran would say, "so roll to the ground, collect ya gear and be ready to shoot him in the neck as soon as ya stand up." Of course that was concerning wild animals but Wolflang had practiced it so much that he now did the manoeuvre with instinct. Wolflang had no idea what had flown passed his ear but he wasn't about to take any chances.

By this time Afeclin had ridden back to assess the situation.

'What's going on?' he asked sliding down off his horse.

'Take cover, I'm not sure what's out there.'

Just as Wolflang spoke another whirring sound buzzed past his ear.

'We're being shot at!' called Wolflang turning around to the direction the arrow had come flying at him. 'I can't see anyone though and I can't tell exactly where it came from.'

Wolflang studied the line of trees opposite him with caution. The forest was thick on either side of the path, for the most part comprising large bankoi trees with their strong trunks and feathered leaves of greens, reds and golds. Bankoi trees were said to be amongst the oldest known on Titania. They were not the tallest of trees but their bodies were thick and mighty with root systems that went deep into the ground. Standing beside the bankoi, the slender white traffita trees looked waif-like and weak.

X-zaivacress vines wound their way around the traffita and bankoi, filling in the empty spaces between the trees like a patterned scarf with their rich green leaves and large deep violet flowers at the end of each arm.

Hiding in amongst the branches and vines was not a hard task. The elves had always used the security of the trees in Taybie Woods to gain advantage against enemies and intruders. From the concealed branches of the bankoi the elves were difficult to discern, let alone hit.

Afeclin was now squatting low in the long grass with his horse standing next to him protecting him on the side the arrows appeared to be coming.

'How could you tell it was an arrow?'

'I caught just a glimpse of it that time,' Wolflang answered with slow breaths, concentrating on the woods all around him.

After a few minutes another arrow came at him from behind, this time plunging into the dirt, a foot away from him.

'There must be more than one out there,' Wolflang suggested in a loud whisper. 'The arrows are coming from a few directions.'

Another couple of arrows came flying at Wolflang, one after the other. The arrows landed in the sand and again did not touch him at all.

'Do you think somebody's toying with me?' Wolflang called to Afeclin, getting more frustrated with the situation. 'Either that or they're a very bad shot.'

'If I had wanted to hit you Wolflang, let me assure you, I would have.'

They both looked up into the trees above them, and there resting on a large branch with bow in hand was Lenna.

'Are you crazy? What are you shooting at us for?' yelled Wolflang in anger.

'Who's up there with you Lenna?'

'Nobody, I was just swinging across from one tree to another so you weren't sure where the arrows were coming from,' Lenna said as she let out a wicked giggle.

'It's not a very funny joke, Lenna.'

'What's this about Lenna? Why the arrows?' asked Afeclin trying to reason with her.

Lenna had no expression on her face as she hung her bow on a branch and produced a small, folded piece of paper from the cord belt of her tan pants. Unfolding the paper she began to read aloud in a voice that was angry but controlled.

'Dearest Lenna, It pains me to be so weak and write this letter instead of speaking to you in person. As much as I love you... rah, rah, rah... it cannot compare to what the world has to offer. So I am abandoning you because I have to follow my dreams, which have nothing to do with you. I will return one day... when I am old and grey and in that day I will marry you... rah, rah, rah... in the meantime have a nice life without me,' she screwed up the paper and threw it to the ground and added, 'or at least that's what I got from it.'

'Please do not tell me you left her a note,' Afeclin cast an angry scowl at Wolflang.

'It was seriously, much nicer than that,' Wolflang said in his defence then turning to Lenna stammered, 'Lenna I... I... I just couldn't seem to tell you...'

By now Lenna was climbing down from the huge tree with her bow over her shoulders. Wolflang admired her agility as she lowered herself to the ground from the last branch.

'It is not about the letter, Wolflang,' she said barely above a whisper, 'I just do not understand why you have to leave.'

'Lenna please don't make this any harder than it is, this is something I have to do.'

Speaking with softness, he reached out his arms to hold her.

She pulled away, her eyes glaring in fury.

'How can you say you truly love someone and then just leave them,' she shouted, tears welling in her eyes, 'it just doesn't make sense!'

Afeclin put a strong, muscled arm around her for comfort.

'Lenna, it is not like he is leaving to get away from you, he is leaving to get away from Tebelligan for a while. He will come back,' Afeclin assured, trying his hardest to help.

Lenna wrenched herself away from Afeclin.

'Do not play innocent in all of this, Afeclin!' she snapped pointing her finger at him. 'You put him up to all of this, didn't you?'

Somewhat pained by the accusation he turned away from her.

'Lenna this has nothing to do with Afeclin. Don't get angry with him. He has done nothing wrong.'

'Yes he has. He's leaving me too. My two best friends in the whole wide world are leaving me!' she wailed, tears streaming down her face.

'Lenna, a friend cannot stick around purely for the sake of friendship.'

Lenna stared at Afeclin with her watery brown eyes for a moment as if contemplating her next move.

'Stay then Afeclin,' she begged, 'stay for me… for us.'

Afeclin looked at her in surprise and wonderment.

'Do you not think I know how you have felt about me all these years? I have known all along,' she continued. 'Stay Afeclin and I will give myself to you for the rest of our lives.'

Wolflang felt his mouth gape wide in shock as a resentful sensation stirred within him.

Would she do that? Give up all we had together and marry Afeclin, a human, if he were to return with her? He shook his head, annoyed by his own bitterness, *would Afeclin give up his dreams to be with her? Does he care for Lenna that much? What is between them that I don't know about?*

☙ ☙ ☙

Afeclin stood silent for a moment, a flurry of feelings surfacing. What an offer she had made. If anything could keep him in Tebelligan, it would be her. For as long as he could remember he had wanted Lenna to be his and now all he had to do was to say yes and return to the Elvin Kingdom with her. Afeclin's mind raced as he longed to take her into his arms and kiss her. Now in this moment was the only chance he would ever have to do that. If he did not strike now, there would be no second chance. It was now or never. His heart was beating at a hundred miles an hour. *Yes Lenna, yes, yes, yes.* Then abruptly he came to his senses. She

62

did not love him and perhaps never would. *Sure, I would be with her but would she really be with me? Would her heart not belong with Wolflang wherever he was? Could she grow to love me and forget Wolflang, her true love?* He thought not. Instead she would be miserable and that would make him unhappy. Besides which, deep down inside of him he knew that his destiny lay beyond the borders of Tebelligan and he needed to put aside his feelings for Lenna and follow it.

'Lenna, I cannot deny that I feel very strongly for you,' he said in a calm and rational voice. 'We both know it would not work. You could not be content with me. I am sorry but I must leave.'

This time Lenna burst into tears. She turned her attention back to Wolflang who stood in silence with a confused scowl on his face.

'Please Wolfy...' she pleaded with all her might, 'please don't go. I will do anything if only you will just stay... pleease!'

Wolflang pulled her close and held her in his arms. She grieved with body-shuddering sobs into his chest as he whispered into her ear.

'I will always love you. My leaving is not about you, Lenna, it never was. I was torn when making my decision. I will be back for you one day, I promise I will, you needn't have thoughts of running into the arms of someone else in fear of being left alone, I won't leave you for long.'

With that he kissed her on the head and said goodbye. He then mounted his horse and began riding away without ever looking back.

'Where is your horse Lenna?' Afeclin asked. 'I take it you rode here or you would never have been able to catch up to us.'

'Over there, beyond the trees, where she can't be seen from the road,' she whimpered.

'I will take you there.'

'No Afeclin, I wish to stay here a moment.'

'Please Lenna, let me help you.'

Afeclin went to pull her up from the ground.

'NO!' she shrieked then whispered with a strained calmness, 'Just go Afeclin, leave now.'

Lenna sat kneeling on the ground, her shoulders slumped, head bowed and her crimson tresses obscuring her face. It pained Afeclin to leave her like that, but it was useless to try any more. Mounting his horse he rode away after Wolflang, feeling a terrible loss within his heart. He caught up to the elf and rode along beside him.

'I never knew you were in love with her too,' the elf said in a low growl that almost sounded like a smouldering jealousy.

'Are you kidding me? After what you did to her, what right have you to be jealous?'

'I… I'm not jealous… she's free to do as she pleases.'

'Just don't speak to me for a while,' was the cold reply as he gave his horse a swift kick in the side as he galloped away.

Chapter

VII

After many hours of solid riding, Afeclin and Wolflang approached the border of Tebelligan. They had not spoken nor stopped for the entire time and now by mid-afternoon they were both hungry and sore.

'How about we stop here for a break and something to eat?' suggested Wolflang daring to interrupt the monotonous sound of horses' hooves clopping against the old paved road.

Afeclin did not reply but kept on riding despite the pain he had been feeling in his backside.

'So, what? Are you not going to talk to me for the rest of this journey?'

Still he received no answer from Afeclin.

'Well, I have to stop at any rate, apart from needing a rest and dying of hunger I need to relieve myself,' Wolflang growled, slowing down his horse to a stop.

Afeclin knew he was being unreasonable but while letting his anger get the better him he had cast aside his own needs as well as his friend's. He let out a loud sigh then turned his horse around and trotted back to where Wolflang had dived off his horse to run behind an aging bankoi.

Afeclin climbed down off his steed and stretched, feeling the relief it brought to his back. Looking to the beautiful stallion whose coat was draped in sweat, he realised he had not only been unfair to his friend but also to their horses.

'There you go pal,' Afeclin whispered to the black horse as he picked a handful of lush grass, which grew up between the stone pavers, and fed it to him. The horse snorted in gratitude as it munched with content, then having had the taste for it, walked to the side of the road and buried his head in the long wide-bladed grass and continued to eat.

'I don't blame you.'

Feeling famished himself, Afeclin scavenged through his bag and pulled out a roll of buttered bread. After a few hurried mouthfuls he took out the silver bottle and guzzled some water down. Standing in the middle of the road he looked ahead to where the border lay only about a mile away. The sun now shone with heat through the trees, across the path on which they rode, blazing down upon him and burning the back of his neck. Wolflang's darker skin could take the strong rays but Afeclin's white complexion was prone to burning and now stung as he wiped his hand across it.

'So you decided to stop after all,' said Wolflang returning to his horse that was also busy grazing in the long grass.

'Don't get too comfortable Wolflang,' said Afeclin in an icy tone. 'This is a quick stop only.'

🐦 🐦 🐦

After a very brief rest and bite to eat they were on their way once more. As they crossed the border of Tebelligan, Wolflang spied two elvin warriors hiding within the mossy branches of the bankoi trees overlooking a decaying wooden sign that read…

TEBELLIGAN 62 KITRA
VISITORS ARE ONLY WELCOME
BY PRIOR ARRANGEMENT WITH THE KING.
TRESPASSES WILL BE DEALT WITH

ACCORDING TO ELVIN LAW.

'Leaving Tebelligan, are ya?'

'Ahh, yes we are,' replied Wolflang looking up into the lush, green trees, abundant with vegetation. The elf looked down upon him through branches he had parted with dirty toes, his greying matted hair falling over his face and his aging bow resting in his arms.

'Interesting,' the warrior said, his whiskered little face appearing to be mulling over the concept of what leaving Tebelligan in actuality meant.

'Do you mean you're leaving Tebelligan for good or just for a holiday?' asked a younger elf in the tree opposite, his head peering over a thicket of x-zaivacress vines.

By now both Wolflang and Afeclin had slowed down their horses to a stop, despite their disinterest in the conversation beginning to take place. The warriors kept chatting and appeared to have nothing better to do with themselves but to bother them.

'I don't know at this stage. We'll see what happens,' answered Wolflang with abruptness.

'Interesting,' the first warrior repeated taking no notice of Wolflang's short reply, 'I don't think I can even remember the last time an elf left the kingdom... oh wait... must have been Rouben.'

'Rousten,' the other warrior chimed in.

'That's it, Rousten! Now that was a long time ago.'

'He sure had a fire in his belly,' said the second warrior with thought.

'Did he ever,' laughed the first, 'wonder whatever became of him.'

'Come on,' whispered Afeclin to Wolflang, 'they have nothing better to do than hold us up.'

Wolflang nodded and the two kicked their horses and continued on their way. As they crossed the border they could still hear the two warriors, their banter audible from quite a distance.

'What a dull job they have,' Wolflang observed, speaking more to himself than to Afeclin.

The elvin warriors' lives had been very uninteresting since the end of the war. All that was left to do was to make sure no one crossed the border that was not permitted. Of course there were systems in place to assure the utmost security in Tebelligan.

Three kitra from the border, to the west of the woods was a small community made up of warriors and their families. Each of the warriors took turns guarding the border by day and night. If by chance there was a security breach that the two on guard at the time could not handle themselves, a call from a short, fat, yaaka horn was made. The warriors in the community would hear and respond with back up forces whilst sending their own messages to other warriors stationed closer to the city. If all the warriors from within the woods could not defuse the problem then the warriors within the city would have been alerted and ready to battle, if need be.

'And yet it would be easy for them to be caught off guard at the moment,' said Afeclin with concern as he looked back to the warriors chatting in the trees. 'They did not even notice us leave.'

Chapter
VIII

Lenna had been whimpering for half an hour or so, feeling sorry for herself. She had not even moved from the place Afeclin and Wolflang had left her. Her insides ached and her throat was sore from the sobbing. Her now red eyes stung. The pain she felt was irrelevant however, compared to the ache she was feeling in her soul.

She did not want to go back home to the city. It felt empty now for she knew Wolflang was not there. Apart from her family she felt there was nothing left for her in Tebelligan.

'What do I dooo?' she asked herself holding her stomach as she crouched over and rocked backward and forward, the dull ache inside of her making her cringe.

What she wanted more than anything was to go along with Afeclin and Wolflang. *I was once told that I should follow my heart in life... Wolflang is my heart, wherever he is, I want to be too...* She considered, *but they would never agree to it, to leave just like that and not tell anybody, besides they would be too far ahead now for me to catch up.*

The more she thought about it though, the less ridiculous the idea became. She would talk herself into following and then talk herself out of it again.

They will have to stop sometime to rest; I can just keep going until I reach them. I have daylight on my side after all.

She stood up and began to walk towards the place she had hidden her horse.

But they also have daylight on their side and if they stop to camp, how should I know where they are? She stopped still and then paced for a moment.

Well, then we will just have to ride like the wind. If we ride with greater speed and without stopping to rest, we are bound to catch up before long, she deliberated.

But... what will mother and father think? She shook her head and sighed. It all seemed so complicated.

I could write to them and tell them. They would understand... wouldn't they? She now ran towards her brown and white spotted horse with excitement, having made up her mind to follow.

'Come Habinna... you and I are going on a little trip,' she said patting the mare's white nose with affection.

She walked the horse through the trees and to the road before flipping the reins over Habinna's head and then grabbing the saddle tightly, she hoisted herself up into the seat.

'Well, here goes nothing,' she said taking a deep breath, then with a hard kick she spurred the horse forward and sat deep into the saddle.

'YAH... Yah!' she yelled as she kicked her heels into the mare again to speed her up.

The ride was exhilarating to say the least. Lenna had always loved to ride. She had received Habinna as a foal when she was just a young elfling herself and was now quite a proficient rider.

Habinna was more than just a horse to Lenna. She had often confided in the dark-eyed mare and the two had gone almost everywhere together. While the mare had aged now and was in the latter part of her life she still had a lot of stamina and when Lenna pushed her, she gave it her all as if she had the spirit of a young horse.

They kept their pace up for a long time before Habinna started to snort and pant. Lenna allowed her to slow down, feeling sorry for the mare who was now draped in sweat having pushed herself to the limit.

'Oh Habinna, you have done well,' she muttered as she patted the horses wet neck, 'I really thought we would have caught up by now.'

Lenna, exhausted herself, considered giving up. 'What am I doing? This is crazy.'

They walked on a little further and Lenna spied something in the distance.

'Whoa!' she squealed, finding renewed energy to continue.

'It's the border. We made it to the border!'

She walked Habinna through the trees that fenced the border of Tebelligan, as she did she held her breath. She had never ventured this far before and now she was about to cross the border and step into another world, one that she wasn't at all sure about and did not know if she could trust. She held Habinna's reins close to her chest and allowed the horse to carry her over.

'Hey, are you leaving too?' yelled an unfamiliar voice from above her.

Lenna looked up into the trees and saw a dirty-looking elf peering down upon her.

'I... I...' she stammered trying to make her mind up as to whether she was going to leave or not, 'I think so.'

She stopped short, 'Did you see another elf leaving?'

'Sure did, and that human fella was with him,' he answered with interest, 'you with them?'

'Yes, I was trying to catch up. Did they come past long ago?' Lenna asked, feeling a sudden modicum of hope returning.

'Not long ago I should think,' he said through blackened toes that reminded Lenna of pieces of coal.

Lenna looked at the road ahead. She could see fresh hoof prints in the dusty red dirt.

'I can't believe the traffic out of Tebelligan today,' came another elf's voice from a tree on the opposing side of the stone road she had just come by. 'Are you planning on coming back or is this a permanent situation?'

Lenna thought for a moment looking into the tree the other voice had come from, but not seeing anyone.

'I really have not given the matter much thought,' she responded, 'I suppose I shall come back at some stage.'

'Well, if you do, be sure to let whoever is on guard know that you are an elf before crossing the border. We have our orders to shoot to wound anyone who crosses without permission,' the elf in the first tree stated with all seriousness, 'and I would hate to see that pretty backside of yours pierced with an arrow.'

The two chuckled.

Lenna frowned, ignoring the joke.

'Come on Habinna,' she said encouraging the mare away from the long grass she had been grazing in, 'we are not far behind and now that we have had a rest we can pick up our speed again.'

Lenna gave Habinna a hard jab in the sides and the mare lunged forward, gaining speed.

They're not far now, not far.

Chapter

IX

Another hour passed without event and the two travellers came to a fork in the road. Afeclin halted his horse and feeling into his bag, retrieved the map. Studying the details, he confirmed the way that they needed to go. The left road would take them through the Woods of Devan to the small town of Desprade; to the right was Pixie Grove.

'This way,' Afeclin called kicking his horse to gallop onward, veering to the left.

Wolflang followed with a jaded sigh.

After travelling all evening in the blazing heat, the sun began to set bringing with it some relief to the weary travellers. A breeze swam through the trees, shaking the traffita's and rustling the green foliage. They had moved along at quite a pace all day and now fatigue was starting to set in.

Afeclin slowed down to a stop and pulled out his map once more. 'We will need to camp in the woods tonight. I estimate that we will make it to Desprade tomorrow, before sun down.'

Camp in the woods? Wolflang shivered a little at the idea. It was not as if he were a stranger to sleeping on the soft mossy ground of the forest, he had done that many times. There wasn't too much danger camping out in any of the woods within Tebelligan. There was the possibility of a chance encounter with a wandering wild pig or the odd snake or two in summer but no real threat. These woods were a different story, however. They were not protected from invaders. *Who knows what lunatics are hiding in the woods waiting for weary travellers to fall asleep?*

Afeclin stopped further along the road and reviewed the map again while he waited for Wolflang to catch up. 'What's wrong?' he called out, noting Wolflang's hesitation.

'Oh nothing... I just hadn't expected...'

He rode up to join Afeclin on the road.

'Shhh... Did you hear that?' said Afeclin putting a finger to his lips as he sat very still, cocking his head to one side.

The two sat in silence, listening.

A slight breeze, a rustle of leaves... *What am I supposed to be hearing?*

Afeclin sat with a look of concern, 'You hear that? What *is* that?'

At first Wolflang thought Afeclin must have been hearing things but then all of a sudden he heard it also. It was only faint to begin with but the sound soon grew.

The noise came from the road ahead and by the sound of it, was getting closer. From what Wolflang could make out, it seemed to be the sound of wagons and marching feet and many horse hooves trampling the hard ground.

'What is that?' asked Wolflang his heart beating fast as the sound grew louder.

'I don't know but I do not think we should be loitering here waiting to find out... come on.'

With that, Afeclin turned his horse and dove into the thick scrub to the left of them. Wolflang followed close behind.

Once they were hidden from the road they stopped and dismounted their horses. Leaving them to graze, Afeclin and Wolflang made their way closer to the road to see what was about to pass by.

'Over here,' Wolflang whispered, 'this tree is perfect for viewing without detection.'

Wolflang climbed the tree with much elfish skill and dexterity, whilst Afeclin clambered up the tree just as the first of the wagons began to pass by.

From the tree limb of the sturdy bankoi, they could see everything without discovery. The trees were thick on both sides of the road with similar vegetation as in Taybie Woods. The dirt road in between however was much wider and well travelled.

As the first wagon rolled by it kicked up unsettled dust and dirt from the dry, hot road. The dust was red and painted everything it landed on. The nearby shrubs, grass, the wagon base and its occupants were all tinted by the red dirt. The wagon was driven by two ugly, mean-looking beasts. Their faces looked a bit like wild pigs with round, fat noses, large teeth and small ears on their huge faces. They were both clad in black leather armour.

'What kind of creatures are they?' asked Wolflang barely above a whisper.

Afeclin shrugged.

'They're trolls,' answered a quiet voice from above them.

They both looked up to see where the voice had come from. Through the dense feathered leaves of the branch above them they could make out a figure.

'Trolls?'

'Yeah, I think they are working for Moorlan,' the voice answered.

'Moorlan?' Wolflang asked with a frown.

'You fellas are not from round here are ya?' the voice commented.

'Well, not really.'

'Shhh! Look!' Afeclin said elbowing Wolflang in the ribs.

Wolflang looked back down to the road. By now several hooded wagons had passed by with footmen carrying swords walking beside them. Now a number of henchmen on horseback came riding by surrounding a large open wagon carrying many pretty young maidens. Through the dusty red cloud that followed the travellers Wolflang could see some maidens who were crying in others' arms, some who spat at the trolls and yelled curses whilst some of them simply sat, staring into the woods.

'What is going on?' Afeclin whispered under his breath.

Just then a slender girl with lengthy dark curls, wearing a long red silk dress jumped from the moving wagon and ran for the woods in their direction.

With lightning speed, Wolflang grabbed his bow and pulled an arrow from his quiver ready to fend off any of the trolls if they tried to follow her but a hand came down from the branch above and grabbed the arrow from him.

'Are you nuts?' the voice whispered with a stern growl. 'You can't fend off that many trolls. Do you want to kill us all?'

'She ran because she saw us in the tree. She is relying on us to help her,' Wolflang answered in desperation.

'You can't help her, trying will only kill her and us.'

Wolflang sat speechless, fuming in the tree as he watched the henchmen chase after the young woman.

It didn't take long for the heavy men to catch the girl as she tripped over her skirts just below the tree they were sitting in. One of the trolls picked her up with a very large hand and slapped her hard across the face. Her large brown eyes watered as a flush of red engulfed her already pink cheek.

'We'll see what Nagrin has to say about you holding up the wagons,' he huffed and snarled.

The girl winced in pain but then held her head up high with grace and dignity.

A fair-haired human man dressed in black descended from a dark carriage that had been following the wagon carrying the maidens and walked toward the courageous girl.

'Oh no, Nagrin,' the man from above breathed.

Nagrin trod with heavy steps, his hands clasped behind his back. His wavy, shoulder-length hair caught the breeze and flew back behind his ears revealing a long jagged scar on the left side of his face that started just below his eye and ended at his chin. His left eyelid was partially closed over his eye looking somewhat deformed.

'So you were trying to make a run for it,' Nagrin said with a loud calm voice then added with sarcasm, 'what, don't like the food?'

'A wagon full of slaves is no place for a general's daughter,' the girl said with defiance.

'A general's daughter? Interesting, which general would that be? Ellaan? Zucuroh?' Nagrin asked with a slight smile.

'Hoashan,' the girl declared.

'Poor naïve girl,' the man above them said, sucking in his breath.

'Oh really?' Nagrin said with an eyebrow raised as he rubbed a hand over the scar on his face. 'Well in that case you are right, a slavery wagon is no place for you.'

The girl looked hopeful for an instant, then let out a feeble scream as Nagrin took a sword from one of the trolls and without a moment's pause or hesitation, plunged it through her heart. The general's daughter fell to the ground in a heap as Nagrin squatted himself down beside her.

He pulled the sword from her chest and without wiping it clean, passed it back to the troll.

'A slavery wagon is much too good for you,' he said with a gloved hand under her chin lifting the girl's motionless face toward him. Then standing up, he faced the rest of the girls watching from the wagon in horror. 'Let this be a lesson to the rest of you. Anyone else tries a trick like that and you will suffer the same fate.'

🐦 🐦 🐦

After the last of the wagons and henchmen on horseback had ridden by, the three in the tree climbed down and tended to the girl.

Wolflang picked up the girl and felt for a heartbeat.

'She's dead,' he said with a look of sickness flooding over him.

'Of course she is, ya can't survive a blow to the heart,' said the man who had been with them in the tree.

'We could have saved her. We SHOULD have saved her!' Wolflang hollered.

'We couldn't have saved her and it was lucky we didn't try,' retorted the man without enmity. 'You saw that man with the scarred face? That's Nagrin. He's what you might call Moorlan's right hand man. Had you killed some of his henchmen he would have killed you. Had he not been able to kill you, he would have put a warrant so high upon ya head ya wouldn't be alive to see next week. Now, I don't know where ya fellas are from but you can't be travelling these woods with a price on your head, it's not smart. There are that many thieves about who would kill a man for the price of a beer.'

'I apologise for my friend,' said Afeclin. 'We are not from around here and are not familiar with these woods but we do appreciate your advice.'

'Ah no matter, listen, the names Typhin.'

Now that he wasn't hidden in the tree the two friends could see whom they had been speaking to. It was obvious that Typhin was human but was only a foot taller than Wolflang. He looked advanced in years as his face and body were weathered but his eyes had a much younger look to them suggesting that he was perhaps middle-aged. He was wearing long tattered shorts with a cord belt around his waist and a short-sleeved green shirt that was unbuttoned revealing a tanned, muscular chest that appeared to be covered in ink pictures. Afeclin could only make out part of a clawed paw and something that looked like a scorpion's tail; the rest was covered by the shirt. The short human wore ankle height cloth boots that were frayed at the tops and his legs were dark from dirt. His hair was short, blonde and curly and light stubble shrouded his face.

'I'm Afeclin and this is Wolflang.'

Wolflang nodded at Typhin, then looking somewhat ill ran behind a tree and vomited.

'Hey, he's an elf, right? Gee I haven't seen an elf since… well since the war,' remarked the stranger with surprise. 'Sheesh, what a day this is turning out to be.'

Afeclin studied the listless girl lying on the ground at their feet. She lay on her back staring up into the trees with lifeless eyes. Blood had now spilled out of her chest that was soaked up by her dress and her once pink cheeks were now a pale white. Afeclin felt a sick feeling come over him also but resisted the urge to throw up.

Neither Afeclin nor Wolflang had ever seen a dead person before now. However, the gruesome sight brought back the vision of the tragedy, which beset his family that Afeclin had witnessed. Trying hard to keep his emotions at bay, he stood back away from the girl crossing his arms and inhaling deep breaths, in through the nose and out through the mouth. It seemed to Afeclin to be another senseless act of violence.

Is this what the world is like? Ruthless and violent?

Before Afeclin had visited the town of his birth he had expected the world to be dangerous and cruel but he hadn't quite anticipated such brutality. The scarred man, Nagrin, had not even flinched when murdering the poor girl. *Is it possible to become desensitised to such violent acts?* Afeclin found it hard to imagine deciding it acceptable to take another person's life. However Typhin did not seem to be bothered by it at all. He was perhaps a little sad but he treated the event in a matter-of-fact way.

'What should we do with her?'

'Leave her there, she'll be found, I'm sure someone will be looking for her,' answered Typhin squatting down beside the girl's inanimate form.

'How do you know?'

'She's General Hoashan's daughter. He won't take her disappearance lightly.'

'Was it because of the General that she died?' Afeclin queried.

'Yeah,' said Typhin looking down at the girl, 'poor kid, she shouldn't have told him who she was.'

'Why is that?'

'You saw that big scar on Nagrin's face?'

Afeclin nodded.

'General Hoashan gave it to him,' Typhin responded covering the girl's face with his hand and with gentle, almost reverent force, closing her eyelids. He bowed his head, shaking it in remorse.

Wolflang rejoined them looking sick and pale.

'What's the matter with you? Ya look like you never saw a dead person before,' laughed Typhin as he stood up rubbing a couple of the dark green bankoi leaves between his hands as if cleaning them.

'Oh I've seen plenty of people die,' Wolflang lied, 'I just think I must have eaten something bad, that's all.'

'Well, that happens,' said Typhin changing the subject, 'listen, where are you two camping tonight?'

'We were just about to find somewhere when we heard the wagons approach,' answered Afeclin, turning his back to the dead girl so he did not have to look at her.

'My friends and I are camped a little further in the woods if you would like to join us,' offered Typhin with a pleasant smile.

Afeclin nodded, feeling reassured that camping with men who understood the dangers of the woods would be far safer than camping on their own. 'We would like that.'

Chapter

X

Lenna had been riding for quite some time along the red dusty track. In an attempt to quicken her pace, she had sped up the exhausted mare between spurts of walking. She was tired and sore herself and longed for a rest but she had come so far out of Tebelligan that she simply had to catch up to Wolflang and Afeclin.

Now, as evening set in, Lenna rode with her head hung. Hope of finding her friends had all but vanished. She had pushed Habinna so hard that the old horse had a hard time keeping up the pace anymore. Her backside ached and she had a terrible thirst.

One ordinarily plans these travels much better I'm sure, she thought to herself.

But she hadn't planned to come on this journey so she was not prepared at all. Carrying nothing but her bow and quiver of arrows that she had fled out the cottage door with early that morning, she was less than ready for travelling. She still wore the clothes that she had been wearing the day before when they travelled to Payden's Pool. Her hair was still matted and dirty.

After such a pleasant day and restful sleep full of beautiful dreams, Lenna had woken with the sun shining in through her window at dawn. She would have slept the whole day away after the New Moon celebrations but it seemed she had forgotten to close her thick drapes allowing the sun to spill in and brighten everything with its glow.

She had barely opened her eyes when she had spied the note on the desk, written in Wolflang's hand-script. She had jumped out of her soft bed with enthusiasm and picked up the note suspecting it was a love letter.

What a fool I was. Lenna sorrowed as she remembered her excitement that morning. How her heart had broken as she read the note and how angry and resentful she had felt.

All of a sudden she heard a sound on the road ahead in the distance. Her heart skipped a beat as she hearkened to the noise. It sounded like horse hooves pummelling the hard ground.

'It's them! Finally... we caught up,' Lenna reported, excitement and energy returning to her being.

'One last run Habinna, and we will have caught up... but let us not chance losing them now.'

She kicked Habinna hard inciting the mare to bound forward and push herself to her limit once more.

Kicking up red dirt as they raced at full speed, Lenna could hear the pounding feet becoming louder and closer, until she knew that once she rounded the next bend in the road, she would see them.

Hurtling around the bend she almost collided with a couple of odd-looking burly men on horseback. They looked at her with a strange expression that was discomforting as they pulled back their horses in reaction.

Lenna, feeling great fear of these men in the pit of her stomach, gave Habinna another hard jab to the sides with her heels, spurring the horse onward.

Passing them on the right she became aware of more riders on horseback. They all seemed to look at her as she flew by. A dozen human women watched her from where they sat in a wagon looking downcast and forlorn. She stared back with intrigue, realising she had never seen a human female before.

'Elf!' rang out in her ears from the men that she had passed.

What appeared to be some kind of procession had come to a standstill. She trudged on with more desperation than ever.

What is this? she asked herself with greater fear rising within her.

As she passed a big black carriage, she could see a scarred man's face through a small window on one side. While she could not hear him, his lips seemed to mouth the words 'An ELF!'

An elf indeed, the words penetrated her soul with indignant pride. *It is as if nobody ever saw one before.* While she was conscious of the fact that there would be a great many people who had never been in contact with an elf before, it made her uncomfortable being watched with curiosity like a wild animal.

'Get that elf!' came a shout from the carriage.

'RUN!' shrieked a few of the women from the wagon. 'You mustn't stop for anything!'

It dawned on Lenna that the women were not simply travellers holed up in a tight space but that they were prisoners and if she did not make haste, she would find herself alongside them.

She gave Habinna a couple of hard kicks to hurry up and speed past the strange procession.

She could hear the drum of horse feet on the ground behind her, gaining on her.

Lenna managed to make it beyond the horses and wagons but her heartbeat was unrestrained as she struggled to keep up the pace. Her eyes searched the woods for some kind of beaten track that she could somehow escape into but the woods were thick with trees and lacked any sign of a rideable pathway through.

Nowhere to go, Habinna started to lag and two big, pig-faced men were on her tail. Fear swept through Lenna like a gush of wind. It enveloped her and made her feel like it was utter hopelessness. Still she kicked Habinna again and again to spur the mare on faster, to gain some distance from her assailants. She gripped the saddle in order to keep from falling.

I don't know how much longer we can keep this up, she thought with despair.

She kept her mind focused on the road searching for some way to flee. They had ridden quite some distance from where they had left the cavalcade stationary on the roadside.

Lenna realised she still carried her bow and arrows with her but there was no way for her to ride at the speed she was and shoot. If she were to stop she feared the men would be upon her. Lenna only wished she had Wolflang's ability of rolling to the ground before firing an arrow but she had not learned such manoeuvres.

So she kept up the sprint, hoping in desperation to meet up with Wolflang but with her eyes peeled for something that could aid her.

At last she saw something in the distance that hung down from the trees.

As she neared it she discovered that it was a large tree limb that draped itself over the road.

If I could just reach that branch and grab hold of it, she thought to herself, *I may be able to pull myself up on it.*

As the tree came closer Lenna started to prepare herself. She put her feet up on the saddle with careful precision, then between the horse's jolting, attempted to steady herself in a squatted position.

In the blink of an eye that tree was right above her. Without any time to think she stood up in the saddle and grabbed hold of the branch leaving Habinna to continue on down the road. There she hung, dangling over the road while she used all her effort and might to swing her legs up over the thick limb and pull herself up.

She managed to scamper up just as the men reached the tree. They came to a grinding halt underneath.

'Come on little elf,' one of the pig-faced men called in a deep gruff voice as he dismounted his horse, 'we're not going to hurt you.'

Lenna sat in the tree, knowing full well she was not yet safe. She looked around at the neighbouring trees to see if there were any that she could leap across to. Alas there were no large trees close enough, she was surrounded by small trees and shrubs.

Well, that will never do, she thought to herself, devastated.

She looked back down at the men, clad in black armour, hovering at the bottom of the tree. One of them attempted to climb up after her.

'You can't get away from us that easily,' he crowed.

Lenna jerked her bow from around her shoulder and snatched an arrow from her quiver. Wrapping one leg around a nearby branch to steady herself, she drew back the bowstring with two skinny fingers and aimed it at the burly man who was heaving himself up the tree after her.

'You want to bet.' The words felt strong but left her lips with feebleness.

The man glanced up at Lenna and stared at her with mouth agape but did not stop climbing.

Lenna let the bowstring go and the arrow soared straight into the man's neck. He let out an agonising wail and as he did so, let go of the branch he was holding and dropped to the ground. He pulled at the arrow, enraged and managed to pluck the fine tipped projectile from his thick neck. Much blood spilled from the wound in a stream down his body and despite the large man's every attempt to stop it, he fell to the ground dead.

The other man looked to Lenna in shock. She held her bow up with the bowstring drawn ready to shoot another arrow if need be.

The man started towards the tree fearless and angry. Lenna did not hesitate, she let the arrow slip, this time making an intentional hit in the leg. The man yowled in pain but still attempted to hobble toward the tree.

'I will get you for that elf!' he yelled in rage.

Lenna grabbed at another arrow. Feeding it into the arrow-rest she drew back the bowstring once more.

The man neared the tree without sign of retreat so she let the string go again, the arrow hitting him in the other leg.

The man groaned in anger and pain and fell to his knees, ripping both arrows out in unison.

When he managed to balance himself back onto his feet he began to totter toward the tree and then looked up at Lenna.

'I wouldn't come any closer if I were you,' she called with another arrow drawn aimed at the man.

The man scratched his face in thought.

'You are one tough little elf...'

He turned around, walked back to his horse and with great effort pulled himself into the saddle.

He rode back toward the procession of waiting wagons, the dead man's horse following close behind.

Lenna bowed her head and breathed a sigh of relief. As she did so she spied the dead man at the foot of the tree. Tears filled her eyes as a sudden realisation came upon her.

'I am a killer,' she said almost choking on her own words.

Chapter

XI

Lenna had been crying into the tree for a while when it dawned on her that there was a good chance she still was not out of harm's way. Looking back down the tree she could see the deceased body of the pig-faced man. She did not want to climb down while he was there but then again she did not want to stay suspended over him either.

Lenna climbed backwards down the tree. Swinging from a low limb she jumped to the ground.

She tried whistling for Habinna but the old mare did not come.

Well, she cannot be still running.

Looking up and down the road with caution, she ventured back out onto the road but kept to the side where the trees lined the track and the leaves hung over the edge shading her from the sun that was starting to sink in the sky.

Tired, hungry and sick over what she had done, Lenna walked on. No longer interested in finding Wolflang and Afeclin, she purely trudged on to locate her horse.

She hadn't gone very much further when she spied something of a dark colour amongst all the greenery. Turning her head in uncertainty she beheld something that appeared to be red fabric lying in the woods on the other side of the road.

Lenna crossed the road, absently checking both ways. As she approached the other side and stumbled into the long grass a couple of feet, she muffled a scream. There on the forest floor lay a girl in a red silk dress with long dark locks and pale white skin. Lenna dared to take a step closer. Holding her breath to block out a pungent smell in the air, she stood almost over the girl's lifeless form. Lenna could see that she had been stabbed with something sharp. Blood stained her chest as well as some of the leaves on which she lay.

Lenna stepped backwards with trepidation, a sick feeling overcoming her again.

This cannot be real, what kind of place is this?

She started to run in the direction of home.

I don't want to be here anymore, this place is crazy! I have to go home, I do not care where Wolflang is anymore.

She stopped all of a sudden in the middle of the road.

What if those wagons are still there? What if those pig-faced men are waiting for me?

She stood frozen on the spot not knowing what to do. She felt trapped, feeling that she could not head for home but realising she had nowhere else to go.

First I will find Habinna, she determined.

She turned around and headed back up the road. As she passed by the girl in red she refused to look and kept focused on the road ahead.

The sun was beginning to disappear behind the trees when Lenna beheld something lying in a ditch nestled under the low branches of bankoi trees.

She ran towards it with an anxious heart, knowing full well that it was Habinna.

'Oh my darling Habinna,' she called as she ran down into the small mossy ditch to be with her horse.

The old mare lifted her head with acknowledgement and snuffed.

Lenna wrapped her arms around Habinna's fine neck and hugged her.

'We are safe now and you do not have to run anymore tonight,' she hushed with a tender murmur into the mare's ear. 'Tomorrow when it is safer, we will return home and forget all about this ridiculous charade.'

The horse lay its head back down and rested with shallow breaths.

Lenna lay next to her, nestled in her soft coat and patted the horse's nose with softness.

'I do not understand why in Titania Wolflang would want to come to this awful place.'

Tears of despair and tiredness began to fall down her cheeks as she gave up her body to exhaustion and fell asleep.

Chapter

XII

After collecting the horses the three made their way through the woods to the area Typhin and his friends had set up camp. The mass of tree limbs colliding overhead this far into the woods blocked much of the setting sun's rays making the woods appear dim and eerie. The haunting sound of the white ghost owl's hoots could be heard echoing through the trees.

In a small clearing two men sat on logs of wood surrounding a bunch of sticks strewn together to make a fire. The smaller, stockier man appeared to be trying to start the fire by rubbing two dry sticks together, without success.

'I've brought some travellers back with me to share our camp and fire...'

Typhin stared at the dismal attempt, 'Ya still working on that, Raan?'

The small man muttered something under his breath.

'The grumbling dwarf rubbing sticks together is Raan. Don't take any notice of him, ya know how dwarves are, always something to complain about,' Typhin teased.

Neither Wolflang nor Afeclin had ever seen any other race before but they had learnt of them. Raan looked somewhat as Afeclin had imagined a dwarf to look with a red bushy beard that had small braids on either side of his chin and thick frizzy hair tied back into a plait. He was shorter than Wolflang and had stumpy little legs. He had a round stocky body that looked strong and solid and he wore a cream shirt that had ripped sleeves with brown pants that tucked into his heavy black boots. His face was old and tired and seemed to have a permanent scowl on it.

'The Goblin is Pitangus, but we call him Pit for short,' Typhin introduced as he circled the log and placed a hand on the goblin's shoulder. 'Now I know what you're thinking; you can't trust a goblin, right? Well, that is right, you should never, EVER trust a goblin; they are definitely not a trustworthy race, however there is always an exception to the rule and Pit... well, he's the exception,' laughed Typhin.

'Hey watch what you have to say about my race,' said Pit sounding wounded. Then he gave a wide smile revealing brown, crooked teeth, 'Actually it's all true.'

Pit was a slender goblin with chalky white skin, piercing grey eyes and few hairs on his bald head. The tallest of the three men, but shorter than Afeclin, he was long and skinny and had a muscular physique despite his thinness. He wore a brown tunic with woven goat hair armbands and had ink markings at the tops of his arms. Afeclin could not make any sense of the dark swirls and lines, which protruded from Pit's shoulders and ended at his elbows. They were not pictures nor did they appear to be writing of any sort. The goblin also wore curious cloth boots that had pointy ends that curled up over his toes.

'This is Wolflang and Afeclin,' Typhin announced.

'Hey, aren't you an elf?' asked Pit.

'Yeah... I am,' Wolflang answered with hesitation.

'Wow I haven't seen an elf in years, not since the Great War anyway.'

'Yeah, elves don't leave Tebelligan nowadays do they?' Typhin asked.

'I guess you could call me the exception to the rule,' said Wolflang with a slight smile.

Pit burst into laughter, 'I like this fellow. Come over and sit down, we will have a nice warm fire to share if Raan ever gets the thing going.'

'The wood you gathered is not the right sort,' Raan groused into his beard, 'it will probably never spark.'

'Well, I guess we will have to have raw owl then,' Pit said with a dismal frown. 'So where are you fellows headed?'

'Lawry castle,' Wolflang said sitting down on a cool mossy log.

'Why would you go there?' asked Typhin with confusion. 'Only wizards go there.'

'Well, my friend Afeclin here is a wizard,' revealed Wolflang in haste. Afeclin shot Wolflang a dark look.

While he felt a certain comfort with the strangers, he was not too sure if they could be trusted with his secret.

'I am hoping the wizard Zallucien will take me on as his apprentice,' Afeclin explained.

'Did you hear that Pit? We have a young wizard in our presence!' Typhin laughed in jest.

'Load of codswallop, magic is,' Raan wheezed.

'Do you know any good tricks?' asked Pit with eagerness.

'Well…' said Afeclin pausing to consider whether it was wise to show off some of his skill or not, *maybe something small and insignificant.*

'I could light that fire without having to rub sticks together for hours.'

'Codswallop!' argued Raan.

Afeclin closed his eyes for a moment concentrating and then snapped the fingers of his left hand. On top of his index finger sat a tiny flame. The flame did not touch Afeclin nor burn him but just danced above the very tip of his finger. Pointing towards the bunch of sticks and allowing the flame to jump onto the wood he then commanded the wood to…

'Burn.'

The fire engulfed the wood in obedience, lighting up the small area they sat in, warming their faces.

'Trickery!' Raan cursed as he fell backwards almost tumbling off the log.

'I don't know Pit but you would think Raan would be happy he can stop rubbing those sticks together, wouldn't ya?'

'You would think so,' answered Pit turning his attention toward Afeclin. 'That is some trick. How do you do it?'

'Magic,' Afeclin smirked.

Chapter

XIII

Lenna roused from a tormented night's sleep to the sound of horse hooves pounding the ground on the road behind her.

She turned to watch what was passing by, nervous that she might be found. It was fortunate for her the riders came from the east and did not seem to see her or Habinna in the ditch. Covered by low-lying branches and feathered bankoi leaves, they could not be seen from that direction.

The riders appeared to be dressed in some kind of dark brown uniform that had silver lines and patterns on the sleeves and chest. They were buttoned up to their necks in argent studs and wore matching wide rimmed hats upon their heads.

While they appeared to be very different to the men that she had run into the day before, Lenna was uncertain whether she could trust them or not. She breathed a sigh of relief as the riders who appeared to be human passed by, disappearing into a cloud of dust, not seeing her from the open side of the thicket.

'Now we just need to get out of here Habinna,' she said shaking the sleeping horse, 'we are going home.'

She shook the horse again hard but the horse did not stir, in fact the old mare seemed very stiff.

'Oh no,' Lenna let out a staggered breath as she stifled a cry, 'no Habinna, do not leave me in this awful place alone!'

It was too late, the mare had slipped away sometime in the night and was now dead.

Lenna fell over the old horse in tears, crying into her coarse hair with all her heart.

The previous day's ride had been brutal for Habinna. It was clear the mare had given her absolute all to protect Lenna. She had ridden beyond her capabilities in outrunning the pig-faced men and had died ensuring Lenna's escape.

'Oh Habinna,' Lenna wailed in sadness, 'you were such a great horse.'

Lenna kissed the old mare on the nose and began to stand up, 'Goodbye my friend... I will miss you.'

Attempting to pull herself together, she took deep breaths. She picked up her quiver and bow and belted them back over her shoulder in haste, then she climbed her way back up the trench and onto the red dirt track.

Bewildered, she looked up and down the road.

I do not know which way to go, Lenna thought to herself with fear rising in the pit of her stomach.

She was deathly afraid of who she might run into if she were to head back towards Tebelligan. She was unsure about wandering into the woods, feeling like she might get lost in all the dense scrub. She also shuddered to think of the girl in red lying dead on the side of the road and the ugly man she had killed further on.

Those men on horseback might stumble upon him. If I go back there, they will find me and figure out that I was the one who killed him.

Her only option seemed to continue down the dirt road and further into the unknown.

Maybe, just maybe, I will find Wolflang yet, she hoped.

Finding Wolflang and Afeclin seemed to Lenna her only chance of surviving outside Tebelligan.

She began by walking and then sped up her pace. Before long she was running along the red dirt track kicking up dust, hungry, alone and now desperate to find her friends.

Chapter
XIV

The ground had been a lot colder and harder to sleep on than it had first appeared. Wolflang had found himself sleeping on rock and although the rock was covered in fresh fallen leaves and moss it provided little comfort for the elf. Adding to the problem, the day's events had kept playing over and over again in his mind. In the early hours of the morning, exhaustion overcame him and Wolflang, tired and achy, fell into a deep sleep.

It was during this sleep, while his body was relaxed and free from the tension built up in him from the previous day, that he saw a familiar being.

A human man, wearing a leather cloak, stood before him and beckoned for Wolflang to follow. His face was shadowed by the cloak's hood apart from his jaw and cheekbones covered in thick, greying stubble. Deep wrinkles around his mouth and down his neck showed that the man was aged and his weathered hands were old but strong.

'You're the hooded man I saw at the celebrations the other night.'

The man nodded and once again beckoned for Wolflang to come with him.

Wolflang, while curious, felt at ease with the old man despite his mysterious nature. He began to walk towards the hooded figure, stepping with lightness on the ground.

The older man led Wolflang to the edge of a cliff. There he beckoned the elf with an open hand to cast his eyes over.

Wolflang came and stood beside the hooded man, looking down into a deep valley beset by mountains.

He beheld a frightening scene before his eyes. For there in the valley a mighty battle raged. Heavy men clad in black armour, not unlike the pig-faced trolls they had seen the day before, surrounded a small multi-raced army.

Wolflang could hear the clang of swords clashing and shouts of anger and fear as men fought for their lives, giving everything they had. Blood flooded the terrain as one by one, the smaller army's men fell to the ground dead.

The men in black, having been victorious, waved their swords in the air and cheered in celebration of their slaughter. It was a sickening sight.

'What is this?' Wolflang asked shaking his head.

The hooded man spoke at last, 'It is a vision of an event that is to come.'

Wolflang felt sick to his stomach. He stared at the strange man with an incredulous frown. 'Why do you show me this?'

'In this moment of time lies a part of your destiny,' the hooded man said as he faded away before Wolflang's eyes.

'What do you mean? I am to die down there?' Wolflang shouted at the already faded figure.

Wolflang's mind raced as he tried hard to comprehend what he had just witnessed. He buried his head in his hands in sorrow and slumped down to the ground.

෯ ෯ ෯

Bursts of sunlight filtered through the large trees, a sweet smell of damp bankoi fragranced the air and a light mist was lifting as Wolflang awoke.

The early morning song of black nali-birds rang out through the woods. With their long red tufts of plumage on top of their heads that stuck up in the air when singing their sweet tune, they puffed up their salmon striped breasts as noise exploded through tiny blackened beaks.

Wolflang rubbed his eyes as he lifted his head out from under his thick brown cloak in which he had been sleeping. Still drowsy from sleep he was somewhat confused by his surroundings at first, then one by one the events came back to him. He remembered Lenna, the sadness in her eyes as he left her alone in the Taybie Woods. On her knees she had appeared heartbroken and confused and Wolflang had refused to look back at her in fear of intensifying the guilt he already felt.

There was the girl in red. The icy stare as she lay on her back looking with blankness into the sky, her once scarlet lips that had turned blue and the blood-soaked dress was more than Wolflang could stand to recall. Then he remembered the dream. The scene of the battle, that shattered his soul at the sight of the senseless killing spree, played over in his mind.

The sick feeling he had had the day before returned to his stomach and a dizziness swept over him like a wave causing him to lie his head back down again. He had been hoping that he would awaken and find that the previous day was all just a terrible nightmare, but even his dreams now haunted him. He wished that he were back home in Tebelligan with Lenna. *And the girl in red?... Well... I wouldn't have known about her... I wouldn't have seen her die by herself on the side of the road. I would still be living in ignorant bliss just like the rest of the elves... but that isn't the point, is it? Regardless of where I was or wasn't, a murder would still have taken place, the only difference would be whether I knew about it or not.*

Wolflang had understood the world was a lot more dangerous outside Tebelligan. He had imagined roughness and thievery but not outright murdering of defenceless young girls. He closed his eyes and winced as he remembered the pain in her eyes as the sharpness of the blade struck her clean through the heart. She had looked to him in her final moment, before she fell. Her eyes had pleaded with him to rescue her from such a brutal fate. *I let her down. Perhaps she would never have died if I had not left Tebelligan after all. Maybe she would never have jumped from the wagon and risked her life if I had not been in the tree watching,* he thought to himself in shame. *If that is so, then her blood is now on my hands.*

'We got to get a move on,' came a voice from above him. Wolflang opened one eye to see who was speaking and saw Pit hovering above him rubbing his hands to warm them as he spoke, a long finely crafted wooden bow was draped over his shoulders. 'Come on, we can't stay here; it's not safe.'

Wolflang lifted his head up and looked around. Afeclin was busy packing the horses. Raan was pouring water over the last of the burning embers from the fire the night before and Pit had rolled up his bedding and was now tying string around it to keep it together.

Wolflang's head dropped back down onto the moss-covered rock that was his pillow and tried to make some sense of what was going on.

'What is happening?' he asked giving a rough cough. 'What is all the hurry?'

This time Afeclin came over and squatted down beside him.

'Typhin and Pit went back to the road this morning after they heard a noise coming from that direction. Apparently some of Hoashan's men were there. They had found the girl and from what Pit could make out they were just waiting for General Hoashan himself to arrive.'

'We have to leave before they start searching the woods and find us to blame for the girl's murder,' added Pit climbing onto his horse. 'I really didn't think they would find her so soon.'

Wolflang's head started to spin again as he stood up and headed for his horse.

'What are we running for? Wouldn't it be better to approach them and let them know just who exactly did kill his daughter?' he managed to ask.

'Are you crazy?' Raan croaked. 'Have you ever met Hoashan? A great general he may be, but he is likely to have your head on a spit before you have had a chance to say, "it wasn't me."'

'He's right kid, I know you want to do the right thing but trust us, you do not want to face Hoashan right now. As far as he is concerned as long as someone pays for his daughter's death, it won't matter who.'

The whole world is crazy, Wolflang thought as he climbed onto his horse. Just then Typhin returned, racing into the camp on his chestnut mare. He stopped just shy of the logs and pulling in the reins tight he caused the horse to thrust her head back in protest.

'They seem to think she was kidnapped by travellers,' Typhin hollered as he jumped down onto the ground from his horse. He grabbed his sword and sheath that had been propped up against a large rock and wrapped the long red strap twice around his waist, buckling it. Next he picked up and shook a thin cloak that had been strewn on the ground the night before. The small human tied the straps of the cloak around his neck. 'We must leave now, without delay,' he hurried as he snatched at a wide brimmed tattered straw hat that had been resting on a tree branch and positioned it onto his head in a haphazard fashion.

'Should we not split up then?' asked Pit with concern. 'We may have a better chance of losing them should they follow.'

'Ya right Pit. The smaller the groups we travel in, the less suspicious we become,' said Typhin, remounting his horse in haste. 'Raan, you take Wolflang east along the coast. Pit, you and Afeclin keep riding through the woods, but be careful not to be seen. I will head back north through the woods and eventually turn around to come back up the old track. We'll meet in Desprade by sundown.'

'The usual place?'

'Yeah,' Typhin nodded giving his horse a swift kick and galloping away through the tall trees and thick shrubbery.

Afeclin and Pit were the next to leave. Urging on their horses they disappeared into the dense scrub and morning mist. Wolflang looked to the dwarf and awaited his command. Raan grumbled something into his beard and after giving Wolflang a wary backward glance he too kicked his horse and galloped away. Wolflang watched as the little man bounced up and down in the saddle, his knotted plait pounding his back as he rode. Giving one last glance around at the campsite, he shook his head trying to relieve the lightheadedness he had been feeling. With a growing uneasiness about heading further into the unknown, he swallowed hard and attempted to catch up to the bounding dwarf.

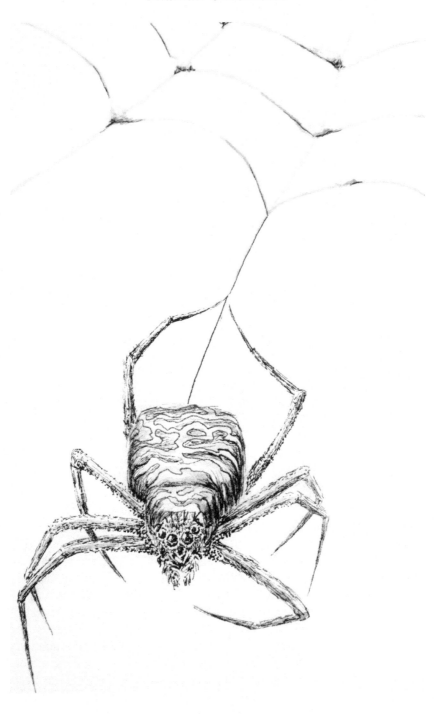

Chapter

XV

After half a day's riding Afeclin and Pit came to a small creek that ran through a shallow ravine. They decided to have a short rest and refresh. The day had become hot and sticky and the ride had been gruelling for them and the horses. Not only had they been travelling up a slight hill but also they had not been following a track. Guiding the horses left and right through the tree-littered woods and keeping constant awareness of low hanging tree limbs and spidery vines was hard work. Obstacles like fallen trees and small anthills made riding exhausting and the humidity was so intense that both riders and horses were draped in perspiration. Now their racing hearts were starting to slow down as they bent over the cooling water and drank their fill from the rocky creek bed. The horses too were pleased at the break and whinnied in relief between snorts of breath as they huffed lungfuls of air.

'I don't think I have ever ridden like that before,' commented Afeclin wiping away the sweat from his brow. He lay back onto the long soft grass trying to catch his breath. The sky above him was masked with dark clouds of purple hues and a damp smell in the air suggested that rain was imminent.

'You get used to it after a while,' said Pit with a breathy laugh followed by a cough.

'Does this sort of thing happen all the time?'

'Well now, you would be surprised how often you can be in the wrong place at the wrong time,' Pit said with a toothy grin as he took his long bow off his shoulders and hung it over an exposed tree branch above him.

'So isn't it a little dangerous then for Typhin to be passing Hoashan and his men on the road. What if they suspect something?' questioned Afeclin leaning down into the gully to splash water on his face and neck.

'Don't you worry about Typhin. He can look after himself,' answered Pit resting his hand on the small water bag that was hanging from his belt. 'He will play the old lone traveller, he's good at that. They may watch him as he passes by but more than likely they won't take much interest in him. Typhin however will be able to listen in and find out what is going on and which way they suspect the killers have gone.'

'The old lone traveller?'

'Yeah, he'll wear his cloak and keep the brim of his hat over his face. He'll hunch over the horse like he's having trouble balancing and cough as if he is about to fall apart,' laughed Pit as he mimicked the actions of Typhin. 'He may get a bit of attention doing it but with that they will also dismiss him just as quickly. You see, there are a lot of old men that pretty much just roam from town to town, bar to bar minding their own business, not hurting anyone else. They just exist for the last part of their life. Mind you most of them have spent the better parts of their lives as soldiers, so when they get too old to fight and they become no use to anybody what can they do?'

'But roam from town to town, bar to bar and mind their own business.'

'Exactly.'

Afeclin took his long black boots off, feeling the relief it brought to his feet to be free from the suffocating, sweat-soaked leather. He stood in the cool flowing water and arched his back to release the tightness he had felt while riding. He looked around, admiring the secluded area they now found themselves in. The trees surrounding the creek all had roots that spilled over the slight gorge, dropping into the

101

water below as if they too were enjoying the relief the cool water brought to their limbs. Known for their varying colours, the bankoi trees surrounding the bank were alive with a myriad of red, green and gold leaves in all shades and hues.

A large silky web hung between two trees on opposite sides of the ravine shimmering as a ray of sun lit it. A large, blue-green miicot spider dangled just below the web, its shell-like square back arched as its spindly legs groped the air with tenderness. As much as Afeclin disliked spiders, he watched the miicot spinning on the breeze with keen interest.

'Is there a war on at the moment?' he asked all of a sudden, hoping to better understand the goings on in Titania.

'Well, I couldn't exactly say the world was at peace, but no, there has been no war since The Great War many years ago.'

'The Great War?' Afeclin asked with awkwardness, embarrassed by his lack of knowledge.

Pit stared at Afeclin with a puzzled look on his angular face, then he chuckled.

'Perhaps you know it better as The Human War,' he said. 'I keep forgetting you were brought up amongst elves and I've been around Typhin so long, I think it is just habit.'

'Habit?' Afeclin shook his head bemused.

'All the other races on Titania refer to the war as The Human War but of course humans refer to it as The Great War.'

Afeclin still felt confused by the whole affair. Of course he had heard of The Human War but he knew very little about it. The elves preferred not to speak of the war as it had brought them so much death and despair, a fact his father had chosen to remedy by cutting them off from the rest of Titania. 'Please forgive my ignorance but I have not learnt very much about it. Why the different names?'

'Well, the war was actually started by humans,' said Pit leaning down into the gully and taking another gulp of water from the creek. He then filled his oxhide water bag as he continued. 'Let me try to explain, you see... there were two kingdoms side by side, Rixsus and Avanleah and they were each ruled by a brother, King Ravash and King Devall. Ravash had a son named Moorlan and Devall had an adopted daughter named Caril.'

Afeclin nodded his understanding and the lanky goblin flopped his curly booted foot on a rock then he leaned over, resting his arms on his knee before continuing.

'Moorlan and Caril fell in love and intended to marry, which to everyone, especially their fathers seemed a very good idea. The two kingdoms uniting as one after the death of the kings was perfectly logical.

A few weeks before the wedding was to take place however, King Devall began to feel uneasy about Moorlan but he couldn't understand where his doubts had surfaced from, so he secretly travelled to Lawry Castle to meet with the wizard Zallucien and ask his advice on the matter. Zallucien told King Devall that he saw great evil in Moorlan and if the two kingdoms were to unite under his rule they would become a terrible force for evil upon Titania. Well, of course the goodly king Devall could not allow that to happen, so without any explanation he forbade his daughter to marry Moorlan.

King Ravash was justifiably upset about his brother's sudden mysterious change of heart and declared war on the Kingdom of Avanleah. To do so he had to bring in armies from the neighbouring countries to help his cause. He enlisted the mountain dwarves telling them that if they did not come and fight, he would send an army of trolls to flatten their mountain. The trolls will fight for whoever pays the most money, they have no loyalties... not even to their own. Dwarves on the other hand attempt to stay out of all conflicts barring their own but will protect their lands at any cost.

King Devall then had to build up his own army. He enlisted some other races to fight in order to protect his kingdom. That is where the elves, goblins and our cousins the hobgoblins come into it. We all fought alongside Devall's kingdom out of fear of what would happen if King Ravash were to take over his brother's kingdom and gain an army twice the size of the one he already had. Before long most of the races on Titania had become involved, taking one side or another, turning what had started out to be a war between two brothers and their kingdoms, into a world war such as nobody had ever seen before.'

Afeclin sat in silence after Pit had finished speaking. It bothered him to learn of the savageness of his own race. It seemed to him that humans were troublemakers, greedy and malicious. He had come to understand his father's feelings toward the world outside of Tebelligan and his distrust of humans. While it was obvious they were not all bad, the girl in the red dress had died an innocent victim and Typhin had done all that he could to help Wolflang and himself, he could see that elves and humans differed a great deal.

'How did Caril take her father's decision?'

'She couldn't understand her father's sudden rejection of Moorlan and begged him to reconsider. Of course he couldn't and so out of respect for King Devall she accepted his decision but hated him for it.

After the war she married another man of her father's choosing and he became the new king soon after that.'

'Did the old king die?' asked Afeclin standing ankle deep in the creek filling his silver flask with the fresh, clear water that flowed through his legs.

'No, he is still very much alive but after the war ended he went a bit crazy.'

'How did the war end? Obviously Devall won.'

'King Devall was lucky. There were many people in Rixsus who were very angry about the way King Ravash had caused so many to die by starting a war over such a trifling affair. They longed to bring the war to a peaceful end. Taking matters into their own hands they hatched a plan to assassinate the King. Once it got out that King Ravash was dead, the war ended and people celebrated. Moorlan, who had assisted his father direct the war, became vengeful over his father's death. He was captured and brought to King Devall.

Feeling sorrowful about the death of so many innocent people and mourning the loss of his only brother, King Devall took pity on Moorlan and instead of having him killed, banished him to the island Norvak.'

'I cannot get over how many people died for no greater cause than a king's pride,' Afeclin said with mourning as he put his boots back on his feet, then stood up and stretched his body.

'Yeah well... it was a long time ago,' said Pit looking up at the sky and then changing the subject, 'we best get on our way; it looks as if it might rain this afternoon.'

The two got back on their horses and continued their ride to Desprade.

Chapter

XVI

The trek through the woods had been tiring for Wolflang. Weaving through the trees whilst maintaining their pace was hard work. Even Raan had found it difficult. Wolflang could see the sweat pouring off the old dwarf as they burst out of the hot woods onto the soft white sand of the seashore. He could hear the dwarf grumbling into his beard as they made their way to the water's edge.

Looking back along the shore Wolflang could just make out the coastline of Tebelligan in the far distance. Letting out a deep sigh he felt a little home sick.

Raan slowed his horse to a trot. After having a swig of water from his decanter the dwarf allowed the horse to walk in the calm water along the ocean's edge.

The dwarf's horse was a little smaller than a regular size horse but even so Raan looked tiny straddling the mare. It amazed Wolflang that the dwarf was able to hold on at times, especially when they rode at such a great pace.

'That was a pretty tough ride through the woods,' Wolflang said trying to make conversation with the aloof dwarf as he too slowed his horse to a walk.

'Woods are nasty areas to have to ride with speed,' said Raan with a breathless rasp, 'you have to be careful. Why I know somebody who had their eyeball whipped out by a low tree branch that hit him in the face as he was riding... nasty.'

'Oww!' was all that came out of Wolflang's mouth as he pictured the poor rider in pain over the loss of his eye.

The sun was hot and the humidity made Wolflang feel hot and tired. The white sand was bright and glistened in the sun. The sun's rays bouncing off the sparkling water stung the elf's eyes and he found himself squinting to block the reflection. In the sky to the south, dark storm clouds were rolling in promising to bring some relief to the heat of the day.

For the next hour, the two waded their horses through the water without speaking. On occasion Raan would grumble a complaint about something to which Wolflang would nod with politeness in order to avoid conversation with the tiresome dwarf.

It was about noonday when the storm clouds started closing in around them. Wolflang watched the clouds, almost pleading with them to rain; feeling it would be a welcome change from the oppressive humidity.

'Where do you come from Raan?' Wolflang asked, breaking the ongoing silence.

'I'm a mountain dwarf. My home is Mount Ibicus or at least was,' answered Raan with matter-of-factness.

'Is it not your home anymore?'

'No not anymore... let's just say I'm not welcome there now,' said Raan, then added with an angry rumble, 'ungrateful brutes, the whole lot of them.'

Wolflang was taken aback by the dwarf's sudden anger. 'What do you mean?' he asked with easiness.

'Ah no matter,' said Raan waving away the question, 'it was a long time ago and I would not expect an elf to understand.'

Feeling a little insulted by the remark, Wolflang was about to give the dwarf a piece of his mind when it started to rain.

'Just what we need,' grumbled the dwarf, 'rain and we're not even halfway to Desprade yet. Come on we'll have to ride it out. Typical that we get lugged with the longest journey when it's raining. Why I bet the others are already in Desprade safe and dry.'

'What are you grumbling about?' asked Wolflang, tiring of Raan's complaints. 'The rain is refreshing. Besides, it has been threatening to rain all afternoon. We could have sped up our pace earlier if you were concerned.'

Raan glowered at the elf through bushy furrowed eyebrows. 'Oh well I wouldn't expect an elf to understand what it is like to feel aches and pains in all your joints whenever you get cold and wet. When that happens you end up bedridden for weeks on end 'cause it's too painful to move. I wouldn't expect you to understand what that feels like; joint pains come from years of hard labour and you've evidently never done a hard day's work in your life.'

'I resent you speaking about my race that way. We elves may not have anything to do with the outside world but we are not sheltered from pain and suffering. Maybe you're right, I haven't done much hard work in my life or suffered the kind of pain you speak of but I have suffered a pain far worse having had to watch my own mother deteriorate and die when I was only young, something you, a dwarf, would not understand!' Wolflang retaliated in anger as he sat back into the saddle and glared at Raan through rain-drenched hair that now stuck to his face.

At first the dwarf appeared to be speechless but then with a skulk he mumbled something into his beard, picked up the reins and gave his horse a hard kick.

'YAH!' he hollered and the horse picked up speed in obedience.

With the rain pouring down upon his head Wolflang sat for a moment watching Raan on his big horse battling the downpour, his long matted ponytail drenched and whipping the little dwarf's back as he rode and once again jounced up and down in the saddle.

Wolflang wondered how Typhin and Pit managed to put up with the intolerable dwarf and why he had let the dwarf get to him.

What's wrong with me? Why in Titania would I ever think to mention my mother to Raan of all people? Wolflang questioned in irritation as he attempted to pick up the pace. His horse plunged through the wet sand, racing close behind the dwarf.

Chapter

XVII

Lenna had run for as long and as hard as she could before she had no more strength in her to continue on at such a pace. Now she trudged on in slow motion, lacking energy and hurting all over.

The heat of the day had not helped either. She sweated from every pore, her mouth dry and in much need of water.

When the grey storm clouds rolled in she rejoiced, willing them to drop their bountiful load on her.

She had never considered herself as weak before but now she did in every way. While her body was weak from exhaustion her mind was weak too and had shown great feebleness in the past few days. Her mind had been powerless against her heart in the decision to follow Wolflang. Her body had done what it had to in order to survive the attack of the pig-faced men and now her mind and heart suffered for it. She was only a shadow of her former strong self and seemed to be debilitating at a rapid pace.

Please rain... please... rain on me... please! She begged the sky as if it would bring some much needed strength as well as relief from the sun and her thirst.

As if a gift from the gods themselves, it started to rain. It was only light at first and Lenna was able to hold her head back with her mouth open wide to collect the rejuvenating water.

Then it began to pour down upon her, drenching her and everything else in sight, making the road pool in places and muddy everywhere else.

Before long, that much needed shower had soaked her to the bone and she began to shiver as she stumbled along through the mud and puddles.

She didn't hear the sound of a wagon approaching from behind through the heavy downpour.

Even once she knew it was there, she did not run from it this time, she just continued on at the same slow pace and kept her eyes fixed on the road ahead. Water bounced off the ground and muddied her legs as she trudged.

The wagon wheels rolled along close beside her following two determined, striped horses that pulled the load.

'Hey Little Elf, are you okay?' came a gruff voice through the rain.

Lenna kept moving onward without turning to see who had spoken to her. Instead she placed her hands over her very telling pointy ears that stuck out through her long dripping hair.

'Oh I understand,' came the gruff voice with an air of compassion, 'it is difficult to be different, people do tend to stare... but you should never be ashamed of who you are.'

'I am not ashamed,' was the unwitting reply that slipped from her lips.

'Oh I see,' responded the voice with understanding then added, 'that is a nice bow you carry there. Was it you who killed that troll a little ways back on the road?'

Lenna stopped dead in her tracks, staring up at the mysterious voice bewildered, unsure whether now was the right time to make a run for it with what little energy she had left or if perhaps this was some person who might be able to help her.

'T..tr..troll?' she managed to ask.

'Yes, that pig-faced buffoon you left dead on the side of the road,' said the voice with firmness.

Lenna stood with fear staring up at the hooded man who had now slowed down his horses to a stop.

'Oh don't you worry about that,' the gruff man said, 'I'm not here to rag on ya! The world is better off with one less troll anyways.'

Lenna stood staring. She didn't know quite what to say. She did feel a little more at ease with the man in the wagon but she kept her guard up.

'And the dead horse... yours?' the man questioned with disturbing bluntness.

Lenna's head sunk in sadness.

'Then perhaps I can give you a ride somewhere?' the man suggested. 'You have an awful long walk ahead of you.'

While Lenna was desperate to jump up into the wagon to give her legs a much needed break, she was not sure whether it was wise to trust the man.

'I am okay,' she said turning back to the road to continue walking.

'Come now Little Elf, my bark is worse than my bite, I can assure you,' he grunted at his own joke. 'I am on my way to Desprade anyhow. You are welcome to join me. I assume you are headed for Desprade too?'

'I do not know where I am headed,' she said with defiance, struggling to hold back tears, 'I do not know where I am. I was trying to catch up to my friends but...'

She stopped still, fighting to prevent herself from crying again. *I have to be stronger than this*, she thought, *I cannot let my weaknesses show.*

As she was doing her best to pull herself together, all of a sudden she felt lightheaded and dizzy. With one hand on her head she tried to grab hold of the wagon with her other hand to steady herself but found that she could not quite reach it. Then she could not see it anymore as her eyesight went dark. Fear raced through her as she tried to gain her senses. *What is happening to me?* she wondered. Then taking a step, she tripped and fell to the ground hitting her head and blacking out.

Chapter

XVIII

Afeclin and Pit were approaching Desprade when it started to rain. The day's journey had been tiring but uneventful. They both looked forward to a rest and seeing the town from a distance was a great comfort.

They donned their cloaks despite the heat, to provide a little protection from the rain as they sat on their horses looking down upon Desprade.

From the hilltop the town seemed small and cluttered. Built within a semicircle of heavily wooded forest area, the town had one main road into it and large stone walls enclosing the treeless edge on either side of the entry. Slanted rooftops, pitched only on one side were lush with turf growing all over them. The houses appeared to be scattered all over the place having no logical order apart from a few main roads that split the town into a number of disorganised sections.

As they had approached the hill, the town had been alive with much noise and activity. Children had run about on the bright green rooftops in absolute joy but now as the rain dropped in excess over Desprade the excitement had depleted and the colour was masked by a grey shadow.

The main road into Desprade was busy with wagons carrying loads of produce for selling at the markets. Most wagons were covered with a canvas or large pieces of thick cloth but many were uncovered causing the peddler's goods to dampen.

'Is it usually this busy?' asked Afeclin watching the wagon drivers speeding up their horses to get out of the rain.

'Yeah, Desprade is well known for its markets so there is always tradesmen coming and going on a daily basis,' answered Pit.

'Where do they all come from?'

'There are a lot of little farms between here and Harlay Dam. Although it may not look like it from here there are a lot of people living in Desprade, so the tradesmen sell their produce within a few days and then leave only to return a week later with more to sell,' said Pit gliding his fingers over his damp, bare head and re-adjusting himself in the saddle. 'Well, shall we get ourselves out of the rain?'

Afeclin nodded and the two rode down the hill to the main road.

By the time they got to the bottom of the hill what started out being a heavy shower had turned into a loud storm. The thunder clapped overhead and lightning crackled in the distance. The two sped up their pace, weaving in and out of the slower wagons to ride into Desprade with haste.

'Over here!' Pit had to yell to be heard over the sound of the storm when they had reached the main street of the small city.

Ducking left into a nearby alley, Afeclin followed Pit to a tiny, two-storey inn tucked away from view of the main street.

'What a strange place for an inn,' said Afeclin climbing down from his steed. 'You wouldn't even know it was here.'

'Smart if you ask me,' said Pit opening a small side door in the wall located next to the main entrance. 'Despite what you might think, this inn is the best in town.'

The side door opened into a small stable and a tall boy came up to greet them.

'Hello gentlemen, can I take these horses off your hands?'

'Take care of them for us, make sure they are well fed and rested,' said Pit handing the boy a silver doucla. 'They've had a hard day.'

The Titanian currency was the doucla, made from gold, silver or bronze and on occasion iron ore which was considered serf's gold. They were medium-sized flat coins that were stamped on one or both sides indicating the city they were moulded in by the blacksmith who forged them.

'That was generous,' Afeclin commented as they left the stable.

'There are times when it is worth paying someone more and there are times to haggle for the best deal,' said Pit opening the door to the inn. 'Now, that boy will work for the coin I gave him. He'll feed, dry and groom our horses fully. He'll even sing them asleep if he needs to. If I had paid him a bronze doucla like everybody else he would just give them a bit of a fodder and leave them to rest for the night. You always want your horse to be in its best condition wherever possible.'

The inside of the inn was much larger than it appeared from the street. While still a small room, it was well-decorated and had a comfortable look with low lighting and high ceilings. A curved bar was located to the right of them as they walked in. A few men were seated at the bar minding their own business but looked up as Afeclin and Pit entered the room. Behind the bar on shelves reaching up to the ceiling were bright coloured glass bottles of various designs. Some round and fat, some tall and sleek, others with more of a square shape to them, all of them were very different and unique with many tints and textures. Inside each of the bottles was a small thick candle that was lit, giving off a soft glow to the bar area.

The other side of the room was full of comfortable lounge chairs seated round about small wooden tables. For the moment they were empty apart from a couple of goblins chatting amongst themselves at the back of the room. Behind the goblins hung an intricate weaving depicting colourful animals in fields of green. The tapestry was so large it almost covered the entire wall as if it had been a painted mural.

Around the room hung what seemed to be ancient souvenirs of various weaponry, breastplates, shields and feathered helmets.

Opposite the doorway they had just come through was a stairwell. *Most likely leading to the guest rooms upstairs,* Afeclin supposed.

Afeclin was so intrigued with the lobby that he failed to notice Pit organise and pay for the rooms.

'We've got three rooms, one for you and your friend, one for Typhin and I and one for Raan. If he has been caught in the rain which he most surely must have, there will be no end of complaints all night from the dwarf,' Pit laughed moving toward Afeclin as he squelched in his soggy curled boots leaving wet footprints all over the polished wooden floor.

'That sounds fine,' said Afeclin startling from his thoughts as he unclipped his wet cloak and hung it on a nearby stand. 'Oh, here, let me give you some money.'

Afeclin fumbled through his bag for his coins.

'Don't worry about that,' said Pit eyeing out the bar, 'how about you buy us a round of drinks while we wait for the others to arrive.'

❊ ❊ ❊

Pit and Afeclin sat on the comfy lounges of the lobby and enjoyed a brew as they rested their bodies.

Afeclin took a mouthful of the dark brown liquid and swallowed. The brew was not as flavoursome as the sweet ale of Tebelligan but it was much stronger and had a hot feeling as it ran down his throat. He let out a loud cough.

'That's strong spirits!' he exclaimed as his eyes started to water.

Pit laughed.

'You think that's strong? That is mild compared to some of the brews I have tried.'

Afeclin looked at Pit with a shocked expression on his face.

'I hate to imagine what you would think of elvish brew then,' he said attempting to try another mouthful of the strong spirits and again bursting into a coughing fit as the heated mixture hit his throat, 'I'm sure you would confuse it with water.'

Pit laughed again as he sat back into the big chair looking content.

Afeclin could see the two goblins still seated under the tapestry on the opposite side of the room. The older one of the two, who looked very similar to Pit with his long face and balding head, kept looking over to their table with interest. The other goblin, who was shorter and paler and had a little more hair, whispered something to his friend.

'Do you know those two goblins, Pit?' Afeclin asked, his voice sounding rough.

'No, never seen them before. Why?'

'They keep looking over here, watching us.'

'Don't take any notice of them,' said Pit not even turning his head to look at the two, 'they're probably eyeing out that big bag you carry so make sure you don't put it down or leave it anywhere, not even for a moment. Being goblins they're experienced thieves and they will rob you of your gold before you realise they've had a hand in your bag.'

Afeclin pulled his bag close as he sat further back into his seat and relaxed letting out a sigh. He tugged at his damp white silk shirt that was starting to stick to his chest. His cloak had kept him from getting soaked through but as they had ridden with speed the wind had pushed open his cloak and allowed the rain to beat in on him from the front. Looking over at Pit he sensed something bothering the goblin all of a sudden and wondered if it had anything to do with the two goblins watching them from across the room.

'Why aren't you like them Pit?'

A roll of thunder rumbled, startling Afeclin and making him flinch.

'Ooh, it's a long story,' said Pit taking another mouthful of the strong brew from his chalice.

'Well, we may have some time before the others get here,' Afeclin encouraged.

'It's really not that interesting, I just stole something I shouldn't have and lived to regret it.'

'You mean the experience had a permanent effect on you?' asked Afeclin trying to push the issue.

'Yeah, you see goblins have rules and in particular one golden rule... never steal anything important. Most people will not worry about a little lost coin or something with little value but if you steal something that is really worth its weight in gold or even sentimental... well... you tend to get into a lot of trouble.

I came to be a master thief. You see, I have been blessed with quick hands and I was never one to follow rules as a youngster. I began to try my luck stealing bigger and better things like jewellery with exquisite diamonds, expensive paintings and ornate boxes covered in jewels. You name it, I could steal it.

One day I passed a big rich man in the street wearing a solid gold chain belt and back then, let me tell you, belts like that were about as rare as a hairy goblin. Needless to say I attempted to pinch it. I strode past him again, pretended to bump into him, skilfully undid the clasp and as I apologised for my clumsiness, zipped the belt out from around him. However, the clasp caught the fabric of his gown and so there I was with my hand on the chain and he with a heavy hand on me.

Well, he turned out to be a very influential senator and marched me out of town to the king and demanded I receive a harsh penalty. I was given the worst punishment a goblin could receive,' he paused, looking at Afeclin who had been sitting and listening with interest. 'What do you think the worst punishment a goblin could receive is?'

After giving the matter some thought he joked, 'Cut off his hands, that'll do it.'

'Precisely,' nodded Pit.

Afeclin looked shocked, 'But you have your hands.'

Pit tilted his head to one side and put a long crooked finger in the air as if bidding Afeclin to wait. 'They took me to the town centre and made me kneel down in front of a large tree stump that was stained with blood. The king had come into town just for the occasion. I was so scared I nearly fainted as they tied my wrists to the block. I wanted to cry or scream or something but nothing came out and as they lifted the axe high in the air I thought it was all over. Me and my hands would be permanently detached and I left with bloody stumps where my hands used to be.

As the axe began to drop a voice piped up in the crowd that had gathered. The blade missed my hands by a whisker and had I not clenched my fists, my fingers would have been hacked off. The voice was that of an old farmer who was well respected around the town. I guess he had seen something more in me or perhaps it was because I was so young that he begged the king to allow me to keep my hands in return for me working for him on his farm that was sixty miles out of town. The king agreed on the condition that I was not to return to the town under any circumstance. So I went with him to his farm and that is where I met Typhin. Typhin was a farm hand there and took me under his wing. We became good friends and there I learnt to make better use of my hands. I was taught to use the bow and arrow so that I could rid the farm of little critters that came to eat of the crops,' he said pointing to his long bow that was leaning against the arm of his chair. 'I learnt to use my hands to build, and sew, and to look after animals. As for stealing, I considered myself lucky to have been given a second chance and I was determined to prove myself worthy of it.'

'So you never stole again, ever?'

'Well, there have been times of necessity, but no, not without a worthwhile cause.'

'Have you been tempted?'

'Amazingly I haven't, the scare that I had at almost losing my hands changed me for the better. I think it was because I was so young. If something like that happened to me now I would probably consider myself lucky and continue on the same path,' said Pit gulping down the rest of his brew and wiping the moistness from his mouth with the back of his hand. 'Shall we have another?'

Chapter

XIX

Lenna awoke to a very loud thunderclap. She jumped in her seat, jolting herself awake.

In the distance she could see the sky light up as a flash of lightning flickered across the horizon.

Rain still cascaded upon her head and body, although the only place she seemed to be feeling it was on her face, stinging her hot red cheeks and getting caught in her long auburn lashes.

She opened her mouth and stuck out her tongue to taste the sweet refreshing water that fell from the sky as she bumped along in her seat.

Looking down at her body she realised that she had been wrapped in a thick blanket that was protecting her from the rain. All at once it occurred to her that she was unaware of her surroundings.

Sitting up in her seat with a shudder, she turned to the man seated next to her driving the wagon she now found herself in. He was bent over with his hood covering his face.

'Where are we?' she dared ask.

'Oh Little Elf, you're awake.'

Lenna recognised his voice as being the man in the wagon she had met on the roadside earlier.

'You had me worried when you fell and hit your head. I thought maybe you were done for. Are you feeling better now?'

'Y..ee..sss,' she responded trying hard to gather her thoughts. 'I hit my head you say?'

'Yes, nasty bump as you fell backwards... I think you fainted or something.'

'Oh...' Lenna was not quite sure how to respond. She did not remember fainting or hurting herself, yet when she felt the back of her head there was a lump that throbbed when she touched it.

'Where are we?' she asked again as another loud clap boomed overhead.

'We are on the outskirts of Desprade,' said the man with his gruff voice. 'Don't worry Little Elf, we will be safe and dry in Desprade very soon.'

Getting somewhat annoyed with being called 'Little Elf' she was quick to answer. 'My name is Le...' then thought better of giving her name to the stranger, 'Letavia,' she lied.

'That's a nice name Little Elf.'

Lenna scowled.

'I am Harrensalick... ahh... Harren for short. It's easier,' he announced with a small cough.

'Oh,' Lenna said looking up at the man whom she still had not seen in his entirety, the heavy rain and thick hood he wore masking his face.

At that moment a figure rode by on his steed. The man seemed to be human and wore a floppy wide brimmed hat with a thin brown cloak. Lenna sat deep into her seat and covered her ears with the blanket, not wanting to be noticed by the human. He looked to her nodding, with a half smile as he galloped past on Lenna's side of the wagon.

The man next to her laughed out loud. 'You going to hide your elvin-ness from others forever?'

'Possibly,' she answered watching the man on the horse, the two of them battling the wind and the rain, 'I am not sure that I trust humans yet... at least not ones from outside of Tebelligan.'

'Ooh? There are humans where you come from?' the man asked with curiosity. 'I thought I heard that only elves were allowed in Tebelligan, these days.'

'Yes, that is true,' Lenna attempted to explain herself to the stranger. 'However, my best friend is a human... but he is more like an elf really, you see... he grew up there.'

'Oh really?' The man seemed thoughtful. 'Well, I can hardly blame you for mistrusting humans. I'm not so keen on them myself.'

Lenna looked up at the man with surprise, trying to see anything more than his dark eyes staring out at her from beneath the hood.

'You see, Little Elf, I'm not a human either,' he said pulling back his hood to reveal a mop of dark grey hair.

His face was odd to Lenna... like none she had seen before, however, it had a strange comfort to it. He had big round ears that stuck out on the sides of his head, a thin nose that looked like it had been pinched and lengthy whiskers protruding from his cheeks on his long white face.

Then Lenna noticed his hands. They were kind of haggard and claw-like with long dirty fingernails that were black.

Lenna stared at the man in curiosity.

'Then what are you?' she queried, her fear leaving her a moment as she studied his features.

'I am a shemalk,' he answered in his sullen demeanour.

'I have not heard of your race. Are there many of you?' Lenna asked kinking her head to one side in wonderment.

'Oh, there are quite a number of us... underground. Ordinarily we don't come up to the surface much.'

'Really? Then why are you here?'

'I was an adventurer in my youth, you might say... longed to see the world, I did. Eventually I grew tired of that lifestyle but by then I was more comfortable living topside... so I built myself a farm and stayed. Have been here ever since.'

'What are you doing here?' she asked with a screwed up nose, 'on your way to Desprade, I mean.'

'I am off to sell my produce at the market,' he answered pointing a hand to the back of the wagon.

Lenna turned to see a number of neat baskets arranged with a variety of vegetables drenched and dripping from the rain.

Just then they came over a ridge and Lenna's heart skipped a beat as she set eyes on the entrance to Desprade. She was happy to be so close to civilisation again, yet she was nervous to be entering a city full of humans and other races that she was unsure of. Knowing she would be the only elf was a strange feeling.

I hope I will find Wolflang here. She sighed.

They came to the front gate of Desprade and had to stop in a line, due to the traffic heading into the town.

'What is with all the traffic?' she asked with interest.

'This is normal for Desprade; it's always pretty busy. Patience Little Elf, we could be here for a while. The rain tends to slow everything down.'

Behind her she heard the sound of a couple of horses riding toward the gates. She sat up abruptly. The trotting reminded her of Wolflang and Afeclin galloping away when they left her in the Taybie Woods.

Could it be?

She turned around to get a look at the riders and as she did one of them darted by her side of the wagon in a mad dash for the city entrance.

It was a little man with a thick plait that seemed to whip his back as he bounced along in the saddle.

She figured that perhaps it was a dwarf. She had never seen one before but she knew they were a shorter race than elves.

Her heart sank as she watched the small man fighting against the rain in an attempt to make it to the city entrance. She never did see the rider who passed by on the other side of the wagon but it was certain they were not the people she was hoping it would be.

She sank back down into the wagon's bench with despair as lightning crackled across the sky in the far distance, suggesting that the storm was moving on.

I hope I will find them here.

Chapter

XX

It was late in the afternoon when Typhin strolled into the little inn. Dripping wet and looking exhausted, he ordered himself a drink at the bar before joining Afeclin and Pit in the lounge area.

Typhin sat down opposite Pit in a comfortable leather chair, moisture dripping down his face. As he removed the wide brimmed hat that he had been wearing, Afeclin could tell that Typhin's curly hair was drenched with sweat more so than water.

'You look a sight,' Pit laughed. 'What took you so long? Did you lose your way?'

'I ran into a little trouble.' Typhin paused putting the strong brew to his lips and gulping it down.

'What happened?' asked Afeclin after allowing Typhin time to rehydrate.

Typhin wiped his mouth clumsily with the back of his hand and took a deep breath as he slid further back into the chair. When he was comfortable he started to speak.

'As I approached Hoashan's men on the road I pretended to mind my own business... which worked fine, none of them took much notice of me and I could hear them talking and discussing the nature of the crime. They had found the place where we camped last night and had seen our tracks going off in different directions. They were just organising a few people to follow the tracks. It really wasn't that long after we had departed and I worried that if any of you stopped to rest at all they might catch up to ya, so I felt I had to do something to delay them. As I was passing them I faked being injured and fell off my horse. Of course a couple of men came running over to help and I said to them in a drunken slur, "The trolls! The trolls! They chased me down. They tried to kill me. All because I said good morning to one of the many lovely girls they had piled into a wagon like slaves. I barely escaped. Took all of me cunning. When I was just out of sight from them, I turned and dove into the bushes and fell off my horse onto a heavy rock, and now I think I've cracked me rib." None of them picked up on my hints, except one rather young man with a bumpy face said, "Hold on a minute old timer, there was a wagon full of girls? What did you mean by that?" and so I had to explain. Through my ramblings I put into their small minds the possibility that the trolls had killed her. However that led to more problems for me. They wanted me to stay there until Hoashan arrived because they weren't sure what he would want to do. My problem was that if Hoashan recognised me he would not believe my story. He would wonder why I would lie to them and then assume that I had killed her. For that reason I couldn't stick around.'

'What did you do?' asked Afeclin sitting forward on the edge of his seat.

'Well, I couldn't leave right away. I had to wait for the perfect moment. I lay around on the cool grass with my hat over my eyes pretending to sleep off a drunken binge, which did have its advantage because they all talked freely in front of me. What I discovered from their conversations was that they were very much afraid of Moorlan and his army.'

'Yeah but who isn't afraid of them? They are strong and very fierce warriors.'

'No you don't understand. Any of those men would fight if told to, that's what they are trained for, but for the last few years the armies round about Titania have been turning a blind eye to the behaviours of Moorlan and his men...'

'They are trying to avoid war,' interrupted Pit with an apprehensive look.

Typhin continued, 'Moorlan would be happy for the armies to try and put a stop to his growing power. He is waiting for them to but nobody wants to see another war begin.'

'At the same time if they don't try and stop him, he continues to go on making small waves around Titania whilst giving him more time to prepare his army,' said Pit with concern.

'It sounds to me like this fellow Moorlan is already in control of the world. From what you say, he can do whatever he likes, whenever he likes and if they try to stop him he will make war,' Afeclin observed.

'That's exactly it, so Hoashan's men didn't know what to do and a few of them were more than a little afraid Hoashan would pursue the trolls for his daughter's sake,' said Typhin putting the cup to his lips and taking another mouthful of the brew.

'You know, I just assumed the armies had no idea what was going on under their noses, turns out they were just ignoring it,' said Pit shaking his head.

'Did you end up seeing Hoashan?' asked Afeclin.

'Yeah, I had a real hard time getting away. It seemed every time I tried to get to my horse without being noticed someone would turn around and wonder what I was doing. Eventually, Hoashan arrived. I tilted my hat over me head so that he couldn't see me face but as it turned out he took no notice of me anyway and went about ordering his men here and there. In all the commotion I took my leave and galloped all the way here,' Typhin said as he wiped the sweat from his brow and gulped down the last of the thick beverage.

'Why would Hoashan recognise you? Does he know you?' questioned Afeclin with interest.

'Hoashan and I have known each other for a long time,' smirked Typhin giving a wink to Pit.

Afeclin waited in patience, expecting the smaller human to elaborate but Typhin instead reclined back into the large easy chair, flipping a coin with speed between his fingers.

'Oh and ya wanna know something interesting?' Typhin said eyeing the other two through his active fingers.

'What's that?'

'There was a dead troll on the side of the road, a little ways short of the girl. He had been shot in the neck with an arrow.'

'What? Really? Was it one of the same trolls you saw yesterday?' Pit asked.

'I assume so, yes. He was wearing the same black armour.'

'I wonder what could have happened to him,' Afeclin pondered.

'I have been trying to figure that one out myself,' said Typhin with a shrug of the shoulders. 'Maybe he caused trouble within their crew and was shot for it. I mean I wouldn't put it past Nagrin to do such a thing if he wasn't happy with the troll.'

'Yeah, but an arrow? That doesn't sound like his style.'

'No it doesn't... and then there is the issue of the horse... ' Typhin let his words hang in the air for a moment.

'Horse?' questioned Afeclin. 'What horse?'

'After I took off from Hoashan and his men, I noticed a dead horse in a ditch. I wasn't about to stop to check it out but I thought it was interesting.'

'A wild horse?' Afeclin suggested.

'No, it had a saddle.'

'The troll's horse?' Pit offered.

'Perhaps,' Typhin mused, 'it could have been killed too.'

'It's very strange though... don't you think?'

At that moment the doors of the inn swung open, letting a cool gust of wind push its way inside the building and circumnavigate the large room before subsiding. In slumped two small, dripping wet figures, a dwarf and an elf.

'I see you're all nice and comfy there,' Raan grumbled as he trudged into the lounge leaving pools of water wherever he stepped. 'Typical that I always get all the bad luck! First I get lumbered with an elf of all people, then we get stuck in a heavy down pour on what you might call the longest route imaginable.'

Wolflang shrugged his shoulders as he combed his hair out of his face with his fingers. 'I've listened to this all day,' he sighed with weariness.

'Well then, that was your first mistake; you should never bother listening to Raan,' laughed Pit holding his goblet high in the air.

'Especially when it's raining,' Typhin added.

'Where's my key? I'm going to go and get dry before I catch my death,' Raan barked at the three seated. They eyed him with amusement, trying not to laugh. 'And don't think any of you are bunking with me tonight.'

As Pit handed him a long silver key, Raan scowled at Wolflang.

'Especially you elf!' he hollered then he turned around and marched off to where the rooms were situated.

With the dwarf gone the attention turned to Wolflang who was drenched from head to toe. He stood with his clothes dripping water onto the polished floor and his little pointy ears sticking out on either side of his head between large amounts of long hair that clung to his face. He looked like he suffered from utter exhaustion.

'You look like a drowned rat,' Typhin remarked.

'Maybe you should take Wolflang up to your room so that he can get dry and have a rest,' suggested Pit.

'We'll meet back here on the hour for dinner,' said Typhin as Afeclin stood up.

'Sure.'

Wolflang made puddles of water and his cloth shoes squelched as he walked. When they were halfway up the stairs, Afeclin looked back at the two they had left, noticing that the goblin had moved very close and was having a serious chat with Typhin. The smaller human's face darkened with concern.

'There's something serious going on with them and I'm sure it has to do with two goblins that were watching us earlier,' Afeclin whispered.

'What on Titania are you talking about?'

'Don't worry, I'll explain later,' said Afeclin realising that now was not the time to fill his friend in on the afternoon's activity, but Afeclin could not help but have a bad feeling about the grave look in Typhin's eyes.

Chapter

XXI

Once they were inside the city, Lenna was determined to search for Wolflang and Afeclin, despite the rain and her being drenched.

'It would be wise Little Elf, to get dry and have something to eat before you go about your search,' said Harren pointing to the inn he had parked his wagon in front of. 'There has to be a dozen or more places they could stay within Desprade.'

'I... I... do not have any coin,' she stammered with embarrassment.

'Well then, this will be my shout,' the odd stranger said with warmth despite his gruffness.

Lenna was taken back by the shemalk's generosity and was not sure what to think of it.

'Why do you help me so, Harren?' she asked searching his dark eyes for truth.

'Oh it's nothing really,' he answered waving her gaze away, 'we are not all monsters this side of the Tebelligan border but as you don't know who you can trust, I feel it is my duty to help you.'

Harren appeared to be sincere so Lenna let down her guard and gave in to his kindness.

'I am very hungry.'

'I don't blame you, you look like you haven't eaten in days,' he said knocking with force at the door to the little inn.

The door opened and a large woman with long greying hair and a freckled face urged them inside.

'Harrensalick, my dear,' the rotund lady said in a joyful voice that boomed, 'how in Titania are ya?'

'Ma lady, my back has been playing up of late, I have a constant aching in my knuckles and I can't hear so good no more but I'm as good as I can be...'

'For a fella my age,' the two sang out together as if it had been rehearsed.

Lenna watched the interlude between the two with interest. It was evident they knew each other well but had not seen one another for quite some time. Lenna thought it amusing to watch Harren make the lady giggle and blush.

Their attention turned to Lenna, as she stood silent in the entrance hall of the inn.

'And who do we have here?' the lady asked with a wide smile and her head cocked to one side. 'Oh my word, she's an elf!'

'Yes she is, her name is Letavia. Thought you might have room for her.'

Harren discussed Lenna as if she was not even in the room.

'She's a timid little thing, come from Tebelligan in search of some friends who came this way, but she ran into a little trouble on the road... killed a troll while she was at it,' he grunted in the lady's ear.

'Oh good grief child, you must have been so frightened, come sit down and I will fetch you a nice bowl of stew and a blanket,' the joyful lady said running off to another room in haste.

'Her name is Marelli, she's an absolutely wonderful cook,' Harren said ushering her into a dining area, 'go on, go on.'

Lenna moved into an undersized room with four tables that filled the small space, there was barely enough room to walk between them. She sat down at a table closest to the window that looked out on the paved street.

'I will go and get us some drinks,' croaked Harren with a half smile, then he disappeared from the room with a bent over hobble.

The room was quaint and feminine. The walls were built with slats of dark wood but there were paintings and small tapestries of flowers and gardens hanging about brightening the panelling. On one wall, a collage of dead insects of varying sizes and colours had been nailed onto a large painted board and gave the impression of looking at them buzzing over a field of green. It was effective if not a little bit creepy.

Fresh flowers in handcrafted pots were presented with great care on a woven cloth that covered the tabletops.

Feeling at ease in such a bright and cheerful room, Lenna forgot about her troubles and sat down in comfort, ready to enjoy a good meal.

Harren returned to the room and sat down at the circular table opposite Lenna. He placed a small pitcher of ale in front of her.

'Drink up, it's a home made concoction... Marelli brews it herself,' he said almost with pride.

Lenna took a big mouthful of the sweet-smelling brew after thanking Harren with graciousness for it. It had a delicious taste but was quite strong as it slid down her throat and made her break into a loud fit of coughs.

'Good huh?' said Harren with a smirk.

Lenna nodded, going red in the face as she tried not to cough again. 'Good,' she managed to say before erupting into another coughing fit.

Once she had gotten used to the heat as it ran down the back of her throat, she began to enjoy the sweet ale as the flavour was quite rich. However there was a little tang to it that didn't seem to meld into the rest of the spices and was a little off-putting. She dared not say anything as she did not want to hurt anyone's feelings but she had the impression the ale was off.

Marelli appeared at the table with two bowls full of thick, hot stew that smelled delectable. Her stomach groaned as the spicy aroma wafted up her nose and she could barely stop herself from diving in and gobbling up the meal.

She was only about halfway through the delicious stew when she became sleepy all of a sudden, to the point where she could not keep her head up or her eyes open anymore.

'What's wrong?' Harren questioned with concern.

'I'm so, so tired,' she said with a giant yawn, 'I can't keep my eyes open anymore.'

'Well, I don't blame you,' Harren said with feeling. 'It has been a gruelling couple of days for you, perhaps you just need a good night's sleep.'

'Yes, like right... now...' her voice trailed off as she slumped over onto the table, missing the bowl of stew only marginally.

Chapter

XXII

After Wolflang had been able to towel dry his hair and change into a sleeveless silk-spun shirt that he brought with him as a spare, he and Afeclin had eaten an early dinner together with Typhin, Pit and Raan in the lobby of the inn. During the meal the three had seemed rather distracted and on guard. As much as Pit had tried to appear jovial and carefree, behind the facade Afeclin could tell something bothered the goblin. While Pit chatted in his usual amicable way, his eyes searched the room with caution and every time the door to the inn opened he and Typhin would glance over as if expecting someone to walk in. Raan was his usual unpleasant self, grumbling into his beard now and then as he rushed through his food. Afeclin didn't know the three travellers well enough to determine whether this was normal behaviour but felt sure there was something wrong. When he questioned Pit about it on the way back to the rooms, Pit had grabbed him by the arm and said in a serious voice, 'Nothing to worry about, it's just this town... we'll be glad to get out of it.'

They had then said goodnight and retired to their rooms for the evening, desiring an early start the following day. The plan discussed over dinner was to continue on with their newfound friends until Afeclin had reached Lawry castle and Wolflang had arrived in Rengal. Typhin had business in Rengal to tend to and the path to Lawry castle was on the way, it made sense to travel together. Afeclin also found it comforting travelling with people who knew the woods around Titania and the dangers that lurked within.

Now in bed, Afeclin tossed and turned for hours but found that sleep would not come. Around midnight he got up, lit the oil lamp beside his bunk and walked over to a chair nearby that he had slung his bag upon when he had entered the room that evening.

In the dim light the wooden space appeared smaller than it was as the corners of the room disappeared into the dark. Two bunks lay side by side against the back wall separated by an old wooden nightstand that held the oil lamp. A small window with a thin green curtain drawn across it was situated above the nightstand blocking out much of the blue moon's glow. A hard wooden chair sat at the end of each bunk and a sheepskin rug was strewn on the floor between them.

With his mind full of turmoil, Afeclin sensed something happening but he didn't know what. He felt the presence of someone nearby, perhaps approaching. He closed his eyes in an attempt to try and understand what he was feeling but his mind seemed to be full of fog and he could not quite grasp the message that his senses were sending him.

Afeclin took his bag off the chair and sat down. Putting his hands on his head he began to rub his temples in a circular motion trying hard to concentrate on an image. Someone was in trouble. Someone in a dark cloak on a horse was stuck, was sinking into some kind of muck. He couldn't make out who the rider was in the extreme dark, nor could he understand why he was having such a vision in the first place. *Does it mean anything?* The vision was interrupted by a forceful knock at the door.

Afeclin grabbed his shirt that was lain over the end rail of his bunk and threw his arms into the sleeves in haste as he opened the door. He felt a cool draft flood inside the room from the outside corridor; the rush of air was so strong that it blew out the flame from the oil lamp darkening the room once again. Afeclin supposed that he would find either Typhin or Pit standing at the door but was startled to behold an unusual looking tall man staring at him.

'Where have your friends gone?' hollered the man without introduction. 'Are they hiding in there with you?'

'I have no idea what you are talking about,' answered Afeclin with some confusion.

'Your friends!' the man hollered again, his black eyes glaring down on Afeclin. 'We know you had been travelling with them.'

Afeclin stared with blankness at the tall man. His features were strong and square, with a jaw that was littered with thick stubble and a large nose that had a mop of hair protruding from it. His hair was grey and stuck up all over the place and his neck was thick and brawny. He was human but taller and larger than Afeclin and his cloak was open revealing a dark green uniform that was free of wrinkles and decorated with fine silver trimmings. He looked like someone of importance. Afeclin wondered who he could be searching for at such a late hour. *Is he speaking of Typhin, Pit and Raan? But they are here in this inn... or are they? Have they left abruptly in the middle of the night without a word?* As Afeclin tried hard to collect his thoughts he was interrupted by the booming voice of the man again.

'WELL? Are you going to tell me where they have gone or do you need a night in the hole to refresh your memory?'

'I don't know what...' Afeclin started, but instead asked, 'who are you?'

The man's face softened for a moment before he threw back his head and roared with a cruel laugh.

'Me?!' he hollered. 'Why, I'm the law around here.'

'Ooh,' Afeclin stared with uneasiness.

'Look I've got no bother with you,' the man said with less volume this time, 'I'm after your friends, you tell me where they are and you can go back to bed. If not you can accompany me to the prison where I think a night in the hole will help you see things more clearly.'

Afeclin did not know what to say. He didn't think the lawman would believe that he had no idea where the others had gone. On the other hand whatever the hole was, did not sound like a good option either.

'To tell you the truth, until you knocked on my door just now, I had no idea that my friends had gone anywhere. As far as I knew they were sound asleep in their rooms,' Afeclin started with uncertainty as the man's eyes closed to a squint and he scowled his impatience. Afeclin hurried to continue, 'As far as I knew they were setting out towards the mountains in the morning but I guess they could have decided to leave early.'

This answer, while vague, seemed to satisfy the man for he relaxed his posture as he mulled over the information.

'Are they heading for the City of Krin beyond the Graandis Mountain range?' asked the man scratching his rough face.

Afeclin's geography wasn't too good but he had remembered seeing mountains quite a distance away on the map that he had looked at the day before. As for names of places near the mountains, he had no idea but hoped he could secure his new friends some time by sending the troops in the wrong direction.

'Let me think... yes... yes, I believe they mentioned the City of Krin and someone they needed to meet there.'

The man thought for a moment and then said, 'I'll send some of my troops that way then and see if we can pick up a trail.'

The man turned around to leave and Afeclin breathed a sigh of relief. Then he spun back to face Afeclin, his eyes fixed on him.

'You'd better not be lying to me,' his voice rumbled, 'these are very dangerous outlaws. Troops are searching all over Titania for them. It wouldn't help to associate yourself with these men or your neck will end up on the chopping block alongside them.'

'I do not know that they are now on their way to the City of Krin, only that they had planned to head there, for all I know they could still be in Desprade,' said Afeclin, his heart beating hard inside his chest.

'My name is Captain Faquin. If you hear anything or receive word from these outlaws it would be in your best interest to let me know.'

The Captain turned in haste and took off down the hallway towards the stairs.

Afeclin shut the door and sat back down on the chair feeling restless and ill at ease.

He wanted to help somehow but didn't know what to do. He only hoped that wherever the three were headed, it was not the same direction as he had sent the troops. He contemplated what the Captain had said about the men being dangerous outlaws.

'I don't believe it,' Afeclin said to himself finding it difficult to imagine Typhin as some dangerous villain, 'there must be some mistake.'

Looking over toward the bed where Wolflang lay sleeping, he sighed. Although in the darkness it was hard to make out Wolflang's face, Afeclin could tell that he was still sound asleep by his deep sporadic breaths. It seemed as though he hadn't even stirred whilst the Captain was at the door.

Afeclin closed his eyes for an instant and within a moment he could see the vision again. Rubbing his temples once more, he concentrated as hard as he could, focusing on the image he was seeing and trying to capture more of a clear vision in his mind.

There was a man. A small man and he was stuck with his horse in what seemed to be a sticky, mud substance. Two other men were trying hard to free him but to no avail.

Afeclin opened his eyes for a moment.

'It couldn't be, could it?' he breathed.

He closed his eyes again and concentrated with all his might to see the people's faces.

Afeclin could only see the backside of the man who was stuck and as he was wearing a cloak he could not tell anything about him in the darkness. He then turned his attention to the other two men trying to help their companion. The taller one of the two was tying a rope to his horse's saddle while the other man, who was very short, was trying to throw the other end of the rope out to the man who was stuck. The faces were blurry at first but then… he could see details. Pit… it was Pit and then he could see Raan. So that would mean the man in the mud…

'It's Typhin!' Afeclin exclaimed louder than he had meant to.

Thoughts raced around his head as he stood up and began pacing the room.

We have to get to them, maybe we can help… but where are they? he thought as he hurried to grab his things together.

Once he had put his boots on he looked over at Wolflang who was still fast asleep. Bending over him, he gave his friend a gentle shake.

'Wake up Wolflang, you have to wake up now.'

Wolflang stirred a little in the sheets but he did not wake up.

Afeclin shook him harder. Then harder still, but the sleeping elf did not wake.

'Come on Wolflang, now's not the time to be dreaming.'

He spied a jug of water on the nightstand next to the oil lamp.

'Sorry about this friend but I did try to be nice,' he said pouring the water over Wolflang's head and face.

The effect was immediate.

'What the hell are you doing?' the disturbed elf cursed between splutters and coughs, staring at Afeclin who was now standing over him, empty jug in hand.

'We have to go,' he said, throwing a pile of damp clothes at Wolflang, 'so get dressed.'

'What's going on? And what's with the water? Have you not heard of gently waking someone?' yelled Wolflang fumbling at his clothes in the darkened room.

Afeclin gave Wolflang a wry look then he walked over to the window and pulled back the coverings a little. He peered out.

The street was empty as far as Afeclin could make out in the darkness. Then all of a sudden a small flame flickered in the shadows across from the inn as if someone were standing there lighting a cigar. Afeclin stared into the dark trying to see who it was. After a minute or two of patient watching, a man stepped forward into the light and bent down to pick something up. The man looked around as he stood up again and then stepped back into the dark shadows. He was wearing a uniform not unlike the one the Captain had been wearing. It was obvious to Afeclin that the man wasn't standing in the shadows for the sake of it. More than likely he was watching or waiting for someone to emerge from the inn, perhaps even them. It also seemed probable that the man outside was not alone but as there was no way of seeing just how many there were hiding in the darkness Afeclin pushed back the sheer curtains.

'We cannot afford to be noticed so don't light that,' he said in a loud whisper as the elf attempted to light the oil lamp.

'But I can't see properly and why can't we afford to be noticed? What is going on?' Wolflang asked with concern. 'Have we been followed here from the woods? Are we in trouble?'

'No, no nothing like that. I will explain on the way, right now you need to trust me,' said Afeclin picking up his bag and cloak then walking to the door, opening it and peering down the hall. 'Okay it is safe, let's go.'

After tying the straps of his damp brown vest, Wolflang threw his bow and quiver over his shoulder in a hurry and grabbed his bag, cloak and shoes. He then followed Afeclin out the door.

They skulked along the hallway, stopping halfway down the stairs so that Afeclin could survey the lounge area.

The room was empty for the most part, only an old man with a large moustache sat in one of the comfortable lounges and he looked as if he had fallen asleep. He had one hand still clenched to his drink and an open book resting on his chest. His grey hair lay over his eyes making it difficult to see if they were open or closed but his heavy breathing and whistling nose suggested he was dozing.

When Afeclin was satisfied that no troops were lurking about they continued down the stairs.

Standing behind the bar was a young attractive woman polishing glasses and humming to herself. The girl's very long and straight, jet-black hair fell around her shoulders in a tidy wave and her pretty face was clean but tired looking. Wearing a black leather vest with a soft white shirt underneath and brown suede pants that suspended just below her knees, Afeclin could see that she was slender but well toned.

'Excuse me,' Afeclin interrupted with a polite smile, 'could you tell me if there is another way into the stables? Other than out the front door, I mean. We want to check on our horses.'

'Ooh your horses will be fine,' said the woman not even bothering to look up or stop what she was doing, 'my brother is the stablehand and he's really great with horses.'

'I am sure he is,' continued Afeclin, smiling through his teeth with growing impatience, 'but all the same my horse has been having a few problems and I just wanted to make sure he was okay.'

'What sort of problems?' the girl's grey eyes looked at him with sudden interest. It was then that she noticed the bags the two were carrying and Wolflang struggling to put on his cloth shoes at the counter.

'Why don't you want to use the front door?' she asked with a wry expression, biting at her bottom lip.

'Well, you know... in case there's any more rain,' Afeclin said lacking conviction, 'we do not want to get wet again.'

'Or could it be that you need to access your horses without being seen by the two jackals guarding the inn outside.'

Afeclin could feel his jaw drop. He had no idea how to answer the girl.

'Jackals?' questioned Wolflang wandering over to a little window in the front door and looking out.

'You know... the troops. Everyone around here calls them jackals. Cowardly dogs that have nothing better to do than follow people around and terrorise them,' the woman explained with obvious disdain.

'I can't see anyone,' said Wolflang trying to peer through the stained glass window in the door.

'Well, you probably can't see much through that window, but they're there. I saw them earlier when I took some rubbish out.'

'Are they waiting for us?'

Afeclin disregarded Wolflang's question and continued talking to the dark-haired girl.

'Okay, I see there is no pulling the wool over your eyes. We need to get to our horses without the attention of the jackals, as you call them, outside.'

The young woman looked the pair up and down for a moment in silence, biting her lip again in interest, then with a twist of her long dark hair she placed it behind her ear and leaned in over the bar, speaking in a hushed whisper.

'Ya see that tapestry over there behind you, with the horses woven into it?'

Afeclin turned around to look at the large tapestry he had been admiring earlier, that covered a good portion of the wall and flowed down onto the floor. In the middle of all the animals there were two coloured horses with what looked like a long horn protruding out of their foreheads.

'Behind the tapestry is a door. It opens into a corridor which leads to the stable,' she continued with furtiveness.

'Thank you,' said Afeclin taking the young woman's hand and giving it a gentle kiss. The girl's pink cheeks blushed red against her snowy white complexion and she smiled revealing two large dimples on either side of her full lips.

Afeclin walked over to the ornate fabric, followed by a confused and nervous Wolflang.

Pulling back the tapestry with one hand Afeclin managed to find the door hidden behind. The door was not locked but took both men to push it open due to the stiffness of its hinges. It seemed to Afeclin that the door was not well used or maintained.

When the door was closed once more the inside of the corridor was pitch black.

'I guess she forgot to mention that there is no light,' said Wolflang with irritation.

Afeclin said nothing but stood in silence, concentrating for a moment. Then clicking the fingers of his left hand produced a small flame that danced above his index finger just like the one he had created the previous night.

Although the flame was small it produced enough light for them to see where they were going. Looking up and down the corridor, Afeclin tried to make out which way to go in the pale light.

'This way,' he said after careful deliberation.

'What is going on Afeclin? Are we in some kind of trouble?'

'No time to explain now,' answered Afeclin with unintentional sharpness.

'But shouldn't we let the others know we're leaving?'

'They have already left.'

'They have? I don't understand…' Wolflang began tiredly.

'I will explain on our way.'

At the end of the passage was another heavy door with rusty hinges. After some exertion the door opened into the stable beside the inn.

A young man stood grooming one of the horses in his care and did not notice Afeclin and Wolflang enter.

'Excuse me,' coughed Afeclin.

The young man, startled, dropped the grooming brush he was using.

'Oh hello, sorry, I didn't notice you come in,' he said looking a little puzzled as he bent down to pick up the brush.

'Actually we came straight from the inn through the corridor. Your sister showed us the way,' Wolflang explained.

'Ooh in some kind of trouble are we? Actually you're not the first ones to come through that door this evening,' the boy said with earnestness, 'three other fellas came through to pick up their horses not more than an hour ago I should think.'

'Did they happen to say where they were headed?' asked Afeclin as he stroked the mane of the horse the boy had been grooming.

'No, but why would they? I'm just the stablehand after all. Nobody tells me anything and that's what I told the captain fellow who came in looking for them.' The boy started pulling hair from the horse brush.

'You spoke to the Captain,' Afeclin said more to himself than to the boy.

'Yeah,' the boy answered, once again brushing the horse's mane.

'I don't suppose you happened to notice which way they headed out of here?'

The boy smirked.

'Well, considering there is a stone wall at one end of the alley, they really could only have headed back to the main street. As for which way they went after that, I couldn't tell you, I certainly didn't walk them to the main street and wave goodbye. However if they were headed out of the city there is only one way to go, through the main gates, the way you came in,' the boy said and then asked, 'Hey, you two aren't from around here are you?'

Afeclin and Wolflang both shook their heads.

'Yeah I didn't think so.'

Afeclin sighed with weariness. He couldn't imagine how he would ever catch up to the others. He barely knew his way around, let alone follow a trail that wasn't meant to be followed. He looked around the room in search of their horses, trying to figure out their next move.

Afeclin spied his horse in the far corner of the stable resting against the gate.

'Actually,' the boy added after a little thought, 'there is one other way you could leave the city unnoticed, but you would have to be crazy to try it.'

'What way?' Afeclin asked almost desperately.

'But you don't understand. It is a dangerous place to go, in fact, nobody goes in there and if they do, they don't come out. The trees are so tall that they block out any moonlight leaving you practically blind. There is mud that swallows you up whole and local legend say that the place is haunted... that's what I'm told anyway but I would not be taking my chances in there. You don't even know if your friends actually went that way... like I said, they would have to be crazy.'

Just as the boy spoke, Afeclin felt the impression return to his mind. This time it felt stronger and much clearer.

'No, I realise it seems strange but I do know they went that way,' said Afeclin with urgency. 'Can you show me which way to go?'

'Is he out of his head or is he always this impulsive?' the boy asked Wolflang with a shocked expression as he tapped a finger on his forehead.

'I don't know,' answered Wolflang looking horrified. 'I'm completely confused.'

'Look we don't have time to waste,' said Afeclin with growing impatience, 'can you tell me where to find this other way or not?'

The boy shrugged his shoulders, 'Why should I care if you decide to enter the Alimest Grove? I can take you to the edge of the woods myself and show you where the path is if you like... after that you're on your own.'

'Thank you.'

Wolflang's face went white.

'We're not really going to go that way, are we?' he asked following the boy and Afeclin over to where their horses were kept. 'It sounds like suicide.'

'We have to. If Typhin and Pit had not wanted to be followed by the Captain, they certainly would not have gone out the main gate. Whereas by going this way (a way that is apparently very dangerous) they would have ensured that nobody would follow them. Nobody would have dared.'

'Nobody except us it seems. What I don't understand is why we need to find them anyhow. If they are trying to get away from the jackals, why not just let them go? Why involve and endanger ourselves?'

'They have done a lot for us. We were strangers to them and to this place. Without their guidance the trolls would have slaughtered us on our first day or we would have been picked up by Hoashan's men and blamed for murder. Now they need our help, the least we can do is try.'

'But how do you know they need our help?' Wolflang questioned with exasperation.

Afeclin was not sure how to answer his friend. Telling Wolflang that he had seen a vision of the trio in trouble was not likely to put the elf's mind at rest. He doubted very much that Wolflang would believe such a thing; after all, Afeclin had never had any visions before. Instead Afeclin ignored his friend's concern and began readying his horse for the ride.

'Only trouble is, I am not sure how we are going to get past the jackals that are watching the front of the building.'

'Only trouble? That's rich.'

'I believe I have the answer to that,' came a familiar voice from behind them.

The three turned to find the young slender woman from the bar standing with her hands behind her back at the door to the secret corridor. She looked at them, her eyes serious for a moment, and then walked with swiftness to where they were standing. Taking Afeclin by the hand she spoke directly to him.

'You're going in search of Typhin and his friends aren't you?' she asked, her voice almost a whisper.

'Yes.'

'I was wiping down the tables in the bar just now when I suddenly had a feeling come over me.'

'A feeling? What kind of feeling?'

'Like a strong impression that something is dreadfully wrong and it has to do with Typhin... but I don't know what.'

As she spoke Afeclin could see the urgency in her deep grey eyes. It was evident she cared for the older man, although when she had served all of them earlier he had not sensed any connection between them. *Perhaps the feelings she has for Typhin are not mutual.*

'My sister, Eliah tends to think of herself as a mystic,' mocked the boy.

Eliah turned and cast a warning glance at her brother.

'Please don't take any notice of him. He mocks what he does not understand.'

'Don't worry I have the same feeling myself,' Afeclin said with kindness then added, 'that is why we must hurry. You said you knew the answer to getting us past the jackals outside?'

'It's easy… you just need a decoy,' she said turning once again to her brother.

'Yeah but who is going to do that?' he asked and then realised Eliah was hinting at himself. 'Oh no… not me! After all, I have to show these fellas where the Alimest Grove is.'

'The Alimest Grove? You think they went that way?' she asked with concern and then answered her own question. 'Of course they would have. It would have been foolish for them to attempt to escape through the main gate. At least this way, even if the jackals get wind of where they went, they are much too cowardly to venture in after them.'

'Are you talking about those men who are friends of father's?' The boy's dark eyebrows rose with interest. Then he smirked as he turned to Afeclin, 'She's in love with one of them.'

'How dare you say that. It's not true!' The woman's face reddened. Then she tossed back her hair with her nose in the air, 'I am just concerned, is all… he is father's friend after all. Father will be most disappointed that he was not here to see Typhin when he was in town but he will be even more disappointed with us if we don't try to help him.'

The boy looked unconvinced.

'You may be right, dear sister,' he said with a careless shrug, 'and that is why I was going to show them which way to go… but here's an idea, maybe you can be the one acting as a decoy.'

'You know that I can't do that Aimish. If I was to get caught, who knows what they would do with me. I don't exactly have a good record with the jackals. Why they would probably lock me in the hole for the next ten years. You on the other hand have never put a foot out of place. Besides you are a really strong rider and they probably wouldn't catch you,' she pleaded, once again biting her bottom lip.

'And if they did?' Aimish asked with reservation.

'You would pretend you were drunk and not completely in control of your actions and the worst you would get is a night in a cell down at the courthouse.'

'That doesn't sound too exciting.' Aimish still sounded doubtful.

Eliah grabbed the front of Aimish's red, patterned shirt and pulled him closer to her, 'Then you just don't get caught. Look I wouldn't let anything happen to you, little brother, but sometimes in life you have to step up and do something to help someone else. You have to trust me.'

Eliah seemed to Afeclin like the kind of woman who could get anything she wanted by using her charm and her brother was no exception. As she pleaded with Aimish her big grey eyes and long eyelashes were bewitching and he could see that there was no way the boy was going to be able to refuse her.

Aimish put his hands up in a stopping motion as if to ward off her feminine wiles. 'Alright, alright, but if anything happens to me…'

'Yes, I will explain to father,' Eliah said completing her brother's sentence.

'Well, you'd better because I am supposed to be here minding the horses.'

'Don't worry. Everything will be fine, but now we really have to get a move on. We're just wasting time here.'

'How do you want to do this?' Aimish asked with a hesitant look on his face.

'I just have to go and close the bar. Have everything ready to go when I come back,' she ordered then disappeared with haste through the passage, opening the door as if it were effortless.

'How did she do that?' asked Wolflang with a mouth open so wide that Afeclin was sure it was about to hit the floor. 'It took the two of us to open those doors.'

'They're very old doors but there is a trick to them,' Aimish answered matter-of-factly as he headed straight for the back right corner of the stable where two handsome looking mares were standing. He then began saddling the first one of them to which he spoke with softness and affection. *Probably his own horse,* Afeclin decided.

When Eliah returned to the stable the three were ready to leave and waiting with their horses at the front door. In her hand she carried a small bottle of ale.

'What's with the bottle?' asked Aimish.

'Have a drink,' said Eliah handing him the bottle.

'What's this for?' he asked gulping down a few mouthfuls of the thick brew. 'Is it supposed to calm my nerves or something?'

'No,' she said taking the bottle from him once again and gulping down a few mouthfuls herself before offering some to Afeclin and Wolflang who both declined. Then she poured the rest of the bottle over Aimish's dark head of hair and shirt. He startled back in alarm.

'What do you think you're doing?' he yelled in anger, giving his head a vigorous shake. Dark ale sprayed over Afeclin and Wolflang.

'You smell too good, if you are to play a drunk [the Gods forbid that you should need to] then you must smell like one. Let me tell you, from many years experience behind the bar, that once you accompany the smell of the liquor with the sweat that will be dripping off you as you ride, you will smell exactly like a drunk. So much so that hopefully they won't want to come near you.'

'Why couldn't I just drink the whole bottle then? If you want me to be convincing.'

'Yes, but I also want you to have your wits about you. Really being drunk would give them the advantage and we don't want that,' she said giving her brother's saddle a quick check to make sure that the strap was tight enough.

'Okay, here goes nothing,' said Aimish as he opened the front door of the stable, 'wish me luck.'

'I will see you in the morning,' said Eliah with a wink, 'ride like the wind brother.'

Aimish mounted his horse as soon as he was out on the stoney pavement and then with only a brief hesitation he strode over to where they knew the jackals were hiding in the dark. As he got closer he started to speed up and then when he was in their general vicinity he hollered some obscene language and spat at them before taking off at top speed down the street.

The jackals reacted just as they had hoped. They yelled back in anger then jumped on their horses and took off after him down the street and towards the main gates of the town.

'Right here's our chance, there's no time to lose,' said Eliah as she pulled her long dark hair out of her face and with a quick twist placed a wiry comb in it to hold it up. She then took down a small lantern from on top of a nearby shelf and hung it over the saddle horn on her horse.

Just as they were about to leave, Wolflang spotted a movement in the shadows. 'There's still someone there,' he said in a panic.

'Surely not, I only saw two earlier,' said Eliah disregarding Wolflang and grabbing her horse.

'No, there is, I promise you, I saw someone.'

'Maybe you were just seeing things, or maybe even a rat. Eliah only saw two jackals earlier, why would there be more now?' Afeclin said trying to reason with his friend. 'At any rate if we wait any longer we will lose our chance to escape.'

'And if I am right? What then?'

'We could possibly outride one of them,' whispered Eliah, 'but surely if there was someone there, they would be curious as to why the stable door is open with faces peering out.'

As if on cue a man stepped forward, out of the shadows, staring with curiosity at the open stable door, trying to see who was in the doorway. Reacting in haste and without a thought Eliah closed the door and stared at Afeclin with anxious hope.

'What now? Should we just chance it and hope that he doesn't catch any of us before we make it to the Alimest Grove?'

Afeclin looked at his horse, stroking the stallion's mane as he considered the problem.

'Well?' asked Eliah with more urgency in her voice.

'I learnt a little bit of "mind provoking" a while back. It is where you speak to another person's mind without saying any words out loud. I have never tried it on people but in Tebelligan I would practice on my father's horses... with disastrous results I might add. It would drive the horses mad and I got into a lot of trouble for it. If I could get inside the mind of the jackal's horse, I might be able to make him run, giving us a chance to get out of here or at least gain a head start. My only concern is that I might upset the horses in here.'

'Do it,' answered Eliah without reservation, 'we've got nothing to lose and we must hurry.'

'Okay,' said Afeclin taking a firm grip of his horse and massaging him with soft strokes, 'you will need to keep quiet so that I can concentrate but you also need to do whatever you can to keep your own horses calm. If they play up they will be impossible to ride. Understand?'

The two nodded and then proceeded to stroke their own horse's mane and hush them with gentleness and affection.

Afeclin bowed his head and closed his eyes but still kept a gentle hold on his horse. Then concentrating his mind on the horse outside he imagined speaking to the horse's mind (this was difficult due to never having set eyes on the animal) but he never let go of the image and kept reinforcing it. With the image gaining strength and growing, he began to whisper to the horse's mind...

RUN...

run away...

run for your life...

be free, my friend...

run and don't stop running till you have gained your freedom!

Hearing the horses around him beginning to whinny and stomp their feet brought Afeclin back from his deep thoughts. Looking around the room, most of the horses were restless and edgy. Eliah's horse seemed a little distraught and she was doing the best she could to calm the distressed animal. To Afeclin's relief both his and Wolflang's horses seemed unperturbed.

Wolflang opened the front door to the stable once again but only enough to peer out. Outside the Jackal's horse was making a fuss. Up on two legs, with loud whinnies and snorts, the horse was clearly disturbed, while the jackal tried to calm him down without success.

Afeclin looked out the door and saw the horse acting up.

RUN! he hollered in his mind once again and this time the effect was immediate. The horse took off at top speed down the road and disappeared around the corner with its owner trying to catch up to him.

'Okay let's go,' said Afeclin mounting his horse.

Eliah and Wolflang followed suit and the three took off down the road as fast as they could, Eliah taking the lead.

They came to the end of the road and instead of turning right onto the main street, leading out of the town, they turned left heading deeper into the town centre.

At this time of night the town was quiet, apart from the odd drunks singing at the top of their voices as they made their way home to their beds.

Most of the windows of the buildings they passed were darkened and only a few streetlights were still lit. Most likely the kerosene had already run out in the lamps for the night, at any rate it made the streets very dark and hard to manipulate. Even the moons were quite low in the sky and as they rode a mist could be felt starting to settle in over the town.

Around another corner and under a bridge they rode as fast as their horses would carry them. At this end of town there were many little houses built in close proximity to each other along the sides of the road. Afeclin glanced at them as they passed by. All the windows were dark and there was not a sound to be heard apart from the clip clopping along the pebble stone road. For the most part it seemed the town was asleep.

They raced through a small alley at the end of the street and came out the other side onto another long road, this time ending with a large open grassy area. Beyond the open space was a dense forest of tall trees. Afeclin assumed this to be the Alimest Grove.

Just as they had left the alley Eliah's horse started to whinny and make a fuss by shaking her head and bucking wildly. Eliah tried hard to control the disturbed mare. She pulled hard on the reins forcing the horse's head back and into submission then she leant forward and with a calm hand, patted the mare's head as she hushed into its ear. This calmed the horse and they continued on.

'We're almost there girl.'

Afeclin could just hear Eliah talking to her horse as they tried to pick up speed again.

'Just a little further and then we can rest.'

As they approached the grassy area, the sound of many horse hooves pounding the pavement came from behind them. With a quick glance behind, Afeclin determined there was about ten or so jackals on horses not far behind them, giving chase.

'We just have to make it to the trees,' yelled Eliah giving her horse another mighty kick. 'They won't follow us in.'

A loud trumpet sounded, giving warning for the trio to stop. It rang out through the quiet street and echoed in their ears. *Too late*, Afeclin thought as he made it through the outskirts of the trees. Wolflang bounded past the first trees just after Afeclin and it was then that the two looked around and realised Eliah was not with them.

'Whoa! Whoa!' said Afeclin trying to stop and turn the horse.

Looking out from the Alimest Grove, he saw Eliah yet again struggling with her horse. The chestnut mare was up on two legs, whinnying with mad thrusts. This time Eliah was doing all she could to stay in the saddle as the jackals came closer and closer.

Without a thought Afeclin headed back out to her. He could hear the faint voice of Wolflang from behind him calling, 'What are you doing? Are you crazy?'

I probably am, but after all that Eliah and her brother have done to get us this far I am not about to turn around and sacrifice her to the jackals.

The jackals were closing in fast and Afeclin only hoped he would reach her in time, although he wasn't certain what he was going to do when he did reach her.

A moment later Eliah had come off her horse and was running as fast as she could towards the grove.

Just as one of the jackals rode up behind her leaning over on one side of the horse getting ready to grab her, Afeclin managed to reach her and grab her hard by the hand hoisting her into the saddle behind him. The stallion's momentum continued forward and as Afeclin pulled hard on the reins he managed to kick the jackal in the head. This caused the jackal to lose balance and fall off his horse giving the two a chance to turn around and head back towards the grove before any of the other jackals caught up to them.

'We had almost made it but the trumpet's sound startled her,' Eliah said with sadness as they rode through the trees to where Wolflang had been waiting bow and arrow in hand ready to strike if necessary.

'It couldn't be helped. You were lucky she made it as far as she did,' said Afeclin breathing deeply. 'The mind provoking really affected her. She was disturbed by it and unfortunately it has been my experience that they don't recover for at least a few days. Why do you think my father was so angry with me practising on his horses?'

'I guess then there is going to be a few disgruntled customers attempting to ride their horses tomorrow,' laughed Wolflang.

Although Afeclin was tired and focused on getting through the woods to help their new friends he welcomed a little lightheartedness from Wolflang. Since the unfortunate execution in the woods, his friend had not been himself and it troubled him.

Afeclin looked out through the woods to where the jackals were gathering. Watching the woods and pacing back and forwards on their horses, it was obvious to Afeclin that the jackals did not want to follow them into the grove.

'Where did they come from? How did they find us so quickly?' asked Wolflang as he too watched the jackals through the trees with one hand gripping the handle of his bow and an arrow pulled in the string just in case one of them was overcome with bravery.

'Who knows,' Eliah shrugged. 'I guess they were alerted somehow, I just hope Aimish didn't get himself captured.'

They watched as a dozen troops on horses congregated on the grassy knoll in front of the Alimest Grove, discussing their next course of action. None of them seemed interested in pursuing the trio into the grove. Behind them the city lay in darkness, a mist settling in over the buildings and the houses aglow from the light of the low moons that tinted the sky in an array of blue, green and silver hues, creating a spectacular effect.

'So what now?' asked Afeclin. 'I assume you can't go back into town. What are you going to do?'

Eliah looked at him for a moment, her expression blank, and then collecting her thoughts answered with decisiveness, 'Now I come along with you.'

'I don't know if that is such a good idea,' said Afeclin feeling uneasy about the thought of putting Eliah's life in any more danger.

'What choice do I have? I can't go back into town; I'd be arrested and very likely tortured. You on the other hand could do with a guide through these woods and I am the perfect one to do that.'

'Have you been through these woods?' asked Wolflang with surprise.

'Yes... no... sort of. Let's just say that I know how to get through and that you could really use my help right now.'

'For some reason I do not feel overly confident,' said Wolflang then added under his breath, 'we're going to die.'

'Well, I guess you're right. It seems you have no choice and your knowledge will come in handy, but what will you do for a horse? You can't ride with me the whole way.'

'Again, no choice. I'm not walking and I am not about to find a horse conveniently tied to the next tree we pass,' said Eliah as she climbed down from where she was seated on the backside of Afeclin's horse. 'However because I am the only person who has any idea which way to go, you will have to ride with me.'

'Hang on a minute, no, no, no. Nobody rides Majenta but me. You'll have to navigate from behind.'

'Mawho?' interrupted Wolflang.

'Majenta, that's what I call him. I felt ridiculous talking to a no-name horse so I gave him a name.'

'Look I don't want to come between you and… Majenta, but seriously, I'm riding him. I can't navigate what I can't see and I won't be able to see if I'm behind you! So move back,' Eliah said with finality in her voice.

Afeclin could see that he again was left with no option but to concede and as much as he hated giving the reins to Eliah, he did so in the attempt to get moving and stop wasting valuable time.

Chapter

XXIII

The journey into the Alimest Grove didn't appear hard at first and to Wolflang it seemed like any other woods he had travelled through. *Looks can be deceiving*, Wolflang realised only moments later when the trees became so thick and tall that in no time at all the sky, moons and light had disappeared from sight. The woods had become thick with blackness.

Everything was quiet and the three had stopped in their tracks in the stillness of the woods. All that could be heard in the dark was the sound of breathing as they sat contemplating moving with blindness into the dark.

'Okay is everybody ready for this?' asked Eliah as she made herself comfortable in the saddle.

'As ready as I'm ever going to be,' answered Wolflang, looking doubtful. 'How are we going to do this?'

'Just keep as close as possible to us.'

'That could be quite difficult since I can't even see you.'

Before anyone could say anything more Eliah let out a deafening shriek.

'Hoooooiyaaaaaaaaahhh!!'

The sound echoed through the woods and as it rang out millions of glowing butterflies filled the air and lit up a visual path through the trees.

'Let's ride!' she yelled and gave the horse a mighty kick that spurred the stallion forward through the glowing lights that flew around their heads.

Wolflang followed trying to stay as close as possible to the horse in front.

Winding around the massive trees and dense scrub they galloped onward. Wolflang kept low to the saddle as he attempted to dodge the low branches of the smaller trees. On occasion however, an even lower branch that Eliah and Afeclin had pushed out of their way swung back and hit him in the face before he had a chance to see it and move.

As he was riding Wolflang happened to glance behind. It seemed that the butterflies were all travelling in the same direction as they were. Because of this, total darkness followed him. *If I happen to fall behind, I will be swallowed up by the darkness once more.* It was no wonder Eliah had told Wolflang to stay close. Fear swept over him. One thing Wolflang knew for sure was that he did not want to be left alone in the darkness of the Alimest Grove. There was something strange about the woods. Something that told him that they shouldn't be there and although Wolflang had never felt much fear before, he was now terrified. He just didn't know what of.

🐚 🐚 🐚

It was a difficult ride, to keep with the glowing anomalies, but they managed to without either of the horses losing their footing on the rocky ground or being wiped out by one of the many low tree limbs.

When the last of the butterflies had disappeared the woods were left in complete darkness once more and the fatigued travellers had to stop. All that could be heard in the stillness of the woods was their heavy breathing as they all attempted to catch their breath. Even the horses snorted and huffed with short hot breaths through their nostrils as they struggled to respire naturally.

'What now?' asked Afeclin unwrapping his arms from around Eliah's tiny waist where he had clung to her as they rode.

150

'Well, which of you fellas brought a lamp? I lost mine when I came off my horse.'

'We didn't bring one, we don't have one.'

'You fellas weren't very prepared. How did you imagine you would ever make it through the darkness of the Alimest Grove without a light?'

'We were not really expecting to be entering blackened groves in the middle of the night when we left Tebelligan.'

'Well then, now we walk,' said Eliah, grabbing in blindness at a low branch and ripping it from the tree. Then swinging one leg over the front of the horse she jumped to the ground.

'Walk? But we can't even see,' Wolflang complained.

Afeclin also reached above him and grabbed at a leafy branch. Pulling it away from the tree he attempted to light it. The dancing flame flickered above his finger for a moment and then went out. Clicking his finger once more he commanded the branch to burn but the branch was too moist from dew and would not light. Again the flame went out the instant it was lit.

'Whoa, how did you do that?' asked Eliah, stunned.

'It's a little trick I know, but it's not really working...' he said pausing to take a breath, 'everything is too damp to burn and the air is so thick I can barely keep the flame alight.'

'Even if you could keep producing the flame momentarily each time it would be something... give us a little light,' suggested Wolflang.

'I can't, it takes a lot of energy and concentration to make the flame appear and stay. If I keep doing it I will just tire myself out and then I will be no good to anyone.'

'How tired could you possibly get clicking your fingers?' asked Wolflang with great annoyance in his voice and making a clicking sound with his own fingers.

'You don't understand the amount of energy your body needs to use to create magic, even the simplest. The greater the sorcerer the greater their ability to harness that energy needed,' answered Afeclin with irritation. 'I mean who am I? I am far from being a great wizard. I know a few tricks so far... that's all and it may seem to you like I am just clicking my fingers but a great deal of energy and concentration goes into it.'

'Okay in that case...' Eliah interrupted attempting to take back control of the situation, 'Afeclin, you lead Majenta but keep one hand on my shoulder, Wolflang you will obviously lead your horse but you also keep one hand on my other shoulder. I am going to lead us all, it will be slow but I have this branch to help me feel my way along.'

It truly was the blind leading the blind and the three were breathless and sweaty from the difficult ride they had just endured, but this part of the woods felt extra hot. There was not a breeze to be felt, the air was very still, thick and humid. Tiny insects danced around their ears as they walked and irritated them to no end, as they had no free hands to swipe them away.

The ground was rough with what felt like strange-shaped loose rocks and thick tree branches littering the path. From time to time one of them lost their footing briefly and slipped. However, because they were huddled together it was easy to recover from the fall.

Afeclin found that with his eyes blinded by the darkness his other senses were heightened. He could smell the raw dampness of the woods surrounding them. There was a pungent smell of decay and rot that Afeclin could only associate with the smell of death, *probably a dead animal,* he hoped. As he perspired he could taste the sweat as it dripped down his face and often into his mouth. The taste was brackish and it made him thirsty. His sense of hearing was also more acute and Afeclin found himself listening to every little sound he could hear. Sounds were all around him. From above him he could hear the flapping wings of a bird, below him, the clashing of rocks and pieces of wood being shuffled about as they trod and around him the faint howl of a wolf in the distance or the hoot of an owl in a tree above them. There were so many little noises to be heard that Afeclin became obsessed with identifying each and every one of them. *There is nothing to fear when you know what the sound is.* But he was not prepared for what he heard next.

It started as a quiet hum that became louder and more distinct as it seemed to get closer, until all of a sudden it was surrounding them.

Everybody stopped still and listened.

'What is that?' asked Afeclin as composed as he could to hide the fear that was sweeping over his body.

'Shhhhh!' hushed Eliah.

The loud hum became more of a drawn out moan as a kind of sadness filled the air.

Afeclin felt as if his heart was about to beat outside of his chest. He could not remember a time when he ever felt as scared as he did at that moment. He had felt some fear as he, Typhin and Wolflang had sat in the tree watching the girl as she was murdered. He had felt a little frightened as they set out in the night from the inn, but now he was so scared he couldn't feel his legs let alone move them. Afeclin supposed that it was the dark that was the real cause of the trouble. There was something frightening about the unknown and the fact that he could not see what was making the awful sound disturbed him a great deal.

'I don't know what to do,' said Eliah with despair, 'I just can't remember...'

At that moment a bright light surrounded them and at last not only could they discover what had been making the awful noise but they could also take in their surroundings.

Not able to bring himself to look up into the bright lights, Afeclin instead looked down to the ground.

'What the...?' he exclaimed louder than he had meant to.

It appeared that they had been shuffling over the resting place of many unfortunate visitors to the grove, for lying all around them on the path were skeletal bones.

Skulls of varying sizes were scattered about the road, indicating many travellers had come this way before and been allowed to go no further. Some of the bones still sat together to form the shape of a person while it was evident others had been knocked apart by travellers like themselves. The sight was grim but looking about, Afeclin was relieved to see that there were no fresh corpses. In fact it seemed that most of the people who had died there had done so many years prior since in a lot of cases the travellers' clothes were either well deteriorated or no longer discernible. Seeing the small graveyard, however did not give him much hope of making it through the Alimest Grove.

'By Ambroza!' Eliah exclaimed. 'We're going to die.'

Wolflang stood in silence, as if frozen, watching the lights dance around his head. His tanned skin had gone pale from fright.

'Wolflang, look away.'

It was then that Afeclin happened to glance above him. In the sky just above their heads were three glowing white apparitions. Their bodies were shapeless, just a white glowing mass. However, their faces not only had shape but also expression. Each of the three ghosts had the look of great pain, suffering and mourning on their faces.

By now the moaning had turned into singing, not a joyful song by any stretch of the imagination, but a depressing lullaby. There were no words and despite the sadness it made one feel the song was intensely beautiful. Starting out in a low key and ever so soft, it grew louder and higher, changing pitch every so often.

'It almost seems like a build up, don't you think?' observed Afeclin with caution. 'Like the song is building up to a grand finale.'

Eliah had looked stunned and very frightened from the moment she realised she had no idea what to do but Afeclin's observation brought her back to reality.

'That's it! Afeclin you're a genius! I know exactly what to do. It is, as you say a build up. Cover your ears.'

Both Afeclin and Eliah covered their ears with their hands. Then turning to Wolflang they realised he was spellbound by the ghosts and unable to respond.

Afeclin grabbed at his friend with both hands and shook him.

'Snap out of it Wolflang,' he said in desperation, 'do not let them get to you.'

Wolflang neither took his eyes away from the deadly apparitions nor acknowledged Afeclin in the least.

As Afeclin looked past Wolflang, he shook his head. Eliah's grey eyes grew wide with concern.

'Afeclin, we have to cover his ears somehow.'

Afeclin looked around for something he could put in Wolflang's ears that wouldn't fall out if not held in place. Spying some cloth still attached to a bony ribcage on the ground nearby, he grabbed at it and pulled it away from the skeleton. The fabric, aged and dirty came off with ease. Afeclin then ripped the cloth into smaller pieces and forced it into Wolflang's ears. Thinking all was fine he then covered his own ears with his hands again and waited. A moment later Afeclin felt Eliah nudge him with her elbow and indicate towards Wolflang. One of the pieces of cloth had fallen from his ear.

Time was short and Afeclin knew it. The ghostly song was getting louder and it was eminent that the pitch was high but he chanced taking his hands from his own ears again to help his friend.

Grappling for his silver flask in his bag, this time he wet the cloth before inserting it back into Wolflang's ear. Then he snatched the piece from his other ear, wet it and shoved it back, in a tremendous hurry.

Hearing the tune beginning to peak Afeclin let the flask drop to the ground as he covered his ears once more. Just as he did the song hit a high, sharp note that was so incredibly loud he was sure it would pierce the soul if heard without aversion.

The sound was like a shrill scream that seemed to last forever. Even through his hands the sound felt like it was penetrating his brain. Cupping his hands even tighter over his ears, his body trembled and shook with violence. The sweat poured off his head profusely and moved with discomfort down his face like rain. The terrible pressure on his mind caused him to fall to his knees and curl into a ball.

The high-pitched shriek that seemed to last forever was in reality only minutes but when the sound had gone the apparitions disappeared also, leaving them once again in complete darkness.

Shaken and wet from sweat Afeclin reached out to Wolflang and Eliah. Both seemed alright but Wolflang was unresponsive.

Afeclin felt about for the skeleton he had borrowed some cloth from. Finding the bony frame and feeling for what was left of the cloth he then tugged the material away from the bones. He managed to get it all off without making too many tears in it. Then he felt along the skeleton for a leg bone and once he had found the longest bone in the leg he broke it away from the rest of the remains.

'What are you doing Afeclin?' asked Eliah with a soft whisper, pulling herself together and in attempting to stand, colliding with him.

Taking no notice of Eliah, Afeclin wrapped the rotting cloth around the top of the bone and lit it with his finger. The cloth took to flame the instant the spark touched it giving light to the dense scrub around them.

'Whoa great idea,' Eliah said with appreciation.

Afeclin smiled and gave a dismissive nod, turning his attention to Wolflang.

The elf appeared deathly white, his eyes stared into space and he stood as still as a statue. Droplets of blood rolled out of his ears but the material had stayed in place.

'Wolflang, are you okay?' Afeclin asked.

There was no reply.

'Do you think the cloth in his ears wasn't enough to keep out the sound?'

'Well, he obviously survived it,' said Eliah and then gave Wolflang a caressing pat on the back as she whispered in his ear, 'Wolflang! Wolflang! It's okay. There is no need to fear, they have gone now.'

'You think speaking to him like a child is going to help?' asked Afeclin with sarcasm.

'You got any better ideas?' said Eliah with defiance. 'I'm no doctor or anything but I have heard that when some people suffer a great scare that they don't know how to deal with they retract into themselves to hide... all I'm trying to do is make him feel safe enough to come out of that state.'

'Okay, okay, see if you can bring him back to life,' said Afeclin finding another piece of cloth to refuel his torch. 'It's strange how the horses don't seem to be affected by the ghosts at all,' he observed waving the flare in the direction of where the two horses stood in the darkness.

'I have read a little of this kind of phenomena,' said Eliah turning to Afeclin, 'it seems it's rare that animals see or hear anything to do with the supernatural, I don't know how it works but apparently it's true.

Look around. There is not one animal skeleton amongst the bones. Do you think all these people walked here?'

After he had wrapped a lot more of the rotting cloth around the bone to keep the torch burning, Afeclin looked down at the ground and noticed he hadn't picked up the silver bottle he had dropped. Bending over to pick up the flask he was interrupted once more by the vision he had been seeing at sporadic intervals for the past hour.

There was something different about it this time. Each time he had seen the vision it had felt desperate. This time there was something a lot more urgent about it but he couldn't put his finger on what.

Picking up his silver bottle and wiping the dirt unconsciously from the spout onto his shirt he drank with thirstiness as he tried to figure out what the new urgency was.

Then it hit him.

'It's happening now as we speak!'

'What are you talking about?' asked Eliah, surprised by the sudden outburst.

'We have no time left… it's happening now. Before, I was obviously just having a premonition… but now it is more urgent than ever. We have to wake Wolflang!' Afeclin explained in a hurried jumble of words.

Eliah looked at him, a blank expression on her face.

'Out the way, Eliah, I need to see to Wolflang myself,' said Afeclin rushing at Wolflang in desperation and pouring water from the flask over his head and face.

Wolflang came out of his trance with a splutter and a cough.

'What the hell are you doing?!' he shouted. 'That's the second time tonight you've poured water on me!'

'I'm glad to see that you're okay but there's no time for idle chit chat. Get on your horse we have to keep moving,' ordered Afeclin without sympathy.

Despite his annoyance, Wolflang did what he was told. Afeclin also mounted his horse and helped Eliah up into the front of the saddle.

'Let's go as quickly as we can for as long as we can, I fear this fire will not last much longer.'

The three of them took off again as fast as their horses would carry them in the dim light. Eliah once again took the reins and directed them while Afeclin held the flame torch high. The light was enough to see where they were riding but did not light up the woods ahead of them very well, slowing them down.

Wolflang followed close behind but seemed to be in a strange mood. He was solemn and had a grave look on his face. He followed almost mechanically as if he wasn't really there at all.

The torchlight began to wane and Afeclin became desperate that they would stumble upon Typhin, Pit and Raan before it ran out. Despite Afeclin's urgency the light did eventually fade and disappear allowing the darkness to engulf them once more. Having stopped dead in their tracks it had also gone deathly silent. Then, as if the gods were answering a prayer, in that sudden silence, they heard voices.

There were two distinct voices and they sounded distressed. The voices were not coming from ahead of them, however, but rather from the right side of them. Scanning the woods in desperation, Afeclin tried to figure out what direction the voices were coming from. He stared into the dark for the longest time but found it difficult to pinpoint the precise direction as the voices rang out in the silent woods. Then just as his eyes were beginning to blur, as he tried to focus on something… anything in the dark he saw a flicker through the trees. At first he wondered if his eyes were playing tricks on him but as he kept his sight fixated on the darkness, he began to see a steady light.

'You see that?' he asked with urgency mounting in his voice.

'See what?' asked Eliah attempting to get down off the horse. 'What is there to see?'

'Wait a moment,' said Afeclin grabbing Eliah around her slim waist and stopping her dismounting the horse, 'see if you can see it.'

'See what?' she asked again. 'How can you possibly see anything?'

'Look that way,' he said, guiding her chin and turning it towards the direction of the light. 'Can you see that glow through the trees?'

'I can't see anything,' she uttered with haste and then added, 'wait a minute… yes… I see it, there is a light. It must be them!'

'Let's head towards the light then. We'll have to walk the horses again. If we do what we were doing before but instead head in the direction of the light we should be able to make it to them,' said Afeclin getting down from Majenta and then helping Eliah to the ground.

'How do we even know it is them?' asked Wolflang coming out of the trance he was in. 'We could be just heading further and deeper into this dark nightmare of a forest. We could end up lost ourselves or even encounter something worse than what we have already seen tonight.'

'You're right Wolflang. There is a chance it is not them but what choice do we have but to check? Besides that light is the only light around for miles and personally I would rather leave the beaten track we are following to head towards some kind of light than continue on towards more darkness... wouldn't you?' said Eliah adopting a diplomatic approach with Wolflang.

Wolflang didn't answer but instead gave a little grunt.

Afeclin was a little disappointed by the behaviour of the elf. Wolflang had come on this journey in search of adventure; it was not like the elf to back away from a little danger. In their youth his friend had always been more the adventurous type than himself. Afeclin had been the voice of reason, the more cautious one putting a damper on all the fun. It seemed as if Wolflang had lost his nerve or perhaps the reality had set in. In games the adventure was fun and exciting but being a part of a real life adventure was not as safe and the outcome was unpredictable, like the girl who was killed with such brutality under the tree beneath them. It was a strong reminder that they were no longer in Tebelligan and that they would now be changed forever because of it.

As concerned as he was for his friend however, there were more important issues at hand like finding the trio who had disappeared into the night and were now in trouble. Afeclin only hoped that it was their light that they were heading towards and not some other horror awaiting them in the dark.

Chapter

XXIV

The journey towards the light was slow and tiring. Now that the three were off the beaten track they had to be careful where they trod. Small bristle bushes and fallen trees were only a couple of the obstacles they had to move over and around. The darkness made their way hugely difficult and their only saving grace being a small light in the distance that had an ever so gradual increase in intensity as they moved toward it.

Wolflang held tight to Eliah's shoulder but kept his sights on the light ahead.

With his body aching from the tiredness he felt and his head in pain after the agonising encounter with the ghostly apparitions, he kept on without complaint.

It was hot in the woods and Wolflang felt as if there was no air to breathe. There was not a hint of a breeze to be felt.

As they walked he could feel his mood begin to worsen and he couldn't figure out why. This was not like him at all but he didn't seem to be able to control it. With his mind full of thoughts of the last couple of day's activities he felt himself despair. *That song!* That paralysing, beautiful song of the ghosts played on and on in his head. Although the song had no words that he understood, it spoke to his soul of great and utter hopelessness and brought to his heart all the sadness he had ever felt in his short elf life. Memories of his mother flooded back to him all of a sudden and then of watching his father's heartache and anguish over the loss of his one and only true love. The memories were painful the first time around but the song... that bewitching song made the recollections unbearable.

The light was the only piece of sanity Wolflang had left and he held on to it as if his life depended upon it. He felt as if the light would disappear all at once if his eyes should stray for just a moment. Sweat poured from his brow stinging his eyes and yet he still remained focused on his target. He craved water but dared not attempt to reach for his water skin for the fear of averting his eyes.

At long last they made it to the light source.

What seemed like an eternity in the dark and the heat of the woods were perhaps only minutes. At first it was light enough for them to see their hands in front of their faces, a little further and they could see the trees about them as well as each other. Within a few more steps they had reached the light source, an old oil lamp hanging from a tree on the other side of a small clearing. Sitting under the tree was a muddied figure hunched over, sobbing into his arms.

The dirty figure startled and looked up at the sound of the intruders. It was hard to tell in the pale light and through the dirt on his face, who it was, but as the figure stood up, grabbing at his bow and arrow in suspicion, they could see for certain that it was Pit.

He stared at them in disbelief for a moment but then as Afeclin took a step forward towards the goblin, he lowered his weapon and spoke.

'No! Don't come any closer!' his shout was desperate then he calmed himself to explain. 'This clearing isn't what it seems, the ground is a kind of mud substance that swallows you up.'

Eliah looked panic stricken at the sight of the devastated goblin and ran through the trees at one side of the clearing, coming out at the other side where Pit stood in helpless anguish.

She reached out her arms to him and held him tight for a moment. Then she pulled back and looked with fear into Pit's watery eyes.

160

'What happened?' she asked almost in a whisper. 'Where are Typhin and Raan?'

Seeing the grief on her face as she dared ask the dreaded question was almost too much for Wolflang. Already struggling with his own demons, he looked away not wanting to hear any more but allowed himself to listen as curiosity got the better of him.

The small amount of hair Pit had on his balding head was soaked in sweat and as he lifted his head up he wiped a trembling hand of long slender fingers over it.

'It was awful,' he began with a shaky voice. 'We were all riding through the woods one minute and then the next... Typhin... he had ridden into the muck... and he knows the dangers of these woods... but I don't know maybe he just didn't notice until it was too late. By Ambroza! If only I had been in the lead, I would have been suspicious of a little clearing like this and avoided it. Damn you Typhin! What were you thinking?'

Eliah was trying to understand Pit's ramblings but was finding it difficult and growing impatient.

'But where is he? Couldn't you save him? What happened to them?' she asked in desperation, grabbing onto his leather vest with tight fists.

'They're gone. Both of them.'

Pit's head hung in defeat.

'What do you mean? How?'

'Typhin was still on his horse and not touching the mud itself, so we tried to get to him before the horse went under, taking Typhin with him,' he trembled as if reliving the story as he told it. 'We tied a rope to this tree and threw the other end to him so he could tie it to the horse's saddle and climb across the rope... it was working fine and he had almost made it. We both had our hands on him and we thought we'd done it... but then the horse went too far under, taking the rope under too and lowering Typhin into the mud. I let go in time but Raan was still holding on and fell in with Typhin. There was nothing I could do. I tried to pull them out but the muck kind of sucked them under.'

'No! It's not true! He can't be gone... No! Surely there must be some way we can get to them. They may still be alive.'

Wolflang and Afeclin had still been standing on the other side of the clearing. As Wolflang listened he felt his heart could take no more, the torment in Eliah's voice was more than he could bear. He looked to Afeclin for some sanity, to his surprise however, Afeclin did not seem to be too disturbed by the situation at all. In fact Afeclin stood scratching his whiskers staring into the clearing as if he were in another world.

Then Afeclin did something nobody could have expected, he jumped up onto his horse and letting out a big cry 'Yaahh!' he rode as fast as he could towards the dreaded clearing. Once he hit the mud the horse became stuck fast and began to sink.

'What are you doing? Have you gone mad?' a stunned goblin yelled to him from the other side.

Afeclin looked at Pit with a strange calmness.

'Get hold of yourself Pit. You know the way out of the woods so I want you to take Eliah and Wolflang and head out of here. Go and wait at whatever town or city you were heading to... if all goes well we'll meet you there.'

Pit looked bewildered. Eliah still clinging to Pit's vest fell to her knees in tears. Wolflang stood in shock trying to comprehend his friend's impulsive move. *What is Afeclin doing? How could he possibly think he knows what to do?*

In a world where he already felt lost, Wolflang did not want to lose his only friend as well but he stood staring in silence at Afeclin sinking into the muck. He wanted to yell out, he wanted to stop him or cry or scream or even say goodbye but nothing would come, nor did he move. He felt paralysed.

Within no time Afeclin and his horse disappeared leaving Eliah, Wolflang and Pit bewildered and confused.

Chapter

XXV

Afeclin looked back at Pit as he became further stuck in the mud. The goblin appeared as white as snow. Afeclin felt for him but mouthed the words 'trust me'.

Although he did not know quite what he was doing jumping into the dreaded mud, it seemed right. It felt like something he should do. He could not explain it and that was why he chose not to. Instead he jumped into the muck before anyone could stop him and talk him out of it. He knew it was insanity but he also knew it was the only way. However, he didn't know what to expect and was nervous because of it.

Afeclin looked at Wolflang before his head went into the mud and was dismayed by the nonchalant expression on the elf's face... *but then Wolflang has been acting strangely since we left Tebelligan*, he considered with sadness.

163

Journey of Destiny

When Afeclin found there was no way he could keep his mouth from going under, he took a deep breath and held his mouth shut tight. A few moments later his eyes went under.

When the top of his head was covered he dared to open his eyes. Afeclin was amazed by what he was able to see; for once submerged the mud was translucent. Tilting his head upwards he managed to look back at his friends who were standing, staring into the mud in horror.

Down he went, further and further.

The mud was so thick that there was no way to take a breath and after a couple of minutes Afeclin became desperate to breathe. Chest tightening, head thumping and body shaking he descended further into the muck hoping with all his might that he had not been wrong after all about his feeling. Majenta struggled between Afeclin's legs, thrusting his body back and forward, fighting for air as they together descended further beneath the ground.

Another minute passed and Afeclin shaking madly started to think it was the end. Perhaps he had too much faith in his own intuition. After all he was far from being a master of the art. *How foolish I am following Typhin and Raan into the pit. What was I thinking I would be able to do?* It was like his very first visit to Payden's Pool many years before when he was just a boy. How clear the memory seemed all of a sudden, the calm cool water, the warm summer breeze and that rich, sweet smell of Tebelligan country. He and Lenna had been floating on a raft out in the middle of the waterhole. Neither of them had learned to swim yet but neither of them were concerned about the water since they were safe on the raft.

The raft was made of three fat logs cut from solid traffita trees and then tied together with the pool's reeds to make it secure. This could be very effective if tightened well.

On that particular day the two of them had been having the most wonderful time basking in the sun, splashing each other with water and joking about. They had known each other for a few years and had developed quite the friendship. They had met in the palace. Lenna's father, being a well-respected chancellor to the King, was required by custom to frequent the court and on occasion his little daughter Lenna would accompany him.

She was the darling of the court and whispers would circulate around the palace of her being a great match for one of the King's sons. However it was the taller human that had caught the young girl's eye and from then on they had become inseparable.

That day would almost end in tragedy for just as they were turning around about to paddle back to the shore one of the reeds

164

snapped on the side Lenna was sitting, disturbing the wooden logs. She had been just a little bit close to the edge and when the log rolled she rolled off it into the pool. She sunk down in the water like a lead weight as Afeclin watched from the top in awe, not knowing what to do. He had nothing for her to grab onto and his arms could not reach her. He found himself calling her name over and over again as if it might help somehow.

When he could stand it no longer a voice within him said, "You have to save her, it's up to you now." So he plummeted head first into the cool water and tried to reach her. Once he was under he could see her again not far away and he tried in desperation to grab the hand that she had reached out to him. As much as he tried, he could not reach her and a moment later he began to feel the pains of needing air. He resisted trying to struggle to the surface and instead attempted to reach her by making wild thrusts with his hands and arms.

After what seemed an eternity submerged in a deep, dark abyss, he managed to grab her hand. Just as he did another face appeared in the water. It was the face of a young elvin boy. The boy put his small arms around the two and swam them back toward the daylight. Gasping for air as they all broke through the surface of the water the boy then let go of Afeclin and swam Lenna to the broken raft drifting a little distance away. Encouraging her to hold on he attempted to swim back to Afeclin. The boy came back to where he had left Afeclin but upon returning found that the human had disappeared. They had found him later, further down the bank, washed up on the shore. To everyone's surprise he was alive and well, just suffering extreme exhaustion.

Nobody knew how he came to be there, least of all Afeclin who remembered nothing more than the boy in the water. The whole incident was very puzzling.

That had been the first time they had met Wolflang. He bounded in like a storybook hero and rescued the fair maiden in distress. After that of course both Afeclin and Lenna decided to learn how to swim but by the time Afeclin was any good it was too late to play the part of the hero. That part had been taken.

It seemed funny to Afeclin to be remembering the experience at such a time. He had not even thought about it for many years. The memory made him feel worse. He felt like that little imbecilic child who didn't know how to swim but jumped in anyway.

Just as it seemed as if life was pretty much over, Majenta fell away from between Afeclin's legs and instantaniously the young human found he could move his feet.

We made it! he thought to himself struggling not to pass out. *Have to hold on just a little longer.*

Before he knew it his legs were free, then his body, followed by his arms. After that he simply fell away from the mud, dropping quite a height before landing on a hard clay floor.

Coughing and spluttering, spitting out mud, he lay on the floor struggling to get air into his lungs. His body still shook and his head still pounded and as if giving himself up to exhaustion he turned onto his back and fell into a deep dreamless sleep alongside his fatigued horse.

Chapter

XXVI

It was daybreak when Eliah, Pit and Wolflang made it out of the Alimest Grove. Weary and sleep deprived they burst through a clump of trees and into a clearing that overlooked a grassy meadow.

The dark had been abysmal in the grove and although they had used the light of the lamp to guide them, the daylight was refreshing as they stepped through the last of the trees.

The journey had been slow and tiring but to their relief, uneventful. Pit had known the way out of the grove and had led them in safety through the darkness.

Everyone had remained silent during the trip. There was nothing to say. They had all lost someone they cared about in the woods and no amount of discussion would change that fact.

Now that they were out of the grove, Wolflang had forgotten all feelings of sadness. He now felt bitter and angry. He regretted having left Tebelligan, where the world was simple. He resented having met Pit and his friends and he was angry with Afeclin for his heroism and stupidity. *What was he thinking jumping into the mud like that? What was he trying to prove? Did he think he could simply magic his way out of there?* The more Wolflang thought about it the angrier he felt.

'Just beyond the clearing is a dirt track which will take us into the back of Rengal. We should make it there by later tonight,' said Pit with a weary sigh. 'There is an inn we always go to on the other side of the city, if Afeclin was right at all and managed to escape with Typhin and Raan, that is where they will go. We will give them three days to get there before we move on.'

'You don't seriously think Afeclin was going to be able to magic them out of the mud do you? I mean come on. I've known Afeclin all my life and as much as he likes to dabble in magic, don't let him fool you... he is no wizard.'

'You think your friend jumped in the mud for no good reason?'

'He just wants to be some hero. He always wanted to be the "hero" growing up,' Wolflang answered with an irritable growl. 'Well, I guess he is now. He died acting the part.'

'I think you underestimate your friend, Wolflang, he is intelligent. He would not have put himself in danger if he didn't think he could help... did you not see his eyes? He knew what he was doing.'

'You base that on knowing him how long, Eliah?' Wolflang snarled. 'He had never been there before; how could he possibly know anything that could help?'

'I cannot believe he made such a brash move without thinking it through first,' she said in a sharp tone with tears welling in her eyes. 'I refuse to think there is no hope for our friends and I will not give up that hope. Afeclin is their only chance for survival and you will NOT convince me of anything else.'

'She's right you know. He knew somehow that it would be okay. I can't tell ya how... but he did.'

'You two can think what you like.'

He mounted his horse, embittered and sullen.

'But don't be surprised when they don't show up.'

Wolflang wordlessly nudged his horse with his feet and proceeded down a slight descent into the meadow.

Pit watched with jaded breaths before mounting his own horse. Eliah swung herself into the saddle of Typhin's horse and gave the animal a soft nudge onwards, trailing behind the bitter elf.

Wolflang didn't want to talk to them. He didn't want them trying to convince him that Afeclin could, in fact, still be alive. The last thing the elf wanted was to get his hopes up only to have them shattered again in a few days. Besides he felt angry and while in his heart of hearts he knew that it wasn't Pit's fault, he wanted to be angry with him anyway. It was silly and he knew it. That was why it was best not to talk at all.

The sun was warm even for the earliness of the day and the air was crisp. It still felt a little strange. All night they had been traveling through the darkness and all at once, it was light again.

Voices of Nali-birds could be heard singing in the tops of the trees that surrounded the clearing. Bright crimson flowers dotted the landscape with the sweetest fragrance that filled the air. Every now and then a blighter rabbit with their round bodies and long floppy ears, bounded out of the grass, hopping away in the direction of the trees. The sun, while low in the sky, peered through the trees with brightness.

Wolflang took in a deep breath, lifting his chin to feel the sun on his face. He closed his eyes and pictured Lenna. He saw her standing in the sunshine, her hair aglow with auburn hues making her appear like a fiery angel. He sighed as he realised just how much he missed her and felt sad for the fact that he had broken her heart to come on this journey, a journey he was at this point regretting. He took another deep breath. *At least we're out of that dreadful grove.* Even the horses seemed relieved. They nodded their heads with cheerful whinnies, occasionally pulling up grass to munch hungrily as they walked through the dewy meadow.

Since coming out of the grove Wolflang had the feeling that he was being watched, like eyes were following his every move. He couldn't understand why he felt the way he did and he looked around with caution. Then out of the corner of his eye he saw something big and brown sitting on top of the grassy ridge at the edge of the clearing. He turned his head to get a better look at what it was and was surprised to behold a large brown bear sitting upright in the grass taking a keen interest in the travellers. The bear's eyes were as black as midnight and they stared directly into Wolflang's.

'There is a bear staring at me, should I be worried?' he asked keeping careful eye contact with the animal.

Pit and Eliah turned to look at the bear.

'Just keep moving at this pace,' the goblin spoke. 'I have a feeling that it is a lawfabex, not a bear.'

'A lawfabex? What's that?' asked Wolflang keeping his eyes on the beast.

'A lawfabex has a head, chest, front legs and paws like a bear but his backside and part of his body are more like a wolf,' he answered with a hushed voice.

Wolflang stared at the beast with interest.

'How can you tell from the front of him that he is a lawfabex?... He looks like a bear to me.'

'Can you see what colour his hump behind his head is?' asked Pit watching the beast himself. 'A lawfabex always has a white hump... bears never do.'

'I can't see his hump.'

'Then there is his colouring... Lawfabexes have a very dark brown almost black coat.'

With the sun's rays beating down on him, the animal's fur had an ordinary brown colouring to it but had every possibility of being darker than it appeared.

'Nope, still can't tell.'

'Of course the best way to be sure he's a lawfabex is by the horn in the middle of his head,' said Pit with a laugh, like he was enjoying a little game.

'Horn? I see no horn... he must be a bear...' Wolflang started, then examining the animal again noticed some kind of blotch in the middle of its forehead, 'oh wait...'

The animal faced Wolflang and kept its eyes on him, making it appear like he had no horn at all but when it shook its head all of a sudden, upsetting the flies that had landed on its face, the small horn instantly stuck out.

'Oh that horn,' he said with surprise. 'Yes, it is definitely a lawfabex as you say... but how did you know?'

'I saw him sitting there as we entered the valley,' the goblin answered with a muffled laugh.

Wolflang rolled his eyes and shook his head at Pit's little joke.

'Is he dangerous? Should we speed up and get out of the meadow quickly?' Wolflang asked feeling somewhat insecure about the way the animal watched him with such interest.

'Of course they're dangerous. Very dangerous, but we don't want him to think we have reason to be afraid. If we speed up it's very likely he'll give chase.'

'How do you know it's a he?' Eliah asked with antagonism. 'Maybe he's a she.'

'Let's hope for our sakes it's not, as with many species the females are way more aggressive,' Pit teased.

'Can't we outrun him?' suggested Wolflang. 'I mean, surely the horses are faster.'

'You have obviously never seen a lawfabex run. They have hind legs like a wolf which make them faster than a horse, when they want to be.'

The trio kept on riding as they had been. Wolflang kept a wary eye on the curious lawfabex. The animal sniffed the air, then appeared less interested, stood up revealing his leaner wolf-like backside and trudged heavily away.

Chapter

XXVII

Lenna tossed and turned as she began to wake the following morning. Snuggling deep into her blankets she felt the relief that comes only after having a nightmare and then waking to realise it was all pure imagination.

What a horrible dream, she thought as she lay with eyes closed enjoying the rest, *I am so glad I chose not to follow Wolflang after all. Who knows what would have happened to me.*

She lay in bed recalling the details of the dream with perfect clarity.

Odd that I should remember it so clearly, she pondered with confusion, *but then, nightmares are like that aren't they? I guess it is because they stir you so greatly... bad things always seem to be harder to forget.*

Lenna remembered Wolflang's note and his painful goodbye. *Yes, it is hard to forget the bad things that happen.*

She turned onto her side and embraced her pillow with warmth, *how glad I am to be home.*

Her joy became confusion however as she began to think about how she came to be at home and safe in her own bed. *Funny... I do not seem to remember that part.*

Lenna held the pillow even tighter as she struggled to remember the details of the previous day. *I am home aren't I?*

The harder she tried to recollect, the more her nightmare became a reality.

She became afraid and obsessed with opening her eyes. *If I open my eyes I will see that I am home and the nightmare will be over... the specifics of how I came to be here are irrelevant... all that matters is that I am home in Tebelligan.*

As much as she tried however, fear kept her from peering out from under the covers. *If I am wrong, then my nightmare will continue.*

The more conscious and awake she became however, the more aware she was of the truth.

Realising that there was no point trying to hide, Lenna opened one eye and looked out from beneath the covers.

She spied a small bedside table covered in a decorative cloth that had pictures of flowers woven into it. On top of the cloth was a small oil lamp with tiny animals carved into its base.

Lenna pulled back the covers over her head, *it is not my room!*

A flurry of emotions raged inside of her from the past few days' very real events - sorrow as she watched her friends leave, excitement trying to catch up to them, fear when she ran into the pig-men, sadness over killing one of them and despair over the loss of her mare. Tears started to fall down her face as she felt the hopelessness of her situation.

Chiding herself for letting her emotions get the better of her again, she got up out of the bed and walked over to a long, skinny table. On top of it a large oblong mirror leant against the wall.

On one end of the table was a large round bowl of water for washing and a piece of brown soap sitting next to it on top of a pretty floral stitched towel. On the other side of the table was a clay pot with fresh flowers that gave a light scent to the room.

In the middle of the table in front of the mirror was a hair comb and a couple of pretty ribbons.

Looking at herself in the mirror jolted her awake.

'Eww,' she said to her reflection with bitterness.

Lenna's face was muddied and dirty. Her eyes looked sore and red and her hair was thick, matted and standing up all over the place.

Using the fresh water that had been provided for her, she washed her face and hands thoroughly before drying them on the towel, leaving black marks all over it. She then washed her dark red hair in the tub as best she could and after giving it a little towel dry attacked it with the comb, pulling out all the knots and making it smooth.

Satisfied with its sleekness, she grabbed pieces of her hair and braided them, weaving the ribbons through it and tying them together when she came to the end.

She looked at herself in the mirror feeling well pleased with the result.

'I have seen worse,' she said to her reflection.

Feeling clean again revitalised her spirits. *Now all I need to do is find Wolflang and Afeclin...* she stopped dead, catching her reflection again in the mirror. 'Wolflang and Afeclin. I forgot to look for them!'

She ran to the door, hesitating as she noticed her bow and quiver resting against a little chair at the end of the bed. She slipped them on over her shoulder and ran out the door to the room.

There was a short corridor with closed doors to other rooms and a staircase that went straight down to the entrance hall she found herself in the night before.

She skipped down the stairs, ran to the entrance door and wrenched it open in haste.

There standing at the door, hunched over her with a grim expression was Harren.

'Whoa!' she exclaimed out of shock and surprise, pulling herself backwards to stop.

'Where are you off to in such a hurry Little Elf?' he asked with a yawn.

'Oh Harren, thank you so much for looking after me last night... I do not know what happened. I think I must have just fallen asleep,' she said in a rush of words, 'but I must go now and find my friends.'

She bounded past him and ran down the stairs of the front deck, having no idea where she was headed.

'Little Elf... it's no good,' came Harren's gruff voice.

Lenna stopped short and turned around.

'What are you talking about? What is no good?'

'After you fell asleep at the table last night, myself and Marelli put you to bed,' he said with his sullen expression. 'You were obviously very tired and I didn't have the heart to wake you... even though I knew how important it was to you to find your friends...'

174

Lenna stood listening with little patience, 'Yes… go on…'

'Well I thought I would see if I could find out where your friends are staying and send them to you…'

'And what did you find out?' she asked with renewed interest moving closer to the old shemalk.

'Well, after much walking of the streets and enquiring at many of the inns in town, in the early hours of the morning I found where they were staying… a little place on the other side of the city.'

'You did? Oh Harren… you are wonderful!' she said with joy, running up the stairs to the inn and wrapping her skinny arms around the tall shemalk's middle.

'Well, hold on there Little Elf, I haven't finished,' he said with an uncomfortable shake of the head, grabbing Lenna's arms from around him and holding them in his clawed hands.

Lenna looked up at Harren with concern.

'What is it?' she asked, her anxious heart beating at an incredible rate.

'It turns out that they had already left… in a hurry I might add,' Harren said with fatigue, 'they were headed for Rengal.'

Lenna let her body slump as she felt the hopelessness return.

'I guess that is it then,' she said with despair, 'I need to give up this ridiculous game of cat and mouse and return to Tebelligan, I should not have followed in the first place.'

'Now, now Little Elf, where is your spirit for adventure?' Harren prodded.

'Gone, lost… I…'

'Chin up,' he said putting a long crooked finger under her face to lift it, 'I was going to be on my way to Rengal in a few days to pick up some supplies but as I have successfully sold all my produce this morning, we could leave now… we'd be there by the end of the day.'

'I… thank you Harren, but I really think I should just give up now and go home,' she said looking into the shemalk's dark eyes. 'I mean, what if I was to make it to Rengal only to find that they had moved on from there too?'

'There is always that chance… '

'You see? I think I am just not supposed to find them and the sooner I stop trying to, the better off I will be.'

'But… '

'But what?'

'I am headed there anyways, so we could go there and look for them and if we don't find them or they have moved on, I can drive you all the way back home again. After all, my farm is not far from the

Tebelligan border, it would be no problem,' Harren offered with mildness. 'What have you to lose?'

Lenna stood staring at the shemalk for a moment. *He really is a kind gentle person*, she thought with interest, *I mean... he does not even know me, yet he has done so much to help me.*

'So... shall we see if we can find these friends of yours? Or will you just return home and never know how close you came?'

Lenna considered. *I guess it would not hurt to go on to Rengal. Once I return to Tebelligan I am not likely to leave ever again, so at worst I can explore a little more of this strange world before returning.*

'Okay Harren, I will accompany you to Rengal,' she said giving him a little half smile, 'at least I feel if I stay with you I am safe.'

Harren bowed his head, 'I appreciate your faith in me, Little Elf.'

Chapter

XXVIII

By midday Wolflang, Eliah and Pit were all tired and hungry. They had been moving at a constant pace all night and day, they had not rested and they had not stopped to eat.

The narrow wood-chip path that they had followed since leaving the meadow was lined with long slender willowy traffita trees and spiral muse flowers. The spiral muse swayed in the breeze, whipping their pale green claw-shaped leaves about and making the violet and lemon-coloured spiral petal bounce like a spring. The busy hum of lumirths or spider-flies as they were better known for their dangly eight legs, could be heard as they buzzed around the flowers collecting nectar with their tiny tubular mouths. Their black and red bodies contrasted against the paler shades of the spiral muse.

The cool, shaded path led them past an open river of fresh flowing water surrounded by long slender reeds. Weary and travel sore they stopped by the side of the riverbed. Here they were able to drink their fill of water and refill their water skins.

'I don't remember a time when I ever felt so hungry,' moaned Eliah more to herself then anyone in particular.

As if a gift from the gods themselves, at that moment a large fleurmire landed in the cool water and began preening itself, unconscious of its audience. The bird had a rotund white body and a long neck. A series of dark red and maroon feathers stuck out and up the back of its neck and rounded its head like a collar. The fleurmire was a royal-looking bird and as such was often found about the palace ponds in Tebelligan. They had been brought there by Endorf as a tribute to his long departed queen.

'Shhhh!' hushed Pit with a slender finger to his lips.

Wolflang having hunted game at the tender age of three understood at once and his hunter skills kicked in that instant.

With careful and deft precision he removed his bow from his shoulder and withdrew an arrow from the quiver. Then with the silence of a snake slithering in the grass he slunk to the edge of the water and pulled back the bowstring.

'Now make sure you aim for the head,' whispered Pit.

'I know what to do.' Wolflang bit back in a harsh whisper feeling great annoyance.

'As if I don't know where to aim my bow,' he grumbled under his breath. He was taught by the most skilled bowman in Tebelligan and although this was a fact Pit knew nothing about, it irritated him. Pit was correct in what he was saying but his father had taught him better and so he knew the best place to shoot any animal, big or small was in the neck. The only thing was, if you were not skilled enough to get the arrow in the right place on the first shot the prey could escape. It would go and die somewhere by itself and was unlikely to bleed enough to track. It was a waste of a good animal. So it was important to take an extra moment to adjust to all the conditions. How fast the wind was blowing, how far away the target was and whether the animal was likely to move all had to be taken into consideration.

Slanting his head to one side and closing one eye to focus he let the arrow go. The arrowhead hit the bird in the spine of its neck, killing it instantly.

'Wow! Nice shot,' said Pit scratching his head, 'that's some skill you got there.'

Wolflang nodded his head and shrugged.

'So who dives in to get it?' asked Eliah standing at the side of the river with her hands on her slim hips watching the bird floating in the middle of the water.

'Well, Wolflang shot it so I guess I will go in and fetch it,' said Pit taking off his dark green boots with the curled toes and beginning to pull up his pant legs.

Before Pit had a chance to get in the water though Wolflang climbed up on top of his horse and began wading the animal through the reeds and further into the river.

'This is how we elves do it,' he said lifting up his feet in the stirrups to prevent them from getting wet as the horse went deeper into the water. When he was close enough to reach the bird he stopped the horse and with a tight hold on the reins he let his body lean over the water where he managed to reach the bird.

Just then they heard a roaring sound coming from further behind the trees.

'What was that?' Wolflang asked placing the bird on his horse, its long, broken neck draping over the horse's back.

'Sounds like a bear,' suggested Pit turning around about to see if he could tell which direction the noise was coming from.

Wolflang and the horse waded back through the water and onto dry land. It was fortunate the river was quite still; the horse was able to walk through it with a reasonable amount of ease.

They heard the roar again and this time it was followed by a little scream.

'Where is it coming from?'

'I can't tell,' said Wolflang trying to see through the mass of trees as he jumped to the ground from the horse's back. As he did, he knocked the bird causing it to fall into his arms.

'Over there!' said Eliah almost shouting, pointing to a bankoi not far through the trees from them in which a little human man was clambering up trying to get away from a huge lawfabex.

On instinct Pit grabbed at his long bow from where he had slung it over a bankoi branch, a little higher than himself. Finding it caught in a jumble of thick stemmed x-zaivacress, he pulled at the bow with impatience, causing the branch to bounce up and down, dropping leaves but having a firm hold on the bow.

At the same time Wolflang, who had run towards Eliah for a better look, dropped the bird, grabbing his bow once more and a fresh arrow.

Pulling back the bowstring, he aimed it at the beast while walking closer to get a better shot through the crowded trees.

The lawfabex bared its teeth, snarling at the small man as its eyes glowed a vicious red. Its massive front claws dug into the tree followed by its skinny wolf backside, climbing with stealth after its victim.

Almost at the bottom of the tree, Wolflang found his angle and prepared to shoot by mechanically considering the conditions around him.

The lawfabex turned its big head to look in the direction of Wolflang. The beast's red eyes softened back to black and stared right into him. Wolflang relaxed his grip on the bow as his own eyes met those of the lawfabex. Standing mesmerised he felt he could see right into the lawfabex's soul and determined that this was not an angry beast at all but rather a hungry animal.

The lawfabex only kept his eye contact with Wolflang for a couple of moments and then continued to harass the man in the tree.

'What are you waiting for Wolflang? Aren't you going to shoot it?' Pit yelled as he tugged even harder at the bow, now with even greater frustration.

'NO,' said Wolflang dropping his bow and arrow and shaking his head, 'I can't kill him.'

'Well, ya can't let him kill the man up there!' Pit called as he pulled hard in desperation to free his weapon. With a mighty tug he managed to release the bow but at the same time snap the string.

'Oh, by Titania!' he cursed.

The man in the tree was frightened for his life and still climbing higher up the copious thick limbs of the bankoi in the attempt of getting as far from the agile animal as possible.

Wolflang in exasperation looked down at the ground, trying to figure out something to do. He saw a small rock in a clump of moss and picked it up.

'Yoo-hoo, bear!' he called out. The lawfabex turned to look again at Wolflang and this time the elf threw the small rock at him, hitting him in the head.

This enraged the lawfabex. Turning its attention to Wolflang he let out a roar as his eyes glowed blood red with anger and he scuttled backwards down the tree, almost falling to the ground.

'What the hell are you doing?' yelled Eliah in distress.

Wolflang tried to figure out his next move. The lawfabex was almost at the bottom of the tree, an angry growl rumbling in his throat.

The small elf then spied his horse by the river, unperturbed by the goings on and grazing soundly on her own while the other horses had disappeared.

Maybe I could lead the beast away from here on horseback, he thought as he ran towards the lonesome horse.

'What are you doing? You'll never outrun him, even on horseback,' yelled Eliah from high in another bankoi overlooking Wolflang.

Wolflang looked back to see where the lawfabex was. As he did so he tripped over something in his path.

He turned to see what it was that had caused him to fall and noticed the bird he had killed only minutes earlier laying in his path. It was then that he had another idea, an idea that would require all the courage he could muster.

He stood. Picking up the deceased bird, he walked toward the lawfabex with limited nerve. Looking down at the fleurmire, he noticed his hands suffered from fierce shaking.

'Pull yourself together elf,' he told himself.

His heart beating fast and his mind racing, he approached the beast.

The lawfabex was now running toward Wolflang with a ferocious jaw agape and saliva dangling from his bared teeth. The elf's knees were knocking together so much that his legs gave way and dropped him to the ground.

The lawfabex slowed down and stalked the cowering elf. Within seconds the animal was on top of him. Wolflang could feel the beast's saliva dribble onto his face and its hot breath all over him.

It was in that moment that Wolflang thought he was going to be eaten. An unglamorous way to die but at least it would provide an escape for Pit, Eliah and of course the fellow in the tree. *Maybe I will be dubbed as a hero. Maybe I will live on in people's minds as the crazy elf who took on the lawfabex. Then again perhaps it is madness sparing the beast his life. The lawfabex certainly is not going to appreciate it. Yet there was something I saw in the animal's eyes…*

He could hear Pit beside the lawfabex trying to hit it with a small wooden log. The beast let out a roar and swiped at Pit with a humongous clawed paw, missing the goblin only marginally.

The bird! Wolflang had almost forgotten about it. He still had it clenched in his hand. With one hand at the beast's throat trying to keep its mouth away from his face, he inched the other hand holding the bird up towards the animal's head.

'Here bear here,' he spoke with softness to the lawfabex. 'I know you're hungry; here's some food for you.'

He waved the bird in the beast's face as best as he could. The lawfabex stared at the bird, then at Wolflang with curiosity for a moment

182

as his eyes regained their onyx darkness before turning his attention back to the bird. He gave it a cautious sniff before wrapping his huge jaws around it and pulling it from Wolflang's grasp. Another look at Wolflang and the lawfabex was gone, running back through the woods from whence he came.

Wolflang laid his head back on the ground, put his hands over his face and exhaled deeply as if he had been holding his breath the entire time.

Pit sat on the ground, staring in the direction the lawfabex had gone. Eliah climbed down from the tree she had been hiding in and ran towards Wolflang and Pit.

Wolflang pushed himself up into a sitting position. As he did so he saw the man whom they had saved climbing down from the tree. The little man jumped from the lowest branch landing two feet on the ground.

The man wore a brown hat and coat that had its sleeves torn off. He had small squinty eyes, a large nose that seemed out of proportion and had a little black moustache that he twitched as he stared at the threesome by the river. After a moment's hesitation the little man ran off through the woods and disappeared out of sight.

'Gee there's thanks for ya!' Wolflang said as he tried to stand up. His legs felt like jelly and he found himself sitting back down on the ground.

'Have you absolutely lost your mind?!' screamed Eliah slapping the elf across the face in anger. 'You put all our lives in danger because of your feelings for that damned lawfabex! What is it with you people from Tebelligan? Think you are all heroes or something?'

'You elves are mad,' added Pit wiping the sweat from his brow.

Wolflang sat dumbfounded with his hand on his now red face.

'Well hey, I did get rid of him.'

'You gave away our lunch to a good-for-nothing animal which you could have killed within an instant. Had you done that we could have taken him to Rengal with us and sold him to a butcher in town for a handsome profit. Instead you put all our lives at stake and you yourself were almost eaten,' said Pit with calm but honest reprove. 'There is no doubt you were lucky, very lucky... but next time you may not be so fortunate.'

Pit took off in silence to find his horse.

Eliah searched Wolflang's eyes with concern and shook her head. She then followed Pit in order to find her horse. She stopped still a moment, looking at Wolflang's mare grazing in peace by the river. She approached the docile animal with gentleness and put a soft arm under her head. Patting her nose with tender words, she examined her ears.

Wolflang watched in interest as Eliah seemed to communicate with the chestnut mare.

'What do you call her?' she asked with renewed calm.

'I never gave her a name.'

Eliah gave Wolflang a cold look, she did not seem amused.

'Then I shall call her Abwahnu,' she said looking into the horse's green eyes. 'In my ancestor's language it means, she that does not hear.'

'She's deaf?'

'Yes Wolflang, your horse is deaf,' answered Eliah through pursed lips.

'Then what does she need a name for if she can't hear it anyway?' asked Wolflang with sarcasm.

'A horse that carries and serves you relentlessly deserves the respect of a name,' said Eliah with impatience, 'even if they cannot hear it.'

She kissed Abwahnu's nose and rubbed her neck. The horse nudged her with appreciation.

Eliah turned to begin looking for Typhin's mare that she had been riding just as Pit returned leading both horses.

'I found them further down the path grazing.'

Wolflang managed to stand on his feet. His right shoulder ached from where the lawfabex had leant his paw on him to hold him down. He massaged it with his hand. It felt wet. Then looking at his shoulder he discovered it wasn't water or sweat he was touching but blood. Examining his shoulder he could find no cuts or marks that would cause him to bleed so. He then checked his body and his head, but apart from a few grazes here and there, he was not wounded in any way as to cause such a loss of blood. Wolflang thought about the beast and decided that perhaps the lawfabex itself had been injured, leaving blood on him.

Wolflang limped to his horse and struggled to mount him with a stiff body. He looked to Pit for a signal for them to move on. There was something unusual in the way Pit held his arm over his stomach. Then as the goblin lifted his arm to motion for the trio to move on, his sleeveless coat flew open and revealed three long bloodstained rips in his shirt. It appeared the lawfabex had clawed Pit after all.

Eliah noticed also and was the first to comment.

'Pit, you're hurt! Why didn't you say anything?'

'It's not that bad, I'll survive,' mumbled Pit as he started off down the dirt road.

'Come on... you should let me have a look at it,' she insisted.

'No really… the gashes aren't that deep,' he answered refusing to stop, 'I can make it to Rengal. I will have it attended to there.'

Eliah threw her hands up in defeat, realising it was senseless trying to persuade Pit to stop. She glared at Wolflang instead. Wolflang bowed his head and tried not to look at her. He felt terrible as it was without Eliah making it worse. He now realised just how foolish he had been attempting to rescue the lawfabex.

In an effort to try to protect the animal, he had put everyone else in danger. In an attempt to save Wolflang from the beast, Pit was injured.

Chapter
XXIX

'Do you think he got stuck in the mud accidentally?' said a sharp voice. 'Surely he wouldn't have ridden into it on purpose.'

'I don't know,' replied a softer, wiser voice, 'I think we might have underestimated our friend here.'

'What do you mean?' came the first voice again with a cough.

'What I mean is, I don't think he's your average young man who dabbles in the arts to impress people.'

'You think he's for real?'

'He's for real alright but it's more than that… it's like there is something within him… something special.'

A snort and a cough followed.

'Load of rot!' wheezed the first voice. 'He's just young and full of spirit. He thinks he is invincible. You remember what it was like being young, you think you can do anything… and from what I remember, you did.'

'I seem to remember you being right there beside me,' laughed the soft voice, 'but no it's not the same, you're wrong. How did he know where to find us? And why follow us into the Alimest Grove? They were safe in the inn, why put themselves in danger? Unless…'

'Unless?'

'Well, unless he somehow knew there was something wrong.'

'Nonsense! You live in a fantasy world. More than likely they were accosted by those goblins that you dealt with or perhaps even the town jackals. What choice would they have but to flee?' grumbled the gruff voice.

'But why attempt the Alimest Grove? They don't know this area but if they felt the need to flee they would have been safer leaving town through the main gate… I'm telling you Raan there is more to this kid than meets the eye.'

'Hey he's stirrin'.'

Afeclin inched his eyes open and looked around him. High above, he could see the swirling mass of mud that he had come through. The mud was clear and looked more like water, a small millpond on the ceiling. It was a strange substance that stayed in one place and did not drip down the walls. Although there was a large amount of mud, Afeclin could still see through to the top where he had come from. It was sort of like looking through a large fish tank.

Blinking a couple of times he focused his attention to the small cavern he appeared to be in. With a tiny amount of daylight streaming in through the mud ceiling he could see the wall of the circular room. Apart from one narrow section of wall, which was clay the same as the cool floor on which he lay, the rest of the chamber was made up of the root system of surrounding trees. A jumbled mess, the roots weaved in and out of each other forming an intricate pattern. There appeared to be no door and no way out.

Afeclin began to sit up and then stopped to hold his head for a moment as he felt a dizziness swimming in his head.

'Are ya right there?' asked Typhin as he got up from where he was sitting and tried to attend to him.

'Ooow, my head. How long have I been asleep?'

'Many hours I think,' said Typhin offering him a drink from his water skin. 'I don't actually know; I hit my head in the fall and passed out.'

'And I lay on the floor for a few minutes after the fall trying to get my breath back and I think I just must have been really tired because I fell asleep where I lay,' added Raan in his familiar croaky voice.

'So what are you doing here? I awoke to find you and your horse here beside us.'

'We came to help you,' he answered in a slow, weary whisper.

'Good help you are trapped in here with us!' snapped Raan.

'Take no notice of him,' said Typhin giving the dwarf a warning look. 'How did you know we were in trouble?'

'It will probably sound strange,' said Afeclin taking a breath and then readjusting his seating position, 'but late last night I got this... premonition... I guess that's what it was...'

Afeclin attempted to explain the unusual vision that had led them into the Alimest Grove in an effort to help their newfound friends.

'Help?' Raan snorted into his beard.

Afeclin began to stand and stretch his legs.

'But what's going on Typhin? Why are the jackals after you?'

Typhin looked over to Raan and the dwarf shook his head with a fierce scowl.

'The captain said you were wanted men. He called you dangerous outlaws,' Afeclin said turning to Typhin with candour. 'I didn't believe him, not for a moment.'

'Well, we *are* wanted men, that part is true,' said Typhin ignoring the grunts of protest coming from Raan, 'but we are hardly dangerous.'

'That is what I figured, but... why are you wanted at all?'

'That's NONE of your business,' Raan growled, throwing a sharp look at Typhin.

'Calm down Raan,' Typhin said with reproach, 'what do ya think he is going to do? We're in here!'

'Its none of *his* business and it's best to leave it that way,' Raan hissed through his teeth.

Typhin ignored the dwarf's protest.

'We are wanted by certain... groups, shall we say, around Titania.'

'Typhin.'

'Calm down old man. I am just going to give him the basics... he knows we are wanted, that ain't a secret now. He deserves some kind of explanation after all the trouble he has gone to.'

Raan skulked in his corner but said nothing.

'As I was saying... certain groups want us for committing a crime that did a lot of good in Titania... but a crime it was nonetheless. Most people tend to be either grateful or indifferent to the matter but every now and then we come across someone who wants to make trouble for us.'

'The goblins at the inn.'

Typhin looked at Afeclin with interest and nodded. 'You are very observant.'

Afeclin shrugged, 'So they made trouble for you after we had left?'

Typhin hesitated, collecting his thoughts. 'Once they had seen the three of us together, they knew exactly who we were and they exited the inn rather quickly. So we discreetly followed them.'

'Where did they go to? The jackals?'

'They were headed that way,' Typhin said with a sly smile, 'however, because of the rain they tended to take the most covered, most concealed way possible. As soon as they were out of view of any town's people we grabbed them from behind and with a sword at one of their throats demanded they tell us what their interest in us was. One of them was a tough little blighter, real tough… but the other one dissolved quite quickly into an explanation. He said that they had recognised us and that there was a reward offered that they wished to collect, so they were off to inform Captain Faquin.'

'That is him, that is the man who appeared at our door!' Afeclin interjected.

'I figured as much. At any rate we put a stop to their telling… at least for a while.'

'What did you do to them?'

'Well we didn't kill them or anything. If Raan had been there, we may have left them a little less intact…'

Raan snorted from his corner.

'…But we gagged them with rotting potatoes, bound them together with cords and threw them in a large rubbish box out the back of some tavern and returned to the inn. We decided not to involve you fellows in all of this, so we joined you and your friend for dinner and then left shortly after you had returned to your room for the night.'

'Weren't you afraid that the goblins would manage to free themselves and make it to the jackals before you made it out of town?' Afeclin asked, remembering the unease that he had felt from the trio over dinner.

'Sure we were, for that reason Raan and I swapped horses. We do that sometimes when we want to be a little less conspicuous. Raan can be a little obvious…'

Raan growled.

'Well, you can be Raan.'

He turned back to Afeclin, 'A stocky little dwarf riding a small horse sticks out in this part of Titania. So we swap horses and he wears my longer cloak, which hides his legs, then he doesn't appear to look like a dwarf, just a smaller person. As for myself, because I am not all that tall, I don't look ridiculous on the smaller horse, maybe a little unusual but not overly noticeable.

As we headed out of town we noticed jackals at the front gate. It may have been nothing at all but we weren't going to take that chance. We turned around and headed for the Alimest Grove. Of course once we were in here, we should have swapped our horses back again but we didn't and I had no end of trouble with that horse. I don't know how Raan can ride him. It was that horse that ended us in the mud.'

'Hey! Watch what you say about Krus. You're just too big for 'er, is all,' Raan wheezed in defence of his steed.

'I've told you before, she doesn't like riding in dark woods like the grove...' Typhin said pointing his finger at the glowering dwarf, 'she gets strange and is hard to control.'

'She doesn't like you, is all,' pouted the dwarf.

'I can understand the horse being a bit spooked by the grove, it's a strange place,' Afeclin said more to himself than anyone in particular.

'I can't believe you had the courage to attempt the Alimest Grove. I am even more stunned that you made it this far,' said Typhin with intrigue. 'How did you know what to do?'

'A friend of yours, I believe, had a bit of an idea what to do. She came with us,' said Afeclin studying the walls of the room with interest.

'She?' asked Typhin, startled. 'Who are you talking about?'

'Eliah, from the inn.'

'Eliah? Why in Titania did you bring her? Didn't you realise how dangerous these woods are?' Typhin burst out, standing up to face Afeclin.

Never having seen Typhin anything but reserved and cool under pressure, Afeclin was not too sure what to expect. Typhin looked angry and concerned.

'Is it really hot in here or what?' he said taking his glare from Afeclin and wiping the sweat from his brow.

'She wasn't supposed to come with us... at least not into the Alimest Grove,' Afeclin tried to explain, 'the jackals caught up to us, I'm not sure how they knew but they did. Eliah came off her horse and had I not managed to get to her first she would have been captured for sure. After that she had nowhere to go but with us which proved to be valuable because she seemed to have some idea what to do.'

Typhin turned back to Afeclin and looked at him for a moment then asked, 'How did she know? I'm sure she would never have entered the woods before.'

'She did not say exactly how she knew,' said Afeclin turning his attention once again to the walls.

'Huh,' bemused Typhin as he sat back down looking like he was trying to figure something out.

'What is it?'

'Never mind it's not important. Did you at least leave her with Pit?'

'Of course I did, I would never have left her with just Wolflang. He is quite someone else at the moment,' said Afeclin beginning to feel with his hands along the rooted walls, 'but... what, is not important?'

'We're gonna die in here anyways,' grunted Raan as if he too were a little curious.

Typhin looked to Raan and then to Afeclin and gave a wry smile.

'Raan, a few minutes ago you were taking all secrets to the grave,' said Typhin with sarcasm. 'What happened to that?'

'That's different, that is,' croaked the old dwarf.

'It is? Why? Because that secret involves you too?' Typhin shook his head, then sighed, 'Alright, but there isn't much to tell, just something I thought was interesting.' He readjusted his position with his back against part of the wall. 'I have known Eliah's father for years. We served in the Elite squad, as Scorpions together. When his wife, Eliah's mother died, Raabarak quit the service and came home to look after and rear his five sons and one daughter. Eliah was only about two at the time and the stable boy, Aim... Aimish I think his name is, was only a baby. Being reared by her father and older brothers has made Eliah tough, ready for a fight and an expert with the sword. Raabarak taught her all that he knew, which had nothing to do with being a lady. Mind you she does have a certain feminine charm that she must've inherited from her mother and I tell you she uses it to get what she wants.'

'Yes, I've noticed that,' interrupted Afeclin.

'Well anyway, on one day that I had come into town with Pit, a sword fight had broken out in the middle of the street and was causing quite a stir with the locals. By the time I got there the fight was over and I found Eliah lying on the ground wounded and unconscious. The older man she'd fought fled when he saw the jackals coming and knowing that she would have been picked up by them and chucked in the hole without her wounds being attended to, I put her on my horse with me and fled too. The jackals gave chase and I had no option but to take her into the Alimest Grove. Although I had only intended to take her in a little way, wait for the jackals to leave and then take her home, a young and foolish one followed us in. I didn't want to have to take her further in but I had to. Pit was still with me and it was the first time he had been through the Grove so I had to shout out instructions to him as we went. I thought we would lose the young jackal while in the butterflies but he was a strong rider and kept up with us. When it was dark again we continued on as fast as we could [it was day so it was not quite as dark as you experienced last night] but it felt more like twilight, making it difficult to see properly and slowing us down. Thankfully it also slowed down the jackal who had not given up on us. I continued on, knowing that the ghosts of the grove would soon appear and sure enough they did. We all stopped dead in our tracks. There was no point continuing on as the ghosts follow and as you would now know you need to cover your ears anyway. The jackal stopped a few feet from us and for a moment you could see by the smirk on his face he thought he had us.

'He must have thought he was pretty good if he was willing to take on you and Pit by himself to get to Eliah,' Afeclin suggested.

'Young and foolhardy that's what he was,' scoffed Raan now sitting, listening and carving a piece of root with a small knife that had a curved wooden handle. 'These young 'uns think they're made of iron.'

'Well his bravery lasted but a moment. Once he looked up into the ghost's face he was a goner. Mesmerised by the haunting song, he could not look away. I must admit I did feel a little bad for him knowing exactly what was going to happen.

I got down off my horse and propped Eliah against a tree. Then I grabbed a handful of clay from the ground, wet it and placed a little piece in both of her ears.'

'Clay. Now that's a good idea.'

'Sorry?'

'Never mind,' Afeclin apologised.

'Okay, well where was I? Oh yeah, I directed Pit to cover his ears and as the song hit its earsplitting peak we watched as the young man fell to the ground in agony. Clutching his bleeding ears, his scream was almost more unbearable then the shriek of the ghosts.'

'It killed him?' asked Afeclin, somewhat horrified.

'Pierced his very soul,' said Typhin with a nonchalant expression. 'He lay breathing slowly for a while but then he was gone. After it was over, we rode back to town and to the inn. Eliah had been unconscious the entire time and when she awoke she remembered nothing. I told her nothing of our journey into the grove. Nor have I told her anything about the grove, fearing she would take herself into it if she knew the secrets of it. I also doubt that she has met anyone else who has made it through, very few try it and even fewer survive it.'

'So you think perhaps she remembers something of her journey with you into the grove after all?' suggested Afeclin when Typhin had finished.

'I think perhaps an unconscious memory is possible.'

'I think there is more to it than that.'

'What do you mean?'

'When we were about to start into the woods she told us she had been in them before...' started Afeclin.

'She did?'

'Yeah but then she changed her mind.'

'Really? That's interesting,' said Typhin, 'maybe she does have a recollection of being in the grove.'

'Fiddle faddle. What nonsense. She was out cold! Some drunk who had made it through was probably boasting at the bar one night, that's all,' argued Raan taking his eyes off his carving to interject his view.

'I guess that is possible.'

'What I don't understand is, if you have this long standing relationship with Raabarak and his family including Eliah, why did you not say more than two words to her when she served us at dinner?'

'Well, that's the relationship we have now.'

'What do you mean?' asked Afeclin turning part of his attention back to the walls again.

'Ahh, well I guess we aren't going anywhere...' started Typhin with defeat, 'Eliah has always had a thing for me. Ever since she was a young girl she has paid attention to me and followed me about whenever I was in town. It was funny and even cute at first but as she got older it became more serious. As she developed into an attractive young woman it became harder not to return her advances. Raabarak could see my struggles and knowing the kind of person that I am, he forcefully suggested I keep away from his daughter lest I lead her on and then really break her heart. Not that I come to Desprade very often but when I do I pretend she doesn't exist. Over time she has gotten over it and now she ignores me right back. It works. I could never give her what she wants or deserves besides I'm a wanted man, that's no life for her.'

'What is your fascination with tree roots?' demanded Raan with agitation.

'Yes Afeclin, you do seem intrigued by the walls,' Typhin agreed. 'Surely you don't think you're going to find a secret door hidden there, do you?'

'That's exactly what I think.'

'Horse poop. Waste of time. We're trapped and there is no way out. You might as well come to terms with it, it will make dying in here all the more easy.'

'I disagree. I would never have dived into the mud if I really thought there was no way out.'

'So you did take yourself into the mud,' said Typhin with awe, 'but how could you know?'

'As we stood there looking at the mud, you and Raan had disappeared into, I started to think about the Alimest Grove as a whole and it reminded me a lot of one of the books I read years ago about the history of wizards. You see wizards started out as a race of people with special abilities and gifts. They understood how to harness the energy around them and use it to make things happen... it is called magic. At first they used it to entertain people. Some entertained the great kings in their courts and some entertained in the streets for money but as they got better and were able to do more, the people started to fear them. Especially monarchs who feared what too much power could do to them and their kingdom. A proclamation was put out that anyone coming across these wizards should kill them. The wizards fought back as hard as they could but once their energy was used they would fall into a deep sleep and be killed. They had to devise other ways in which they could survive. The wizards retreated into woodland areas to hide and found that if they developed spells to trap people they could remain safe and live out their years protected by the woods. Some built castles to live and develop their skills in within the woods where people could not reach them. It occurred to me that this is exactly what the Alimest Grove is.'

'Okay, that does make sense but we are still buried in one of the traps that they developed. They would not have designed a way out. I mean look around the edges of the floor, plenty of people have died here, as is intended.'

Afeclin looked to the floor where a few skeletons lay in a heap here and there. It did have the feeling of a burial chamber.

'No if they really wanted just to kill people they would have made it so that people drowned in the mud. Not so that they could sit in a chamber until they died. What is the point of that?'

'What is the point of the chamber then?' growled Raan, his patience floundering.

'I believe it is a safe haven, I have read of them. They used them a lot in the first centuries when their magic was quite limited and undeveloped. If they were retreating into the woods and found they were followed by people trying to kill them, or perhaps to even figure out the whereabouts of their hideout, they would lead them to a swampy area and disappear into the murk. If people were silly enough to follow, they would be swallowed up and drawn into a small cavern, like this one, and would not be able to escape. Meanwhile the wizard knowing the secret to the haven was able to escape the cavern through some kind of trapdoor system, I'm guessing, and make it safely back to their secluded dwelling.' Afeclin followed his hands along the walls trying to find something unusual that could be the key to the trapdoor.

'I hope that means you know the secret of this haven.'

'Well no, how could I? But it is enough to know that there is a way out and we will keep looking until we find it,' answered Afeclin as he pulled at a knobbly piece of root.

'I for one do not believe in such dribble so I will not make a fool of myself searching for something that isn't there,' grumbled the dwarf.

'If you want to die Raan, that's your choice, but I certainly hope that when we find the door you will change your mind and come with us out of here,' said Afeclin with reproach.

'Well, I think it's worthwhile spending my time trying to find a way out,' said Typhin following Afeclin's example.

The two searched and searched. Every lumpy bit of wood was given meticulous scrutiny. They looked for notches in the roots and they tugged hard at any lengths that were poking forward but nothing proved to be a way out. After a couple of hours of close examination they had to admit defeat and one after the other gave up to rest.

'I told you didn't I? Said you were wasting your time. There is no way out... we are here to die,' cackled the old dwarf not even lifting his eyes from a piece of bone he was now whittling away at.

'Come on now, Raan... we had to try.'

Afeclin sat down against the wall and buried his head in his hands. He felt tired and hungry but frustrated more than anything. What a fool he had been letting his intuition get the better of him again. It seemed very clear that he had been wrong about the cavern and yet there was still a small voice deep inside telling him that it all made sense.

How could that be? he thought to himself. *What have I missed?* Then he looked up and stared for a moment at the small area of wall that was not disturbed by the root systems of the trees above. In fact the roots stopped in perfect, almost obedient formation around the clay area that was roughly the width of a door.

'Of course!' Afeclin exclaimed slapping his head and standing up.

'What's got into him?' asked Raan, looking up from what he was doing with sudden interest.

'What's the matter Afeclin?' asked Typhin, ignoring the dwarf. 'Did you get another idea?'

Afeclin stood staring at the wall, not hearing the other two. Approaching the rootless section of wall, he placed both hands onto the clay. The wall felt cold, damp and hard and did not appear at all to be a way out. Focused on the fact that he had to be right this time, he pushed his hands hard against the wall as if trying to shift it. The wall did not shift but his hands began to sink into the clay. Another big push and his hands disappeared. The interesting thing was that once inside the wall he found that he could move them with ease. It seemed that the wall must have been not more than an inch thick.

'I've found it!'

'Is it some kind of door?'

'That is precisely what it is, however it doesn't open like a regular door,' said Afeclin trying to explain, 'in fact it is more like a doorway that you simply walk through.'

'Walk through? How can we walk through the wall?' asked Typhin with scepticism.

'You won't catch me walking through walls,' grumbled the dwarf, 'load a rot!'

'I'm going through. Pass me the reins of Majenta,' Afeclin said pointing to his horse who had been standing in silence against the wall. 'I'm going to walk through and try to take Majenta with me but if he resists because he thinks he can go no further, you'll have to give him a push.'

Both Typhin and Raan looked at Afeclin in disbelief.

'He's gone mad.'

'I must say Afeclin, this doesn't sound right... we can't walk through walls. Maybe if we were immortal beings...' Typhin was cautious, 'or even if we were wizards but...'

'Relax, it will be fine,' said Afeclin with a knowing smile, 'we are not transfiguring ourselves. We are simply going through a wall that is not as solid as it appears to be.'

Typhin still looked doubtful but was at least willing to go along with the plan whereas Raan was his usual stubborn dwarf self refusing to believe or try anything out of the ordinary. Afeclin gave a shrug and let one arm sink further through the wall while in his other hand he held Majenta's bridle. He coaxed the stallion closer to the wall but just as the horse felt the clay at his nose he made a sharp tug backwards, not understanding what he was supposed to be doing.

Afeclin decided to try something new. This time he let his body sink into the wall and when he was almost standing on the other side of the door he looked to Raan and Typhin who stood amazed. With a wink at them he pulled his head back and found himself standing on the other side of the wall. Once again he was in darkness. In his hands he could feel the reins between his fingers and he started to give a gentle pull. At first the horse seemed to advance toward the wall but then there was a mighty tug and Afeclin could feel Majenta resist with vehemence. Afeclin had to hold tight and pull hard to stop from giving in to the powerful stallion.

The tugging game with the horse seemed to last forever. In the end Majenta was so disturbed that he kicked up his front legs to push away from the wall. Just as he brought his hooves down on the wall his legs and body went straight through the clay, the force landing him partially on the other side so that he was now half on one side and half on the other.

'Okay fella,' Afeclin whispered into the horse's soft ear and then stepped backwards allowing Majenta to come all the way forward.

The air was thick and dusty this far below the ground and it made Afeclin's throat tickle, so much so that he let out a loud cough to clear it. Just as he did he heard a clicking coming from high on the wall. He looked up to see where the unusual sound was coming from. All at once a flame sparked to life on an ancient looking carved wooden torch held up by a tree root that was wound around it. Then no more than a few feet further along the wall, another torch lit up, lighting a little more of what appeared to be a passage.

Torches continued to light themselves one by one revealing a long dark passageway. The passage was as straight as a sword, never bending one way or the other and the lights seemed to go on forever. The walls of the passage were made of clay and void of decoration apart from the tree roots that came through the wall in very specific positions for the purpose of holding each torch.

After a couple of minutes of waiting and wondering whether Typhin was having a hard time persuading Raan to step through the wall, Afeclin watched as the lights one by one began to dim. In no time at all he was left in darkness again.

Growing up, Afeclin had never had any problem with the dark. He never feared it. At times it was his friend. It provided an opportunity for quiet and reflection, a time to ponder his abilities and an escape from reality. Now in the dark, Afeclin grew tired and irritated by it. There had been something very frightening about the dark in the woods, a fear of the unknown, a feeling he was not used to or comfortable with. In Tebelligan he felt safe, perhaps naively so.

'Afeclin. Are you here?' a voice interrupted and startled him from his thoughts.

'Typhin, I was beginning to think you were not coming.'

Afeclin gave a big cough in order to relight the passage. The torches almost sparked to life again with obedience.

'Nice trick but an unusual chant,' Typhin teased as he studied the passage in its full light.

'I won't argue with you there, but whatever lights the way,' said Afeclin with a grin. 'Is Raan coming?'

'I tried to convince him but that dwarf is so stubborn,' answered Typhin waving his muddied straw hat in frustration.

'Shall we wait and see?' suggested Afeclin.

Typhin looked thoughtful for a moment as he considered the question.

'No. Leave him be, if he changes his mind he'll find us.'

'Do you think he can shelve his disbelief for long enough to walk through the wall?'

Typhin had a grave look of concern on his face, 'A couple of years ago I would have said he'll get over it. He'd make some lame excuse why he couldn't leave us and follow... but the older that dwarf gets the more peculiar and prideful he becomes, so I just don't know. I would die for that dwarf but if I was to lie down and give up just because of his stubbornness... well... I would have been dead long ago.'

The two started the long journey down the passage. After a couple minutes Afeclin looked behind and could see the first of the lights, where they had entered, beginning to fade. He sighed. It didn't seem like the dwarf was going to change his mind this time.

'How is it that Raan refuses to believe in the supernatural after all he has seen in these woods? I don't see how he can explain it all away.'

'You don't know much about dwarves do you?' retorted Typhin with a grin.

'I had never met one until recently,' Afeclin scratched at his whiskers in thought. 'I don't really know about humans and I am one. The only race I could tell you anything about is the elves and even then I couldn't explain what has been going on with Wolflang as of late.'

'Oh? Acting strange is he?'

'You could say that. He has always been the adventurous type but now that he has the opportunity, he seems like he just wants to go home or crawl under a rock and hide. I don't know what has got into him.'

'Well, I don't know anything about elves,' Typhin paused with a weary sigh, 'gee this passageway seems to go on forever.'

The passage continued on and on and showed no sign of ending.

198

'No, I have never known any elves before,' Typhin seemed lost in thought, 'on the other hand I could tell ya all about dwarves. I've known Raan for a very long time now.'

'The problem with dwarves,' he continued, 'is that they don't believe in anything. They believe in nature and they trust it. Everything else is trickery and illusion and in their minds can be completely explained if investigated properly.'

'They do not believe in the gods?'

'Not at all. They believe it's all a load of hogwash invented by wizards to scare and control humans and other races that are gullible enough to believe in it.'

'What do humans believe then?'

'Different people believe different things. Some follow one god, some follow another and some don't care either way. Some humans believe so strongly in the god Ambroza for instance that they refuse to associate with anyone who believes in the god Islaraan and therefore there have been many conflicts between these groups.'

'What about you Typhin? Do you believe in anything?'

Typhin sighed, 'I grew up following Ambroza. It was what my family believed but after all that I have seen and experienced, I feel that even if the gods are real and are there, they don't do anything to help us and so I just do my own thing. The only god I see prevalent in our society today is Hazifa.'

There were four gods known in the world of Titania. Ambroza, was the almighty ruler over all and father to the other three gods, Islaraan, Hazifer and Afeclinella. The twin brothers, Islaraan and Hazifer were said to be the exact same in stature, strength and intelligence but the polar opposite of each other in attitudes. That being that Islaraan was said to be the founder of everything good, wholesome, kind and wise, whereas Hazifer was said to be the founder of darkness, evil, loathsomeness and disease.

The youngest of the gods and the daughter of Ambroza was the goddess, Afeclinella. Afeclin was well acquainted with the goddess due to the fact that the elves followed and worshipped her. Afeclinella was revered as the god of daybreak, purity and innocence. The elves were a spiritual and superstitious race. When things were going well and there was peace within the land it was said that the elves were well favoured by the goddess and that she was pouring her blessings upon them. If anything went wrong however, or if a natural disaster was to strike, it was said that the goddess was angry with them and therefore punishing them.

'I'm guessing with a name like Afeclin the elves must worship the goddess,' suggested Typhin as if reading Afeclin's mind.

Afeclin smiled. 'Yes, well when a strange human boy comes to live in an all elf community under peculiar circumstances what is a wise old king to do...?'

'Name him after the goddess they worship to gain favour and blessings from her?'

'You could say that.' Afeclin shrugged.

'Well, who knows Afeclin, son of the goddess, maybe you are a good omen sent by the gods. You are certainly the most courageous human I have ever had the good fortune to meet.'

Afeclin felt a little embarrassed.

'I don't know about that, I haven't got us out of this place safely yet.'

'Still had it not been for you coming to the rescue I would still be sitting inside that chamber spending my last precious days in this world with a grumpy old dwarf.'

The two walked on down the long unbending passage. As they walked Afeclin spoke at length of the unusual circumstance he was found in as a baby and of his childhood with the elves.

'So you're technically a prince as well as the son of the goddess?'

'Well, I don't know about being the son of a goddess but... yes... I guess, technically I am part of the royal family,' answered Afeclin with thought. 'I don't think however that I am really in line for the throne.'

'What would happen if both your elder brothers were to be killed by some peculiar accident and your father grows too old to rule over his people, would you then become the king?' asked Typhin, with interest.

'I don't know... I think my father would want me to be king but I don't think the elves would accept a human king, even one that has grown up in an all elf world and so my father would have no choice but to pass the throne to someone else.'

'Well, you're the bravest prince I ever met and I have met my share of princes. Many of whom I would loathe to see on the throne even though they were born into royalty.'

Afeclin half smiled as he turned his head around to see behind him. In the distance he could see the torches dissipating one by one like candles being blown out. Beyond the torches was complete and utter darkness. Afeclin found himself wondering about the dwarf. *Is Raan really going to sacrifice himself for his pride?* It seemed crazy... but still it appeared that the dwarf had not attempted to follow. Typhin looked behind also, the smile slipping from his lips as he thought of his friend.

Afeclin had no idea what to say. He did not know Raan well enough to be able to add any words of encouragement. He was about to break the silence when Typhin let out a yell.

'I see the end of the tunnel!'

Afeclin looked towards the direction they were travelling and sure enough there was a small light in the distance that grew as they walked on.

Soon they were so close to the source of the light that they could now tell that it was sunlight streaming into the passage and in their excitement began to increase their speed. First walking a little faster, then a slow jog and until they were so close that they could almost feel the sun's rays. They started to run.

In no time at all they burst out of what seemed to be a cave entrance and once again into the tree-littered forest.

Pockets of sunshine streamed with warmth through small spaces between verdurous foliage and their sudden noisy appearance startled hundreds of birds from high branches. The squawk of impatience echoed through the woods as the birds took flight. Leaves and feathers fell from on high like rain.

Wild black sheep with uneven horns that spiralled on either side of their head and were overgrown and mossy, ran to the safety of further trees, congregating together. From the security of the flock they stood still, their beady eyes watching the three muddy intruders with cautiousness, ready to run again if necessary.

Afeclin looked behind him to see where they had come from and was surprised to find they were surrounded by nothing but woodland and sheep. Trees of varying sizes and volume stood firm in every direction he looked. Afeclin then noticed Typhin's reaction as he too spun about and could not see the cave from whence they had come.

'Where in Titania are we?!' Typhin exclaimed with volume. 'And where has the cave gone?'

'I do not know,' said Afeclin still turning himself about looking for the entrance as if he must have just missed it with his eyes, 'maybe it's invisible.'

'Well then, let's test that theory,' said Typhin with curiousness. 'If it's invisible by rights it should still be here, we just can't see it.'

Typhin walked back in the direction they had come. A straggling lamb skittered about from his hiding spot and out of the way of the fair-haired man.

'Are you in the passageway yet?' Afeclin called to him when Typhin was a good distance away. Typhin appeared to be walking about in the woods. He did not vanish and there was nothing unusual.

Typhin walked back to where Afeclin was waiting, watching.

'I didn't vanish or anything did I?'

Afeclin shook his head.

'I didn't find the entrance to the cave either. You would never know that we have just come from deep under the ground,' Typhin said with thought, as if still trying to figure it out. 'Could you imagine what the dwarf would say about that! He'd have trouble explaining where the entrance went. It just vanished the moment we stepped out into the sun. "Load of hogwash" he would say and "it's all trickery." It is? Well then, I would like to have him explain it to me.'

As he said this Typhin mimicked Raan to perfection, capturing his gruff voice and mannerisms. He pointed his finger the same way Raan would point a finger and pretended to play with a long beard under his stubbly chin the way Raan would tug at his long filthy plaited beard. Afeclin could see that he was well practiced at copying the dwarf. They both laughed.

'That's one thing about dwarves, they're thick skinned,' he said with affection going off on a tangent, 'you can't hurt their feelings and they don't care if you have some fun at their expense. They're loyal as a dog, grumpy all the time and boy, can they fight. You should see Raan when he is in a battle. He may be a stumpy little man but he is vicious when he needs to be and strong too. They could never be bribed or tortured (they're much too proud) and you'll never find a truer friend. Of course they won't tell you they like you and the only way you know is if they decide to stick with you. The day that a dwarf decides to stick with you is the day that you have been blessed and cursed all at once. They are the best companions to have with you and they will never let you down but they have the worst habits I've ever seen and the foulest moods...'

Typhin stopped talking, he looked very thoughtful and concerned for a moment.

'You're worried about Raan, aren't you?'

Typhin nodded his head with sadness, 'You know I really thought he would have caught up to us by now.'

Afeclin tried to think of something to say that was helpful. He ran his fingers through his hair and it was then that he noticed the thick dry mud that was gluing his hair together.

'Well you know, if he didn't figure out the... uh... interesting chant that is needed to light the passage he could be slowly trying to make his way in the dark,' Afeclin said after a moment's hesitation as he flicked mud out from underneath his nails.

This comment seemed to cheer Typhin enough to break him out of the mood he was in and concern himself with their location. Looking around he scratched at his whiskers. 'It would be helpful to know where we are,' he said.

Afeclin stopped picking at the dirt and walked over to a muddied Majenta who was grazing in the shade of a large tree.

'I have a map that might help,' he said as he rummaged through his garboa cloth bag and pulled out the ancient map he had been using only days earlier to guide their way along the roads once they were out of Tebelligan.

'I don't know that a map is very useful unless you know the location of where you are on it,' suggested Typhin looking over Afeclin's shoulder as he unfolded the map.

'Here is Desprade,' said Afeclin ignoring the older man's comments, 'and behind there would be the Alimest Grove. Do you agree?'

Typhin grabbed at the map to get a better look. 'I'm afraid my sight isn't what it used to be,' he said squinting as he examined the parchment. 'This map is older than I am. A lot of these roads no longer exist and there is much missing.'

'Well, I did get it from Tebelligan,' sighed Afeclin, hanging his bag from Majenta's saddle horn, 'from elves that have not left their country for almost two decades and even then it was for the purpose of war, not to sketch new maps of countryside they care very little about.'

'You're right of course,' apologised Typhin, studying the map. 'You see here's where you would have entered the Alimest Grove, correct?'

'Yes, I think so.'

'Well now assuming you came exactly the same way we did,' Typhin began, 'first we headed north along the path with the glowing butterflies and past the spooks of the forest. To get out of the grove, however you need to head south because the grove will take you all the way to the ocean. Firstly you have to go east for a little ways, which was the direction we were going when that horse got us stuck. So that would have put us around about here.'

Typhin pointed to a spot on the map within what they figured to be the Alimest Grove area.

'The door out of the cavern was on the south side of the room and the corridor continued straight ahead from the door which would also have put us in a southerly direction. As we walked we definitely saw that the passage did not change direction in any way nor did it veer to the left or right... therefore we must have headed south and according to this if we keep heading this way we'll make it back to the main road that goes to Rengal,' said Afeclin with certainty.

'You could be right, of course,' Typhin responded, once again scratching at his whiskers. 'But how do we know for sure the door (if you could call it that) to the cavern was on the south? After all the place is enchanted with wizards' spells. It's just as likely that although we could see through the mud to the top, it could be that it is mirrored or backward and if that is the case we could be heading north.'

'I never thought of that... but how do we know?'

Typhin looked up into the sky. 'The sun is high being about the middle of the afternoon, so at this stage we can't tell by the sun which direction we are headed but if we wait an hour or so and see which way the sun starts to drop we'll know exactly the way to go.'

'So we wait.'

As he looked up into the sky, his stomach groaned and he realised just how hungry he was.

'I'm so very hungry.'

'I suppose you didn't think to stop and grab some food to bring before you left the inn?'

'No... at that time food was the last thing on my mind,' he said now realising that it was perhaps a wise thing to make some preparations before leaving with such haste. *A lamp, food and extra water could have been very useful on this trip.* In his urgency to leave he had not considered any of the items. It was fortunate he remembered to grab his own bag. 'But I will remember that for next time you are swallowed by mud,' Afeclin teased as he sat down on a pile of dry leaves covering the soft mossy floor of the forest and rested his back against an old tree stump.

Typhin smiled at the remark. 'Yes, well, I do hope that next time you ride in to save the day you will be more prepared,' he joked, kicking at something on the ground.

Afeclin's eyes fell on a young ewe grazing under the trees.

'I don't suppose we could catch and cook ourselves a bit of sheep?'

'We could do that, but for the effort you have to go to, to prepare it for cooking... like cutting off the fleece, then skinning it... well it is a lot of work when we are only going to be here a short while,' said Typhin scratching his face as he continued to kick at the ground, 'besides it's very messy. We are better to wait for a good meal in Rengal.'

'I guess you are right,' said Afeclin. 'It would be a different story if we were camping here.'

'HA!' Typhin exclaimed as he bent down and pulled at a tree root lodged in the ground.

'What is it?'

'You see that tree stump you're leaning against? That is an old monkey leaf tree. When the monkey leaf dies, slowly its roots make their way to the surface,' he said handing Afeclin the piece of root he had dug up, 'their roots are full of nutrients they get from being so far down in the ground and they are very filling to eat. Try it.'

Afeclin took the piece of root and sniffed at it with careful suspicion. Then figuring that it must be alright if Typhin said it was, he took a big bite. He mulled it in his mouth for a moment and then began to chew it. It seemed okay, so he took another bite, then another and another. He was halfway through the rotting piece of wood when it struck him that it did not taste so good after all. In fact it was the foulest tasting, most awful flavour he had ever had the misfortune to encounter.

'Blahhhh!' he spat out the wood with disdain.

Typhin burst into laughter.

'That tastes terrible... how can you eat that stuff?'

'Ya don't unless you're starving to death,' Typhin answered with a teasing laugh, tears streaming down his cheeks.

'I can't imagine eating it then either.'

'You should have seen your face,' Typhin spat, rolling around on the ground in hysterics.

'I don't see what's so funny,' said Afeclin tiring of the older man's nonsense.

Afeclin got to his feet and ran to his horse. He grabbed the silver flask from his bag and was grateful to find a little water left in it. He drank a mouthful, swished it around in his mouth and then spat it onto the ground. The taste on his tongue was unbearable, like nothing he had ever experienced before.

'I think I would rather die than eat that again,' said Afeclin, trying to lick the taste off his tongue and onto the underside of his untucked shirt.

Typhin sat up from where he had been lying on the ground in a fit of laughter. He wiped away the tears from his cheeks and took a few deep breaths before speaking. 'You know you would be really surprised what ya would eat when you're starving.'

Afeclin coughed and spat again on the ground.

'Can't imagine it.'

'Let me tell ya something, those little roots are a starvin' man's best friend. They give you strength and fill ya up and they are in abundance in the southern parts of Titania. I was actually surprised to find one here, only I recognised the stump of the tree. The trees thrive in the north therefore they don't die and the roots stay underground. They have saved me from starvation and worse on more than one occasion.'

'What do you mean worse?'

'Well for instance, when I was a soldier my battalion and I found ourselves surrounded by habatchiees in the Woods of Carbowna. With no food or water available we were able to stay alive for over two weeks until help arrived by just eating the monkey leaf root. Not only that but we had the strength to keep the habatchiees at bay. We would never have had the chance to starve in those woods for we would have been slaughtered first and made into pig's meat. Keeping up our energy and strength is the only thing that saved us.'

'What are hab…habat… What did you call them?'

'Habatchiees. They are a dirty, stinky race of dwarf who inhabit the island Boanga. They are a nasty race that have in the past caused a lot of trouble with the inhabitants of the south of Titania,' Typhin explained.

'Why are they so dirty?'

'I don't know. I don't think they have any interest in cleanliness. It's not their thing,' said Typhin with a grin. 'I guess their stink serves them well; it certainly keeps people away from them. Like on the battlefield they are referred to as the skunks. Nasty stinky rodents… that's what they are.'

'What trouble were they causing with the southern inhabitants?' asked Afeclin. He was very curious about the different races of Titania.

'It comes down to history,' started the older man as he took a swig of water from his small, muddied water-skin that was hidden under his shirt and was attached with some kind of leather clip to his belt. 'Hundreds of years ago, it is said that the habatchiees lived in union with the mountain dwarves as one tribe, in the lower, southern part of Titania, at the edge of the mountain. As history goes [or at least this is how Raan tells it] an old silver-haired maiden found her way through the mountains to where the dwarves lived. She managed to befriend them and gain their trust by offering to cook and look after them if they allowed her to stay. Dwarves are terrible cooks and since they believed that she had nowhere to go, they allowed her to live in their village. What the dwarves didn't know was that she was really a witch and her interest lay in the land they were living on. Something about a curse on the land and her ancestors being buried in the area. So she caused trouble and division among the dwarves, turning families and friends against one another. Where the dwarves had previously lived in content, free from war and hatred, they began to bicker amongst each other.

206

Where they had never had a chief or leader before, they contended over the right to have a high chief of the village. Eventually in all the fuss and commotion they managed to burn down the entire village and those who did not want a leader took off into the mountains and became the mountain dwarves.

The one dwarf aspiring to be chief led his followers over the waters to Boanga. His name was Habatchiee.

So what do you know, hundreds of years later they want their land back because history dictates that it was theirs first. In the meantime however, many different races had settled in those parts. No one knows what became of the old witch or whether there even was one. So needless to say they started a war against the new inhabitants of the land in an effort to drive them away. They would have succeeded too had it not been for certain resistant groups that refused to give up the land and of course the soldiers that were called upon to help.'

'I wonder why they were so desperate to get their land back after all those years.'

'You never know with dwarves. Never underestimate them. You never know what's going on in the head of a dwarf. They think differently than you or I, they have a different mentality altogether. You just ask Ra...' Typhin said stopping as he considered his friend then continued with aggravation, 'RAAN! Boy that dwarf infuriates me!'

Typhin lay back on the ground and placed his straw hat that was now thick with dry brown mud, over his face to shade his eyes from the sun. After a moment he put his head up and looked at Afeclin, the rim of his hat still low over his eyes.

'You should keep that root in your bag, you never know when you may need it,' he said, laying his head back down to rest in the sun.

Afeclin put his hands behind his head and lay down to rest on the mossy ground in the shade of a bankoi. Strangely enough the root had managed to ease the hunger pains he had felt. It was as he was beginning to imagine having to live off monkey leaf root to survive that he realised the taste had gone from his mouth. Although the flavour was no longer there, the horridness of it was etched on his brain forever. He would do as Typhin suggested and keep some in his bag, just in case, but he hoped with all his might that he would never have cause to use it.

There in the warmth of the sun both he and Typhin drifted off to sleep.

Chapter

XXX

'Yahhhhhhhhhhhhhh!!'

Afeclin and Typhin were startled awake by a strange cry that echoed through the woods and the sound of wings flapping as a dozen or more birds took to the sky in fear. Sheep scampered this way and that stopping only to hide and watch from deeper in the woods.

'What was that?' Afeclin asked as he leapt to his feet, rubbing his eyes to clear them so he could scour the area.

'I… don't know,' mumbled Typhin as he reached for his sword in haste and stood poised, ready to take action if necessary.

There was neither person nor animal to be seen anywhere.

Afeclin and Typhin looked at each other in confusion. Then all of a sudden as if from nowhere there appeared a familiar dwarf on horseback.

'Raan!' Typhin uttered in surprise.

'You were expecting the jackals maybe?'

Typhin shook his head.

'I thought you were done for this time,' he said, 'can't live without us huh?'

'Hmph,' grunted the dwarf in his usual careless way, 'more like I realised you couldn't live without me.'

'That will be the day,' teased Typhin raising his eyebrows, 'but I am glad to see you, old man.'

Raan leaned forward and pushing his legs straight out, he allowed his stumpy body to fall to one side of the horse and then jumped down to the ground.

'Listen to me now, there are weasels after him,' he said with a stern growl, shaking a finger at Afeclin.

'Weasels?' questioned Afeclin. 'And what do you mean they are after me?'

'You know, shemalks,' continued Raan, now speaking directly to Afeclin, his short arms flailing with impatience. 'When I was in that hole I saw them… up top, through the mud. It is amazing how well you can hear everything above when you're in that hole. They were confused by the fact that your tracks went no further than the mud but they decided to follow the other tracks made by Pit and your friend. They kept referring to the *young wizard*, saying, "How are we going to find the young wizard? Where did the young wizard go?" and things like that. I could only assume they were talking about you.'

'But what are shemalks or weasels?' asked Afeclin with concern. 'Apart from being large rodents, of course.'

'Well they are a bit like large rodents,' said Typhin, 'but they're actually a race of people who live underground most of the time. They grow whiskers out the sides of their faces, have big round ears that stick out and longish faces, that kind of give them the look of a weasel.'

'Not to forget their claws,' added Raan.

'They don't have claws exactly,' corrected Typhin, 'just long slender nails that they use to dig with… but the main reason they are referred to as weasels isn't because of what they look like but because they are clever and sly. They're good fighters and silent hunters, just like weasels.'

'You don't tend to see them much… above ground,' said Raan taking a sip of water from the flask that he had grabbed from his saddlebag.

'For the most part you will never see any of them. They never venture far above ground,' continued Typhin. 'However there are some renegade shemalks that have decided for whatever the reason to live above ground.'

'The only problem is that they work for whoever pays them the most. They have no loyalties anywhere and with wages the way that they are these days bounty hunters are the best paid workers. Shemalks are the most skilled hunters in Titania,' Raan added with a gruff cough.

'So they are bounty hunters,' said Afeclin mulling over the information.

'Well… yeah.'

'And if they're after me it is because there is a bounty on my head?'

'That's right,' said Raan with intolerance. 'Now you can appreciate the severity of the situation.'

'Well, don't look at me like that. I haven't done anything! I am surprised there are not weasels or shemalks after you fellows…'

'There has been from time to time but the bounty on our heads isn't worth their trouble anymore.'

'What will they do if they find the others?'

'Whatever it takes to get the information they need to find you, torture if necessary… boiling water over the head, knife under the fingernails or they may even start cutting limbs off…'

'Raan!' hollered Typhin hitting the dwarf over the head with his hand. 'You don't need to go into detail.'

'Just telling it as it is,' defended Raan, 'there's no use sheltering the boy from the truth… from the danger he has put everyone in.'

'Why are they after me? It doesn't make sense.'

'Did you meet anyone before you met us? Did you upset anyone?' suggested Typhin.

'No, I didn't, I certainly have not made any enemies… yet… that I know of,' answered Afeclin, feeling confused. 'I don't know anyone outside of Tebelligan and the people I have come across would not have known I was a student of wizardry. To look at me I appear very ordinary. The humans I have met and seen in passing have been much the same as me. My clothes are of fine quality but are in no way showy. I cannot understand why anyone would be so interested in me. Interested enough to send a pack of weasels after me to hunt me down at whatever the cost.'

'It doesn't matter why or who,' said an irritated Raan shaking his fists and stomping his feet while the pitch in his voice rose a couple of notches, 'all that matters is that we find Pit before the weasels do. They're not going to believe a story about you diving into mud and sinking away.'

'You're right Raan,' said Typhin looking to the two horses standing by and then at the sky. 'We need to hurry to Desprade and now that the sun has dropped...'

Typhin looked at the sky again, 'Well I'll be a son of Afeclinella... would you look at that.'

They all looked up.

'The sun is sinking behind us meaning that we came out of the tunnel heading east therefore...'

'Therefore this way is south... not straight ahead,' Afeclin completed Typhin's sentence pointing to the right of them.

'Well? What are we standing around fer? If we know the way, let's go,' said a now red faced dwarf as he led his horse to the monkey leaf tree, climbed on top of the stump and from there it was quite easy for him to mount his horse, 'and don't think you're riding with me Typhin.'

Typhin looked at Afeclin's horse, 'I guess I'm bunking with you then am I?'

'I'm getting used to it now but it will slow us down of course,' Afeclin answered with a sigh.

'You're right it will,' Typhin said with a pause his eyes resting on a large ram that had bravely wandered closer than the others. 'Raan, I think if we could get hold of that sheep there, you could ride him into town and sell him to a butcher once we're there. What do you think?'

'Ridiculous,' he answered with a snarl, 'I am not riding a stupid, lame-brain sheep!'

Typhin was not listening. Instead he had already begun trying to catch the animal. He signalled to Afeclin to creep up on it from the other side.

Afeclin understood and began to inch toward the oblivious animal being careful not to arouse suspicion.

The sheep must have had an inkling something was not right and edged away from the two closing in. In its effort to keep an eye on Afeclin and Typhin however, it did not realise it was moving closer to Raan.

With reluctance, Raan removed his feet from the iron stirrups. He wormed his body with great agility for a stumpy little man, taking a rope from his horse's saddlebag that was positioned behind his leg. He made a loop in the rope with his stubby fingers. Then dropping the rope in front of the sheep's head he managed to place it over its horns and around the unsuspecting animal's neck. Before the sheep had a moment to react he tightened the noose.

'That is how it's done boys.'

The sheep struggled, jumping and kicking for a minute while the dwarf pulled hard on the rope preventing him from getting anywhere. The sheep finally admitted defeat.

'You see that? That is one stupid animal,' Raan said with disappointment. 'No fight in it at all.'

'Well isn't that fortunate for us then? Since we don't have time to train an animal for you to ride,' began Typhin amused by the dwarf's reaction to the animal.

'I am not, repeat NOT riding that lame-brained animal into town,' Raan interrupted with a growl, 'I'll look ridiculous.'

'Come on Raan you'll fit quite nicely and with all that wool he is bound to be a comfortable ride,' Typhin pleaded.

'NO,' Raan snapped.

'Come on, you don't have to be so stubborn all the time…'

'I am not being stubborn! I have a horse, Afeclin has a horse… the only person here without a horse is you!' croaked Raan. 'YOU ride the sheep and get a hurry on because we need to get moving.'

'You think you will look ridiculous riding it. What about me? My legs will drag on the ground.'

Raan had already trailed away, sending the message that there was no way he was going to concede.

Typhin looked to Afeclin with despair. Afeclin shrugged his shoulders.

Typhin's head dropped, 'I guess I have no choice then.'

'You can still ride with me,' offered Afeclin. Deep down he was hoping that Typhin would reject his offer, as the heat from the day would make it hot and sticky enough in the saddle without an extra rider.

'No. It will slow us down too much,' Typhin answered, patting the sheep to calm it. Then he looked at Afeclin and smiling said, 'It's okay, I will lag behind but that won't matter… better to allow you two to go on ahead with swiftness.'

Typhin retied the rope around the ram's neck and nose and jumped on the animal's unwilling back. The disgruntled sheep bucked several times and tried hard to run away. Typhin held tight to the rope but was not yet centred and so slid down the back of the sheep. He held on tight as the animal carried on trying to make a run for it. Typhin was pulled across the grass hitting a few rocks as he bumped along.

'Owww,' he moaned, getting to his feet when the sheep came to a standstill.

Afeclin tried hard not to laugh but found himself unable to resist. He turned his back and attempted to mount his horse, chuckling into the saddle as he did so.

A frustrated Typhin shuffled back his unkempt, mud-stuck hair and attempted to mount the animal once more. This time the sheep did not buck but shot off at a fast trot.

'Let's go!' Typhin hollered bouncing on the sheep's back. 'I don't know how far he'll go before he's worn out... so I'd better keep moving.'

Afeclin caught up with Typhin in no time and the two rushed along despite the smaller animal's height.

It seemed to get hotter as the afternoon waned but the trio did not stop for rest. Even Typhin, while lagging behind managed to keep the sheep moving at a good pace to the astonishment of Afeclin and Raan.

Afeclin glanced behind to see how Typhin was getting on. While the ram itself was quite large, Typhin's slender legs were almost dragging on the ground. His almost naked torso which was covered in ink pictures and his strong muscular build looked out of place on top of the woollen, weak-minded animal. Raan was right. He did look ridiculous and Afeclin could not help but laugh every time he turned around.

Raan was no better.

'Come on Typhin is that as fast as your animal will go? Oh that's as fast as it can go.' 'Make sure you don't break its back before we make it to Rengal,' and 'you must be pretty warm in your woollen saddle,' were just some of the taunts the dwarf would shout back to Typhin with a mighty laugh. It was the most jovial Afeclin had ever seen Raan.

While it was obvious that Typhin felt silly, he was good-humoured about the whole affair and remarkably quick-witted.

'Are those flies hanging around your animal... or you Raan?' 'Hey at least my animal is going to make me a pretty sum when we get to town.' And 'you'll be paying people to look after your animal, whereas people will be paying me to take mine off my hands,' he would reply unperturbed.

They had been riding for hours in the heat of the day. The humidity and the sweat were getting to Afeclin as he shifted uncomfortably in the saddle. His bottom was sore and perhaps bruised. He had never ridden so much in his life. He had never needed to. The monotonous sound of horse's hooves against the gravel was no longer soothing but rather irritating and he grew tired of the constant bouncing in the saddle.

The forest appeared to be getting denser as they rode on and it got to the point where they could no longer see into the woods at all. In fact the thought came across his mind that it would be an excellent place to hide, *especially if you're a weasel with a bounty to collect.*

It was as he was contemplating these thoughts that he noticed an old rugged sign on the side of the road.

As they passed, Afeclin slowed down his horse to read. There was only one word painted on the sign that appeared to be in ancient script. It said Malveen. It didn't mean anything to him except... *it is somehow familiar.*

Afeclin pulled on the reins to bring his horse to a complete stop and then began rummaging through his bag. *It will annoy me to no end if I continue on without at least trying to find out what this strange word means.*

Raan slowed his horse, noticing that Afeclin had come to a halt.

'What are you doing? What is the problem?' he grumbled, turning the steed.

Afeclin said nothing but took out a small book from his bag and began hunting through it.

'This is neither the time, nor the place for catching up on your reading.'

'I just have to check something. It will not take long,' Afeclin answered shuffling through the pages.

'We have still got a ways to go you know...' the dwarf began with an angry growl then shifted to a note of surprise, '... well I'll be horns waggled!'

Afeclin looked up from his reading for a moment to see what Raan was getting wound up about.

He saw Typhin in the distance, still riding his Ram.

'I can't believe that sheep has been able to keep up the pace,' he said bemused. Then he called out, 'Hasn't your sheep given out on you yet?'

'I know! I'm surprised at this one's stamina,' Typhin called back as he got closer to them, 'not bad for a dumb animal, heh?'

'Here it is!' Afeclin exclaimed, ignoring the banter going on between the other two. 'Malveen... it is a code word to wizards which means place of rest. I knew I had seen that word before. As it turned out I wrote it down in my notebook years ago thinking one day it may be important.'

By now Typhin had caught up to them and was sitting resting on his sheep stretching his legs out and massaging them.

'And is it important?'

'Well, yes it is for me,' Afeclin answered, the excitement in his voice rising. 'This sign marks the entrance or way to Lawry Castle... the possible place of rest for wizards.'

Afeclin began taking in the surroundings noting a large tree that hung out over the road and some rocks further up that had a funny shape to them.

'What are you doing?' asked Typhin watching Afeclin with curiosity.

'I am making sure I don't miss it when I come back.'

'You mean you're not going to take the path now?'

'Well, I would ordinarily but I need to go to Rengal first and make sure Wolflang is okay.'

'No, no, no,' said Typhin in sudden opposition, 'you must take this path here and now.'

'Well, it's not just that, you know,' continued Afeclin a little puzzled by Typhin's outburst. 'Wolflang doesn't know that I am alive. He will be thinking that I died in that muck. I know he will and he has been acting so strange...'

Afeclin's mind drifted back to the previous night's activities when with bravery or stupidity he had jumped into the mud. He again saw the look of his friend. The drained, unemotional face of Wolflang upset him a great deal. 'I at least need to say a proper farewell.'

'I understand, really I do...' began Typhin as he struggled to keep his sheep still, '...but let's put it this way. I have been through these woods many, many times in my life and this is the first time I have ever seen the road leading to Lawry Castle. I have never seen that sign before.'

'Then maybe I need to mark some trees so that I don't get lost coming back this way.'

'No... you see and I can't believe you don't already know this young wizard... the path changes all the time. One minute it is here and the next it has changed and the entrance is somewhere else. They say... I mean I have heard that if you are meant to find it you will happen upon it. If not you could spend weeks going around in circles trying to find it but ya never will,' Typhin explained.

'Oh,' Afeclin sighed, 'I cannot believe I have never read any of that. It makes good sense of course... I should have realised.'

'Well, don't beat yourself up about it,' Typhin joked and then added in a serious tone, 'but you know, the fact that we just stumbled across the path is perhaps a sign that you must follow. After all this is your destiny, is it not?'

Afeclin looked at the path. The path itself was visible for a few metres only and then the forest became so dense that it looked as if the path went nowhere at all. It did not look very important or inviting.

Afeclin glanced at Typhin who was still struggling with his ram and then to Raan for some kind of confirmation or as if the answer was in some way written on the dwarf's face. Of course his reply was typical of the little man and not helpful in the least.

'Load of hogwash, paths do not change.'

'Just like tunnels do not disappear, I suppose,' Typhin winked at Afeclin.

'Well of course they can't. What in Titania are you on about Typhin?'

'I guess you didn't notice that when you came out of the tunnel from under the ground it was not there anymore and couldn't be accessed. It had just disappeared.'

'Of course it didn't. What rubbish you speak. You need your head checked!'

Typhin looked at Afeclin with regret, 'I knew we should have pointed it out.'

They both laughed.

'Crazy! The both of you,' Raan grumbled turning his horse back the way they had been traveling, 'well I'm not hanging around here waiting for you two to decide what you are doing.'

Raan continued down the road at a hurried pace that was indicative of his irritation.

'It's time to decide,' said Typhin ignoring the disgruntled dwarf, 'if this is your destiny, you must take the path now.'

'What if it isn't?' asked Afeclin feeling doubt now that the castle was almost in sight.

'Afeclin,' Typhin said with a fatherly hand patting the taller man's leg, 'I have seen many magicians in my time and never would I have said that any of them would amount to anything. You on the other hand have something else. Something in your veins, an intuition that I could believe you were born with... I don't know... all I do know is that no one else would have, not only followed us in the dead of night, into the Alimest Grove no less... but having found us, jumped into thick mud not knowing what to expect. You put your life on the line for us... or maybe you didn't. Maybe you knew you would be okay. If that is the case then I would definitely say you have wizard blood pumping through your body... only a wizard could have known.'

Afeclin nodded, not knowing what to say.

'... But I hate to leave without seeing Wolflang. I just need to know that he is alright.'

'Don't you worry about your friend. We'll look after him. I'll explain to him what happened and that you are alive and well. He is welcome to journey with us until he finds his own path so don't you concern yourself with him.'

Afeclin bowed his head, so many thoughts rushing through his mind that he could not think straight.

'I guess you are right.'

Afeclin started digging through his bag. He found what he was looking for and pulled out a small, thick piece of wood that was painted a dark blue colour. From the top of the wood hung multicoloured feathers that were tied on with pieces of woven wool. Afeclin thumbed it through his fingers and stopped when he came to a little word carved on the side of it. Armatto, it said in elvin script, which meant… greatest friend.

'Could you give this to Wolflang for me when you see him,' Afeclin requested, climbing down from Majenta '… he will understand.'

'Of course I will.'

Typhin dismounted the sheep and Afeclin handed him the piece of wood. He tucked it into a long pocket he had in his pants. Then with the other hand he took Afeclin's hand and forced it into a fist. He made a fist himself. Then he pushed his hand hard against Afeclin's and holding it there said, 'Good luck my friend.'

'Goodbye and thanks for everything,' Afeclin said as he remounted the stallion and then after giving Typhin a brief nod, kicked Majenta in the sides and galloped away in the direction of Lawry Castle without looking back.

Chapter

XXXI

Afeclin rode with nervousness and excitement through the woods toward Lawry Castle.

He scratched at the dry, crusty mud on his bristly face. He wasn't used to such growth as he had always kept his beard trimmed and tidy. Now the extra hair irritated him.

As he scratched he worried over Wolflang. He was troubled by leaving without having ridden on into the city to say goodbye to him. He was concerned about what would become of the elf if he kept up his strange behaviour. Afeclin was cheered however by the trust he had in his new friend Typhin. He felt sure that the older man would look out for his friend whether Wolflang would accept it or not.

The woods were very dark, not black like the Alimest Grove, but dark nonetheless, despite the daylight that existed beyond the grey clouds that covered this part of the woods. Afeclin wrapped himself in his thick cloak, bringing the hood right over his head as a chilling breeze whistled through the trees and swept around him and Majenta.

The narrow stoney path wound tightly through tall eerie trees that towered over him and looked down upon him. The trees were bare, stripped of their leaves and yet there were no leaves to be found anywhere on the path or the forest floor. The naked branches were warped, twisted and gnarled and hung over the path like long slender arms that reached out to grab him. Their roots spread around about, between the trees and spilled over onto the path, pushing through the stones and sticking out all over the place as if trying to trip them. On occasion Majenta's hoof struck a looped root and the horse fell forward, losing his footing and half tumbling. He had to strain to stop from falling over.

As the wind blew, the trees swayed and their movement seemed strong and deliberate as if each tree was filled with its own spirit. The thin papery bark of the trunks were torn in such a way that the trees appeared to have lifeless faces with pained expressions of mourning and despair.

A thick mist spread along the floor of the forest. It snaked around the trees and grew stronger the further in they travelled. Before long Afeclin's visibility had become so poor that moving forward became a very slow process.

Then came a whispering, a breathy whisper that seemed to come from high in the trees and then buzz around his ears.

'Turn back, while you still can,' it seemed to say and, *'leave now, do not go any further. You have been warned...'*

Afeclin shivered.

He stopped the horse and sat for a moment trying to urge himself to continue onward, further into the unknown. He felt the unremitting murmurs in his ears but also through his body. It made his headache and his heart beat with wild palpitations inside his chest. An uncontrollable force shook him from his core. Even Majenta was uneasy this time as the stallion turned around about in a nervous circle. Afeclin pulled hard at the reins attempting to gain control again of the frightened animal.

The whisperings were relentless and cold, sending a chill up Afeclin's spine. Terror was beginning to paralyse him to the point where he could not move. Afeclin was not even sure if there was anything to be afraid of but there was something very strange and unnerving about the woods that struck fear to his very soul.

With his brain pounding, making him feel dizzy, Afeclin rubbed his temples with his thumb and middle fingers trying hard to think. It was then that he looked down at his chest and noticed a peculiar glowing through his shirt. Pulling his shirt forward, he found the rock that Endorf had given him still hanging around his neck, radiating its brilliant blue. It was warm to the touch and as Afeclin held it in his hand and closed his eyes, it seemed to give him the courage he needed to go on.

Ignoring the voices he was hearing Afeclin urged Majenta to face the direction they had been heading and gave him a mighty kick. The obedient horse spurred forward kicking up his front legs as a last protest before moving. They then darted through the trees, being able to behold only what lay a few feet ahead of them. Reacting almost with instinct to each sharp turn, they bolted as if trying to escape with their lives, as if some beast or other were in hot pursuit of them.

They galloped solidly for another hour, Afeclin fixated and focused on getting through the wood and Majenta obeying every kick, every pull from the bridle.

At long last they came to a descent that led out of the leafless trees and into an open valley, which was rich in colour and flourished with vegetation. All at once there was no more mist and grey clouds masking the sky and now that the sun was allowed in, its shine was resplendent.

Shielding his face with his hand, Afeclin attempted to see what lay ahead in the valley. He was blinded for a moment as his eyes adjusted to the sudden brightness.

The trail continued on through the valley until it reached a small, peculiar-looking cottage. Afeclin pulled on the reins to slow Majenta and as they walked down into the valley he was able to get a better view of the unusual building.

The stone walls of the cottage were uneven on all sides of the dwelling and the windows were small and odd-shaped, apart from a large window at the very front. The thatched roof was steep and pointy a little left of the centre and a tall stone chimney protruded out from the highest peak. From that point the roof had a disproportionate wave that spilled over the building, meeting the walls at differing heights and extending over, creating asymmetrical eaves on each side.

The cottage was not pretty to look at. It appeared old and in disrepair. Even the flowerbed under the front window was weedy and ill-maintained.

To one side of the walls a large Braga-bell tree shaded what appeared to be some kind of garden that held a collection of rocks and boulders. They were all different shapes and sizes and were unique in colours and patterns.

The other trees, surrounding the cottage, were withering in the heat. All in all, the place looked lonely and unkempt.

Upon reaching the secluded dwelling Afeclin sat looking at the faded blue painted door, contemplating knocking. He didn't have to sit for long before an elderly man with a long grey beard emerged from inside the house.

Not seeming to notice Afeclin, the man went about watering what looked like dying plants scattered around about the cottage whilst producing a tuneful hum. He seemed to be quite content in his own little world.

The old man wore white and blue robes that Afeclin was sure must have looked quite elegant once upon a time but were now tattered and faded. His balding head was a little red from the sun and on his face he wore an extraordinary pair of spectacles with blue, hexagonal lenses that masked his eyes.

'Et um,' Afeclin coughed alerting the old man of his presence.

The old man looked up in surprise as he patted his chest as if to calm his heart.

'You mustn't do that to a man my age,' he huffed in a croaky little voice, shaking a wrinkled finger at him, 'the heart can't take such a shock! I could have keeled over and died and then where would you be... unless... that was your intention... to do away with me? In that case, don't think it will be that easy. I have no intention of surrendering myself to any green bean. I will die fighting!'

The elderly man stood in a fighting stance, shaking his fists. *He means business.* Afeclin tried not to laugh; however he did admire the old man's gumption.

'Look old man, I have no intention of fighting or hurting you, I...' Afeclin began to explain.

'OLD MAN?' the elderly man wheezed. 'Who are you calling an old man? Why I am barely 150 years older than you, I am in my prime... old man indeed!'

Afeclin threw his hands in the air with apology.

'I am sorry I didn't mean to offend you old...' he started but then bit his tongue.

The old man scowled.

'I had best be on my way,' Afeclin said feeling sheepish as he pulled the reins tight to one side in order to turn Majenta. 'Goodbye.'

The old man nodded and turned his attention back to what he was doing. 'Old man indeed.'

Afeclin looked about the valley. Beyond the small clearing, the area was surrounded with crowded trees. He rode to one side of the cottage to see if the path continued beyond.

Nothing.

Just more trees.

No path or track to speak of. It all seems to end here at the cottage.

Afeclin sat confused wondering whether he had missed something earlier and if so what to do next. He rode back to the front of the cottage where the old man still stood watering his weeds, humming away.

'Excuse me… sir, but I wondered if you could help me,' Afeclin asked with gentle refrain.

Without looking up from what he was doing he gave an astute answer, 'You are looking for Lawry Castle, are you not?'

'Well yes, as a matter of fact I am.'

'Don't look so surprised. Why else would you be in this part of the woods?' the old man ranted. 'Unless you're here to do away with me… in that case…'

This time Afeclin interrupted hoping to avoid another scene. 'I can assure you the only reason that I am here is to find Lawry Castle. Do you know where it is?'

'Of course I do,' scoffed the man.

'Well, do you think you could tell me where to find it?' Afeclin felt anxious. 'I need to speak with the wizard Zallucien.'

'What do you want with him?' The old man then stood up straight and folding his arms on his chest added with a mocking tease, 'Oh, so you think you are a wizard do you?'

'That is none of your business.'

'You are not cut out to be a wizard,' he said laughing, 'but don't get so sensitive about it; I'm just making an observation, that's all!'

'And what would you know anyhow?'

The old man gave Afeclin a stern look, his eyebrows furrowing. Then he relaxed his arms as if he didn't really care anyway.

'The wizard Zallucien is dead,' he stated giving up the charade.

'DEAD?'

'Dead! But if you are still interested in the castle it is just beyond the trees behind this cottage. Good day.'

With that the old man disappeared inside his house.

'Dead?'

His body went limp for a moment as he tried to come to terms with this new information.

'How could he be dead?' he said feeling confused and disorientated. *The great Zallucien dead? How could such a thing have happened?*

Afeclin plodded toward the trees behind the cottage once more. This time he got down off the horse and leaving Majenta waiting he walked into the woods.

He had to push aside bushes and tree branches to get through the scrub but after squeezing through a large bush he found what he was looking for or at least the remnants there of.

What looked like the makings of what once was a fine castle were scattered all over the ground. Large pieces of granite and broken stone dotted the area. All that was left standing were the foundations and sections of wall on either side of the floor.

Afeclin climbed over some of the large stones, which judging by their rounder shape looked to have come from a tower. He lumbered up onto the massive foundation flat. Here he could see black soot marks patterned all over the leftover walls where evidence of a fire had surged.

'Whatever happened here?' he said, barely above a whisper, as if in respect to the grave of this wondrous building. He could not fathom the idea that such a mighty and powerful building was now but a ruin. Wizards from all over the country had come to study and learn from the most renowned sages of all time here within its walls. It had been a fortress, a stronghold and a sanctuary of protection at times when wizards were reviled as the plague.

Afeclin closed his eyes and tried to imagine what it had looked like at that time. He had read so much about those years and its history that he felt like he knew the building's soul. And yet here it was not even a shadow of its former self.

He put his hand on one of the walls and ran his fingers along the black markings as if trying to sense what had gone on. As he did this he was unaware that eyes were upon him, watching through the trees, his every move.

Afeclin sat on a piece of fallen stone to think. He was tired, achy and when he stopped and thought about it he discovered he was famished.

Now that he had come this far it seemed such a long way to go to Rengal. Instead he considered sheltering in the old ruins for the night.

First he needed food and he wondered where he could find some. It seemed that the obvious place was in the old man's cottage beyond the trees but there was no way he was going to knock on the door and beg for something to eat.

Afeclin rummaged through the bag that he still wore over his shoulder. He found the piece of rotten root that Typhin had given him earlier that day and seriously considered eating it.

Putting the root up to his lips he tried to make himself forget the taste long enough to take a few bites. It wasn't working though. The thought of the foul tasting bark was enough to put him off eating altogether.

Instead he took the blue rock he was wearing and turned it over in his hands. He had forgotten all about it over the past few days' journey and had always meant to give the fascinating stone a more thorough examination.

It was about the length of his index finger and had an odd pear shape to it. It looked smaller in the palm of his hand than it had in the Elf King's. Afeclin's large human hands almost swallowed the incandescent object. The rock's glow seemed to come from deep inside. It was a stunning piece of stonework. It had perfect formation and contained no cracks or flaws in its crust as if it had been forged by the gods themselves.

Afeclin's thoughts were interrupted by a sudden rustle in the trees nearby.

He jerked his head up and was surprised to see the old man sprinting toward the ruins.

'What is it that you have there, friend?' the old man asked pointing at the illuminating stone with interest.

'Oh so it is friend now is it?' Afeclin commented with a wry smile.

'Where did you get that?' he continued ignoring Afeclin's tone. 'Who did you kill to steal it?'

'It is mine! I didn't steal it nor did I kill anyone for it.'

'Very snippy for someone so innocent,' croaked the old man sounding eager to cause trouble. 'I don't care either way… but… how much do you want for it?'

'It's not for sale.'

'Everything's for sale,' the elderly man wheezed beginning to climb the large boulders of the ruins. 'It just depends on the price. How does fifty pieces of gold sound?'

Afeclin stared at the man who was now standing no more than a foot away from him. He was confused. Why the old man was so desperate to get his hands on the rock was beyond him. Fifty gold pieces was a lot of money. He had only brought enough coin with him to see him to Lawry Castle as he had refused to take any more than that from Endorf. Now he had next to nothing left. With no food and nowhere to sleep the old man's offer was tempting.

'I said it's not for sale,' he replied with firmness, making up his mind.

'It is just a rock.'

'Yes, well it is not for sale,' Afeclin said again with resolution.

'Think wisely boy. I can see you have nothing and now that your precious wizard is not around to train you, what are you going to do? How will you find yourself another wizard to take you on if you do not have the means to seek one out? Whereas I am an aging old fool who would receive great joy out of such a rock in my collection. I will pay you 75 gold coins, not a piece more but I will also invite you into my home for a hearty supper and a good night's rest before you get on your way in the morning.'

Again Afeclin felt tempted as he held the rock in his hand once more feeling the warmth from its glow. *If it is just a rock, why does the old man want it so badly? Is he just a senile old coot who finds joy out of a little rock garden and pretty stones or... is there more to it?* Afeclin felt sure that there had to be more to it and wondered what it was that was so important to the aging man.

'Thank you for the offer,' he answered with bowed head, 'but I cannot sell it. It is simply not for sale.'

The elderly man scratched his balding head and observed Afeclin with curiosity.

'It is just a rock,' he repeated.

'That it may be... but I cannot part with it. As crazy as it sounds, I have no idea why it is so important but I feel that in some way... it is.'

The man sighed and turned around. 'Well, why don't you come inside and have something to eat anyhow,' he said with near kindness, 'I don't imagine you'll find your way to eating that dried up piece of root.'

Afeclin stood watching the nimble old man climb down the large boulders. He was certainly light on his feet for his age. Afeclin wondered whether he should go with the man. His stomach said yes but his mind questioned whether it was a genuine offer or a ploy to get the rock from him.

As if hearing Afeclin's thoughts or sensing his reservation the old man responded, 'I am not going to try and steal your rock away from you. I can't promise however that I won't continue to try and persuade you to sell it to me but you have my word that I will not harm or trick you.'

Afeclin stood speechless for a moment before coming to the realisation that a good meal might be worth a little risk. He placed the rock back under his shirt and then getting to his feet hurried to catch up to the old man who had already disappeared into the scrub.

Besides, he considered to himself as he rushed through the trees, *this might be a good way for me to find out exactly what happened to Zallucien and Lawry Castle.*

Chapter

XXXII

After travelling all day on a bumpy stone road, sitting for long hours on the hard wooden bench of Harren's wagon, the boredom overtook her and Lenna drifted off to sleep.

When she awoke, the petite elf was surprised to find herself nestled into Harren's body.

She sat up with abrupt uneasiness, wiping a drip of moisture from around her mouth that had trickled off her lip.

She looked at their surroundings and attempted to gather her thoughts as she shook the drowsiness from her head.

No longer enveloped by trees, they barrelled past houses and stores as they raced down a tired old street of what appeared to be a city.

Lenna sat upright, rubbing her eyes in disbelief.

'Are we here already?' she asked with a yawn.

'Yes Little Elf, we have made it safely to Rengal… as promised.'
Lenna sat still, amazed by the city's size.

People were everywhere.

People of differing races, sizes and heights scattered themselves about the city. They bustled about in stores, on sidewalks, in wagons, on horses and crossing the roads. Lenna found the other races fascinating to observe, their mannerisms and speech being so much different from what she was used to.

She watched a couple of humans arguing in front of a store window, with discreet observation. They appeared to be married, the man being scolded by the woman who belted him over the head with her satchel. Lenna giggled to herself. She was pleased to be able to study other passersby without them taking much notice of her. With her thick hair covering the tops of her ears, it wasn't so obvious she was elvin. Her larger eyes did not attract much attention, as they were not as much a stand out feature of her race.

Lenna did not find Rengal very attractive. Unlike Tebelligan, which was by comparison a much smaller, compacted city, there appeared to be a lack of colour and art. Rengal seemed decrepit and in disrepair as the buildings they passed were crumbling and faded.

'Not much to look at, is it?' Harren stated watching Lenna with interest.

'It is not a beautiful city,' she said with sincerity, 'but it is very big.'

'It's the biggest on the continent, Marrapassa,' he professed with a smile, 'but you are right it isn't so pretty anymore.'

'You mean, it once was an attractive looking city?' Lenna asked as she tried to imagine how Rengal might have looked a long time ago when the buildings were new and fresh.

'Yes, it was quite the metropolis in its day, alive with colour and music. It boasted many cultural influences and was fresh and exciting.' As Harren spoke his eyes lit up with reminiscence. 'Then of course came the Great War. Rengal was one of the cities most affected by fighting and conflict. Architecture was destroyed, fires were lit that surged through the streets and buildings with many inhabitants were killed. In later years, after the war had ended, they tried to rebuild the city as best as they could with the resources that they had, but funds were limited. War had made the people poor and they suffered from the losses of their loved ones. Rebuilding a city was something that was not high on one's priorities.'

Lenna felt sad for the people and the city. 'War is a terrible thing,' she said with passionate sensitivity despite having no direct experience with warfare. She had heard Afeclin's story many times in the past. The way he was found, a baby in a cradle within a village ravaged by war, tugged at the elf maiden's heartstrings. *No person should have to go through that,* she had often thought.

Harren nodded with thoughtful repose as he jolted to a sudden stop, allowing some small children playing with a ball and twigs to cross the road safely.

Lenna's eyes fell upon a discoloured sign in the distance that read Waterfeln Inn and her mind focused on the reason she had come to Rengal in the first place. Making her mind up she scuttled down the side of the wagon without a word.

'Hey where are you off to Little Elf?' Harren called after her as she ran across the road in front of him.

'Just going to check out this inn to see if my friends are here,' she called back to him, her face flush with excitement.

Lenna bounded up the rounded front steps to the inn, missing every second one as she flew with speed.

The entrance had two large green doors with long slender window panels cut into each side. She peered through.

Beyond the entrance hall was a nice looking crescent shaped bar with dark green glass panelling along the front edge surrounding it. Behind the bar was an elderly looking gentleman with short greying hair, a long grey moustache and wearing an emerald green bow tie around his neck.

She opened the door and walked into the building, wringing her hands as she approached the man at the bar.

'Excuse me,' she said with a shy cough.

'Yes ma'am how may I help you?' the man asked, his moustache twitching. 'Do you need a room?'

'Well, I don't exactly know yet,' Lenna stammered, flicking her hair back over her ear. 'You see I am looking for some people.'

The man looked at her with deep surprise. 'You know ma'am, I don't mean to stare but you are the second elf I have seen today… and I haven't seen an elf for twenty years or so!'

Lenna stared at the man in disbelief, a million thoughts rushing through her head at once.

'You saw an elf?' was all she could manage to spit out.

'Yes ma'am, he checked in with another fella and a gal not more than a half hour ago I should think,' the man answered with candour. 'Would you like a drink?'

Behind her, Lenna heard the door open and she spun around on her toes hoping to see Wolflang.

'Oh it is you, Harren,' she said with some disappointment.

'Yes, I came in to check on you. Is everything alright?'

Lenna nodded. 'He is here just as you said, I mean, in Rengal as you said. He has checked into this inn.'

'Oh that is good news, Little Elf,' said Harren in his less than enthusiastic way.

Lenna frowned with sudden confusion and turned back toward the barman.

'What did you mean they checked in with a gal, you mean a woman?' she asked, jealousy starting to build inside of her. 'What woman?'

'A human woman ma'am, very nice looking too. They were altogether, the three of them… of course they all took separate rooms.'

Lenna attempted to push away the feelings of resentment and anger building inside her. She felt like she had been replaced. *Who is this woman and where did she come from?* Lenna realised that the best way to find out was to ask Wolflang herself.

'Are they here now?'

'No ma'am, they left soon after they had taken their things to their rooms,' said the man as he wiped down the counter top with meticulous care.

'Oh,' Lenna's smile fell. 'You do not happen to know where they have gone do you?'

'Sorry, ma'am I don't.'

'Well, thank you for your help.' Lenna turned back to Harren who had stood to one side of the counter listening. 'The main thing is that I know where they are staying now, so I will just wait here until they return.'

'Very well Little Elf, I will be on my way,' said Harren with a voice that sounded almost disappointed. He staggered out of the inn.

As Lenna watched him go, she was full of her own thoughts, *I shall sit and wait for Wolflang and surprise him when he comes in the door, and won't he be surprised!*

She walked to a little sitting area across from the bar and on the other side of the entrance. A couple of wooden bench seats lined with decorative cushions were placed opposite each other, one against a large arched window that looked out onto the street and the other against the opposing brick wall. A number of small trees filled the perimeter of the room and a window in the ceiling allowed the sun's rays to stream into the room making it warm and light.

It occurred to her that she had not bid Harren goodbye, nor had she thanked him for all he had done in rescuing her from her pitiful state and helping her find her friends.

Looking out the window of the inn she saw Harren standing beside his horse. The shemalk looked forlorn as he spoke to a burley man in a green coat. The man appeared to be handing Harren a small coin bag.

Harren took the bag, opened it and tipped it, allowing a number of gold doucla to fall into his long clawed hand.

I have never seen anyone so miserable when receiving gold coins before, the elf thought as she watched the unusual interlude, *perhaps he is sad we have to part ways... and I never even said goodbye.*

The thought stirred her very soul as a sudden realisation came upon her. Over the past few days the old shemalk had grown on Lenna, despite his persistence in calling her *"Little Elf"*.

I must say goodbye! she thought as she bolted toward the door in a sudden panic that she just might miss him if she did not hurry.

She pulled open one of the heavy doors and went to run toward the wagon but as she did the big man in the green coat stood in her way.

'Oh excuse me,' she said veering around the broad man.

The man moved in the direction she had tried to pass, again standing in her way.

'Uh, do you mind awfully, I'm trying to pass,' she said with slight annoyance in her tone.

Then she went to pass the other way and he blocked her again. She looked up into his face. The big man had the face of a pig and she recognised that he was a troll.

'Oh my,' she breathed as she turned to run in the opposite direction calling out to Harren for help.

'HARREN!' she screamed at the top of her lungs.

The old shemalk kept driving and never looked back.

She tried to run back inside the building but as she went to grasp the door handle, the door flung open on her and hit her in the head as another pig-faced troll stood in her way.

'Where do you think you are going?' he asked with a large grin on his face revealing dark rotten teeth.

Before she could think or react the first troll had his hefty arms around her, lifting her off her feet and over his shoulder.

The tiny elf screamed and kicked and thumped the troll's back with her fists. She bit him hard on the arm, causing the troll to growl in anger. The other pig-faced troll grabbed the back of her neck and gave a gentle squeeze.

'We can't have you making a big fuss and alerting the troops now can we?' he said with a dirty snarl.

Lenna felt her body go limp.

Chapter

XXXIII

The Westkey Link was a small tavern situated in the heart of Rengal on the main artery through the city. Every evening it was busy with city workers and travellers unwinding from a hard day.

Wolflang looked around the room and studied the various people in it. A couple of drunken humans and a group of loud goblins celebrating were at the far end of the black wooden bar from where he sat on a tall metal stool. Behind him, on one of the circular tables there was a serious game of cards happening between a mean-looking troll, a hobgoblin and a busty woman with long golden curls. A dwarf had fallen asleep at another table in a tight corner nearby, his heavy boots resting on the table as he balanced the chair backwards on two legs. Between the tables people were standing about everywhere, talking, singing, drinking and making merry. The atmosphere was loud and crowded in the dingy room, which bought a little peace to the troubled elf's mind after the previous night in the silent and sinister Alimest Grove.

Since coming to town, Wolflang had been the subject of much interest. People had stared as he had ridden down the main street. Some had called out to him and others had even tried to touch him, as if he were some treasure that was unique and special. While for the most part none of the attention was antagonistic toward him, it made the elf rather uncomfortable to have people stare and point at him.

Wolflang had walked into the tavern with his head hung low and his hair shuffled over his long pointed ears in the hope that no one would take any notice of him. Now in looking around the room it seemed that nobody even cared.

The tavern had a hefty wooden corner door into the place that was held open by a heavy bag of sand. A large stained glass window with green trimming covered the front wall, which was a floral design with the tavern's name spelt out between leaves and flowers. In front of the window, a long plank seat with dark green cushioning sat against the wall seating a number of black and red uniformed soldiers and one uncomfortable dwarf. The floor was tiled with small, brown clay squares that were neither dirty nor polished but aged, well worn and in some places, chipped. The wall behind the bar was painted with a mural of chalky grey and white. Splashes of green added a little colour to the scene, which portrayed Rengal in its earlier days.

Tired and depressed, the weary elf downed one drink and then another.

'Another one,' his voice was hoarse as he spilled a couple of coins on to the counter.

'You'll want to take it easy with those drinks friend,' said the barman refilling the glass again with strong liquor. 'This stuff is potent… it will knock you out if you drink it too quick.'

Wolflang wanted to say something like, "I can handle it" and "I need this, I have had a hard couple of days, want to hear about it?" but the room was beginning to spin and he couldn't quite focus on anything. All he could manage in a low voice was, 'I'm not your friend.'

'We meet again,' came a voice from the seat beside him.

Wolflang looked up and tried hard to focus his eyes on the person before him. At first he didn't recognise the big nose and squinty eyes but then he focused in on the man's dark moustache.

'Hey you'rh… the man I rescued from the bear earlier today,' he said squinting his own eyes to see better.

'Lawfabex,' the man corrected.

'Right, lawfabex.' Wolflang nodded.

'You are one crazy elf,' the man said with a smirk.

'Yeah, I've 'eard that before.'

'Hey, I didn't say it was a bad thing, some people would call it bravery even.'

'Yeah, well... I'm not even shhure why I did that.'

'But me, I would call it stupidity,' the man said raising his eyebrows as he picked up his drink and walked to the back of the bar.

Wolflang watched as the arrogant little man sauntered away.

'Sstupid or crayse, I saved your life,' Wolflang called out after him, 'you still haven't thanked me for that!'

Outside on the street laughter and mocking taunts could be heard echoing into the bar. Some of the patrons moved out the door to see what all the commotion was.

Wolflang hunkered over his drink for a moment staring into the now empty glass. He had no interest in getting up and going out on the street to see what all the fuss was about. *I couldn't care less.* He was about to order himself another drink when he heard someone from outside yell, 'Don't you realise you're on the wrong animals? The dwarf should be riding the sheep! Ha ha ha.'

Wolflang's ears rang with the word dwarf. He thought for a moment and realised there were plenty of dwarves around town and that it could have been anyone... and yet... something inside him said that he should at least check.

Lurching sideways from the stool, his head spun as he balanced himself on his feet.

He concentrated hard as he walked toward the door focusing on each step and treading with utmost care so as to not stumble and fall. The room had become cloudy and his eyes stung from the smoke, which made his vision begin to blur. He bumped into a goblin as he attempted to pass a small group entering the bar.

'Sorry, wass'anaccident,' Wolflang slurred as he struggled to balance.

'Get out of my way,' the goblin retorted, giving Wolflang a hard shove to the chest. Wolflang stumbled and tripped over his feet, falling backward onto the floor.

He looked up at the goblin in shock, feeling annoyed and embarrassed. The elf's hair fell behind his back, exposing his ears.

'Will ya look at this fellas, an elf,' the goblin laughed, 'should've realised from those buggy eyes.'

'Little far from the Tebelligan border aren't ya liddle fella?' another teased with a patronising tone. 'What happened, did ya get lost?'

A roar of laughter carried through the crowd as other patrons began to take notice and join in the fun.

Wolflang went red in the face as he became enraged by the taunts. He scuttled to his feet and hurried away from the crowd inside the bar, fearing what he may do if he let his anger get the better of him.

By the time Wolflang made it to the door he was grateful to be heading outside. He now, more than anything, needed fresh air.

Walking out the front door of the bar, he rubbed his eyes to clean them and took deep breaths to calm himself. As he lifted his fingers from his face he managed to see what the fuss outside was about. Coming down the main road of town were two persons, one riding a horse and one riding a sheep. The one riding the horse appeared to be a dwarf and the one riding the sheep seemed to be a bit too big for the animal.

Wolflang blinked several times and tried to focus on their faces. He staggered forward a little. With laughs and mocks ringing in his ears he studied the faces with intense interest as they rode further into town.

As the two riders began passing the tavern, Wolflang managed to make out their faces at long last. He recognised Raan first; his snarled face was far from happy as usual. The other person was a proud-looking Typhin who rode, with his nose in the air, astride a sheep of all animals.

Wolflang watched as they passed and half expected to see Afeclin bringing up the rear, but he was not there. He was nowhere to be seen.

'Ssso where issee?'

Despite the noisy street, the question caught Typhin's attention the instant it left Wolflang's lips. He turned his head and looked back at the elf, bringing the ram to a halt.

'You know who I am talking about don't you?!' he added, no longer capable of holding back his anger. 'The one who dived into ssick mud attempting to ssave your sorry lives... and yet, here y'are... alive and well and where issee?'

Typhin removed himself from the sheep's soft back and marched in silence toward Wolflang, dragging the animal behind.

'You never tisappeared into mud, did you?' Wolflang garbled, his anger fuelled by the goblins inside the bar, now directed at Typhin with all sense and logic leaving his being. 'Wassall a tchick wasn't it?'

'Wolflang. Come with us so I can talk to you, you're not making any sense right now. It's evident you've drunk too much and we need to discuss this,' said Typhin reaching out his hand to grip Wolflang's arm.

'You sink I'm ssupid don't you! You sink because ima elf I don't know anysing!'

He pulled away from Typhin's grasp with frantic flailing of arms. Then pulling back his arm with fierce intent, he swung wildly and hit Typhin square on the jaw. The force of the punch knocked Typhin to the ground.

Wolflang stood towering over Typhin who now lay on the ground rubbing his jaw.

'You pack a nice punch,' he said looking up at Wolflang with a surprised expression.

Wolflang shook his head in despair. *What am I becoming?* he thought to himself. He looked around at the people standing and staring, once again pointing at the elf. He felt sick with extreme fatigue. Without a word he took off with a stagger down the street looking to get away from the crowd that had gathered.

'Wolflang, wait!' He heard Typhin in the distance but Wolflang kept on walking.

'You there!' a voice came from one side of him.

Wolflang kept moving in the same direction with his head down.

'I said, you there!' the voice came again, this time more authoritative. 'Halt right there.'

Wolflang did not stop nor did he look.

'Right, if that is the way you want to play it.'

Before Wolflang could even think, two sets of hands came out and grabbed him with force.

'Get your hans-hoff me,' Wolflang protested with unrestrained vehemence, 'who you hink you are?'

Glancing up, he saw his harassers. They were two large, bearded men wearing the exact same attire. Bronze stripes were painted across the arms of what appeared to be a uniform and peculiar emblems of flying creatures were sewn onto the torso.

Wolflang determined that they must be lawmen and he stopped struggling so as not to create more trouble for himself.

'You want to go for a little walk? We'll take you for a little walk,' said the larger of the two with a deep laugh while he tied a rope around Wolflang's wrists. The other chuckled with a wide smile, sharing the joke.

'Look I'm sorry,' pleaded Wolflang, 'I didn't recognise who you were... I... I'm new here.'

'Come on, you're coming with us,' the other continued without sympathy.

'You can't go getting drunk and punching out the locals. The mayor doesn't accept that kind of behaviour in his city,' added the larger man.

Wolflang's head seemed as light as a feather all of sudden. Then he felt his legs collapse beneath him and his eyes close as he hit the ground.

Chapter

XXXIV

After Lenna had awoken from her unconscious state, she had found that she was sitting on a horse, tied to a saddle and travelling along a dirt track surrounded by treeless plains. Her bow and quiver had been taken from her. The two trolls rode ahead leading her horse along the beaten path.

What am I doing here? she had asked herself with confusion. *Where are they taking me?*

Thoughts had rushed through her mind as she attempted to remember the last moments before she had blacked out.

The troll was in my way, then he went to grab me and I called out to Harren, but he did not seem to hear me... he rode away. I did not get to say goodbye to him because the troll was in my way... the same troll that was speaking to Harren... giving him gold coins.

Lenna shook, as if she had been struck by a bolt of lightning, *they gave him gold... why?*

The immediate answer that came to her mind she did not want to believe.

Perhaps it was a coincidence? Surely Harren did not drive me all the way to Rengal to hand me over to the trolls, he was trying to help me find Wolflang... right?

While she had struggled to accept that Harren was anything less than a kind-hearted saint, there was evidence to the contrary. Had she really hit her head when meeting Harren or had she been hit by something? Had she really been so tired that she fell asleep at the dinner table or had she been drugged? It was possible. But *that gold...* it could not be explained away.

So what? He had been promised gold if he could bring me to Rengal? she surmised, pained by the prospect. *I trusted him!*

Feeling hurt and betrayed, she focused her attention on escape.

She had thought about kicking the horse to spur him on and away but the troll in front of her held the reins so she did not imagine she could flee without him coming too. Then she had worked on the rope that bound her wrists to the saddle horn. While the rope was wrapped around it several times, she thought that her small elvin hands and wrists were perhaps slender enough to squeeze them out.

It had taken some time and effort and it had been very painful on her hands, bruising them and tearing the skin, but she managed to free them.

At first she had determined to bide her time and wait for a good opportunity to jump from the saddle and make a run for it. However, a hiding place was not forthcoming and as they travelled further and further away from Rengal or anything else recognisable, Lenna had begun to feel the urgency to escape.

She had noticed that the two trolls paid little to no attention to her, they plodded along on their horses with their heads down, feeling the rampant heat of the day.

Lenna studied the plains in every direction. Behind her, the slender dirt track through small spiky bushes that dotted the landscape went backwards as straight as an arrow for kitra. To the right and left of her as far as her eyes could see, grainy red sand filled the spaces between thorny ball-shaped shrubs but there did not seem to be anywhere to flee.

Deciding to make her escape, Lenna allowed her body to slither from the saddle. She landed two feet in the hot sand and lingered by her horse as she watched to see if the trolls had noticed her movement. She held her breath a moment and swallowed hard feeling an ache in her dry throat. Then without further hesitation she ran with speed, in absolute silence, back up the track in an attempt to gain her freedom.

Despite the heat and sweat that poured from her brow, she ran as fast as her legs would carry her. Every now and then hot red sand poured into her thin, strappy shoes, burning her feet and toes. Regardless of the pain she felt however, she had managed to push on and keep moving at a good pace, taking herself further from her assailants with every burning step.

It was a long time before either of the pig-faced trolls had even noticed her missing, however it did not take them long to catch up to her on horseback once they had realised she was gone.

She cried in pain and fear when they bounded up to her and blocked her with their horses. She was breathless and tired and the hot sun not only beat down upon her from above but also reflected off the sand, sapping any leftover energy she had.

Lenna stood, wanting to run but realising that it was futile. There was nowhere to go and the heavy trolls being on horseback were at a huge advantage.

'You enjoy travelling by foot so much, let us oblige you,' one of the rough trolls roared with a laugh.

Now, hours later, Lenna walked along the beaten track, with feet burning and blistering in the hot red sand, her hands bound together in front of her. A troll on horseback held the rope, pulling her onward. Every now and then he called things down to the elf to torment and upset her.

Lenna tripped over her feet as she struggled to keep up the pace. The heartless troll jeered and tugged the rope hard, forcing her to rise to her feet. The pain in her wrists was almost unbearable and she winced as she stood, but she continued on with pride.

Chapter

XXXV

It had been a simple meal - a few forest berries mixed with herbs, some potatoes and roasted squirrel doused in honey; nothing like the cooking in Tebelligan which was rich, flavoursome and very elaborate. The meal seemed to be a mixture of whatever was available at the time but it was tasty and very filling. Afeclin felt so full afterwards that he just wanted to rest.

'Why don't we adjourn to the living room. It is much more comfortable there,' croaked the old man.

'Sure,' said Afeclin with a yawn.

It occurred to Afeclin that he had not even asked the old man his name. He had been meaning to ask the man many questions over dinner but had been so famished that he had dived into his food and almost hadn't come up for air. Now he felt embarrassed as he sat down in a large velvet easy-chair in the front room of the cottage.

'Thank you for your hospitality,' he said with a sheepish grin, 'I cannot believe I do not even know your name.'

'My name is Daubin,' the man said with half a smile.

'And mine is Afeclin.'

'Ah-ha… like the Goddess.' The old man raised an eyebrow.

'Yeah, like the Goddess.'

'Well, Afeclin, I am sorry that I can't offer you some spirits but you see I don't drink,' said Daubin.

'Oh that's quite alright.'

The older man walked out the room only to return a little later with a small tray carrying two silver mugs.

'Perhaps you would like to try a herbal brew instead… my own concoction,' Daubin suggested holding out the tray to Afeclin.

'Thank you,' Afeclin said with politeness as he took a steaming mug from the tray.

Sniffing the hot liquid first he put the silver mug to his lips and took a small sip. The flavour was like nothing he had ever tasted before. It was sweet and it was bitter all at once and the heated brew warmed his belly.

'It is very good.'

'Well, it is also very good for you,' Daubin said as he too took hold of a cup of the hot brew and sat down on another soft velvet chair facing Afeclin. 'I don't suppose you have reconsidered my offer, have you?'

'No, I haven't… I just would not feel right about it,' Afeclin answered taking another sip of the boiling brew with care so that he did not burn his tongue.

'I expected as much.'

There was silence between them and Afeclin decided that now was as good a time as any to enquire about the castle.

'How is it that you live directly in front of the castle? Have you always lived here?'

Daubin sighed and then took a long thoughtful sip of his drink. The old man appeared to be considering the question.

'I was in the employ of your wizard,' he answered with a serious air, 'no one could ever see the great Zallucien without first seeing me.'

'Oh!' Afeclin sucked in his breath, gaining a new respect for the old man.

'Yes,' Daubin continued ignoring Afeclin's added interest, 'I was the third gate to the mighty Lawry Castle.'

'What do you mean third gate?' Afeclin asked. 'And what about the other gates?'

'Well you must have come through the other two.'

'I did not see any gates.'

'That is because they are not gates in the physical sense just as I am not a gate as such,' the old man snapped with a gruff cough. Sitting back in his seat he readjusted his robes and continued speaking, 'No, they are gates in a different sense. The first gate is the entrance which changes all the time and is almost impossible to find if you are looking for it... you obviously stumbled across it... accidentally.'

'The friend of mine whom I was travelling with told me that you only find the entrance if you are meant to,' interrupted Afeclin.

'What a lot of hoohaa,' Daubin said with insult. 'Why would you be meant to find the entrance to the castle if it is destroyed and the wizard no longer alive?'

Daubin has a point. It was something that Afeclin had been wondering about all evening... *Why was I meant to come here? Was there a reason for it or was it just dumb luck?* After giving it more thought he had an answer for the old man.

'Perhaps I was meant to come here and learn for myself what had happened.'

The old man looked almost impressed but his reply did not reflect what was going on inside of his head.

'Perhaps.'

'So what about the second gate?' Afeclin asked.

Daubin's spectacles had begun to fog up from the heat of his drink. He bowed his head and removed the glasses. Using a piece of cloth that was sitting on a little table beside him he cleaned the lenses, taking great care not to touch the glass with his fingers and then without ever looking up at Afeclin placed them back on his nose.

'The second gate is the trees,' Daubin continued, 'you may have noticed them talking to you on the way here.'

'Yes, I thought I was hearing things.'

'Oh I can assure you that you were hearing things alright,' the old man went on, 'they were whispering to you were they not? Telling you to leave or face certain doom?'

'Something like that.'

'The whispers are relentless and cold; they seep through to your soul and freeze your body from within, to the point where it is almost impossible to push on. You found the courage to continue... many do not, many turn back and never return.'

'And you are the third gate,' said Afeclin, adding with cheek, 'the dotty old man who makes you feel as if you are completely lost and probably sends you on a wild goose chase so that you really do lose yourself.'

Daubin took another mouthful of drink and then rested his mug on the table beside him.

'Something like that,' he said imitating Afeclin with a smirk as he again bowed his head and cleaned his spectacles that had fogged up once more.

There was something very strange about the way he did it. The way he kept his head bowed and did not look up until his glasses were back on his face.

'What is with the spectacles,' Afeclin dared to ask.

Daubin put the frames back on his nose and then looking at Afeclin answered, 'Blind as a mole. I cannot see a thing without them... I mean seriously you do not get to be as old as I am and retain the blessings of perfect sight.'

'I have never seen blue lenses before. Is that common in this part of Titania?'

'Actually it was quite by accident,' the old man said sitting forward with a little giggle. 'I was crossing over Blue-Stone Creek one day when I happened to look down into the water at the blue fish swimming around and wouldn't you know it my glasses fell right off my face. When I finally fished them out with a stick, they were blue.'

'The water made them blue?'

'Yes, it is the only creek in the world that can do that... but anything that touches the water, anything at all... will turn blue.'

Daubin sat back in his chair once again and relaxed. The room fell silent.

Afeclin looked around at the small room. Behind Afeclin's chair was a large window that was now covered by heavy red velvet drapes. In the corner of the room stood a tall lamp that was lit and had a brilliant glow providing the room with plenty of light. After all the darkness of the previous night the lamp was very comforting.

There was not a lot of furniture in the room apart from the two large chairs and the table.

There was a small trunk to one side of the room and a crimson red rug that covered the floor. The real feature in the room however was the walls, which were covered from floor to ceiling in paintings of varying sizes. Some depicted people, some were landscapes and some Afeclin could not understand at all but liked them just the same. Each of them was a work of art, painted with lots of colour and detail.

One painting caught his eye in particular. It was of two elderly men with long grey beards. The taller man had an arm around the shorter man and the two looked like great friends. The shorter man looked very happy with a wide smile, which showed his two front teeth were missing. Despite a strange expression his eyes looked kind and intelligent.

The taller man was smiling too but his expression was more of a knowing one.

Afeclin supposed that one of the two men were Daubin but he didn't know which. The picture seemed like it was painted a long time ago. They both had hair on their heads and looked a little younger. Of course Daubin did not have teeth missing, which made Afeclin think that perhaps the taller one must have been him, but having never seen the old man's eyes left Afeclin wondering.

He asked the question, 'Is one of the men in that painting you?'

Daubin turned in his seat to look at the painting, 'Yes, yes that is me.'

'So you must be the taller man?' asked Afeclin.

'Actually I am the shorter one believe it or not,' the old man answered with a sigh.

'Oh you are?' said Afeclin with surprise. Then he added with delicate tact, 'But the teeth? You have all your teeth I see.'

'Yes, well that is true. You see that picture was painted before Zallucien fashioned me a pair of teeth to wear,' said the old man with a self-conscious bow.

'Oh I see,' said Afeclin with apology then he turned his attention to the other man in the picture, 'so who is the other man in the painting?'

Daubin let a little smile spread his lips, 'That my dear is your beloved wizard.'

'Zallucien?' Afeclin said getting to his feet to have a closer look at the painting.

All his life Afeclin had wondered what the great Zallucien looked like and now here he was, depicted in colour and alive in paint.

'You must have been very good friends,' suggested Afeclin as he returned to his seat.

'Ahhh that we were.'

'Whatever happened to him Daubin?' Afeclin asked in a hushed voice.

'That was a long time ago,' the old man said with a sorrowful sigh as he also looked at the painting, 'nearly twenty years ago.'

Afeclin did not want to beg the old man for information so he sat in silence, scratching at the dry mud in his hair while he waited in patience.

Minutes passed and not a word was spoken between them.

When Daubin did start to speak it was with a quiet whispering, as if what he was about to say was so delicate and so secret that even the walls themselves were forbidden to hear.

'He had an apprentice by which name... oh, I shouldn't speak his name.' He put his fingers to his mouth as if to prevent the name from escaping his lips. 'This young man had great talent. He was very fluid in his art and he worked hard and improved greatly day by day. Zallucien was very proud of him and claimed that he was the best he had ever seen.' He paused and pursed his lips together as if attempting to hold back any emotion that he was feeling. 'Years went by and the young wizard became reckless. Dabbling in things that he shouldn't, opening up books of dark magic that were best left unread and meeting in secret with undesirables. Over time it got progressively worse and Zallucien was beyond knowing what to do about the uncontrollable wizard.

Fed up with the young student's arrogance and disobedience he finally refused to teach the young wizard anymore or allow him access to his books. It was hard for him as he was very fond of the boy and had seen his potential for good. Unfortunately, evil was overshadowing all that the young wizard did and Zallucien was unable to ignore it any longer. He could not, in good conscience, continue to train him when his student took what he learnt and used it for dark purposes. The young wizard was furious and left hastily but not before causing a monstrous explosion that blew up the entire building, destroying everything and killing my dear friend.'

'It was lucky that it did not take you,' Afeclin suggested.

'Yes,' Daubin said with uncertainty, 'I was blessed to survive... but what of that? I ran into the burning building, found Zallucien and managed to carry him out but it was too late for him. Too much smoke had seeped into his lungs and he could not recover. There was nothing I could do.'

'I am sorry.'

'Why? You didn't have anything to do with it. Or did you?' the old man wheezed in a sudden irrational tone.

'Considering I would have been only a couple of years old at the time it is highly unlikely,' said Afeclin with renewed calm, hoping not to get the old man riled up again.

'Yes, well I suppose...' Daubin started with a shrewd scowl.

'I only meant that I am sorry for your loss. It must have been hard and awfully lonely all these years.'

'Well, I appreciate you saying so,' Daubin replied returning to his milder manner. 'I do miss my friend and I have been living alone for so many years now that I am afraid I am not very good with company... I guess I am a little suspicious of it.'

'I suppose I could understand that,' Afeclin said with sympathy. 'Have you ever considered moving to town or somewhere where there are other people... I mean what purpose do you serve staying here?'

'This is my home, I cannot leave it,' Daubin answered shaking his head.

'But there is nothing for you here now.'

'Perhaps not but I am more of a loner anyway,' the old man said with a shrug of his shoulders, 'besides loneliness isn't so bad.'

Afeclin felt sad for the old man and began to understand his peculiar nature. *Being alone for close to twenty years would certainly make you strange to other people. You might even forget how to act around others. The more time spent alone the more uncomfortable and odd it would feel in the company of others.* Afeclin had felt that discomfort since being in the old man's presence. Now he understood why.

'There is something I do not understand though,' said Afeclin changing the subject to address something that had been bothering him about Daubin's story. 'I thought I read that Zallucien had the ability to see good or bad in people. If so, how did he not see that this wizard that you speak of was evil from the beginning?'

The old man seemed to be taken aback by the question and took a moment to gather his thoughts and respond.

'Yes, well to explain, every wizard is born with a gift... or ability you might say. Zallucien has the ability to see a person's aura. Everybody and everything emits an aura. It is a light or glow emanating around all things that have a life force. Zallucien could determine whether a person was a friend or enemy depending on the colour and size of their aura. Most people have a yellow or green aura that indicates they are generally good-natured. Some people have a blue or purple aura and that is indicative of exceptionally good and extremely trustworthy people. Then there is white, reflecting absolute purity, but only the gods are that pure. On the other end of the scale there is black, which is pure evil, brown which is evil and red which would be the mark of a very bad person. Orange is in-between and a person with this colour aura could be good with bad tendencies or bad with good tendencies. There are a lot of people who have an orange aura. It doesn't always mean much. I mean, a person with an orange aura could grow and change and become almost pure for instance.'

'So a person with an orange aura could also become very evil,' said Afeclin with a wry smile.

'Well,' coughed the old man, 'yes… yes they can.'

'And this… no name wizard had an orange aura?'

'Yes, yes he did.'

'Is that normal for a wizard to take on an apprentice who had an orange aura? I mean isn't that a bit of a risk when you are teaching him an art that can be lethal in the wrong hands?'

'You are right in what you are saying. It isn't normal; in fact most wizards would not choose to teach anyone who did not at least have a blue aura. Zallucien was often requested to interpret the auras of hopeful wizards,' answered Daubin with a sad look.

'Then why would Zallucien of all people choose to train…'

'I know what you are trying to say,' interrupted Daubin with a scowl, 'Zallucien strongly believed in this wizard's ability and felt deep down that he was good. He believed the young apprentice needed to be taught by someone who was not evil for him to have any chance. Zallucien didn't want this young man with amazing talent to end up being trained by the only person who would take him, Zarome.'

'Zarome is Zallucien's evil twin brother is he not?' asked Afeclin remembering something else he had read.

'Yes, you certainly know a lot about your wizard,' sighed Daubin. 'Zallucien knew that if Zarome got his claws into the young man that he would surely turn to the side of evil but on the other hand, if he was to train him himself he would maybe become a great force for good.'

'Well that is understandable, I guess,' said Afeclin considering.

'Don't be so naïve!' growled the old man, changing his temperament yet again. 'It was stupid, reckless and it killed him. I told him not to teach the boy but he didn't listen. Now, that dark sage is out there and the last I heard he was in alliance with the warlord Moorlan. The two of them are cooking up something. I fear that another war could be imminent.'

Daubin's hands shook and his lips quivered. He had once again become that crazy old man Afeclin had met when he first arrived. It was like he had two personalities. One that was intelligent, full of the wisdom of his years, in particular those spent with Zallucien, and one that was given to bouts of peculiar rantings.

The room went silent as the two sat, with eyes wandering around the room, not knowing what to say after Daubin's brazen outburst.

Afeclin found himself playing with the rock around his neck.

'Why are you so interested in this rock?' Afeclin dared ask, breaking the silence as he pulled the leather holding the rock up from under his shirt. 'And don't tell me you're a rock collector because I know you know something about it.'

The man sat in silence. Leaning back in his chair with elbows on the armrests, he clasped his long slender hands under his chin.

'It is a moonrock,' he said with a simple grunt.

'A moonrock,' Afeclin repeated, puzzled, 'as in, from the moon?'

'Yes, the blue moon, Glendell.'

Afeclin sat stunned for a moment looking at the rock in his fingers. 'So how did a rock from the moon get here? Did it break off and fall to Titania?'

'Of course pieces of rock do fall from the moons from time to time and land here, yes... but they are dead pieces of rock and certainly do not light up like that piece in your hand does,' Daubin said with a renewed air of intelligence.

'So what about this piece? Why is it alive?' asked Afeclin staring with fascination at the rock.

'That piece did not fall, it did not accidentally come to be here... it was brought here.'

'From the moon?'

'Yes.'

'What? You mean someone went to the moon, took this rock and brought it back to Titania?' asked Afeclin with an incredulous shake of the head.

'Not just anyone...' Daubin hesitated, 'a god.'

'A god?' Afeclin repeated, the words falling out of his mouth. 'But then how did I come to have it?'

'Well now, that is an interesting question,' the old man answered leaning forward for emphasis. 'How did you come to have it? They are only given by the gods themselves in very rare and special circumstances. So either you found it accidentally, you killed someone for it or you are someone tremendously special and of great importance to the gods.'

'I don't know about that,' Afeclin mumbled with an unpretentious air, 'but I was found as a baby with it hanging over my crib in a village that had been destroyed. I was the only survivor.'

'Very interesting,' Daubin said mulling over the information.

Afeclin went on to tell the old man what Endorph had said only nights before about the rock and how it came to be in the King's pocession after it had been left in the village ruins.

'That is very interesting,' Daubin repeated staring at Afeclin in curiosity.

'I had been thinking it was a wizard who had brought the rock to my father because I had learnt something about how wizards can send secret messages to people with their minds...'

'Yes, it is called mind transference.'

'Of course, that's it. Anyway I assumed it was a wizard but are you telling me it could have been a god? That thought never occurred to me.'

'I can't say either way since I wasn't there... but... I do think that it is more likely that it was a god than a wizard. I have never heard of a wizard giving away a perfectly good moonrock. Especially to a baby!' said Daubin, his shrewd eyes peering into Afeclin's. 'No, I think it would be someone who knew your full potential. There would be a good reason why you were saved as a baby. It was not just chance.'

'I wonder which god,' marvelled Afeclin.

The old man shrugged. 'The trouble is it could have been any of them... even Hazifer.'

'I was afraid you would say that, but how will I ever know for sure?'

Daubin shrugged his shoulders again, 'You won't... not until he, or she chooses to reveal himself to you but I shouldn't worry too much... with a name like Afeclin I would think the Goddess has had a hand in this.'

The old man's words made Afeclin feel better. He sat back further into the big soft chair and yawned. He had forgotten how tired he was. Afeclin felt as if he could fall asleep there and then but he was aware that he needed to move out to the ruins where he had planned to spend the night. The thought of leaving the comfortable chair however was enough for Afeclin to force his eyes open a little longer.

'Would people actually kill for the rock?'

Daubin had a stern look on his face as he answered, 'If someone knows what it is, yes they may try to kill you for it. The rock contains many powers that if in the hands of the wrong person could become a deadly weapon. You must never let anyone touch it or even see it... if they don't know you have it they won't bother you. If they do find out you have it and they want it, do not give it to them, even if threatened. They can't take it from you without injuring themselves... having said that... if they kill you... the rock goes cold and then they can take it.'

'So what you are telling me is to guard it with my life?'

'Yes, yes indeed.'

252

'Huh,' said Afeclin wondering whether he was up to such a task. Then he asked yawning loudly, 'What kind of powers does it have?'

'I don't know myself, that will be something that you will have to learn for yourself.'

'I wonder if this rock is the reason why there are weasels searching for me,' Afeclin said more to himself than Daubin.

'There are weasels looking for you?'

'Yes, apparently. I have no idea why; after all I have not made any enemies. I have some kind of bounty on my head, I guess. Maybe it has something to do with the moonrock?'

'Couldn't say myself, but I would be very careful if I were you, those shemalks are crafty people and they will use whatever means they can to get to you. If it is the moonrock they are ultimately after, they will do whatever it takes to get it,' said Daubin with a grave look. 'You must take great care once you leave the woods of Lawry Castle tomorrow. Do not take anything for granted.'

'I will be careful, I just hope they haven't caught up with my friends.'

'Hmm, that would not be good,' Daubin said with a stern look.

'No, it wouldn't. It worries me.' By now Afeclin felt so tired that his eyes just shut by themselves. 'Thank you for dinner,' he said with an exhausted yawn and then added mumbling, 'but I really must go and re…'

Afeclin gave in to his drowsiness and drifted off into a deep sleep.

Chapter

XXXVI

Wolflang woke to find himself on a hard bed in a tiny stone room.

Looking around the room he tried to recall how he had come to be there. He attempted to sit up but his head ached an awful amount and he had to lie down again.

The room was very bare. It had a hard cement floor with a bucket in one corner. High in a big wooden door was a small window that had vertical iron bars inserted into it. On the opposite side of the room was another little window that appeared to go to the outside. This window also had built-in bars and was again high in the wall.

How long have I been asleep?

Wolflang rubbed his temples with his fingers trying to rid himself of the pain in his head while he attempted to make some sense of his situation. It was then that certain memories came flooding back to him.

He remembered drinking at the bar and then seeing Typhin riding a ridiculous black sheep. He recalled his anger at Typhin and remembered hitting him. He also recollected two burley men annoying him and then... nothing, blackness.

So how did I get here?

He looked around the tiny room again. *What a strange place this is.* It was not the room that he had paid for at the inn with Pit and Eliah. He couldn't imagine why he would choose to sleep in such a hovel. It was neither nice nor comfortable. He wished he could remember something more.

Dragging himself to his feet, he walked over to the door and tried to open it. The door had no handle however, and appeared to be locked.

'What kind of place is this?' he whispered to himself. 'How does one open the door?'

He looked up at the hole with the bars in the top of the door. Standing on tiptoes he tried to see out but he was too short and the window was just too high for him to reach.

He looked around the room for something to stand on. The bed was the right height but appeared to be attached to the wall with big metal bolts. Then he spied the wooden bucket. He picked it up and looked inside. It was empty but black with filth and had a foul stench to it. He turned it upside down against the door and stood on top.

Looking through the bars he could see a small corridor that opened up to an undersized room where there was a large man seated at a wooden counter. The man had untidy black hair and a long dark moustache. He wore a somewhat familiar maroon uniform with emblems on it and tall leather boots that were muddied to the ankle. He had his head down in an industrious manner and appeared to be writing with a feather quill.

'Hey you there!' Wolflang called through the bars.

The man turned his head in part toward Wolflang's room then put his head down again and continued what he was doing.

Wolflang tried again, 'Excuse me! I'm not sure how to open the door to my room. Can you help me?'

This time the man stared at Wolflang a moment before letting out a roar of laughter.

'Well, I'm glad you find it so amusing,' said the elf with embarrassment, 'but... you see... I don't remember coming here so I don't know why I am here or... where I am for that matter. So if you will just help me open the door I can go.'

This seemed to make the man laugh even harder. Wolflang grew frustrated.

When the man stopped chortling, he responded in a flat voice, 'Prison doors are not made to be opened from the inside, they are made to keep people in.'

'Oh,' said Wolflang with a sigh, then shook his head as it dawned on him what had been said. 'Wait... I'm in a prison?'

The man in uniform nodded his head as he burst into laughter again. Turning himself in his chair he returned to what he had been doing, his body continued to convulse as he chuckled.

Wolflang frowned. He had heard of prisons before but he had never seen one and knew very little about them.

The elves did not imprison people in Tebelligan therefore prisons were nonexistent there. Endorf had no tolerance for crime but had such a great love for his people that when wayward elves were brought before his court he would send them to work underground in one of the many mines that existed around Tebelligan. A few months of hard work underground straightened them out more often than not.

There was not much crime in Tebelligan. Elves being a peace-loving people tended not to cause trouble to their neighbours. So crimes were never very serious and were dealt with in a swift manner.

There had only been one time Wolflang could recall that a serious crime had to be dealt with by the king. That particular elf had been referred to as 'killer' to which Endorf with a heavy heart had pronounced a penalty of death.

Despite being five years of age, Wolflang could still remember standing on a beach with his father in a crowd of elves. He remembered watching as one old elf, with hands tied in front of him, was escorted down the pier to a boat, his teary wife following, comforted by friends. A larger man carrying a heavy boulder trailed behind them.

Endorf had given some kind of small address to the people. Included in the speech was a reading of the elf's crimes. He had concluded with an announcement of his punishment, which was to be death by drowning. The boat then floated away for the retribution to be administered offshore in a private manner. The crowd, satisfied, dispersed and returned to their homes.

'Umm... why am I in prison?' asked Wolflang stirring from his thoughts.

The man seated at the desk seemed to be a prison guard. Leaning back in his chair, the man sighed. He placed a cigar in his mouth and lit it with a small oil lamp that had been sitting on the desk adding extra light to the windowless room. After a quick puff he stood up. Having adjusted his pants first, he then rummaged through some parchments on the desk and after finding what he was looking for, the large man walked toward the cell where Wolflang had been detained.

'Disturbing the peace, drunk and disorderly behaviour, striking another person and failing to stop for authorities,' the guard said reading from the parchment he held in his hand.

'What is that?'

'That is the report of your crimes of this evening and the reason you are in that cell,' the large man stated. 'Any questions?'

'Yes, how do I get out of here?'

The guard took another puff of his cigar as he raised his eyebrows. 'Well you don't. Lord Xerlais the Judge Supreme will come and visit the prison and decide whether you should be further punished or exonerated. Until then you are stuck here.'

'Well, when do you expect him? How long before he comes?' asked Wolflang fearing that he might have to stay in the prison for a couple of days.

'Well, he's out of town at the moment but don't worry I expect him back either next month or the month after,' the guard said sucking on his cigar.

'Next month or the month after? Are you joking? I have to stay here all that time?'

'Hey, don't worry,' the hefty guard said almost laughing again, 'the good thing for you is that after spending so much time in prison he is bound to free you without need for further punishment. Let me tell you prison is a breeze compared to some of the punishments I've seen him dish out.'

'Somehow I don't feel any better,' said Wolflang with despair.

The guard sniffed the air and let out a little sigh. 'Well, they don't put people in prison to make them feel better,' he said readjusting his pants again. Then he walked back to the desk and sat down puffing on his cigar.

Wolflang jumped down off the bucket and looked around him. He couldn't imagine being stuck within the four walls of the prison cell for any period of time. However, there didn't seem to be any way to escape the confined space.

Picking up the wooden bucket again, Wolflang placed it under the window on the other side of the cell. Standing on it once more he attempted to look out.

It was a little higher than the other window but the elf managed to get his eyes above the ridge just enough to see.

The pavement of the street outside was level with the window, which meant that the prison cell was, to a degree, underground. In fact if it were not for the bars preventing him from escape, he could have climbed up out of the cell onto the street.

Outside it was beginning to get dark. Wolflang could see a man in the distance with a long rod lighting the street lamps. Very few people were out and about. Wolflang figured that it must have been close to midnight.

Studying the iron bars in front of him, Wolflang tried to wobble them to see if any were loose. As he expected, they were as solid as could be.

He looked back at the small cell. It had become quite dark inside. He let out a yawn and decided that perhaps it would be best to try and get a good night's sleep. It occurred to him that he had not had much sleep since he left Tebelligan days earlier. He also feared being awake when the darkness set in. He did not want to remember the events of the previous night and was concerned about the feelings the darkness might evoke. With that thought in mind he lay down on the bunk and closed his eyes. In the morning he would try to figure out what to do about the mess he was in… if there was, in fact anything he could do.

Chapter

XXXVII

Afeclin was awoken by the sound of a loud knocking at the front door. Rousing himself enough to stand he looked around the room. He was alone in the small sitting room but he had the feeling he was alone in the whole house.

The knock came again, this time seemed more desperate.

Perhaps it was Daubin, thought Afeclin as he found his way in the darkness to the front door of the cottage.

Afeclin opened the door with a yawn, his eyes still half closed.

There was something very large towering over him. It was both tall and wide and its skin had a golden hue. Afeclin rubbed his eyes in disbelief. Then looking again he realised that it wasn't his imagination at all. A large, golden dragon stood before him in the clearing at the front of the cottage. She was without a doubt as big as the house, with

259

beautiful round eyes, a long neck and large white teeth. Afeclin thought that perhaps he should feel afraid but for some reason felt quite at ease with the beast.

The dragon roared and growled as if she were trying to tell him something important. The strange thing was that for some reason Afeclin understood her.

'Come with me,' she seemed to say. 'I know where they are.'

'Wolflang?' he asked hoping that the dragon would also understand him.

The dragon nodded and answered, 'Him as well.'

'Will you take me to him?' asked Afeclin feeling a little excitement brewing from within.

'Of course,' she said nodding her large head as she extended a long clawed limb to Afeclin.

Hesitating for only a moment, he climbed up the beast's arm and onto her back with skill.

Afeclin could not explain how he knew so much about dragons or why he was so comfortable with the large beast but he was. He sat down on the dragon's back and held onto two of the sharp spikes that stuck out at the base of the animal's neck.

The dragon turned herself around and started to flap her impressive golden wings as she began to run with large clawed feet along the ground.

Within seconds they were in the sky, flying high above the trees. The wind blew through his hair and tousled it back over his shoulders. It seemed to be a little harder to breathe at this altitude, not to mention chilly but the feeling of flying was magnificent. It was like nothing he had ever felt before. His adrenalin surged as his heart beat faster. He felt invincible and strong like he was untouchable from such a height.

They flew low over the water where they were almost hit by the tail of a mammoth whale. The dragon had to pull up all of a sudden to avoid hitting the monstrous seacreature. They flew over masses of trees as if they were one of the birds and over a large sleepy desert, coming to rest at the foot of an enormous mountain.

'Where are we?' questioned Afeclin after they had come to a complete stop.

The dragon once again roared and growled in the back of her throat.

This was the place where they were to meet his friends.

Afeclin looked around about but he did not see anyone.

There was a cluster of trees behind where they had landed between the desert and the mountain. The trees were clumped together in tight formation and it was hard to see very far in, kind of like an undersized woods. The mountain itself was rocky, steep and void of any vegetation besides a few small trees here and there.

The place seemed to be deserted.

Then he heard noises coming from inside the woods.

'Afeclin!' he heard a voice shout.

The voice was familiar to him, but he couldn't place it. It was a woman's voice and she called in desperation to him. Staring intently into the woods he tried to figure out who she was.

An attractive woman appeared from the trees. Afeclin gaped in disbelief.

'Lenna?' he asked staring at her.

'Afeclin!' she called as she ran toward him with arms stretched wide. 'Oh my love I'm so glad you're here!'

Lenna reached Afeclin with speed and throwing her arms around his neck, she kissed him with heated passion.

Afeclin could not believe how she came to be kissing him but was not afraid to kiss her back. For as long as he could remember he had wondered how it would feel to kiss her soft lips and now here he was and it felt good.

Pulling herself away from him but keeping the embrace, Lenna cried in his arms. It was obvious she was trying to tell him something but was having a hard time getting the words out through all the tears.

'P...p...please... forgive... me. I... am... just so... s...s...sorry,' she managed to say, 'I do... l...l...love you... Afeclin.'

She took a deep breath as she tried hard to control her emotions, 'I... love you more than... life itself!'

Afeclin could not believe what he was hearing. Only in his dreams had she ever said anything to him like that. He tried to find the words to comfort her.

'Lenna, there is nothing to be sorry about,' was his awkward reply, 'and you know that ...I ...love you... also, I always have.'

It seemed to cheer her and they kissed once more.

This time as their lips touched Afeclin felt something like a knife hit him in the back.

'Urrgh,' he gasped in pain, gripping her arms tight.

'What is it? What is wrong?' Lenna asked, panic-stricken.

'My back... something in my back,' Afeclin muttered as he fell forward onto the ground.

Lenna could now see what the problem was and she screamed in horror.

'Afeclin, there's an arrow in your back,' she said with fear in her voice.

Afeclin could feel Lenna trembling as she helped him sit up a little and held him tight making sure he would not lie down onto the already penetrating arrow.

Afeclin could feel his mind slipping away and was finding it hard to breathe.

'Help!' Lenna called frantically.

Afeclin looked forward towards the woods, the direction the arrow must have come. His eyes began to blur and he blinked them hard to try and see who it was that was coming out of the woods at that moment carrying a bow in his hand.

'Just hold on,' he could hear Lenna saying, 'don't you leave me again! Not this time!'

Afeclin tried to hold on, he squeezed her hand but he was finding it very hard to focus. He tried to concentrate on her face. She had aged a little since he last saw her, if such a thing were possible. She no longer looked like a naïve girl but instead an intelligent woman with years of life experience.

Another face came into view; it was the figure from the woods carrying the bow. Afeclin could not believe his eyes.

'Wolflang?' Afeclin questioned. 'It was you?'

'They're holding Matara in a cave on top of the mountain,' Wolflang seemed to say to Lenna as he put a firm hand upon Afeclin.

Afeclin could not keep his eyes open any longer. He took a big gasp of air and then felt his body go limp.

Chapter

XXXVIII

Lenna had walked beside the troll's horse all the evening and well into the night after it had become dark.

While the red sand no longer burnt her feet as it had cooled after the sun had gone down, they still ached from the scalding they had received earlier in the day. Lenna's hands and wrists continued to hurt from being bound together and from the wounds she had inflicted on herself trying to escape. She had discovered that if she kept up the pace and held her hands in such a way that the rope being held by the troll was loose, she could ease the pain and friction caused by the tight bonds.

Now, late at night, the path before them was lit only by a blue-green haze that emanated from the moons in the sky and saturated the mist that had risen over the desert plains. Lenna could barely see her surroundings but the shadows suggested that the landscape had not changed in the least.

Tired, sore all over and having a tremendous thirst for water Lenna heard something that brought a little comfort to the troubled elf. *Running water!*

She could hear it in the far off distance, somewhere in the beyond darkness, and as they continued moving forward, the sound became louder suggesting that they were moving toward it.

When they made it to the water source, a flowing river in the middle of nothingness, Lenna went to run to the water's edge to take a drink but the troll holding the rope that bound her wrists pulled her back with a sharp and abrupt jerk, sending a surge of pain through her body.

'I just want some water,' she said trying her best not to sound weak.

The troll looked at her in uncertainty, then after some assessment, turned to the other troll.

'What do you think Haizu?'

Haizu looked at Lenna with little pity but seemed to make his own judgement of her and their surroundings. Then with a smirk he gave a directional nod.

The first troll climbed down off his horse and went to Lenna, untying the rope from around her wrists.

'Don't you be trying anything clever,' he said with a low growl, 'it wouldn't be wise.'

Lenna nodded with fatigue.

She ran down to the water's edge and drank with great thirst, cupping the cool water in her hands and putting it to her mouth as soon as she could get it there. After she had drunk enough to quench her dry throat and body she waded into the water to calm her sore, tired and aching feet. She dangled her arms and hands in, washing the dried blood from off her wrists and allowing the water to relieve her blisters.

Despite the darkness the river seemed large and wide.

What if I were to swim away right now? she contemplated letting her body sink a little into the refreshing stream. *I am a strong swimmer and it would not matter where I ended up, downstream or the other side as long as I was free from the trolls.*

As she thought it over in her mind, taking into full consideration the tired state she was in, something in the water swam up and bit her in the leg attaching itself to her.

She shrieked in fear and pain as she ran from the water shaking her leg in desperation trying to loosen the little creature's grasp.

The trolls chuckled. 'I told you it would be unwise to try anything.'

Out of the water she could see the creature that had attached itself to her. It had the shape of a flat-headed fish with large teeth that had bitten through the fabric of Lenna's pants and into her flesh, holding tight to her leg. It had a long tubular tail that had also attached itself to her with strong suction, causing a burning sensation though her body.

'Help me get it off... please!' she begged the trolls between shrill screams and violent shaking.

The two trolls looked at each other laughing at first and then Haizu rushed to his horse and took from the saddlebag a small cloth sack.

The troll carried it over to Lenna who was still screaming and flailing her leg around.

'Just stay still a moment and calm down,' said the troll with aggravation. 'I'm gonna help ya.'

Lenna sat still, clenching her fists and teeth as she tried to control the pain. She watched Haizu as he opened the cloth sack and took out a round metal object, that appeared to be fire steel, and a small square piece of flint.

'What are you going to do? Light a fire?' Lenna screeched through gritted teeth.

The troll nodded as he took a small round empty tin from the sack and a piece of cloth. Placing the cloth inside the tin, he rubbed the steel and flint together and as the flint dropped onto the fabric it took to flame. Haizu then picked up the flaming tin and waved it at the strange creature sucking on Lenna's leg.

The creature let out an ear-piercing squeal, letting go of Lenna and dropping to the ground in a frantic recoil. As the troll held the flame again close to the strange fish, it rolled itself back toward the river with jolted movements, its tubular tail pounding the sand in feverish aggravation.

The glow from the small fire died and Lenna sat on the ground staring up at the two trolls trying to regain her breath.

'What was that?' she managed to ask.

'That was a deadly hervit leech,' was Haizu's short and simple reply as he packed up his tinder sack. 'They inhabit Harlay River from here to the ocean in the south.'

Lenna examined the tooth marks on her leg. Some had cut into the skin while others were just deep indentations. On her stomach where the tubed tail had been attached, there was a round red mark.

'What was that thing doing to me?' she said, her lips quivering as she massaged her aching thigh.

'Why, sucking your blood of course, or at least attempting to,' said the other troll in clear amusement of the situation. 'Had you swam out there, hundreds of those little critters would have had your blood for dinner.'

Lenna's heart almost stopped beating, swimming out there was exactly what she had been considering doing. She could feel her body shudder at the thought of what could have been, if she had made a dash for it before she had been attacked.

That little creature saved my life. She shook her head at the irony of it.

All of a sudden there was a sound from the waters, a ringing of a bell and a distant shout.

'Ahoy there! You the group I have been sent here to collect?' came a far off voice in a small circle of light that appeared to be coming closer to the shore.

Lenna realised what they had come all the way to Harlay River for.

'We are going to cross?' she asked in fear, not wanting to go anywhere near the dreaded waters.

'Yeh, we were told to meet you here... we have the elf,' Haizu yelled back to the boat, taking no notice of Lenna.

'Alright, prepare yourselves for boarding,' came the voice again in reply.

Lenna watched in silence as the light from the boat intensified as it neared the shore.

When the boat made it to the edge of the water, it stopped just shy of the beach.

Lenna had expected something of a bigger vessel judging by the light that had emanated from it, so she was a little surprised by the size of it, a small boat with two tall masts. It had the appearance of a miniature ship.

'This is as far as we can go with 'er,' the same voice called out. 'This ship has a long keel underneath and it will get stuck if I try to get 'er any closer.'

Lenna's heart went into a panic. She took several steps backward, shaking her head vigourously.

'I am not going to go back in that water,' she said with defiance.

'You will be going in if I sez you're going in,' said one of the trolls with an impatient growl.

'But I will be eaten alive!' she squealed with insanity. 'There is blood dripping down my leg, won't they be attracted to that?'

'She's got a point, Brackin,' said Haizu eyeing the wounds. 'If she walks into that water, those leeches are going to not only be upon her but us also.'

Brackin's pig face seemed to pale in colour as he mulled over the situation.

'We'll just have to carry her then,' he said picking her up from the ground and slinging her over his shoulder like a rag doll. This time Lenna did not fight or fuss, she just stayed still.

'Come on, let's get going then,' Haizu growled with urgency. 'The elf is expected on the other side, and as it is we might just make it there by daybreak.'

Haizu took the lead. After taking his saddlebag with him, he waded though the water with speed and climbed up into the boat in safety.

It was then Brackin's turn. He readjusted Lenna on his shoulder and then after a brief hesitation waded through the cool water with the elf.

At first there seemed to be no trouble and the troll focused his attention on getting to the boat. Then all a sudden he stopped.

'What are you doing, ya fool, keep moving,' Haizu yelled from the boat.

'I felt something brush past my leg,' said Brackin as he turned on the spot, watching the dark water with intense fear.

'Keep moving!' Haizu's voice came again.

Keep moving, please keep moving, Lenna repeated over and over again in her mind, keeping her eyes closed in fear of looking down and seeing the boney spine of the flat-headed leech poking out of the water.

Brackin started moving again but quickened his pace, dragging his legs through the water that was now at his middle.

'Ahhhh,' the troll groaned in pain, 'one's got me!'

'Just keep moving, Brackin, we'll get it off you when you get in the boat.'

Lenna held tight to the troll's shoulder as he made his body shudder, trying to shake off the creature.

Please don't drop me! Lenna thought, terrified of being thrown into the brink.

'Ow! Another one Haizu!' Brackin called out, continuing to take small shuffled steps towards the boat.

'Look at me, Brackin, you're nearly there.'

'I can't! There's another one attached to my stomach.'

Lenna dared open her eyes and could not believe what she saw. They were surrounded by dozens of the creatures, flopping their tails in the water, taunting them as they circled.

Looking behind, she was grateful to see that they had almost made it to the boat.

If only he will make it.

Within another moment, a leech attached itself to Brackin's back, the troll howled in pain.

'Pass the elf up,' yelled Haizu when they were close enough, 'then we can get you aboard.'

Brackin held Lenna up in his strong arms, allowing Haizu to take her and get her safely inside the vessel before turning his attention back to the other troll.

'Hey, we can't be putting him in the boat with that many hervits attached to him. Do you want them all over us?' said the captain of the vessel, holding the troll's arm and speaking in a quiet and serious tone.

The troll nodded his understanding.

Lenna sat watching, speechless by the brazen attitude of Haizu who agreed to get the boat moving.

A shout came from the side of the boat. 'Hey help me up!'

Haizu leaned over the edge and made a gesture by raising two fingers to his head and then waving them away as if to say farewell.

'Hey! Don't you leave me!' came the angry yet terrified reply.

Haizu turned his back on the troll in the water as the vessel began to turn and head back the way it had come.

'Don't you leave me here Haizu!'

The shout was followed by a muffled scream and the sound of much splashing about. Haizu did not look back as the troll was being drained of his blood and before long the splashing stopped and the waters became quiet and still again.

Lenna crouched with her back up against one of the high sides of the boat and sat in silence, still watching the small three-man crew work to put up the dark sails and get the craft coasting at a good pace across the rushing river waters.

She could see the dark bearded face of the captain who stood at the helm steering the vessel. He had an icy stature, bathed in a green and blue glow from the moons. He had a weathered face that was wrinkled and scarred. His long black hair was greying and matted and he wore what looked to be a black and red uniform that was tattered and old.

Haizu stood at the front of the craft looking up into the starry sky without remorse. While Lenna cared less about what had happened to the other troll after he had tormented her all afternoon, she was a little surprised by Haizu's nonchalant expression. *Doesn't he care at all?* It was hard for her to understand but the evidence was there. He had allowed his companion to be eaten up by leeches without a shudder of regret.

'Blanket miss?' came a voice from above her.

It was one of the crew members holding a grey worn blanket out to her. Lenna took hold of the blanket with gratitude. It was not that she was cold by any means; it was a very warm evening. However, she wrapped herself in the cover and found it comforting to be nestled into the soft wool.

While she knew that she was headed for the other side of the Harlay River, she had no idea what was in store for her beyond that. What she understood was that someone was waiting for her on the other side, expecting her on this very boat, *perhaps the same person who sent Harren to collect me and bring me to the trolls in Rengal.*

She felt little anger anymore; in fact she felt little of anything at all, other than a numbness that filled her soul and a throbbing in her thigh where she had been bitten by the leech. Lenna sat, holding the blanket for support watching the others on the boat. No more thoughts of escape, she had no more energy to try.

Chapter

XXXIX

Afeclin's body jolted him awake as he took a gasp of air.

The smell of food cooking wafted up his nose and tickled his nostrils as he looked around the small room.

It took a few minutes for him to figure out where he was and what he was doing. He was confused and it did not make sense. One minute he was dying at the bottom of a mountain in the arms of the woman he loved, the next minute...

'I'm back,' Afeclin whispered, his eyes resting on the familiar painting of Daubin and Zallucien. Then he breathed a sigh of relief.

'It was all just a dream?'

Afeclin mopped the sweat from his brow with the back of his hand. 'It seemed so real.'

'What seemed real?' questioned a voice from the doorway.

271

Afeclin looked up to see Daubin leaning up against the doorframe with a sharp knife in his hand.

'Oh, this dream I had,' answered Afeclin stretching his arms and his shoulders. There was an aching in his back that made him wince. 'I could have sworn it really happened.'

'How do you know that it didn't? I mean maybe you were sleepwalking,' suggested Daubin.

'I doubt it... I flew on a dragon after speaking its language. I caught up with the girl that I love and I was killed... by my best friend no less,' said Afeclin looking at the knife in Daubin's hand and cringing. 'Can you please get rid of the knife? It is making my back ache.'

Daubin had a strange expression on his face as he looked at the knife and then at Afeclin and scratched his head. 'Al...right then, whatever you say.'

The old man disappeared out of the doorway and Afeclin sighed as he tried to massage his aching back. He was still shaking after the night's dream. It had all felt so real and he could not get the images out of his head; the pained expression on Lenna's face, Wolflang appearing from the woods and shooting him in the back. He wondered what it could mean... if anything.

Daubin reappeared at the door once again.

'I meant to tell you that I have fixed us some breakfast if you are interested in joining me for a bite,' he said, waving the knife around in the air as he spoke.

Afeclin winced once again.

'Oh! So sorry,' the old man said as he hid the knife behind his back. 'Come have something to eat... it will do you good.'

Afeclin agreed to come. He was beginning to feel a little hungry and it was likely to help him get his mind off the dream.

He stood up out of the old comfy chair and stretched his back as much as he could. Looking back at the chair he had slept in all night, he noticed that a spring had broken through the fabric and was positioned right where his back had been leaning. He examined the spring; it was thick and solid and had a pointy bit at the end.

'Well, that at least explains the backache.'

🐾 🐾 🐾

Breakfast was an arrangement of various kinds of bird eggs with swamp rat done in a thick brown sauce.

Afeclin had always thought of rats as vermin. In Tebelligan rats caused so much destruction and illness that the elves had to devise ways to destroy them. Some would drown them. Some would set large cats onto them but the most effective way known was to set up traps of

272

poison. Rats were motivated by food. All the elves had to do was leave a bunch of food scraps laced with venom from deadly orcal ants out overnight and in the morning they had themselves a graveyard of rats. Of course once the rats were poisoned to death you would never consider eating them. They were pests and the elves despised them. No elf would ever consider eating such a vile and hated creature.

For Afeclin the thought of eating rat now was a little off-putting but the way it had been cooked with the thick brown sauce oozing all over, it smelt delicious.

He cut a piece off the rat's hind leg and closed his eyes before placing the bite in his mouth. Afeclin imagined he was eating squirrel again to settle his stomach. To his surprise though, it was good.

'So you had an interesting sleep last night eh?' asked Daubin as he placed a wooden fork full of food into his mouth.

'Hmmm, yes,' Afeclin answered with a full mouth. Swallowing quickly he continued, 'Thank you for allowing me to stay... I had not intended to intrude but I think I just fell asleep.'

'You did indeed... but I didn't have the heart to wake you, you looked as if you hadn't slept in days,' Daubin said with bits of food spitting from his mouth as he spoke.

'Well I haven't had much sleep in the last few days,' said Afeclin trying to rub his achy back once more. 'I guess I'm just not used to it.'

'So what is wrong with your back this morning?' asked Daubin. 'Did you sleep on it funny?'

'You could say that. Actually one of the springs in the chair I slept in broke during the night which made for an uncomfortable and painful sleep.'

'Oh I see,' said Daubin, 'well that certainly does explain things.'

There was quiet for a few minutes as the two continued to eat their breakfast in silence.

As he sat peeling the shell from the bird eggs, Afeclin began to think of his dream again. He saw Lenna's stunning dark brown eyes looking into his with absolute adoration... a look that he had only ever seen directed at Wolflang. Then he remembered the pain of the arrow in his back and seeing Wolflang's face as he approached bow in hand.

'Aaargh,' groaned Afeclin throwing bits of shell down on the plate in irritation, 'I can't get that dream out of my head.'

'Tell me about your dream,' suggested Daubin with interest.

Afeclin related the dream to the old man with perfect clarity.

'Ahh, it was just a dream,' said Daubin when Afeclin had finished. 'It doesn't mean anything.'

'But what if it does? What if it was some kind of premonition?... What if I was seeing how I am to die?'

'It's possible I suppose. Have you ever had any premonitions before?' Daubin asked as he shoved eggshells one by one into his mouth and began munching on them. The crunching sound was irritating and grated on Afeclin's nerves.

Afeclin stared at the old man a moment, trying to ignore the sound coming from his mouth.

'Yes, I have had a premonition once. It was actually on the way here... but it was a little different.'

'Different in what way?'

'Well for a start, I wasn't asleep.'

Afeclin began to tell the aging man all about the premonitions he had about his new friends in the mud the night before last. He continued with recounting the events that had led him to the cottage.

After Afeclin had finished, the room fell silent once again. The old man appeared to be thoughtful as he mopped up the last of the sauce on his plate with a piece of bread and placed it in his mouth in a clumsy fashion.

'Very curious,' Daubin said as wiped the sauce from around his mouth with the back of his hand.

'Yes, it is rather strange,' agreed Afeclin with a nod.

'But you see, you knew the first one was a premonition. This time you're not sure... so perhaps it was just a dream.'

'It felt so real... like the first one,' said Afeclin.

'It may have felt so real because you got hit in the back with a spring,' suggested Daubin scratching his balding head.

Afeclin sighed. 'I thought of that... but I am just not convinced.'

Daubin gave Afeclin a discerning look. Afeclin could tell there was great intelligence beyond the opaque blue lenses that covered the old man's eyes. It made him wonder.

'At any rate if it wasn't a premonition you have nothing to worry about, but if it was a premonition consider yourself lucky,' Daubin said interrupting Afeclin from his thoughts. 'You can prepare yourself for that moment in time where you meet your doom... and when that day comes you can do one of two things...'

'And what is that?'

'Say goodbye to your loved ones first or when the moment arrives... duck.'

'You can do that? I mean you can change the outcome of events to come?'

'Well, why not, it's not history… it hasn't happened yet. So why wouldn't you be able to stop it from happening by changing something you do?'

'I suppose you're right,' said Afeclin feeling somewhat cheered.

⁊ ⁊ ⁊

After breakfast Afeclin helped Daubin with the cleaning up.

Having spent some time with him, Afeclin felt the old man did not seem so strange anymore. When he had first arrived, he thought that Daubin was a dotty old man who had lost all sense years ago. Now he could see that Daubin was kindly and much more intelligent than he made out to be. His years of experience with Zallucien were invaluable and Afeclin felt sure Daubin knew much more about things than he let on.

The problem now is where to go from here.

Afeclin needed to find someone to train him but he didn't know of any other wizards or where to find them.

Perhaps Daubin will know.

He decided to ask.

'I thank you for your hospitality Daubin. You have been more than kind. I suppose I really should be going.' He paused for a moment, 'But I wondered if you knew where I could find someone else to train me. I am very serious about learning the art but the only wizard I knew of was Zallucien.'

The old man looked at Afeclin in curiosity while he scratched his hairy chin. He opened his mouth as if to say something but didn't. Instead he paused and thought for a moment and then waving a slender finger in the air said, 'I happen to know that the wizard Crymonthon lives on the southernmost side of the North Island within the Swamps of Basca.'

'Oh really?' Afeclin said feeling a little hope returning.

'He is an idiot of course,' said Daubin making a dismissive gesture by waving a hand in the air, 'but he knows his stuff. He will be able to teach you well, I think.'

The older man did not seem so sure. Afeclin could feel the little piece of hope he had slipping away. He now felt that he would have a better chance of learning the art if Daubin were to teach him.

An idea came to his mind but then left as sudden as it had come, leaving Afeclin grasping for the lost thought but unable to retrieve it from his mind.

How strange.

'I have a map… I think, for the island,' said Daubin all of a sudden interrupting Afeclin's thoughts again.

275

The old man ran from the room, returning moments later with a large rolled up leather parchment.

He unrolled it in a hasty and careless manner.

'Here,' he said, putting a long slender finger on the map, 'is his castle. It is not as protected as Lawry but you will need to know certain things.'

Afeclin studied the map, following Daubin's instruction.

'The only way in…,' Daubin continued, 'is this area here. It doesn't appear to be a way in but if you look hard enough you will find it.

Then once you are in you will be presented with three paths that you can take.'

Daubin traced the map with his fingers as he spoke.

'You must follow the peepinco bushes.'

'Peepinco bushes?' questioned Afeclin.

'The fool has a thing for peepinco berries. He likes to grow them everywhere,' said Daubin shaking his head.

'Huh, interesting. Anything else I should know?'

'When you get to the castle, you cannot just knock at the door… if you do you will be considered uninvited and an enemy. You may be in for a terrible fate.'

'So what do I do instead?'

'You must light a fire with a green flame in the small fire pit at the side of the castle,' said Daubin.

'And then what?'

'And then you wait until you are invited in for an audience with the wizard.'

'So that is it then… just wait?' asked Afeclin with suspicion.

'Yes, you wait for as long as it takes… hours… days… it could even take weeks, but you wait until he is ready to see you and if you leave before that time, you will never be able to seek an audience with him again.'

'Weeks?'

'They're not my rules. I told you he was an idiot but if you want to see him you have to play by his rules,' said Daubin shaking his head, 'and with the way the world is now, I'm sure he will be on his guard.'

'I see,' said Afeclin with a sigh. Then something said earlier dawned on him, 'Hang on… did you say, green flame?'

'Yes, most importantly, it must be a green flame. Any other colour and it will be assumed that you are an enemy.'

'But how do I make the flame green?' asked Afeclin with concern.

'Well you mustn't be much of a wizard if you can't do that,' Daubin croaked. 'I guess you will have to figure it out.'

Afeclin felt a little embarrassed that he didn't know how to make a coloured flame. It would be something he would have to work on while on his journey to Crymonthon's castle.

Daubin rolled the leather parchment back up again and handed it to Afeclin. He then accompanied Afeclin out the front door of the cottage and the two said goodbye. As they shook hands Afeclin happened to notice an odd-shaped mark or scar on the older man's wrist as his sleeve slid up his arm.

'Well goodbye then,' said Afeclin as he turned around and started walking towards the trees where Majenta stood grazing in peace. As he walked he thought about the mark. He had seen something like it before... it was sort of the shape of a long, thin dagger.

It was then that an idea occurred to him. It was the same thought that had come to him several times that morning but could never seem to hold on to. He focused intensely for a moment, refusing to let the idea escape from him again. This time he managed to think the thought through. He spun around to face the old man...

'Daubin, do you think you can do something for me?'

'I suppose so,' he answered with a cautious look on his face.

'Could you just take your glasses off,' he said stepping forward a little, 'then look at me and tell me what you see.'

'Afeclin, if I was to take my glasses off I wouldn't see a thing. So how could I tell you what I see?' Daubin laughed as he crossed his arms.

'I see,' said Afeclin giving a little nod. He turned to leave again but then hesitated and looked back at the old man who was still standing at the door.

'For what it is worth I think Zallucien was right,' Afeclin said turning to face Daubin. 'I think he was right to train that dark mage. Despite what has happened since, he was right to try. No other good wizard would have given him the chance, so he would have been put on the wrong track to begin with. Zallucien at least tried and who knows what good lurks inside of him now because of it. It could be what has kept him at bay all these years, perhaps his dark side has taken longer to grow.'

When Afeclin finished speaking the old man stood silent. He seemed thoughtful.

Afeclin shrugged his shoulders and then turned back around and continued walking to his horse. He felt disappointed and he shook his head.

'Afeclin, you have a true purple aura with an orange fringe… rare, very rare indeed.'

Afeclin turned around to face the old man once again. This time Daubin stood looking straight at Afeclin, thumbing his glasses over in his fingers.

'Zallucien?' Afeclin asked with anticipation.

'Yes my friend, I am the wizard Zallucien of whom you seek,' the old man answered bowing his head as if in defeat.

'I knew it, I just knew it,' said Afeclin rushing to the wizard and shaking his hand in excitement.

'When did you figure it out?' Zallucien asked with intrigue.

'An idea about you has come into my head several times today,' Afeclin admitted with pride, 'but before I could think it out properly I would lose the thought. This time I simply refused to let the thought go when I caught sight of the picture on your arm. It reminded me of the lightning dagger I had seen in pictures, worn by only the greatest of wizards.'

'Your mind is strong,' Zallucien said with approval. 'Of the few visitors I have had over the past twenty years, nobody has ever been able to push past my mind spell.'

'Mind spell?'

'Yes of course,' answered the old wizard, 'I must protect my identity. I cannot have people playing with ideas about who I am, or they are likely to figure it out. You, my dear Afeclin, managed to push past my mind spell… that requires a very strong mind.'

Afeclin felt honoured to receive such a compliment from the great Zallucien himself and he bowed his head. There was so much he wanted to ask the wizard but for that instant he fell silent allowing himself time to absorb the moment.

'Why do you need to hide your identity? Why can't people know that you are here, alive and well… I mean what is the point of all this secrecy for the few weary travellers who happen to find themselves here?'

'First of all… nobody finds themselves here accidentally. They happen upon the path for a reason. It is as your friend told you… those that are meant to find the path will do so,' the old wizard said with weariness. 'As for myself, I decided after my good friend Daubin was killed that I would retire. I simply had nothing more to give as a mentor.'

'But why become him? I mean, wouldn't it be simpler just to tell people you have retired?'

Zallucien responded with a sigh, 'People travel from all over Titania to see me. They encounter hardships, sickness, injury, nights without sleep, days without food, they may be robbed or even attacked. After all that… to finally arrive here and find out that I have been killed is devastating enough but to get here and have me simply tell them that I will not help is another thing altogether. People will not take no for an answer, just like you will not, now that you know the truth.'

Afeclin felt guilty. Zallucien was right. He did not think he could leave without at least trying to persuade the old mage to teach him. *How can I? I have come so far.* Afeclin understood Zallucien's point perfectly.

'The other reason…' Zallucien continued, 'is that I think it is better for the dark mage to believe that he succeeded in his aim of killing me and destroying my work.'

'Ohhh…' Afeclin said with thought, 'that makes sense. I mean you don't want him to surprise you with another attack… and with him thinking you are no longer a threat you have a chance to gain the upper hand.'

'Hmmm, you're right of course,' Zallucien said with a little sadness. He moved across to where a large boulder lay to the side of his rock garden and sat down. With his bony elbows resting on his knees and his head in his hands, his beard came close to touching the ground.

The old man seemed contemplative and troubled.

Not knowing what to do or say, Afeclin felt rather uncomfortable.

After a few minutes of quiet Afeclin dared to break the silence.

'So what does it mean then?'

Zallucien looked up, not understanding the question.

'I mean my aura,' Afeclin added realising he had not made himself very clear. 'What does it mean to see more than one colour?'

The old wizard shuffled himself on the rock and rearranged his robes. 'It is rare… very rare. Most people will be one colour or another, not two distinct colours.'

'But what does it mean?'

'As I told you last night the purple indicates a pure and true heart but the orange would indicate a part of you that is undecided.'

'But what does that mean?' Afeclin persisted.

The old man put a finger to his lips as he considered the problem.

'It would mean that on the whole you are a good person but there is an uncertainty about your character. Usually I have found that the reason is due to family history, for instance a relative with bad blood.'

'Bad blood?'

'Yes. Say perhaps that you have a long lost aunt who happened to be an evil temptress. Her blood would run thick with hate and despair and all things evil. You possibly would have inherited some of those genes and while you are a good person and have been taught well, there could be evil intentions lurking within you, that you do not know about because they are buried.'

'Ooh,' said Afeclin with sorrow, 'I guess that means that I would have absolutely no hope of persuading you to train me. You would never come out of retirement for someone that possibly had bad blood racing through his veins.'

'Twenty years ago I would have seen your potential and said to myself, "I must train him for here is someone special," I would not have worried about the orange…'

'But now?'

'Well, now of course it is different. I would not like to chance preparing another dark wizard to send out into the world. I have a responsibility.'

Afeclin bowed his head.

'Is there no way I can convince you?' he pleaded.

'I am sorry,' said Zallucien with earnest regret, 'I am sorry for myself as much as you. I know you would make a fine pupil… but I simply cannot. That is my final word on the matter. I wish you a safe journey. Maybe you will be able to reunite with your friends in Rengal if they still be there. Good day.'

With that the old man put his thick blue glasses back on his face and turned and marched himself back inside the cottage.

It was as if the old wizard could not be around Afeclin any longer, as if the temptation to change his mind was far too great.

There was no way that he could force Zallucien to train him. His best bet was to head east towards the sea and try to find a way to cross. The wizard Crymonthon was now his only hope.

Afeclin walked towards Majenta and patted his mud-beaded mane. He took from his bag a carrot that he had found in the kitchen earlier that morning and fed it to the stoic animal. The horse munched it, whinnying his gratitude.

As he hoisted himself up onto the saddle a gust of wind blew around him.

Within the wind Afeclin thought he could hear a very soft and gentle voice whispering in his ears.

'Stay,' it seemed to say, 'do not give up.'

Afeclin looked about him feeling uneasy.

There was not a soul around.

'Perhaps it's those trees again,' thought Afeclin giving Majenta a little nudge with his heels.

As they began to walk down the long path and back up the hill Afeclin began to consider his problem of how to make a green flame.

Another gust of wind whistled in his ears.

'Stay,' came the whisper again.

Afeclin looked about with confusion. He did not understand.

'Where is that voice coming from?' Afeclin whispered to himself. 'Why would it want me to stay?'

Then Afeclin's eyes rested on something he had not noticed before. Under a tall clump of trees to one side in front of the cottage was a small fire pit.

That gave Afeclin an idea.

Climbing back down off Majenta he searched the ground for sticks and fallen branches. Then he placed them in the fire pit and covered them with dried bits of moss.

He produced a dancing flame above his finger then he flicked the flame with the forefinger of his other hand. The flame fell onto the dry kindling and immediately roared to life, crackling and spitting as it started a sizeable fire in the pit.

'Now,' said Afeclin rubbing his hands in front of the fire more out of habit than for warmth, 'how to turn the flame green.'

Afeclin opened his bag and pulled out a small, dark red book. It was a very old wizard's handbook. Although Afeclin had read it cover to cover numerous times over the years, he hoped that maybe it would provide a clue to changing the flame's colour.

He thumbed the aging pages lightly as he looked through the book.

The first section of the book contained recipes, herbal remedies and concoctions to cure or fix anything from a headache to an ingrown toenail. This section was the number one reason that Afeclin had brought the book with him. He had figured it could come in handy at some stage. However it didn't provide any solution to the problem at hand.

The rest of the book was made up of basic spells and incantations that, when done to the specifications, could dazzle onlookers, surprise friends or upset adversaries.

Afeclin reminisced about many of the spells he had tried. Most of them had gone well but every now and then when his concentration had been low his spell would produce disastrous results.

While the spells themselves were fairly basic, written in a form that even a child could understand, being able to produce a spell was an art. It required meditation and concentration and an inner belief in oneself. Afeclin had always enjoyed meditating even as a very young boy. Clearing his mind of all that was going on in his life at that time, breathing in and out with long controlled breaths and focusing on a far-off place enabled him to enter another realm of being. It was there that he was invincible and courageous and everything he wished he could be in reality.

Afeclin chuckled to himself as he came upon a spell Lenna had tried once when she had borrowed the book from him in order to get revenge on the palace record keeper whom she loathed.

Hompelnoo was a nasty, red-haired, big-nosed elf who punished anyone and everyone he came in contact with that put his oversized snout out of joint. He was employed within the great library of the palace to take care of the books and keep records of the dealings of the kingdom.

From time to time Hompelnoo had offered small lectures at the library on varying subjects on which he was well acquainted and enjoyed the satisfaction of expounding his knowledge to all who would listen.

On one particular day, Lenna had arrived late for a lecture with Hompelnoo. Having stepped into the library one minute too late, the silence in the room was deafening.

With Hompelnoo's sharp squinty eyes directed on the tardy elf, she was made to sit in the corner wearing a funny-looking boar skin pig nose, constructed by Hompelnoo himself. Around her neck was hung a sign that read, "I'm a pig because I take up other elves' valuable time."

The whole ordeal left her humiliated and devastated beyond belief.

Lenna had then begged Afeclin to allow her to borrow his book of spells. Afeclin did try to persuade her to let him perform the spell himself but the stubborn elf was determined that for maximum satisfaction, she had to do it herself.

She chose a spell that would give Hompelnoo a bad case of lice. She wanted to see him driven crazy with an itchy scalp.

The key ingredient for the spell was a strand of hair; just a single strand was all that was required. Afeclin warned her that she must be very careful to make sure it was one of Hompelnoo's even if it meant pulling a strand of hair straight from his head. However Lenna was not about to walk up to the elf she feared more than death and pull his hair.

Instead she planned to bide her time, looking for hair, watching for a piece left behind in a hat or hanging cloak. As it turned out she didn't have to wait too long, for only a couple of days later Lenna was at the library looking through a book when Hompelnoo leaned over her in his pompous, self-important way to see what she was reading. As he leant over, Lenna was surprised to see a strand of hair fall onto her page. Placing it in a page of her notebook she took great care in getting it home. Later that night she contrived the spell. The next morning she awoke to an itchy scalp. She had developed a bad case of lice. The strand of hair that had dropped had been her own. The poor elf maiden spent the following days in vicious scratching. Afeclin managed to cure her of the lice using a herbal concoction out of the same book. The unfortunate side effect was that clumps of her hair began falling out due to the remedy. *She would not speak to me for a long time after that incident.*

The thing that amazed Afeclin the most though was that Lenna did manage to conjure up the spell. However, after her harrowing ordeal she was unwilling to try another spell ever again.

Afeclin reminisced as he sat stoking the fire. He laughed again at the thought of Lenna suffering such indignities. He wondered what she might be doing at that moment in Tebelligan. Knowing Lenna as well as he did, he guessed that she had most likely locked herself in her room, grieving over the loss of her precious Wolflang and the life they could have had together.

Feeling resentment rising within him, Afeclin waved away such thoughts and continued looking through his book. Every now and then he added more sticks to the fire as he flicked through the pages.

The spells were in no particular order, just a random jumble of hexes and enchantments. There was a spell that could give an enemy nightmares, a spell that could make them old, one that could make them deaf, blind or mute or, all of the above. There was a spell that could conjure a rain cloud that would follow the receiver around, a spell that could cause thunder and lightning in a person's home and a spell that could give a person the face of a bat or make hair grow all over one's body. There was a curse that would cause worms to grow out of one's nose or a hex that could make one think and act like an animal. There were many other vile and disgusting or frightening spells and curses.

The spells were relatively harmless. None would cause any physical harm nor pain as far as Afeclin knew. They were designed more for humiliation purposes and for that reason no spell was permanent.

Afeclin had been unwilling to try spells out on the unsuspecting, except his brothers on occasion and instead had tried many on himself. The spell named "sightless wonder" had worked like a charm. He had been blind for three weeks before the spell had worn off. His eyes had turned to stone and he had been unable to blink but had found life as a blind man very interesting and educational. His other senses were heightened during that time and he had to rely on his instinct. He was very pleased however to have his eyesight back after the enchantment had faded. How wonderful it had felt to see colour and light once more after living in pitch darkness for weeks. It was much the same feeling as being in the Alimest Grove and not being able to see. Only, the Alimest Grove was much more frightening.

Even though the spells had a humiliation factor about them, Afeclin had been prepared for the outcome of any spell he tried and made a point of making the most of each experience.

While there were many interesting spells in the book none of them were very useful in helping him obtain his goal of conjuring a green flame.

He put the book down on the ground next to him and sat thinking for a moment. He knew it had to be something simple. He closed his eyes and tried to meditate. He focused his mind and energy on the fire. In slow and deliberate breaths he inhaled and exhaled all the while maintaining concentration. He opened one eye just a fraction. As he did so he happened to notice a leaf with green and red stripes fall from the branches of the tree high above him. It floated down almost in slow motion, spinning and circling as if dancing on the breeze. As the leaf hit the flame and was consumed by the heat, the fire turned green.

Afeclin smiled but inside his heart was doing somersaults.

'So it is the leaves from the tula blossom tree,' he remarked in triumphant relief.

He knew this type of tree well as they grew in abundance on the most southern part of Tebelligan and were the type of leaves that were used in the big balloon that was burst at midnight every New Moon ceremony. Because of the lightness of them, the leaves tended to dance and float as they fell to the ground giving them a spectacular effect.

Once the leaf had disappeared in the flames the fire went back to its original reddy orange hue.

So I need more leaves.

Afeclin looked around at the many tall tula blossom trees surrounding him. The only problem was that the trunks were so tall that the leaves were much higher up.

He had never seen such old tula blossoms before. He wondered how he could reach them or whether he needed to scour the ground for recently fallen leaves.

He received a swift answer, for just as he was considering the problem another red and green leaf pulled away from the branch and began to fall, then another from a neighbouring tree. Then another and another, until there were leaves falling every which way and landing with beautiful accuracy in the fire giving the flames a moon-green glow.

It took a moment for him to register just how it was happening but then the realisation hit him that he was willing the leaves to fall himself. Just as Afeclin thought in his mind that he needed another leaf, another leaf would pluck itself from the tree and fall into the flames giving off a sweet aroma that filled the air as the smoke sailed on the breeze and floated around him.

Feeling happy with himself he shifted his body into a comfortable position on the ground in front of the fire and went back to meditating. All he could do now was wait.

Chapter

XL

A few hours of travelling over the water with an unsettled stomach, that was not accustomed to surging water currents, made sleep a near impossibility for Lenna.

In the early hours of the morning as she was drifting off, her body having given up to exhaustion, a large bell rang at the top of the mast.

'Land ho!' came a shout on deck from one of the crew.

Excitement raced across the deck as the crewmembers readied the boat for entering the shallower waters. Lowering the sails to slow their approach and preparing the anchor to drop when close enough, the crew worked with speed and vigilance.

Lenna stood for the first time in hours. The last time she had to stand up was to be sick over the side of the boat. She was pleased to be getting on to dry land at last but nervous as to what awaited her.

She walked to the front of the small craft and watched the shoreline as they neared it. She was amazed at how much better she felt just seeing the land up ahead and knowing they would soon be upon it.

They sailed as far into the shoreline as possible before dropping the anchor.

As the morning sun was starting to heat up Lenna looked out over the body of water between where the boat had anchored and the beach. It was quite the distance still.

She licked her dry lips, dreading how they were supposed to get across. There was no way she was going to set foot in the water and chance being attacked by the terrifying leeches.

After a few minutes of waiting however, she noticed two men hop into a rowboat on the shore and begin to paddle out to them.

Lenna breathed a sigh of relief as she watched the muscular men manipulate the water current and guide the boat in safety to the waiting vessel.

Upon reaching them, one of the men stood up inside the small boat and beckoned for Haizu to bring Lenna onto the boat. When she saw the man's ugly pig face appear over the side of the boat, Lenna hung her head in bitter disappointment. *Not another troll, I should have known.*

She was hurried into the waiting rowboat and ushered onto a wooden bench.

'Hey, Haizu, she okay without any ties?' asked the troll as he began to row back to shore.

'Oh yeah, she ain't going nowhere,' Haizu answered, giving Lenna an intimidating smirk.

Lenna shook her head in fear. While it had crossed her mind to attempt another run for it once they reached the beach, she had come to realise that it just was not worth her time or energy. Without any means to escape with speed, she would be recaptured and treated with malice again, which was something she did not think she had the strength to cope with anymore. No longer was her plight about getting back to Wolflang or even Tebelligan, now it was just to survive whatever lay ahead.

As they neared the shore, Lenna was most pleased to notice that beyond the desertlike beach, which was wide and sandy, there were woods and trees of varying sizes and colours in the distance. She could not have had any idea where they were but the change of landscape was refreshing all the same.

One of the trolls alighted from the boat and waded the passengers to the sandy shore. While he was only ankle deep, Lenna could not watch him trek through the water.

Haizu leaned forward with a sly smile. 'They only feed at night,' he said giving her a wink.

'Oh,' she said relaxing a little.

After they had stopped, Haizu took her by the arm and helped her out of the boat in an almost gentlemanly way, if that were possible. As she alighted the small wooden craft Lenna's eyes caught sight of something pretty shimmering in the sand. Her feet landed very near to it as she jumped down into the soft shore. Faking a little trip in the sand, she fell to the ground and collected the object in her hand before standing again and pretending to brush herself off.

The troll looked her up and down with a shake of his head, 'What is that you have in your hand elf?'

'I..I..It's nothing,' she stammered with unease.

'Show me!' the troll growled.

'It's just a… '

'I said SHOW ME!' he yelled in Lenna's face. She cringed as a putrid smell of hot, stale breath swept over her. She held open her hand, showing off the small and delicate object.

'A shell?' Haizu questioned, shaking his head with annoyance. 'Hurry up, get a move on.' He then guided her up the beach toward the woods.

They were on a slight incline, climbing a small sand dune. Before they made it to the top a figure appeared as if from nowhere and wandered down to greet them.

The man was dressed in black from head to toe, wearing a wide rimmed hat with a single feather protruding from it. He had blonde wavy hair that flowed back behind him as it caught the breeze and he walked with an arrogance, which was both pretentious and narcissistic.

'Well here we are finally. You are a brave one, I must say,' the man in black said as he took her by the hands.

The man in black had a scar across one side of his face and over his eye, deforming it somewhat. He seemed somehow familiar to Lenna but she could not place where she had seen him before.

Rengal perhaps? But it couldn't have been, maybe Desprade… but I cannot place him there either.

The scarred man noticed the dried blood and marks on her leg and shouted, 'Haizu, what on Titania happened here? I gave you direct instructions that the elf was not to be harmed in any way.'

'Master, she was thirsty when we reached the river, so we allowed her to have a drink. We weren't to know she would try to swim for it and one of those leeches got her.'

'I was not swimming,' Lenna protested with defiance, 'I was simply cooling myself and my burning feet, since you made me walk through the desert in the scorching sand.'

'You did what?' questioned the man in black with exasperation.

'Master I...' Haizu began but was cut off by the man's observation of Lenna's wrists and hands. 'What is this?' he questioned, all patience wearing thin. 'It looks as if you blockheads have tied her too tight and dragged her across the desert.'

'I... I...,' Haizu stammered trying to get the words out to explain, 'that is we, didn't want her to escape again.'

'Escape?' the scarred man repeated with a confounded expression. 'Where did you think she was going to escape to... in the desert?'

'I, I... I'm sorry master,' Haizu said bowing his head in shame.

'Idiot! Don't you know how valuable the elf is to us?' the man in black said taking off his hat and swiping the troll numerous times over the head with it.

'Yes sir,' the troll said taking the beating with humbleness.

Lenna was quite surprised to see the heavy brute taking such treatment from a thin, waif-like man.

He must be a man of considerable power, Lenna pondered. However, she felt less afraid of the man in black than the trolls.

'I apologise for the treatment you have been given during your travels here,' he said with a slight bow.

Lenna was quite put off by the man's patronising attitude toward her.

'Treatment? Being brought here against my will is terrible treatment alone,' she burst out, fuming.

'Quite so,' said the man with no sign of animosity toward her, 'your freedom has been taken from you. I can understand your anger towards us.'

Lenna felt more than anger at that moment. She felt great hatred toward the scarred man. *How dare he attempt to understand anything I have been through.*

Feeling volatile, she spat into his face.

Unperturbed, the scarred man wiped the spit from his cheek with his hand and then without warning grasped her own face and squeezed.

'Now listen here elf. It is true that you are very valuable to us, but don't let that make you feel invincible. I can make your life very comfortable or I can make your life extremely difficult. It would be in your best interests to treat me with respect.'

Lenna stared in icy detest, but said nothing.

The scarred man let her go and turned to begin walking back up to the top of the mound. The trolls followed pressing Lenna to continue also.

Once they reached the very top, overlooking the other side, Lenna was shocked to see what waited for her at the bottom of the hill.

It was the same cavalcade that she had passed on the road that first day out of Tebelligan when the trolls had chased her.

I should have realised, she moaned.

That instant she recognised where she had seen the scarred man before, *he was the one looking out of the window from the black carriage.*

While horses grazed in a grassy knoll just in front of the wooded area, girls that she had seen stuck together in the wagon were now guarded in the open area by a dozen trolls.

Some girls sat and talked, others paced or stretched their legs while they had opportunity to. They all looked to Lenna as the trolls helped her down the sandy bank.

'Here is your chariot for the next few days,' the man in black said motioning to the large wagon the girls had been huddled together in as they travelled, 'I hope you will find it comfortable, Little Elf.'

While Lenna was annoyed by the condescending nature of the scarred man, what irked her more than anything, sending a chill down her spine as the words came out of his mouth, was hearing him use the name 'Little Elf' just as Harren had… the person she had trusted with her life.

'My name is not Little Elf,' she said with bated breath, lifting her chin with pride.

The scarred man raised an eyebrow with amusement, 'No?' he said. 'Then what should we call you instead?'

'Letavia.'

Chapter

XLI

Wolflang had been sitting all alone in his prison cell for two whole nights with only the sketch of Lenna for company. He had been fed nothing more than stale bread and fermenting cabbage.

Now it was the morning of the second day and the sun streamed through the small cell window.

The two nights had felt like an eternity and he had begun to feel like a caged animal. During the day he had paced back and forward in the tiny room not knowing what else to do with himself.

He had found himself desperate to refrain from any type of reflection on the past day's activities. He didn't want to think about Afeclin and whether he was or wasn't alive. Lenna would come to his mind and he would see the attractive elf with her big brown eyes staring at him with a sorrowful 'why?' expression on her face. He didn't want to think of her either; it was much too painful. Brushing away thoughts of her and home he tried hard not to think at all.

Avoiding his thoughts had worked well enough during the daytime but at night he was at the mercy of his unconsciousness. Afeclin disappearing into the mud, Lenna, the girl in the red silk dress, the ghosts of Alimest Groove and the hooded man who called on him with a vision of his destiny, swept in and out of his dreams, haunting his nightmares and denying the elf's mind any peace.

Now he sat on the bunk and tugged at his pointy ears.

Rengal had been nothing that he had imagined.

Home in Tebelligan he had grown up listening to his Great Uncle tell wonderful tales of the magnificent city of Rengal.

As a young man his Great Uncle Clavinus had lived for a time in Rengal before the human war. Clavinus had enjoyed living in the busy city. It was modern and exciting. It was home to many different races and life was a faster pace than the quiet, slow Tebelligan lifestyle.

Wolflang had made up his mind at a young age that some way or another he would make it to Rengal.

Now here he was trapped within a prison cell with no money in his pocket, no way out and only his thoughts to keep him occupied, which he was avoiding at all costs.

Rengal itself had been most disappointing as far as cities went. It was dirty, smelly and seemed to be poverty-ridden as there were beggars on almost every street corner. Maybe once upon a time it had been a beautiful city full of charm and life but now the buildings were old, decrepit and falling apart. The streets were full of holes and everything appeared to be grey, bleak and unkempt.

The problem that Wolflang faced now was where to go from Rengal. A part of him would flee and return to Tebelligan in a heartbeat and back into the arms of his love. The other part of him supposed that it was weak to feel that way and that there was something out there for him. He just had to find it.

It was as Wolflang pondered these questions that his thoughts were interrupted by the sound of a bolt sliding and the door to his cell crack open as the rusty hinges creaked.

A large man appeared at the door. Wolflang recognised him by his uniform with the winged lion emblem, which he had discovered was a symbol of the armed order in Rengal. He was one of the prison guards.

'You have a visitor,' roared the guard as he made way for a cloaked figure to enter. Then closing the door Wolflang heard the bolt slide back into position.

The cloaked figure sat down next to Wolflang on the bunk and then pulled back the hood that hid his face. Wolflang was surprised to see that it was Typhin.

'I am not upset with you for attacking me the other day,' Typhin said with honesty.

'Oh really?' Wolflang said without feeling, 'I don't know that I am sorry about that.'

'It's okay… I don't expect you to be sorry about that,' said Typhin in his mild manner, 'truth is, had I been in your position I probably would have thought the same thing and reacted the same way.'

'Humph.'

'You and your friend did Raan and myself a great service the other day. You risked your lives to save people you barely knew. We are greatly indebted to you.'

Wolflang looked up at Typhin with a disdainful expression on his face. 'If you really feel that way why has it taken so long to come? I've been sitting here for two days in this hell hole.'

Typhin laughed.

'You have not been here for two days yet. That's nothing, Pit and I were imprisoned in one of these cells for weeks,' he said standing up and looking around the room. 'I see you got one of the nicer cells too. You even have a view of the street.'

'Are you crazy? This room is disgusting... and it stinks too!'

'Try living in it for a few weeks and see how good it smells then,' Typhin said with an eyebrow raised.

'You're not going to leave me here, are you?' said Wolflang with sudden concern.

Typhin looked back at Wolflang and gave him a wry smile.

'The reason it took so long, as you say, to come was that I needed to raise some money to get you out. Fortunately I was able to sell the ram I rode into town and make a handsome profit. Enough that I was able to use Afeclin's share to bribe the guards.'

'Afeclin's share?'

'Yes of course. He helped catch the stupid thing, he deserved half of the profit,' Typhin said sitting back down again next to Wolflang. 'He is not here to collect his share, so his share naturally goes to you. He would want it that way.'

'Thanks… I guess,' Wolflang said trying to understand, 'but where is Afeclin?'

Typhin opened his cloak a fraction and put his hand into a concealed pocket. He pulled out something that was wrapped in a red silk handkerchief.

'He found the path to Lawry Castle and although he wanted to come here first and make sure you were safe and say a proper farewell, he decided to take the track there and then because it is mystical and there would be no guarantees that he could find it again. After all, the whole reason for him leaving Tebelligan was for the purpose of finding that castle,' said Typhin, placing the wrapped item in Wolflang's hands. 'Before we went our separate ways Afeclin asked me to give you this.'

Wolflang unwrapped the silken handkerchief and uncovered the wooden ornament.

'Armatto,' Wolflang whispered as his fingers traced the inscription in the wood.

He looked to Typhin again. 'I can't believe he kept it all this time! I made this for Afeclin when we were very young.'

'Yes well, I guess you mean a lot to him,' Typhin said standing up again and placing the hood over his head once more. 'Shall we...?' he motioned toward the door.

Wolflang being lost in his memories forgot for just a moment where he was. Startling himself from his thoughts he jumped up off the bunk.

'Yes, let's go… please.'

Typhin thumped at the prison door, 'Okay we're ready to come out!'

Presently a sound was heard just outside the door as the bolt was slid across and the heavy door opened.

The guard allowed the two to walk out.

As Typhin walked past the guard he handed him some silver coins.

'As promised.'

'Pleasure doing business with you,' the guard nodded as he took the coins and put them in a concealed pocket in his uniform.

'Is that legal?' Wolflang dared to ask as they walked out the door of the prison building and onto the street.

'Of course it's not legal but they don't get paid enough to be loyal. What I gave him just now was equivalent to a month's pay.'

Wolflang could see Typhin grin despite the dark shadow the hood cast over his face.

'So what's with the hood?'

Typhin looked around with cautiousness.

'We've been discovered here and we must move on,' said Typhin a little above a whisper as they walked down the busy street. 'It was a risk for me to even come and get you.'

'Who are you running from?'

'Don't concern yourself too much with details... it's a long story,' he answered avoiding the question. 'You should be more concerned about what may come knocking at your door looking for your friend. I wouldn't be surprised if they are in the city somewhere.'

Wolflang stopped dead in his tracks staring at Typhin.

'What are you talking about?'

Typhin paused and motioned for Wolflang to continue walking with him.

Wolflang followed in obedience.

'What is going on?' he said as he ran to catch up.

'Without all the details,' started Typhin allowing an elderly man to pass him before continuing, '...we happened to find out that some bounty hunters are searching for Afeclin. We don't know why or for who they work but they lost his scent when he jumped into the mud and have since followed yours hoping you will lead them to Afeclin.'

'Bounty hunters?' Wolflang stared feeling very concerned. 'And you're saying they could be in town with us now?'

'Well, let's put it this way... they weren't that far behind us and they could have got to you easily in the prison cell had they tried. I would assume they have lost your scent and as you are not the one they are after, have not been able to find you.'

'So should I be concerned or not?' asked Wolflang with confusion.

'Not so much concerned as perhaps cautious,' said Typhin with guidance. 'Get out of the city and away from here before they do happen upon you. You are welcome to journey with us until you find what you are looking for. We are getting ready to leave right now.'

Wolflang considered Typhin's offer for a moment. *It would be nice to journey with people who know what they are doing and where they are going.* The only problem was that they seemed to be in some kind of trouble and although Wolflang did not know what, he did not want to be experiencing more hardship due to association with those who were considered criminal.

'I don't think so. I appreciate you getting me out of prison but... I think I need to figure out what I am going to do on my own,' said Wolflang with gratitude then added, a little embarrassed, '... and for what it is worth I am sorry for attacking you as you rode into town, I wasn't thinking straight.'

'Well, don't worry about it, a bit of Rengallian brew will do that to you... trust me, I know,' said Typhin with a laugh. Then he stopped at a street corner and took Wolflang by the hand. Forcing his hand into a fist and then making a fist himself he pushed it against the elf's.

'Good luck with your journey,' he said in sincere friendship, then added, 'I heard about your venture with the lawfabex and I must say I am very impressed. You are most brave... that can be very useful... you should find something worthwhile to do with it.'

Wolflang felt embarrassed at the memory of the lawfabex and of Pit's injury.

'By Afeclinella... I had forgotten... is Pit alright? I mean... how are his injuries?' asked Wolflang with sudden concern. 'I should have killed the beast when I had the chance. I don't know what came over me. I really don't.'

'Don't worry about Pit, he has had much worse than a mere claw scratch,' said Typhin with a laugh. 'It really wasn't as bad as it had looked, no serious damage done, a few stitches and he was fine.'

'Well that is a relief to know.'

'Yeah, well Pit is now boasting about his 'lawfabex attack' and showing off his wounds proudly. It gets a lot of attention, especially from the ladies... if you know what I mean.'

Wolflang smiled at the thought of Pit acting like his injuries were much worse than they had been and having half a dozen gorgeous women swooning over him trying to help make him feel better.

'Well, anyway good luck to you also,' Wolflang said. 'Don't get caught by... err... whoever it is that you are running from.'

Typhin nodded.

'The inn we have been staying at is up that road, in case you have forgotten,' said Typhin pointing to a road on the left. 'You will find all of your belongings where you left them.'

Typhin looked around with caution once more, gave a nod of farewell to Wolflang and then continued on down the street without another word.

🦋 🦋 🦋

Wolflang easily found the inn. He walked up the stairs of the Waterfeln Inn and pushed open the heavy doors. At the bar stood a young woman with golden curls busy serving drinks to a couple of old dwarves. She barely looked up to see Wolflang enter. He hurried past them, turning into an entryway that led to the rooms. He wandered down the long sunlit hallway which was lighted by an elongated slender window in the ceiling. The pale brick walls were old but well maintained and x-zaivacress vines crept along them. With the sunlight streaming inside the

296

building and the greenery all the way along the walls, the corridor had the feeling of being outside.

On the way to his room he could hear a tuneful melody played out with skill on a fiddle. Passing the room that the music seemed to be coming from, he noticed the door was ajar. Stopping to look through the open slit, he smiled to himself as he watched a dark-haired woman move her fingers with exactness over the strings while she drew the bow across them adroitly producing a harmonious, beautiful sound. The woman rocked her body, feeling the music she played with tenderness. She turned her head toward the door and Wolflang was awe-struck to see that it was Eliah.

Stepping back away from the door, the wooden floor creaked under his feet. Afraid he may have given himself away, he hurried into his own room across the hall and shut the door.

Wolflang collected his belongings, making sure he had everything that he had brought with him.

He felt inside a little concealed pocket in his bag to see if he had any money left. To his surprise he pulled out a couple of gold coins. Having never had gold coins himself before, he wondered where they had come from.

'Typhin!' he said shaking his head in disbelief as he realised the older man must have given him more than Afeclin's share of the money from the ram.

It also occurred to him that Typhin must have known that Wolflang would not accompany them where they were headed. For this reason he must have made sure Wolflang had enough money to get by.

'Probably promised Afeclin that he would look out for me,' Wolflang said to himself feeling agitated that Afeclin and Typhin thought that he couldn't look after himself.

He threw the coins on the bunk with disgust and turned to walk out the door.

Before shutting the door, he stopped and looked back at the golden coins lying on the bunk. They glistened in the sunlight that streamed through the window.

Wolflang shook his head again as he fought the desire to leave without the money and show everyone that he did not need any help.

'Gold coins are gold coins after all,' he said forcing himself to go back into the room.

He stormed back to the bed and picked up the coins with disdain.

'If Typhin and Afeclin were here I would throw you at them,' he growled at the coins as if they could hear him, 'but since they are not...'

Wolflang was interrupted by a tap at the door.

Eliah was standing in the doorway, her fiddle was held against her chin and the bow she tapped against her leg.

'Your door was open... am I interrupting something?' she asked with a knowing smile.

Wolflang turned red at seeing the beautiful woman at his door witnessing the strange interlude with the gold douclas. Her green eyes stared at him with a bemused expression as she leaned against the door with her long black hair cascading down her back and her head cocked to one side.

'I was just... that is I... what I mean to say..., ' Wolflang stammered as he searched for a plausible explanation for his bizarre behaviour.

'Just talking to yourself?' Eliah asked with kindness.

'Well...'

'It's okay, everybody does it,' she said smiling, then added whispering, 'especially the ones who say they don't.'

Wolflang felt better. He was also surprised at how kind she was being. The last time he had seen her she had not been in the best of moods with him.

'What's with the fiddle? Where did you get it? I didn't know you played... it sounded really nice,' Wolflang gushed in a fast flurry of words.

Eliah smiled, taking her fiddle from her chin to show Wolflang.

'Typhin bought it for me yesterday,' she said stroking the instrument with fondness. 'I have always played, since I was a little girl... my mother played. I guess I started playing to try to be nearer to her through it. She died when I was very young... I never knew her.'

'I lost my mother when I was young too,' he said realising that it felt nice to have some small connection with the dark-haired human.

She nodded with a slight smile, perhaps feeling the kinship too.

'Why aren't you with the others?'

Eliah looked down at her shoeless feet and sighed.

'Typhin thought it was best that I didn't go on with them,' she said with sadness.

'Oh! Well, that is understandable I guess, after all they are wanted criminals... or something,' Wolflang said with confusion. 'What is all that about? I mean, why are they being chased all over the countryside? What have they done?'

Eliah shrugged her shoulders, 'I don't know. Typhin hasn't told me anything. He says it is in my best interest that I don't know. And I don't think I really want to know anyway.'

Wolflang smiled at Eliah with the sudden realisation that the dark-haired beauty was in love with Typhin. The way she twirled her hair when speaking about him and the way her eyes lit up with the mere mention of his name was fascinating to Wolflang. He wondered if Lenna acted the same way about him when he was not around.

Ignoring the intrigue that he felt, he changed the subject. 'So what will you do now then? Will you be journeying back to Desprade?'

'No, it's too dangerous for me at the moment,' she answered in thought. 'Typhin believed it would be best if I go and stay on my aunt's farm 'bout a kitra outside of the city.'

'That sounds like a good idea.'

'What are you going to do Wolflang? I thought you might be tagging along with the boys.'

'No, I feel it is better to go my own way.'

'You mean you don't want to get caught up in whatever Typhin's problems with the law are,' Eliah said with a teasing smile.

'Yes… well, that too,' said Wolflang, '…so I will go my own way and seek out my own destiny.'

Eliah looked at him with a kindly expression on her face, then with fiddle still clasped in her hands, went to Wolflang and bending over she threw her arms around his neck and gave him a big, soft hug.

'I wish you well my friend,' she said in her sweet voice as Wolflang copped a mouthful of dark hair. Then she turned and left the room.

Wolflang stood staring for a moment as the door to his room closed behind her.

🐚 🐚 🐚

Wolflang walked down the cobbled street leading his horse, now named Abwahnu, behind. He was not sure where he was headed or what he was going to do.

Wishing an answer to all his problems would just present itself, he stopped in front of the old tavern, the Westkey Link, that he had drunk at only days earlier, and stared inside at the long curved bar.

The room was almost empty this time and seemed a much more inviting place as it was free from the smog and the crowd.

No! He thought to himself, *That would not be wise.*

Taking a step to move on, he stopped again this time putting a hand into a pocket in his pants and pulling out one of the gold coins.

'One drink for the road perhaps?' he suggested to Abwahnu who looked away with disinterest.

Making the decision to go inside the drinking hole, Wolflang looped Abwahnu's reins around the horse pole and went inside.

'Oh our elvin friend has returned,' said the rotund barkeeper as Wolflang approached the bar.

'Yes, can I get a drink please?' asked Wolflang, bowing his head in shame.

'Oh, we do have manners today,' said the barkeeper with a laugh. 'What will it be?'

'Something, not so strong this time… I think.'

'A wise choice,' laughed the jolly barkeeper. 'May I suggest a bit of Rengallian Rum? It has a sweeter flavour and it is not nearly as potent.'

'Sure, why not.'

The barkeeper picked up a clay bottle from behind the counter and poured the thick rum into an empty goblet that he had just cleaned with his apron.

Wolflang sniffed at the drink.

The liquid was a greeny-brown colour and had a sweet, spicy smell to it that reminded him of fermenting apples.

He took a mouthful and swished it around before swallowing.

It had an unusual flavour. It was not terrible and it was not all that strong, but it was an acquired taste all the same.

Wolflang let out a sigh, *I wish I had some idea where I am headed.*

He was about to ask the barkeeper where the closest neighbouring town was situated when he heard a voice pipe up from beside him.

'You look like you have the weight of the world on your shoulders, young elf.'

Wolflang turned to find an old man suddenly seated on the bar stool beside him.

The old man's hair was matted and silvery grey. His face was wrinkled and worn and a mass of stubbled hair grew out all over it. He wore a brown leather cloak that had a hood draping down the back. Wolflang had not noticed him when he had walked into the bar and he wondered where he had appeared from.

'Wait, you can tell I'm an elf?' Wolflang asked surprised that even though he had tousled hair over his ears, he was recognised as an elf all the same.

'I've known my fair share of elves in my time… it is obvious to me…' he said and then added leaning in close, 'I don't think anyone else here has really taken any notice of you.'

'Oh, that's good. When we arrived in Rengal… everyone stared at me as if they had never seen such a person before.'

300

'If they had been born less than twenty years ago, the likeliness is that they haven't,' the man stated with raised eyebrows.

Wolflang nodded. 'That's fair I guess.' He then turned back toward his drink and sighed again.

'Drowning your sorrows are you?' the man asked with an affable smile.

'I have some decisions to make and I am not sure how to make them based on my limited knowledge of the world outside Tebelligan,' Wolflang answered the man with openness, surprising himself at how frank he was being with the stranger.

The man nodded with understanding. 'It's a hard time in a young man's life when he has to decide which path to choose... it's even harder if he doesn't know what his choices are,' the old man stated as he took a mouthful of brew from the chalice he held in his hand.

Wolflang stared at the older man, a little surprised by his wisdom and insight.

'Yes you are right, how can I know which way to go if I don't know my options,' he said feeling instant ease with the man, 'but how do I find out what my options are?'

'That is a difficult one...' said the old man considering for a moment then adding, 'well let's concentrate on where your talents lie. I have seen that you are very brave and can fight well... even when drunk.'

'You saw that?' asked Wolflang dismayed.

'It was hard to miss, and what about that run in with the lawfabex? A very brave act that was.'

Wolflang looked at the man in surprise.

'How could you know about that?' he asked bewildered, covering his face with his hands.

'Word gets around,' the old man answered with an intriguing smile.

'I don't even know why I did that,' Wolflang said trying to explain his actions. 'I know I should have killed the lawfabex... and I could have quite easily. I mean I have killed plenty of animals in my life. It's just that when I looked into his eyes I felt like I could feel his soul or something and I just knew he desired nothing more than some food. I sound crazy, I guess.'

'On the contrary, I believe what you say and I also believe it is what makes you braver than most. To act on your intuition despite everyone else is very brave.'

'Well, I don't feel terribly brave.'

'Nevertheless you have a gift and you should use it,' the old man said in a serious tone. 'Have you ever considered joining the legion?'

'Legion?'

'The Legionaries; War Soldiers. They train in preparation for an outbreak of war and in the meantime do their best to patrol and protect cities and towns that lack in law enforcement... basically they attempt to keep the peace around Titania but have the ability to fight when needed.'

Wolflang was intrigued by the prospect of joining the legion. It seemed like something he would want to do. Being part of the solution to the problems in Titania and helping people was something he could do, something that would feel worthwhile, where he could be useful.

'I think I would like to be a soldier.'

'Then that is what you should do,' the old man said nodding like a proud father.

'Where do I go to join? Do you know?' Wolflang asked with enthusiasm as his heart started to race at the thought of this new adventure.

'I know someone who leads the Scorpius Brigade who are settled on the North Island,' the old man said as he took another sip of his drink. 'I also happen to know that at this moment he is interviewing new recruits in the Dewby forest which is about 80 kitra south of here.'

'Really?'

'Yes, his name is Tay Flaigon. He is an old friend of mine and when you find him, if you tell him that Old Ursidaen sent you, I am sure he will see you for an interview. The rest is up to you.'

'Wow, thank you. I don't know what I would have done had I not run into you. The Gods must have sent you or something.'

Old Ursidaen gave a kind smile of browning crooked teeth. 'Anything is possible.'

Wolflang felt so comfortable with the old man that he now had the impression that he knew him or that they had met before. Even his face seemed somehow familiar.

'Could we have met before?' Wolflang probed, searching the old man's eyes. 'I mean you seem so familiar.'

'Humans have not been allowed in Tebelligan since the war which was before your time so I don't see how it is possible.'

'You're right of course... but still...'

'Now listen carefully,' Old Ursidaen said ignoring Wolflang's interest. 'When you get to the Dewby Forest you must find the tree with the largest trunk. You got that? The largest. Find it and when you do, look up.'

Wolflang was not sure he understood but he gave a nod to the instructions anyway.

'Do you want a refill?' a voice interrupted from behind the counter.

Wolflang turned his attention to the barkeeper.

'Do you think I could get some water?' Wolflang asked, thinking he was better off staying sober before he headed out of the city.

'Some water?' laughed the barman with an eyebrow raised. 'Ooh-kay.'

'I still say you seem very familiar,' said Wolflang turning his attention back to the old man who... all of a sudden wasn't there anymore. *Now, where did he go?*

Wolflang scanned the room, but the man had vanished. He ran to the door of the tavern and looked out onto the street. It was alive with people and horse-hitched wagons heading in and out of the city. However, he could see no traces of the old man.

Wolflang wandered back to the bar and sat down scratching his head baffled.

His stomach ached and it occurred to Wolflang that he had not eaten much in the past few days.

'Can I get a proper meal before I go?' he said still looking around the room, distracted by the disappearance of the old man. 'Did you happen to see where the old man I was speaking to just now went?'

The barkeeper shrugged his shoulders and shook his head, 'I'm sorry, I didn't take any notice.'

'Oh,' said Wolflang.

'Let me get you that meal,' said the barman sidling through a door into the kitchen area.

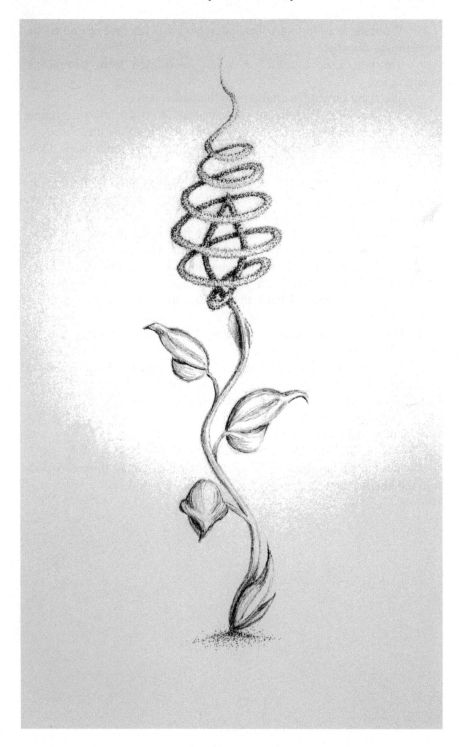

Chapter

XLII

Afeclin had sat by the fire determined to prove his dedication to Zallucien, two days straight without food or water and without moving his position.

It required mental and physical stamina and Afeclin was resolute in proving he had both.

He had kept his mind occupied with meditation and prayer.

Prayer was something he had not done a lot and he felt a little strange attempting it. While the elves were very strict about their religion they tended to keep it to themselves. Endorph had directed Afeclin as a young boy to pray to the Goddess. When Afeclin had questioned how one goes about praying, the old King had given a simple reply, "Just speak and she will hear you."

As much as Afeclin had grown up with an extreme interest in the mystic and supernatural he had never had a complete understanding about the gods and their roles. He believed in them but he hadn't been able to bring himself to talk to someone he could not see.

While he was spending his time meditating he had decided that it wouldn't hurt to try a little prayer, after all he figured he could do with all the help he could get.

To make it easier for himself, while meditating, he imagined himself in the presence of the Goddess herself. In his mind he approached her crystal throne where she sat in the middle of a large manicured garden with green trees standing in straight formation and colourful flowers blossoming out of the ground in lines of blue and pink and silver. Her hair was long and silvery and it flowed around her like gushing waterfalls. Her eyes were as blue as the bluest ocean and her skin white and soft. Afeclinella wore a long argent gown that had crushed crystals all through the fabric making the Goddess sparkle in the sunlight.

While she didn't smile at all, Afeclinella had a kindness that radiated from her that made her most desirable to be in the presence of.

Afeclin approached her throne with nervous anticipation.

'Afeclin, you come, finally,' she said in a soft voice that was both haunting and beautiful.

Afeclin bowed before her with humbleness, 'Your Majesty.'

'Oh, Afeclin enough of the formalities, why have you not come to see me before?'

'I... I... I...' Afeclin struggled to find his words. 'I just didn't know how to speak to someone I could not see.'

'I know,' the Goddess nodded, 'you are not the only one, many of my followers do not talk to me anymore. People feel foolish. But I ask you Afeclin, how is one supposed to come to know me if they will not converse with me?'

'I understand your problem Your Majesty but it doesn't make it any easier to speak to you and know that you are actually listening.'

'I always listen Afeclin.'

Afeclin dropped his head in shame.

'I am not angry with you Afeclin. I am glad you have come to me now,' she continued.

'I come to you, Your Majesty, for help,' Afeclin admitted.

'What is it that you desire of me?' the Goddess asked with magnificence.

'I want more than anything to become a wizard. I know it is in me, I can feel it.'

'Yes, I feel that too.' Afeclinella agreed.

'But one doesn't just become a wizard, great or otherwise. One must be trained and taught the very principles that must be followed,' said Afeclin.

'I agree completely.'

'The greatest wizard that ever lived is in that cottage over there,' Afeclin said. While his hand was technically pointed in the direction of Zallucien's house, in the garden of the Goddess he was pointing at a large tree. Nevertheless Afeclinella seemed to understand. 'However, he refuses to train me and while I understand his reasons I can't help but feel that he is wrong... is that wrong?'

'It is never wrong to follow a desire within oneself that is good and true,' she answered with wisdom.

'...But I cannot make him train me.'

'No, that is true and neither can I. I cannot make a person do something they do not want to do. The gods do not force anyone to do anything. We give people the opportunity to make their own decisions. This has both good and bad consequences but regardless they retain their freedom,' Afeclinella explained with delicate reasoning.

'I see,' Afeclin said bowing his head again as his heart sank.

'Still...' the Goddess added with thought, 'I don't see you being trained by anyone else.'

'You do see me being trained though,' Afeclin asked with concern, 'don't you?'

The corner of Afeclinella's mouth rose just a little and there was a smile within her eyes.

'Faith...' the Goddess said as she started to fade away, 'you must have... faith.'

'Before you go, I wanted to ask,' Afeclin called in desperation, 'was it you who protected me as a baby with the moonrock?'

'No,' she said, disappearing before his eyes, 'that was someone much closer to you than I.'

And then she was gone.

When Afeclin had opened his eyes after speaking with Afeclinella he was surprised to see that it had started to get dark.

He had wondered what to make of his conversation with the Goddess. What had started out with him imagining he was in her presence had ended with him feeling like he had, in actual fact, been before her.

He had been able to hear her voice in his ears. He could smell her fragrance, which was enchanting, and once she had faded away he could not imagine her back as much as he tried.

Even now a day later it seemed impossible but the memory still felt real.

The dream I had the other night also felt very real, he thought to himself, feeling confused and unsettled.

'Maybe I am crazy,' Afeclin said to himself.

'No you are not crazy,' came a voice from behind him.

Afeclin shifted his body around to see Zallucien standing behind him.

'At least, you're not crazy for the reasons you think you are. If you are crazy for a completely different reason… well… that is not for me to say,' Zallucien said strolling around the fire and sitting down cross-legged on the other side opposite Afeclin.

Afeclin sat opened-mouthed for a moment and then asked, 'How do you know the reason I think I might be crazy?'

'Well, there is that dream that plagues you for a start and then of course there's the fact that you have been sitting here for the past couple days watching a green flame. Onlookers might call it crazy, but not me. I know that you needed to learn how to make a green flame, which you succeeded in doing, congratulations. Now I assume you are sitting here in practice of going to visit my old chum Crymonthon.'

Afeclin let out a disheartened sigh.

'I was hoping to prove to you just how dedicated I am.'

'Ahh… but it will take more than dedication to prove that you will not turn evil as soon as I turn my back.'

'I know that,' Afeclin said bowing his head, 'but I had to try something. I need to be trained and I just know that you are the one to do it. I have studied hard the books that have been available to me. I have worked hard to improve the magic I have learned. I feel destined to do this… like I have been prepared all my life. In an all elf village this was the only thing that ever felt natural or normal for me. I could never become a dark mage… I know that of myself. I don't need an aura to tell me what I am, for I already know. I want to do good and help people and rid the world of its evil.'

Zallucien sat in quiet reflection, listening with interest. He was not wearing the strange blue spectacles Afeclin had come accustomed to seeing him in. This time through the wizard's eyes he could see the profound essence that he embodied.

'Please teach me,' Afeclin pleaded. 'I will be a good student… I will do what I am told and the moment you see my aura start to change for the worse you can stop the training. I won't let you down… please give me a chance.'

There was quietness between the two for a few minutes while Zallucien pondered and Afeclin sat, awaiting his reply.

The afternoon sun was high in the sky warming everything its light touched. Afeclin, although seated in the shade of the tree, could feel the heat emanating from the ground nearby. The fire also had a warm glow that radiated heat onto his face resulting in an abundance of warmth being felt. The smell of ash and smoke drifted around him and up his nostrils, at times causing him to cough or sneeze.

'If I agree to teach you, I will have to have complete adherence to my methods. You must trust me, and you must obey my rules, no questions asked,' Zallucien said with a stern furrow. 'Do you agree?'

There was now not a shadow of the battering old fool that Zallucien had played days earlier. In his place was an intelligent, strong and knowledgeable man who could be quite frightening to look at. Indeed, a strong and very powerful wizard.

Behind his dark eyes lay a lifetime of dedication to the art. The wrinkles around his eyes showed pain and stress from the things he had had to live with and endure.

This was the man who had been imprisoned for forty years by a dark queen and nearing death had managed to escape and free over a thousand prisoners.

This was the same man who exploded into a fireball when attacked by a family of dragons, killing the dragons and freeing a town full of people who were being devoured by them, one by one.

His cause was always good and from what Afeclin had read of this noble man… he never asked for anything from anyone in return.

Afeclin revered Zallucien and only hoped that he could someday be even half the man that his mentor was.

He did not have to consider for an instant whether he agreed to the old mage's demands.

'I will do all that you ask. I only hope I can live up to what you expect of me. I do not wish to let you down.'

Zallucien looked at Afeclin and narrowed his eyes, then relaxed and half smiled.

'I believe that.'

It felt good to know that Zallucien believed in him but it also made Afeclin more determined to show him that he was not wrong for doing so.

'Shall we go inside then?' suggested Zallucien. Then he added with a grin, 'I will show you to your room and to be honest you could really do with a good wash.'

Afeclin nodded and attempted to stand up. After having sat in the same position for days, his legs were numb and jellylike and his first attempt to stand almost landed him in the fire. When he tried again he managed to stand but he did have to hold onto something. He grabbed at the nearby tree he had been seated under, getting to his feet with relative ease compared to the pain he now felt in his legs. As the blood flowed back into his feet they began to cramp and he found he couldn't walk for a few minutes until everything had settled.

By now Zallucien was at the cottage door and called back to Afeclin.

'What are you waiting for?'

Afeclin shook the life painfully back into his legs and then hobbled into the cottage as fast as he could.

'Thank you so much Zallucien... for giving me a chance and all,' Afeclin said when he had caught up to the older wizard.

'It is not me you need to thank. You have a real friend in the Goddess.'

Afeclin stopped in his tracks, surprised.

'You spoke with the Goddess?'

'Yes. She was quite adamant that I needed to train you... so much so that she was willing to vouch for you.'

'Really?'

'Yes, so you see, you really are not crazy after all,' Zallucien said with a wink.

So it was true! He had not imagined his visit with the Goddess. She had helped him by giving her word that Afeclin was worth training... *that has to mean something!* At any rate he now had two people he could not let down.

'This will be your room,' Zallucien said showing Afeclin into a small chamber that housed little more than a bed and side table with a lantern on it.

It did seem a little cramped, unlike the large spacious rooms of the castle he grew up in but it was only for the use of resting one's head so Afeclin wondered, *what more could I want?*

'It's perfect,' said Afeclin with gratitude.

'Well, there's no need to exaggerate,' said the old man, 'but we wizards live a humble existence and there is simply no need for extravagance. Come, there is more I want to show you.'

Chapter

XLIII

Wolflang had been riding for a number of hours in the hot sun headed for Dewby Forest. The path he followed was through open fields that had very few trees and shade was limited.

Long seedy grass blanketed the ground surrounding the sandy path, withering in the heat of the day.

Qwiaquet bugs hopped about the grass on long slender legs chirping busily. The occasional dracasia or desert dragon-lizard as they were better known for their spiky scales and tiny wings would scamper across the path and propel themselves into the air in an attempt to catch one of the bounding bugs for lunch. Abwahnu's hooves made a weary shushing sound as they shuffled through the hot golden sand.

The sun beat down upon the back of Wolflang's neck and the sweat poured from his brow to his face which ran into his eyes, stinging them and making it impossible to see. Adding to the irritations he already felt, many tiny red-winged rausmoth flies that lived in the sand delighted in torturing him further by dancing and buzzing around his face.

Even though he was trying to conserve his water supply, Wolflang's throat was dry and he had a terrible thirst. As a consequence, he had soon drunk all the water from his waterskin. He decided that he needed to keep a look out for some small creek where he could fill it up.

'I can't believe this day,' he said to himself. 'I can't remember another day this hot since I left Tebelligan.'

After another couple of hours journeying, when he was feeling close to dehydration, he heard something that sounded like a running stream close by.

Wolflang rode his horse in the direction he suspected the sound was coming from. He had to stray a little from the beaten track but at last, nestled in some long grass, he found it.

'Looks like a good place to rest a while,' he said to Abwahnu who, having wasted no time, was drinking water from the flowing river.

Wolflang squatted down beside the cool stream and after gulping down handfuls of the refreshing water, threw some on his face and behind his neck. He pulled the piece of string that he had tied his hair back with earlier that day and wet his long, mousey hair to cool himself further. He then sat down in the shade of a tall leafy bush to rest with a package he had bought from the tavern before he left.

Opening the package he found a small loaf of bread, a block of cheese and two figs. Cutting a chunk of the cheese off, he ate in hunger as if he had never enjoyed a large meal before he left Rengal.

After snacking on some of the food, he rewrapped what was left and placed it on the ground next to him. He then lay back onto the long grass, pushing it down to flatten it and then resting his head on his folded cloak. Looking at the cloudless blue sky, he listened to the sounds from the stream for a while before drifting off into a restful sleep.

He awoke hours later, to find a strange man looking down at him.

'Huhhh!' Wolflang uttered, sucking a short, sharp breath in as his body jolted awake.

'I didn't mean to startle you, brother,' said the man in an accent that was unfamiliar to him.

Wolflang rubbed his eyes to clear them. Then sitting himself up he finally saw who had approached him. Before him stood a very tall, half naked, black man, holding a long spear in one hand. Around his waist hung what looked like a small loincloth and he wore no shoes upon his feet. His body was very muscular and he appeared to have several scars on his arms and torso. His head for the most part was bald with long matted hair that began just above his ears and ended at his waist. It was decorated with feathers and bits of straw.

Wolflang had never seen anyone so dark before and was surprised by how green the man's eyes were.

'Hallo there, brother,' the man said in his thick accent.

'Ah, hi,' answered Wolflang staring at the unusual man before him.

'I wondered if you minded my sharing your little river with you?' asked the man with politeness.

'No,' said Wolflang looking around at the small trickling stream, 'I mean of course not, be my guest.'

The man nodded in thanks, then dropping to his knees, cupped the water in his hands and drank of the cool stream.

The man's muscular body was thick with droplets of sweat and rausmoth bugs stuck to him like glue.

After the man had drunk his fill, he splashed water all over his body and wet his thick hair. When he stood back up again he looked refreshed.

'I needed that,' he said with a grin, then added, 'my name's Oomall.'

'Uh, I'm Wolflang,' he said offering his hand in friendship.

'This is how my tribe's people do it,' Oomall said squatting down as he took Wolflang by the hand and then moved his hand into an upright position to grip the palm more firmly, making their forearms and elbows meet.

'Your tribe's people? Where are you from?'

'I come from the West. My tribe is situated just west of the Graandis Mountain Range,' Oomall said pointing a finger in the direction he spoke of. Then joining Wolflang on the grass added, 'Only... I left there a year ago.'

'You left? Why?'

'It's sort of a long story...' Oomall began bowing his head, 'but I was cast out.'

'Cast out?' Wolflang repeated with surprise. 'What did you do to deserve that?'

'I was in love with a girl who was so far above my tribal standing that I had no right to even speak to her. She was the Chieftain's daughter and I, no more than a lowly hunter.'

'I should have known it would have something to do with a woman... ' Wolflang muttered under his breath.

'Sorry? What was that, brother?'

'Oh, I was just thinking that no tragedy would be a tragedy without a woman involved,' Wolflang said shaking his head. 'So what happened?'

'Well, I began to realise that for me to be even able to stand half a chance with her I would have to become a warrior and compete for her hand in union... it's basically the same as you might call marriage,' he interjected by way of explanation. 'I trained harder than anyone I knew. I changed the way I hunted... using my bare hands and body instead of my spear when hunting larger prey. I ate a lot of food to build myself up and I worked my body every spare minute of the day.'

Wolflang sighed as he thought of Lenna. It was unfortunate that he didn't care for her so much that he would sacrifice everything just to be in her presence. The truth was that he was willing to risk losing Lenna to live his life.

'You must have really loved this girl.'

'I just knew she was the one for me and I was determined to do all I could to prove it but that's not the half of it. Later I discovered that she also had had great interest in me for the longest time but had been forbidden to mingle with those below her station. However, once I found this out we started meeting in secret. Before long, we were in love and determined to enter into a union,' Oomall related.

'Even so, first you had to prove yourself worthy,' Wolflang interrupted.

'True... which I planned to do by competing for her. Unfortunately on the day of the competition I found myself unwell and while I know I put in a good effort... my sickness got the better of me and I lost. She was then promised to the victor, which devastated her,' Oomall said with sadness.

'But how did you end up being cast out? Surely not because you lost.'

'To make a long story short, I was found in her tent...'

'In her tent? Is that all?'

'In a compromising position...'

'Ooh...'

'...on the day of her union.'

'I understand now,' said Wolflang feeling a little sorrowful for the man.

'Had they come in two minutes earlier they would have found me in an even more compromising position... if you know what I mean,' Oomall gave Wolflang a wink, 'and had that been the case I would have had my neck on the chopping block. They would have ensured that I was given a shamed man's death, for chopping off a man's head also chops off his hair. It is believed in our culture that to cut one's hair is a sign of disgrace and the Gods won't accept you into their afterlife if you are disgraced.'

'So that is a pretty hefty punishment then, to die and enter the afterlife disgraced all in the one swing of the executioner's axe,' said Wolflang stunned by the brutality of Oomall's tribe. 'I guess you were pretty lucky.'

'Lucky, huh,' Oomall said with a sorrowful laugh. 'I was once almost a warrior, almost in union with the girl of my dreams and now here I am... worthless, a good-for-nothing nomad who is forced to wander this world aimlessly for the rest of his days.'

'But why?' Wolflang asked, amazed at Oomall's attitude. 'Why must you wander aimlessly? Why can't you settle down somewhere, or find something to do, something to get involved in?'

Oomall looked at Wolflang with a wry expression on his face. 'What would I do? I am a hunter... possibly a warrior, these are all I know.'

'Hunters make good money in the city. You hunt for beasts and then you sell them making a handsome profit,' Wolflang said thinking about the money Typhin had made selling his sheep.

'What would I do with money? We live off the land; we have little use for money. Oh, I'm not stupid, I have seen what money can buy but we are simple people who live a simple existence.'

Wolflang felt very sad for Oomall, *he seems to be more lost than I am... or at least was.*

He sat thoughtful for a moment.

'Well then, perhaps you need to put your warrior training to good use. I am on my way to join the legion, to become a soldier. I want to fight the evil in this world... to make a difference, to be useful,' Wolflang said with passion. 'Why don't you come with me?'

'By the Gods!... I had never considered joining with races other than my own to fight the wickedness in this world,' Oomall exclaimed in thought. 'In my year of traveling I have seen much that has angered me and made me sad for the evil that exists in Titania... but as a tribesman it is our belief that what the outside races do is really none of our business. We believe in keeping out of wars and such strife.'

'I hadn't considered it either. Being an elf we view all affairs outside of Tebelligan as having nothing to do with us. However, earlier today I met an unusual man who put me on this path,' said Wolflang. 'I felt completely lost in a world I could not understand but now I feel there may be something I can do, that I can make something of myself.'

Oomall sat in silence for a while appearing to be deep in thought. When he did speak he changed the subject.

'So you're an elf. I wondered where you came from. I have never seen anyone with such pointy ears and your skin's darker than other people I have met. To be honest I would not have even known what an elf was until now.'

'At least you haven't stared and pointed at me,' said Wolflang with a grin. 'I imagine you must have people stare at you also being so dark yourself.'

'Yes brother, it is true, people are always curious about you when you're different. When I enter a town or village, children always run up to me and touch my arms to feel my skin because it is different to theirs... but I don't mind, at least they don't fear me or look at me like I am an enemy.'

Wolflang sat thinking, when he heard a sudden crack of a stick breaking behind him. He looked around in time to see a black sack coming down upon his head. He tried to make a move to avoid it but it came down too fast and a second later he was in darkness.

Wolflang struggled and kicked. He tried punching out at whoever had ambushed him but found each time he did so he hit nothing but air.

He could also hear noises of a struggle. It sounded like Oomall was also being attacked.

'Who are you? What do you want of me?' Wolflang yelled in anger and frustration.

Wolflang cried out in pain as something hard and very heavy hit his head, within a moment he had blacked out.

Chapter

XLIV

Lenna had spent the past couple of days in a cramped wagon, squished up against human women that bickered between each other and complained about every little futile thing that bothered them, making an uncomfortable journey, unbearable. No one was all that nice to Lenna; either out of jealousy or spite the women looked down on her and treated her with animosity. So Lenna sat alone and kept to herself.

Inside the large wagon, a wooden bench ran around the inside perimeter and two large benches sat in the middle providing seating for the captives. Lenna sat on one of the outer benches and drooped her arms over the side of the wagon watching the wilderness and countryside as they rolled by. At times she would sit and study the beautiful shell that she had found on the beach. It was shiny with a pearly crust that was curved with ripples. Depending on the sun's light shining on it determined its colour at any given time. Sometimes the shell would look more blue with a hint of green and at other times it was more pink with yellow swirls. While just an inanimate object, the shell brought a little comfort to Lenna. It was something she could own and hold onto and in some ways felt like a little piece of home even though she had collected it far from the Tebelligan border. Collecting shells was something she had enjoyed doing with her mother and sister when they would visit the ocean together in her youth. So she treasured the shell as a precious item, one that had great value to her. The stunning crustacean also reminded her of the mysterious shell that she had found only days ago on the path to her home. Lenna thought about the ancient script carved into its delicate crust and the peculiar glowing that had attracted Lenna to find it in the first place. She had hidden it inside a crafted wooded box in her room with the intention of showing Afeclin and finding out something more about it. How differently things had turned out for her than she had envisioned at that point.

For weeks she had done little more than imagine her life with Wolflang. Now here she was trapped in a wagon full of human women, destined to serve as a slave, owned by some strange man in black.While she did not feel that any woman, regardless of her race, deserved to be a slave, she was quite grateful to see the other women leave the overcrowded wagon. Even to take up their serving positions in little inns or drinking houses that the cavalcade visited as they moved from town to town.

Once she could see through the cart to the other side, Lenna spotted a young shy woman with curly blonde hair; her blue dress was stained and ripped. She had looked more frightened than Lenna had felt and all the other women seemed to ignore her. Lenna took it upon herself to cross over to the other side of the wagon and talk to the girl to see if she could comfort her.

'Hi, are you okay?' she had asked with somewhat timidness herself.

The girl had said nothing but nodded with a sheepish expression.

'She's mute,' shouted a busty brunette with a big voice from the other side of the cart where Lenna had been seated prior to moving, 'might as well not bother wit' her, she can't answer anyway.'

Feeling annoyed at the woman's attitude toward the girl's disability, Lenna had tried even harder to connect with her.

'My real name's Lenna,' she had said in a hushed tone. 'I gave the man in black a different name because I don't want them to address me by my real name. I know, it doesn't change the situation much, but I kind of feel it hides some of my identity. Does that sound silly?'

The woman had shaken her head vigorously and in that instant, Lenna had known she had found a friend.

'I only wish I knew your name,' Lenna said with a sigh.

The girl leaned over and after smoothing a heap of sand in the bottom of the wagon, wrote the letters to spell her name.

'Sarvina?' Lenna said with surprise.

The girl nodded and gave a shy half-smile.

'That is really pretty.'

From that moment onward, Lenna and Sarvina had kept close together.

The man in black, whom the women touted as Nagrin the nasty, seemed to take an interest in the developing relationship between the two and was supportive of it, giving Lenna and Sarvina the opportunity to remain together whenever they had alighted from the wagons. To Lenna, Nagrin was a strange man and she couldn't quite figure him out. When the women did as they were told and everything was going well he was a gentleman, kind even, but when he did not get things his way or if they disobeyed him, he was downright cruel.

Lenna learnt in no time to keep her mouth shut, even though she found it difficult not to assert her opinion. She was unfailing in doing what she was ordered to, avoiding any retribution.

Lenna had heard the women talking during the trip about one of the girls who had been killed by Nagrin because she jumped from the wagon and attempted to escape. They talked of how the girl hadn't got very far because she had tripped over her long silk dress. It had reminded Lenna of the woman in the red dress, who lay on the forest floor having bled to death, and made her feel ill again.

'Was it a red silk dress?' Lenna questioned to the surprise of the other women.

The women disregarded Lenna and continued chatting amongst themselves. Sarvina squeezed Lenna's leg for attention and then having gained it, nodded with vehemence.

'It was red?' Lenna asked looking for confirmation.

Sarvina nodded again with sadness and fear behind her eyes.

'Oh,' Lenna said, having a greater understanding as to why Sarvina seemed to be as afraid as she was. Nagrin was not one to be reckoned with.

There didn't seem to be many trees around in the western part of Marrapassa, the land had lush, green rolling plains that covered miles and miles of terrain in every direction they could see. While the sun shone with harsh rays in the sky, heating up the countryside, it wasn't the kind of heat Lenna had experienced only days ago in the desert. It was humid, the grass looked wet as if it had rained only recently and a cool welcome breeze swept across the prairies bringing relief to their clammy skin.

Sarvina and Lenna were the only two remaining in the wagon when they arrived in the city Zurrid a day later.

They were driven in through the main entrance, which was a large arch built of rich red stone with black wrought iron gates that opened onto the main streets of town. A high dark green hedge, that had bursts of tiny pink flowers all over it, covered the front edge of Zurrid. Rooves, of varying colours and styles could be seen floating just above the hedge. It was a very pretty sight to behold in the middle of the green plains.

The streets were not paved at all but were green with grass. Dirt tracks where the wagon wheels rolled along the ground sat in the middle of lawn but were just an extension of the dirt road they had been on.

All the houses were built with black rock and were quite similar in design. The roof was the feature of each little cottage that gave them uniqueness. Some rooves were pitched at higher degrees than others, some had little windows in the upper part of the roof while others had an ordinary shape to them but each were bursting with ultra bright blue, yellow or red coloured shingles. Gardens, abundant with vegetation and flowers, crept around the outside of each house, beautifying the little town further.

They drove straight through the middle of the town, passing many houses and little storefronts all the while being watched by local onlookers with interest and fear. Looking back at the black coach that Nagrin rode in, Lenna could see why. It was creepy and evil looking and the trolls who walked or rode along with the cavalcade appeared menacing. Their arrival was far from unassuming or without a certain amount of pageantry.

At the far end of town they came to a large two-storey inn with a high pitched purple roof. Under the front eaves swung a white sign with dark purple writing, 'The Violet Spraide'.

The wagons came to a stop and Lenna knew this was to be their new home.

One of the trolls unlocked a small door in the front of the wagon that made for easy movement on and off the vehicle. He hollered at Lenna and Sarvina, ordering them out of the wagon. The two women obeyed in haste and as they descended to the ground they were hurried across the grass to the front porch of the inn.

As they were about to step up on the stone stairs that led to the entrance, Lenna was whisked away by Nagrin.

Both Lenna and Sarvina looked to each other with distress. *What does he want with me now? Don't tell me I am not going to stay with Sarvina.*

Nagrin led Lenna back to the wagon with a tight grip on her arms. She looked him in the eyes with all the courage she could muster, waiting for whatever was to come from the dark, fair-haired man.

'I need you to watch over Sarvina,' said the unnerving human, his eyes firm and serious.

Lenna was not quite sure what to say. She was confused and surprised by the request from Nagrin the "nasty" of all people.

'I can see you two have become quite close but she is not strong like you. I want you to keep her safe, speak on her behalf, make sure that no-one has any reason to harm her,' Nagrin said with startling compassion. 'Will you do that for me?'

Lenna stared into the man's dark eyes searching for reason behind his sudden care. *He's in love with her*, she realised with sudden horror. *How can such a thing be possible?* It seemed implausible, but there it was staring her in the face. The dark man had always shown kindness to Sarvina and once Lenna had befriended the blonde woman, Nagrin had been rather hospitable to her also.

'Of course I will,' she said, *but not for you.*

'Good,' he said lessening his grip on her, 'I will come back from time to time, when I can and check on her. If these people treat her badly, you be sure to let me know.'

Lenna nodded, still watching with curiosity the sincere expression on his face that went against the name the women knew him as. *It is almost like he has two completely different personalities*, she thought with interest, *one evil and one a saint.*

They joined the others inside the lounge area of the spacious building. The room was stuffy and hot making it difficult to breathe. There were plenty of panelled windows at the front and back of the room but none had been opened.

'Open a window, for crying out loud!' Nagrin ordered, looking to Lenna with agitation as beads of sweat dripped down his face.

Lenna ran over to a front window desperate for airflow and began to turn the decorative handle to unlatch the window. She found it difficult to see through the glass panels as the glass itself had been blown by a glassblower which had left a large round patch of colour in the centre of each panel.

Just as she managed to push out the panelled window frame allowing a cool breeze to sweep in through the building, she heard a voice yell from the hallway stairs behind her.

'What do you think you are doing?'

Lenna spun around and spied a grey-haired lady dressed in a long green patterned dress with a white apron hurry down the stairs.

'I, I...' Lenna tried to push out her words, 'it was hot.'

'The master does not like to have the windows open at this time of the year, it lets in all the insects,' the lady yelled in distress as she ran to the window to close it.

'Ahem,' came a cough from Nagrin who was standing behind them, still in the middle of the room.

The lady turned around in surprise.

'Oh master Nagrin, I did not expect you for another couple of days,' she said with an awkward smile that revealed yellow teeth.

'Lord Spraide is no longer the master of this inn. His mysterious disappearance rendered this inn available for Lord Moorlan to purchase. I trust preparations are in order?'

'My apologies master,' the lady said looking very pale as she reopened the window. Then stiffening in pride she added, 'Yes, everything has been prepared... the former staff have been dismissed apart from Tesletta, the cook and Briale, the housemaid.'

'And of course you... I'm sorry what do you do?' Nagrin asked with his arms held behind his back, pacing in front of the women and looking down on her with scepticism.

'I oversee this establishment, I manage the staff and make sure everything is running properly and smoothly, I was under the impression that you needed my assistance as Lord Moorlan would not be running the place himself... I...' the lady explained with urgency.

'Alright, alright, it appears that we do need your services. You don't need to be getting yourself frazzled,' interrupted Nagrin.

'I am not frazzled!' the lady pronounced with an indignant sniff, folding her arms across her chest.

Nagrin looked at her with a wry expression causing the lady to feel uncomfortable and uncross her arms bringing them to the sides of her body.

'I will be leaving you in charge of this establishment, but I am trusting you to run it well. This is to be the best inn in town, no excuses,' Nagrin threatened. Pointing to Sarvina and Lenna he added, 'These are your two new waitresses. They are primarily to work the front of house and serve customers, however, they are at your disposal to work under your direction as you see fit. But I warn you that whenever I or Moorlan himself come to visit, I expect to see these women in top shape... do I make myself clear?'

'Perfectly,' she said through clenched teeth and pursed lips.

'Well then, we will be leaving you to it, these girls may need some training,' said Nagrin, turning to leave as he motioned to the trolls to ready the wagons before turning back to the lady, adding in a low supercilious voice close to her face, 'and open the windows, you need to let some air into this place.'

The lady nodded but her look was venomous, which frightened Lenna. She wondered if the older woman's agitation would be taken out on both her and Sarvina despite Nagrin's demands of keeping them in "top shape".

The lady opened all the windows on the main floor with begrudging effort. Then returned to Lenna and Sarvina, looking them up and down with a forlorn sigh.

'I suppose if this is all they have left me to work with, you will have to do,' she said standing straight with a single hand in an apron pocket. 'My name is of no significance to you. We are not friends nor will we ever be, therefore you will address me as Madam and you will only address me if I call on you. I understand that this isn't the situation you desire to be in, but nor I. Things were working perfectly well under the old management, and I had staff that already knew what they were doing. I did not need to start at the beginning again and train them. It just seems pointless to me... besides which I am understaffed now. I had at least three more workers, so I hope you like working hard because you are going to need to... do I make myself clear?'

Sarvina nodded and Lenna piped up with a 'yes madam'.

'What's wrong with you missy, the bugs got your tongue?' Madam questioned Sarvina, her nostrils flaring.

'Madam, may I just interject here, Sarvina canno...' Lenna started but was silenced by Madam's raised hand in a stopping motion.

'Did I ask you to speak?'

'No Madam but...' Lenna tried to continue.

'Silence!' Madam yelled at Lenna having used up all her patience. 'I don't want to hear from you, either of you... just stay put and I will send Briale down here to show you around and get you into your uniforms.'

Madam started off toward the entrance hall where the stairs were and then spun back around. 'Know this, if either of you try to escape, both of you will be punished for it. I can make it so that you will keep in excellent shape as Nagrin expects... but suffer greatly you will... so do not even consider it.'

Once Madam was gone, Lenna looked to Sarvina who bit her nails in distress.

Lenna went to her and pulled the girl's hand from her face. 'Don't worry Sarvina, we are going to stick this out. If we just keep our heads down and do what we are asked, everything will be alright.'

Sarvina seemed to question with her eyes.

'I am sure of it,' Lenna answered with an assuring smile, but deep down she felt very uncertain about their futures in the inn.

Her eyes scanned the room with interest. Along the main wall, where there were no windows, there were two large open fireplaces with heavy-looking mantles sitting just above. On top of each mantlepiece was a couple of marble statuettes at each end and some brass figurines between them. Above the left fireplace, in the middle of the mantle sat a large bronze-wood clock that had a gentle tick as the second hand moved. Lenna had never seen such a fine crafted timepiece, not even within the palace of Tebelligan. Its shiny wood, glowed from the red stained finish and brought out the natural patterns in the wood that it had been crafted from.

Close to the fireplaces were a number of round tables with cushioned chairs seated around about them while the rest of the lounge had large soft couches and armchairs around the edges of the walls.

In the middle of the room, covering a large portion of the dark red floorboards was a green, red and black carpet that was soft looking and had frayed edges. It was all in all a comfortable looking space.

Lenna's thoughts were interrupted by the sound of footsteps entering the lounge area and Lenna turned to see a woman not much older than Sarvina or herself standing at the entry. The woman wore a dark green dress with white lace trimming and an apron much like the outfit Madam had worn but simpler. Her long brown hair was held up in a messy knot on top of her head while pieces of hair fell down the sides of her face. She was attractive but in a plain way and was tall and slender with broad shoulders. In her hands she held a pile of folded sheets.

'You must be the new bar girls, my name is Briale and I am the housemaid,' she introduced with formality. 'I am afraid I have not had the time to ready your bedchambers... but you see we were not expecting you so soon.'

'Perhaps we can help you,' suggested Lenna feeling an instant ease with the tall housemaid.

Briale gave a tired smile. 'That's very kind of you but with all that you will have to do, I doubt you will have time to help me. Come, I'll show you to your room.'

Lenna and Sarvina followed Briale up the long spiralling staircase to the second floor.

At the top of the stairs, a balcony looked down upon the main entrance, its balustrade wound around the top floor. Briale led them around the platform passing many rooms with numbers on the doors that were all painted with different colours. Once they had made it the whole way around they came to a small dark corridor that had a tiny panelled window at the other end.

'This is the staff quarters,' Briale announced as they entered the walkway. 'First door to your right is Madam's. You would have to be desperate or have a major emergency on your hands to ever knock at her door. Opposite is Tesletta's room, have you met her?' Lenna shook her head. 'She's the cook... nice lady... when she's not cooking but keep out of her way as much as you can when she is, she has a frightful temper and does not appreciate people in her kitchen.'

They walked on. 'This door on the left is my room, then there is a couple of rooms empty since, I am sure Madam explained, we are understaffed now with the changeover,' Briale continued with a sniff. 'Here is the tub-room, it's just a room with a tub for washing, Madam insists on cleanliness. The tub is big enough to soak your whole body in once a week and there are buckets of fresh water to wash your face and hands daily.

The room at the very end is for the both of you, Madam insisted that you share. I don't know why, but it is quite comfortable for two.'

'It is fine, we do not mind,' said Lenna, grateful to be stuck with Sarvina, 'do we?'

Sarvina shook her head with a smile.

'You don't talk much, do you?' Briale observed.

Lenna stepped in to explain.

'Sarvina cannot speak, she is mute,' Lenna said as she tucked her hair back behind her ear. 'I tried to explain to Madam but she would not listen.'

Briale stared at Lenna for a moment with surprise.

'What is it?' Lenna asked with confusion.

'Oh I don't mean to stare... I didn't know... I mean I have never met an elf before.'

Lenna realised at once what she had done and felt a little embarrassed by it. 'Oh, it's alright, I get that a lot.'

'You have no idea what that will do for this establishment. People will come to stay here just to be served by you,' said Briale her voice rising with excitement.

Lenna now understood why Nagrin had gone to such an effort to make sure that he had her. She was to be a side attraction apart from a slave, Lenna would be good for business. She sighed. 'Do people need to know?'

'Why wouldn't you want them to? You're an elf, you're special and you will be treated as such,' said Briale as she opened the door to their room.

Inside the small chamber was little more than two unmade beds, a small wardrobe and a dresser. Between the beds there was a small window with the blown panelled glass that was similar to the windows on the lower level.

Briale walked to the wardrobe and took out two dark green dresses the same as her own.

'These will be your uniforms, however I think yours may be a bit big for you,' she said to Lenna. 'I can take it in for you though... I can sew a little.'

'Thanks,' Lenna said with absentmindedness, her thoughts returning to their conversation in the corridor, *It is dangerous being special, humans look at you as if you are a possession they can exploit. I shall really have to keep my head down.*

'Here are your sheets. I am sure you can make your own beds,' said Briale placing the bundle she had brought upstairs with her on one of the bunks. 'I will allow you time to organise yourselves and change into your uniforms, then I will have to show you what you will be expected to do for the dinner service tonight. I'm afraid you will have to get to work right away, as I said we're...'

'Short-staffed,' Lenna interrupted with an eyebrow raised.

'Yes,' Briale responded with a smile.

'Can I ask a question though? What happened to the previous owner?' Lenna asked hoping she was not stepping over any lines by doing so.

Briale had a concerned look on her face. She continued towards the door, then closing it, she turned around.

'I don't know terribly much...' she started in a serious undertone, 'but about a month ago, a man came in and asked to speak to the proprietor. He offered him a large sum of money to buy this establishment, but my old master was not interested. He said it had been in the family for generations and no amount of money would ever match the sentimental value. The man left after warning him that he would regret his decision. A couple of weeks later my master went missing and has not been seen since. Then we received word that the inn had been bought by Moorlan, though what he wants with an inn in Zurrid, I have no idea, and we were told to dismiss half our staff and prepare for slaves to come in and work. It is all very strange, especially our master's disappearance, seems all very mysterious and underhanded... and if ya ask me, I'd say our master didn't just disappear, but was done away with... if you get my drift. Not that I will miss him at all. I am glad to see the back of him quite frankly. However I don't know that our new master is any better... At least he manages us from the Island of Norvak. Although I don't fancy having the trolls wandering in all the time, they are a drunken and crude lot but at the end of the day, what choice do we have?'

Lenna nodded with understanding. She was able to follow little about what was going on around Marrapassa and who people were, but it was clear that she was not the only person trying to make sense of the goings on.

Briale opened the door again and a draft flooded into the room from the corridor.

'I must tend to my other duties, get dressed and meet me downstairs,' said Briale in a rush of words, 'and don't worry I will let Madam know about Sarvina. It is best to come from me.'

Chapter

XLV

Awaking to the sound of a crackling fire, Wolflang opened his eyes and gazed around. The sun was now lower in the sky and although it was not cold or dark yet, a fire burned to one side of him. On the other side of the fire he could make out a shape. He tried to sit up higher to see better but found that he was unable. As he looked down he discovered that he was bound to the tree he was sitting against.

Sudden shock and fear swept over his body like a tidal wave.

Where am I? Why am I here? What are these scoundrels going to do with me? raced through his mind, over and over.

The wind was still for a moment, the fire died a little and Wolflang was able to better see the figure beyond the subdued flames.

It was Oomall and he was tied to another tree on the opposite side of the fire. His body was slumped and his head was down. His arms were wrapped around the tree and there appeared to be blood oozing out the top of his head.

'Oomall!' Wolflang called out trying to wake the dark man.

'So you're awake are ya?' An unfamiliar face appeared in front of him from behind the tree.

'Who are you?' asked Wolflang struggling in the ropes. 'What do you want of me?'

The man, or creature, as he appeared, sniffed the air with disgust.

'I'll ask the questions,' came another voice and another strange man appeared in front of him.

The men had an unusual look to them. Their faces were long, pointy and hairy. They had small noses with hideous whiskers that poked out from each side of their faces. Their hands were long and slender with sharp, clawlike nails that were dirty. Even their movements were unusual. They moved more like animals than people. With their arms bent in front of them, hands dropped and fingers curved, they had the look of weasels.

'Tell me where to find your friend,' the second one wheezed.

'My friend?' asked Wolflang realising full well that they were speaking about Afeclin and that these creatures must have been who Typhin had warned him about. 'You have him over there.'

Wolflang nodded his head in the direction of Oomall hoping that by doing so he wasn't further endangering his life.

The weaselly creature glared at Wolflang through his beady eyes and grew angry. Lifting a hand high above his head, he brought it down fast, hitting Wolflang hard across his face, digging his nails in at the last second to leave a deep scratch.

'Ahhh!' Wolflang cried out as his cheek stung.

'You know full well that I am referring to your magical friend,' the man screeched in anger. 'Don't waste my time!'

'Well, I regret to inform you that he fell into a large mud puddle and we couldn't get him out.'

The man looked at Wolflang and snarled.

'Yes, the mud,' the weasel said with thought. 'The tracks disappeared into the mud.'

'That's because he drowned in the mud,' Wolflang said with as much sadness as he could fake.

The weasel nodded at another one of the creatures that had just appeared as if from nowhere.

Before Wolflang had time to think, the newest creature was at the elf's neck wielding a knife against his throat.

Wolflang could barely breathe in fear of the knife slicing him.

'He is a mystic, a magical mutant,' said the weasel that appeared to be in charge. 'He would have found a way out. Where did he go?'

'I don't know, I haven't seen him,' Wolflang said with gentle caution.

The weasel nodded again and the one holding the knife pressed harder, this time leaving a slight laceration. The cut throbbed in pain and he could feel blood trickle down his neck to his chest.

'I thought... he... he was... d.dead... He is... only... an amateur magic... user,' Wolflang said trying to keep his speaking and breathing very slow so as not to allow the knife to cut any further.

'I see,' the creature said standing thoughtful for a moment, eyeing Wolflang intently.

The man then nodded to the first of the creatures, making a motion with his head directed toward Oomall.

The first creature understood and made his way over to the dark man tied to the other tree. First he stopped by the fire and pulled out a long burning metal rod. He then pulled Oomall's head back by his long hair, rousing the man to consciousness.

Oomall looked around with surprise.

The head weasel nodded again and gestured something with his clawed fingers.

The creature held the burning rod up to Oomall's face in obedience.

'Do you still insist that your friend was a mere amateur and not capable of escaping from mud designed by people just like himself, many moons ago?' the head weasel pressed.

Wolflang looked at Oomall who was frightened by the closeness of the glowing iron to his face and hair.

Wolflang was struck dumb. He didn't know what to do. He had been trying to protect his friend from the foul creatures but was beginning to wonder whether Afeclin even needed his protection. *After all Typhin did say that the path to Lawry Castle was enchanted and could not be found through searching for it. Then if they did by some miracle stumble upon it and make their way to the castle, surely the great Zallucien could stop the weaselly creatures from harming Afeclin. Therefore does Oomall or myself really need to die for Afeclin's sake? He wouldn't want that.*

By now the rod had burnt Oomall's face twice and Wolflang could stand it no longer.

'STOP!' he yelled with defeat. As he did so he felt the blade cut him again,'I will… tell you… what I… know.'

The head weasel motioned to the man with the rod to stop what he was doing and for the man holding the knife against Wolflang's throat to relax his grip.

'By all means elf, enlighten us with your knowledge,' the weasel said with a nasty grin.

'All I know is that he has made it to Lawry Castle to be trained by the great Zallucien,' said Wolflang hoping that the mere mention of Zallucien's name would frighten the weasels from their cause.

On the contrary it did the opposite.

The weasel stood looking at Wolflang with interest.

'Well now,' he said after a moment of thought. 'The truth at last. That wasn't so difficult was it?'

The weasel laughed with wicked intent.

'You know of course or perhaps you don't, that the castle was burned to the ground many years ago and the "Great" Zallucien killed.'

'What? That's not true.' Wolflang cried out in shock, 'That can't be true!'

The weasel raised a knowing eyebrow and gave an ironic smile, then he went to walk away.

'Kill them.'

'What?… Wait!' Wolflang began with urgency.

All of a sudden there was a loud growling sound that made everyone freeze on the spot.

Oh no, not a bear! thought Wolflang looking around him, trying to figure out where the growling was coming from. He felt like a piece of bait tied to the tree.

The bear appeared out of the scrub and stood up on his hind legs revealing a slender wolf-like backside.

'It's not a bear, it's another lawfabex,' Wolflang breathed as he tried to sit further back into the tree.

Coming down to the ground it growled and swung its massive paws with sharp claws at the two cowering weasels, tearing flesh and breaking a leg of the one holding the rod. The two ran away in fear through the trees chasing after their leader who had disappeared into the scrub the moment he had heard the beast. The wounded one hobbled in pain as the lawfabex chased close behind.

Wolflang had watched in surprise and horror. He could hear frightened screams in the distance and growls from the animal. Then realising that the beast could come back at any moment, he struggled with the ropes, trying to loosen them.

'Oomall. Oomall! Are you able to free yourself?' Wolflang called in desperation as he tried in vain to loosen the ropes that bound him. It appeared that Oomall had been trying to squeeze his hands out his bonds.

'I can't seem to get free. The ropes are too tight.'

'We have to get out. What if that lawfabex comes back?'

Wolflang remembered back to days beforehand when he had been lucky he had not been devoured by a lawfabex much like this one. It was an experience he was in no hurry to revisit. He sat, body shaking at the thought of the beast returning.

'Hey don't worry brother, that lawfabex surely won't be back. He's got enough to eat out there, he doesn't need us,' Oomall said, trying to remain calm, as if sensing the deeper fear that was inside Wolflang.

The two sat in helpless horror, listening to the gruesome sounds further away in the woods, hoping the beast would not return for dessert.

After a while all was quiet again and all the two could do was sit and watch the fire dance and swirl in front of them and hope that someone would happen upon them.

'Do you have any idea where we are?' Wolflang asked.

'I can't be too sure but I think we are on the outskirts of Dewby Forest,' Oomall said looking around.

'Really?' Wolflang said with a laugh. 'You mean those… weasels brought me where I wanted to be?'

'Well, I guess if you wanted to get to the Dewby Forest, then the answer is yes.'

'I'll be a son of a human,' Wolflang said quite amazed at the fact that the creatures had done him a favour.

'You're forgetting one thing, brother,' Oomall piped up putting a damper on Wolflang's delight, 'unless someone comes along and frees us we ain't going anywhere. And if we don't get freed before dark then we are sitting ducks for bears.'

The sun was now disappearing behind the trees. It would be dark soon.

Wolflang's heart sank. The chances of someone "just happening by" was slim to none. However, the longer they sat, the more chance there was that a bear, another lawfabex or perhaps some other ghastly creature would happen upon them.

Wolflang's fears were realised all too quickly, for sitting amongst the trees not far from them was the big, brown lawfabex. His thick stubby horn protruding out of his forehead was now red and entrails dripped from his blood-soaked jaw.

The beast approached them this time, with particular interest in Wolflang.

Sniffing and snuffling, the lawfabex examined Wolflang while the elf shook like a leaf in front of him.

Staring into the beast's large brown eyes, there was a familiarity. Wolflang hadn't noticed at first but this lawfabex was the same lawfabex that he had encountered days earlier.

Wolflang wondered what it could mean. *Is this beast following me or is it by chance that our paths have crossed again? Did the lawfabex save me on purpose or is he just hungry again and happened upon something to eat… coincidentally when my life was at stake?*

The elf looked the beast in the eyes, 'We meet again.'

The lawfabex stood tall all of a sudden, growling and baring his bloodied teeth, startling the frightened elf. Wolflang cringed as the lawfabex dropped, allowing his sharp claws to fall onto the ropes that held Wolflang, loosening them just a little. Then the beast grabbed at the ropes with his teeth and attempted to chew through them.

Both Oomall and Wolflang watched, stunned by the gesture.

The rope was broken and Wolflang was able to free himself. He jumped up off the ground and stood staring at the beast in silence.'Thank you,' he managed to say.

The lawfabex grunted and did a kind of nod with his enormous furry head.

Then remembering that Oomall sat waiting to be released, he dared focus his attention on the dark man. He was not quite sure if it was quite safe to trust the beast, he was still a wild animal after all.

Wolflang backed away from the lawfabex, keeping careful eye contact with it as he edged around the fire closer to Oomall.

Oomall was released in haste and the two stood staring at the beast, with a nervousness of someone holding a snake wondering when or if it may just choose to strike.

'They really gave it to you, brother,' said Oomall motioning to Wolflang's face and neck.

Wolflang wiped the blood from his face with the back of his hand.

'Oh, I'm sure it looks worse that it feels,' he said rubbing the blood from his hand onto his garboa cloth pants.

It occurred to Wolflang that his horse was nowhere to be seen and that he hadn't laid eyes on Abwahnu since they were abducted from their resting spot.

'I've lost my horse,' said Wolflang with frustration. 'What a day this is turning out to be.'

'Don't worry, brother, you can always walk. I walk everywhere,' said Oomall motioning to his shoeless feet.

'I guess I will have to now, but I was hoping to get where I am headed before nightfall.'

The lawfabex grunted and growled and motioned with his nose.

'I think he's trying to tell you something,' said Oomall with interest.

'What do you think he's trying to say?' whispered Wolflang as if trying to hide his ignorance from the beast.

The lawfabex kept motioning with his nose towards his back. He was clearly trying to tell them something.

'I think he's offering you a ride, brother.'

'No,' laughed Wolflang thinking it ridiculous that a wild animal should offer to carry a person, 'that can't be it. Could it?'

But the more Wolflang watched the beast's gestures the more Wolflang thought Oomall could be right. He decided there was only one way to find out and that was to ask the lawfabex himself.

'Are you offering to carry me on your back?' he asked only half expecting a response.

The beast nodded his hefty head.

'By Afeclinella!' Wolflang exclaimed with excitement.

'Should I?' he questioned Oomall with apprehension, hoping he wasn't about to do something stupid by accepting the lift.

'Do it brother. He obviously likes you. If he really wanted to eat you he would have done it by now.'

'Either that or he wants to take me home to feed the family.'

Wolflang approached the lawfabex with caution. The beast turned around and lay down as low as he could, making it easier for Wolflang to climb on his back. Wolflang was amazed by the intelligence of the animal. It was what he had seen days earlier when he had chosen not to kill him. *Could this be the beast's way of thanking me?*

Once Wolflang was seated in safety, the lawfabex stood up on all fours preparing to depart.'Are you going to come with us?'

'No, I think I will make myself a new spear and catch me a fowl for dinner while the fire still burns,' he said approaching Wolflang and doing his tribal handshake to say goodbye. 'I thank you for not allowing those creatures to burn my hair. It means a lot. Farewell brother... until we meet again.'

Chapter

XLVI

Afeclin followed Zallucien down a long sloped hallway where they came to a dead end.

Looking around there didn't appear to be any doorways just a corner of stone that seemed to go nowhere.

Zallucien knocked on one of the stones.

Rat-tatta-tat- tat-tat-tat-tat

Stone by stone the corner of the wall in front of them disappeared to reveal another hallway beyond.

Zallucien led Afeclin through the bricked hallway a little way and then down an old narrow stairwell that veered to the left. The stone stairs were uneven and off balance and the rocky ceiling was very low. Afeclin found he had to lower his head and tread with care to make it down the staircase without falling. As they moved further into the dark, hollow rocks with short candles stuck into them lit up by themselves along the edge of the wall and began to dim as they passed. It reminded him of the mysterious corridor Typhin and himself had travelled through on their way out of the Alimest Grove only days earlier.

Once they reached the bottom of the long staircase there was a small chamber. On the other side of it was an opening into a large spacious room.

Zallucien stopped just shy of the opening and commanded Afeclin to do the same.

To one side of the opening there was a small shelf that jutted out from the stone wall. On top of the shelf sat a large oval-shaped crystal. The crystal was pure white and from a distance had looked much like a gryphon's egg. Zallucien put his hand around the crystal with a firm grip. At his touch the crystal glowed pink, then blue and then a deep dark purple. It was then that he took his hand off the glowing rock and entered the large room. Afeclin followed close behind.

'I am the only one who can touch the crystal, for anyone else to touch it, it is the kiss of death… that includes you… at least for now.'

'I understand.'

'I have a spell on the crystal and this room. You cannot enter the room without first touching the crystal and only once the crystal turns purple is the spell lifted. As I said you cannot touch the crystal therefore you can never enter this room without me,' Zallucien said with a stern, sharp look at Afeclin that made him want to cringe. 'We are now deep under the remains of Lawry castle. This room is actually the only surviving remnant. What that dark mage did not know was that I felt he was up to something and being the cautious person I am, put a spell on this room. I was in here when the castle blew up… the spell saved myself and this room. Unfortunately I did not know that Daubin had entered the castle above and not having been in the only secure room… well… I needn't tell you again what happened.'

'I see,' said Afeclin not knowing what else to say.

'This is my sorcerer vinderha,' Zallucien said with pride, his arms stretched wide. 'In other words, my sorcery room. It is the room where I study, where I practice and where I invent. Almost all magic I conjure up takes place in this room. Feel free to look around.'

Afeclin was spellbound by the size of the wondrous room. He had not expected to find himself in a room so big under the remains of Lawry Castle.

In the very centre of the room sat a big round stone platform and in the middle of that stood a tall bookstand that was carved with intricate detail in the shape of a gryphon's claw holding a crescent-shaped wooden board.

To the left of the platform was a long wooden workbench that had a single shelf underneath. On the shelf were varying sized pots and containers. Behind the workbench and against the wall were shelves that housed all sorts of bottles and jars full of very interesting items. From what Afeclin could make out there were some jars with body parts of animals, some with fine powders or herbs and there were many, many bottles with all sorts of strange, different coloured liquids inside.

Further along the wall and extending to the doorway, there were cupboards with doors. *I wonder what strange and wonderful things they house?* Afeclin could only imagine. *Maybe larger jars with larger animal parts, monkey heads for instance.* Afeclin stood wondering for a moment and then shaking his head turned his attention to the other side of the room.

In the very corner, close to the doorway they had come through, an old open fireplace was situated. Fresh logs sat on a cast iron grate ready for lighting. On the mantle above the fireplace sat a crafted wooden ship with a bright painted hull and cloth sails.

'You like my ship?' asked Zallucien with interest.

'It is a beauty,' answered Afeclin, captivated by the craft.

'It took me four years to build it,' Zallucien said adding, 'she looks so grand I almost wish I was small enough to sail it. I didn't leave out a single detail… so if we were that small she could be sailed.'

'That's some effort.'

'Yes well, I have had a lot of time on my hands in the past twenty years.'

Clearly you have, Afeclin thought to himself smiling.

Afeclin saw something bright and colourful flicker out of the corner of his eye. He turned to examine it properly. In the middle of the wall was a large oval mirror. However, it did not seem to work like a mirror and when Afeclin stood in front of it, instead of seeing himself he saw the colours swirl through it again.

'Wow,' he exclaimed, 'what is this?'

'It is my window to the world,' said the old man standing closer to the mirror. 'With this I can see any corner of the globe, any town, any river, any sea. I can oversee any war or dispute. It is like looking out a window only I don't just get to look out at my own backyard, I can see anyone's backyard. It keeps me in touch with what is going on around Titania.'

'How does it work? Will it show you anything you ask to see?'

'Well… not quite. It shows me things that are going on around the place… things of interest. The window determines what I will be able to see on any given day. I do not get to choose… but it always shows what happenings are of most importance in the world.'

Afeclin was most intrigued by the mirror and wanted more than anything to see it in action, however he decided he had plenty of time for that and he still had the rest of the marvellous room to explore.

Afeclin turned catching sight of a large thick feather mattress strewn on the floor in the corner. 'Is this where you sleep?'

'Oh no, I have a chamber in the cottage down from your room,' Zallucien answered and then added by way of explanation, 'as you start to do more and more sophisticated spells you will come to see that it is very taxing on your body. There are many incantations that will leave you feeling weak. You will find you will have no energy left and feel the need to rest or even sleep. That is why I keep a mattress handy. There is nothing worse than waking up and finding yourself on the hard stone floor.'

'That does sound awful.'

Behind the mattress was a glass aquarium that covered the wall… that *was* the wall. Hundreds of fish of different colours, shapes and sizes swam about inside. Plants rose up from the bottom and chunks of colourful coral decorated the interior and provided excellent hiding spots for the playful fish.

It was as he was looking through the aquarium that he noticed there was a room on the other side. Looking along the wall he discovered a couple of wooden doors with an elaborate design of dragons carved into them. He ran to them in excitement.

'May I?' he asked the old wizard with one hand on the doorknob ready to open it.

'Be my guest,' Zallucien said bowing his head and waving a hand at the door.

Afeclin turned the knob and opened the door.

He gasped as he stood at the doorway looking around the huge hexagonal room.

It was a library, one like Afeclin had never seen before.

Zallucien joined Afeclin and they walked into the room together.

'Look up!' he said with a finger pointing upwards.

Afeclin looked with astonishment at the winding staircases that led upwards in what appeared to be an underground tower.

There were levels and levels of bookshelves leading all the way to the impossibly high ceiling. The shelves were full with books in all sorts of colours and sizes, organised in neat rows. There were ladders to reach the higher books on each level leaning up against the shelves. The bookshelves appeared to be full but there were also books piled up in neat stacks all over the room. *These must be the ones that do not fit in. Either that or they have been borrowed from their home higher in the tower and have not been returned.*

There were comfortable seats positioned around the room and one small sofa against a half wall that was the only one without a shelf other than the aquarium wall.

In the middle of the room was a large wooden desk which had scrolls rolled out on it held open by pots of ink with feather quills of varying sizes sticking out. On one side of the desk, large books were piled up. On the other, interesting tools lay about. In the very corner next to the tools was a frightening dragon skull that had a piece of coal stuck in one eye socket and an emerald stone in the other. The skull was small, nothing like the size of the dragon's head in his dream.

Afeclin had never been so impressed and he almost couldn't contain his excitement. *I just want to dive into the books and start reading.*

'This room is amazing,' he said, turning around in circles in an attempt to see it all. 'I've never before seen so many books.'

'It's the largest collection in the world,' Zallucien said with pride, 'everything you could want to know about, the history of the world, the Gods, magic, plants, animals, moons, races, you name it. It can be found in these books.'

Afeclin felt his jaw drop. It was evident his education was just beginning.

'Have you read all of these books?'

'I have read most of them… but I continue to read. You may look at me and think I would know just about all there is to know but that is far from the truth; there is always something more to learn.'

Afeclin nodded in agreement.

'You seem eager to begin reading, my young apprentice,' Zallucien observed as Afeclin took a book off one of the many piles on the dusty stone floor and began flicking through the pages with interest.

'Oh, is it that obvious?' Afeclin looked up from the book with a self-conscious grin.

'Do not get me wrong, it is a good thing,' Zallucien assured, 'a love of reading will get you far as a wizard. Wizardry is not all about spells and magic… it is about understanding the universe we live in and working with it. Sometimes by using magic and forces we understand how to evoke and control. Other times a knowledge of how things work is enough to take control. Remember knowledge in itself is power.'

'A knowledge of the history of wizards and the traps that they would set in woodland areas got me and my friends out of an underground safe haven.'

'That is exactly my point,' Zallucien said raising a finger. 'With magic a wizard can get himself out of many situations. But the magic can also leave him worse for wear, requiring days to rest before moving on. Having knowledge of how things work got you out of that haven the way that had been invented all those years ago using the magic that was already there within those walls.'

'Well, I certainly could not have got us out with my own magic.'

'That is why you have come to train with me... is it not?'

'Yes... the kind of training I need now though, unfortunately doesn't come from books.'

'You are right of course, and that is why I am going to start the intense training straight away,' said the old man with a thoughtful nod and a scratch of his beard. 'It is not my usual way. Normally I would require my apprentices to spend their first two years with me reading and learning of the great books in this library before I will train them in the way of the arts. It is perhaps an old-fashioned idea but one that I find of great importance. A worldly knowledge is the key to advancing in wizardry.

You, my dear Afeclin, have spent your youth in reading and discovery and are therefore ready to advance to a higher learning. It is still important that you continue to read but you must do so in your own time. You may never take books from this library. They must be left in this room but instead carry a journal with you and write the things you find important to remember, in it. Also write a journal of your own, of your life and the things that you learn as you learn them. All wizards write journals of their lives. The very top level shelves are full of wizards' journals... an interesting read when you get around to it. They date back to the dawn of our craft.'

Afeclin looked up at the tower trying to see to the very top level. It was a long way up many flights of stairs.

'You have proven to me that your mind and will power are very strong, that will be a great strength to you,' said Zallucien with a serious look on his shrewd face. 'However you have also proven that you care a great deal for those around you and while that sounds like a good thing, unfortunately it will be one of your greatest weaknesses.'

'Caring is a weakness?' Afeclin asked with confusion.

'It is of course,' the old man answered. 'Look at your dream. It is when you care the most that you are off guard, vulnerable... hence why you are killed.'

'That was just a dream though... wasn't it?'

'...No,' said Zallucien bowing his head as if about to deliver some terrible news. 'You had what is known as "Cuthbire's Claw". It is a dream wizards have concerning their death.'

'Cuthbire?'

'Cuthbire was an evil sorcerer that lived four or five hundred years ago, well before my time. In his youth he attempted to fight off a fireball using basic magic but in doing so he was hit and his hand was badly burnt causing it to deform in such a way that it looked kind of like a claw. So outraged by the deformity and uselessness of his hand, he cut it off and replaced it with the talons of a mammoth golden eagle.'

'... But why would a dream be named after some wizard and his clawed hand?'

'In those days, so I am led to believe, if a wizard was to die it was directly or indirectly related to Cuthbire. Most times a wizard's life ended by the claw of Cuthbire slicing through his heart. He became infamous for it and feared because of it.

He was so mighty and so incredibly crafty that no wizard stood a chance against him. It was said that the God Hazifer gave Cuthbire a vile of his own blood to wear around his neck for added protection and strength.'

'I don't understand. What has all that got to do with a dream of your death?'

'I was getting to that,' answered Zallucien with impatience. 'In order to help wizards even have half a chance of defeating Cuthbire, the God Ambroza, father of all gods, gave wizards everywhere a gift of foresight in the form of a dream. A premonition of their own death.'

'But what is the point of it, I mean how did it help defeat him?'

'Think about it. What will you do with the knowledge of your own death?'

'Well, of course I am going to do everything I can to stop it from happening.'

'Precisely, a wizard can have a death dream even years before it is due to happen. He can prepare for that day and if he has prepared well he may be able to change his fate.

As for the name, they are really just death dreams but it was nicknamed Cuthbire's Claw because it was the part of the dream that the wizards feared most, the part where Cuthbire would claw them.'

'Oh I see,' said Afeclin with thought, 'so was it because of a death dream that you decided to put a spell on this room?'

'No, not at all. It was, as I said a feeling I had that I needed to be careful but I obviously was not ever supposed to die by the dark mage's hands… not at that time anyway, I never had a warning about it,' Zallucien said as he wandered over to the small sofa and sat down. 'Truth be told it would have been very useful to have a Cuthbire's claw at that time. I could have prepared myself and my old friend Daubin as well.'

'… But you wouldn't have foreseen his death.'

'No, true but having known exactly what was coming, I could have told him to keep away or gotten rid of the dark mage before he did any damage…' He bowed his head in sombre reflection, 'Truth be told there is a lot of things I could have done… had I… had I but known.'

'How did the dark mage not take into consideration that you may have had a death dream, or as you say, Cuthbire's Claw, about what he was about to do? Surely he would have to consider that you have prepared for the outcome and may still be alive.'

'Actually, I'm not sure that he even knows what one is. I don't remember telling him about them. I don't usually tell apprentices about death dreams unless they actually have one… and he never did… but those who follow Hazifer do not receive the gift of Cuthbire's Claw. It would go against the reason it was intended for, which is to fight the evil of this world.'

'Then how can you have any doubts about me?' asked Afeclin with scorn.

'My dear apprentice, I wasn't sure it was a death dream at first because it is very unusual for one so young and not yet apprenticed to be given such a gift so early in their life. Then, there is the reason that I had no interest in training you… so I was not willing to see it as it really was.'

'Oh.'

'Cuthbire's Claw is perhaps the more depressing of the three gifts of the gods…'

'Three gifts?' interrupted Afeclin.

'Yes of course, one from each of them. You didn't know?'

'No, I did not. What are the other gifts?'

Afeclin sat down in a hard wooden chair opposite the old wizard.

Zallucien sat forward on the sofa. 'There is a greater gift and a lesser gift. The greater gift is given by the God Islaraan. It is a gift of natural power, given at birth to all those with magic in their genes. It lies dormant until such a time as it is needed,' Zallucien said pausing only to readjust his robes. 'The lesser gift is given by the Goddess. It is similar to the greater gift but it is more of a natural ability than a power. It also was given at birth and likewise lies dormant until it is time to use it.

You have seen my natural ability. I am able to see the aura around people and read it to understand more about that person.

The dark mage has the natural ability of hearing. When his name is said he can listen in on the conversation. No matter where he is in the world he can stop what he is doing and focus in on a conversation about himself.'

'Hence, why we cannot mention his name.'

'Mentioning his name would be the worst thing I could do. He would hear my voice and then know that I am alive. His name has not escaped my lips since the day he brought down Lawry Castle and killed my friend.'

'His name is of great importance then. Don't you think you should let me know what it is so that I will not accidentally speak his name without the knowledge that it is, indeed his name. The one I am not supposed to speak?'

Zallucien sat in silence for a few minutes scratching at his long white beard in thought.

'You are right,' he said, pointing a long slender finger at Afeclin. 'There is always a chance that you could announce the name innocently without knowing that it is in fact the name of the dark one. But there is just as much chance if I was to reveal it to you that you would accidentally speak it out loud because the name is in your head. The simple truth is that if the name is not in your mind it will not be on your tongue and if it is not on your tongue, it cannot slip off your lips. Besides there is only one place that you would come across his name and I guarantee that in that day you find it you will also come to realise that it is in fact the dark one being spoken of.'

'I will just know?'

'You will know without a shadow of a doubt,' the old man assured.

'Well, alright then,' Afeclin nodded, then changing the subject added, 'I seem to remember that you have an ability related to lightning. Is that your other gift?'

'It does not surprise me that you would know that,' said Zallucien with a smile. 'You are correct; it is the gift from Islaraan. I have the power to call lightning from the very sky and use its electrical force to my own advantage. I can mould it, shape and control it. A very difficult skill to master if having to learn it. I have seen extraordinarily good wizards die attempting to control lightning. It is a real blessing to be born with the power, I can tell you.

The other good thing about your own gift is that you can use the power for a lot longer before tiring. For instance a learned wizard can control the lightning and can do so for a short time only, whereas I can do it for hours on end before I need to rest.'

'What about the dark mage? What is his other gift?'

'That I do not know. I wish I did. He never discovered it during his time here... not that I know of anyway. If he did, he never told me about it. Of course it would be handy to know exactly what we will be up against in time.'

'How will I ever know what my gifts are?'

'Don't you worry about that. They will reveal themselves in time,' said Zallucien with a kind look. 'In the meantime you might want to try to remember if you had any strange or unusual experiences when you were young. They might provide a clue.'

Afeclin thought for a moment. Flashes of his childhood came to him as he searched his mind for the strange or unusual. He remembered something he had only thought about days before. He could not believe he had forgotten the memory again.

'I did have this one experience that I could not explain,' Afeclin began. Seeing the old wizard's sudden intrigue he continued, 'I almost drowned... but before I managed to lose my life, something happened, and I found myself washed up on the bank alive and with no idea how I came to be there.'

'Interesting,' said Zallucien with a look of curiosity. He pushed himself up out of the sofa and stood up stretching his back as he did so. 'It sounds to me like you may have the power to teleport from one place to another. It has never happened again?'

'No never.'

'We must explore that possibility in your training. If teleportation is your gift we will find out. In the meantime it is getting late. We must go and have ourselves a meal and then retire to our chambers early tonight. Tomorrow we will rise at dawn and you, my young apprentice, will start your training. It will be vigorous and hard work. It will require your mind to be strong as well as your body being fit. The more you strengthen yourself, the more endurance and power you will be able to sustain. As for tonight... let us rest.'

Afeclin took a deep breath as he glanced once more around the large room before following the wizard back to the cottage. He could feel the excitement within him beginning to bubble. There was so much to learn but he knew he had found himself the best master to teach him. This was the moment he had dreamed about as long as he could remember. He wanted so much to share it with his best friends Wolflang and Lenna but they were not there and that was something he needed to get used to. *Perhaps I could write to Lenna and tell her of my progress, after all, if this death dream is correct it predicts the two of us to be together in time.*

'You may not write to anyone and speak of your progress,' Zallucien said as if reading Afeclin's mind. 'It must not get out that I am alive or that I am training you. You may of course write to people but of where you are and what you are doing, you may not.'

'Did you just read my mind?'

'Yes, it is very easy to do,' Zallucien said with a wry smile as they walked up the steps of narrow stone corridor. 'You must learn to put a block on your mind so that it cannot be read so easily. As strong as you have proven your mind to be, it is not nearly as strong as it needs to be because it is untrained. You must learn to control your thoughts to make it stronger otherwise it will become your weakness. If the dark wizard can read what is in your mind you are without power. He will be able to perceive any move you are about to take… making the element of surprise impossible. He will know what you fear and where your weaknesses lie and he will use them to his own advantage. You will be powerless to stop him.'

'There is so much to learn,' said Afeclin with a weary sigh.

'Yes there is, but with a good meal and a full night's sleep, your mind will be well rested and ready to acquire knowledge. Your brain is an organ that must be exercised to become strong. It will certainly be getting well worked here. Most nights you will retire early, exhausted from the day's activity, with your brain aching. You will get used to it of course but it is the only way to learn and certainly the only way I teach.'

The two walked on without speaking. Afeclin could see he would have to put in a painstaking effort to gain favour with the old wizard but that did not deter him in the least; in fact he was even more enthusiastic about the challenge before him and being able to prove himself.

Tomorrow we begin. Tomorrow my life will start. My journey to becoming a Master of the Art. It is but a dream away.

The old wizard looked back at Afeclin once more and gave a dubious smile as if to say, 'Oh really, young apprentice?'

First thing, I must learn to keep my thoughts to myself.

Zallucien seemed to nod in agreement.

Chapter

XLVII

The lawfabex was soft and warm to ride and it did not make Wolflang's backside sore. While he sat on the shearer wolf part of the animal, his hands dug into the warm fur of its bear part, either way it was a comfortable ride.

He had no idea where he was going so he allowed the lawfabex to keep on walking forward through the forest hoping they would come across a tree that appeared to be larger than all the rest.

Then it became too dark to see anything properly.

The moons could not shine their light well enough through the trees and the beast stopped walking altogether. He growled something at Wolflang.

'I think you're right, it's too dark. We should camp here the night,' Wolflang said giving the lawfabex a rub. 'Thank you for the lift my friend.'

Wolflang slid off the back of the large animal and stood beside him.

'You have done a great service for me today,' Wolflang said patting the beast's head. 'You are not indebted to me though, so if you are not here in the morning when I awake, I will understand.'

Wolflang lay down upon the lush grass under a tree and rested his head upon a root that was sticking up out of the ground. To his surprise the lawfabex lay down next to him giving off a cozy warmth.

Wolflang was astounded by how comfortable he now felt with the beast. He supposed it was silly not to keep on his guard with such a large, wild and unpredictable animal but he couldn't help it. There was something about the beast that took away all of Wolflang's fears. He had never felt so safe since he left Tebelligan, even the dark did not bother him so much while in the presence of the lawfabex and he could feel himself drifting into a gentle, harmonious slumber.

His last thought before he closed his eyes was that of wonderment, at how bright the stars were in the forest all of a sudden and how unusual it was that they seemed so close.

Chapter
XLVIII

Finding himself snuggled into a warm, furry coat, Wolflang opened his eyes and looked around. A heavy mist had settled over the forest during the night, which made it hard to see any more than a foot in front of him.

He was still sleepy and since there didn't seem to be anything he could do until the mist cleared he allowed himself to fall back to sleep, snuggling back into the sleeping lawfabex's fur again.

The next time he awoke it was to the sound of a horse's hooves pounding against the grass-covered turf. Wolflang sat up and instinctively reached for his bow and arrows. That was when it occurred to him that along with his own horse, his bag, quiver and bow that he had hung on Abwahnu's saddle when he had rested by the stream were also gone. *Damn!*

In the distance Wolflang could just make out a figure on a horse. As he was not willing to take any more chances on strangers, he searched the ground for something sharp that he could use as a weapon if the need arose.

The best he could find was a large, round and somewhat heavy rock. He picked it up and stood poised ready to throw it, if need be.

Now that the mist had cleared and the sun was up, rays of sunlight streamed through small glades all over the forest. Wolflang watched as the rider rode into a clearing close by.

'Oomall?' he questioned when the rider was close enough to make out.

'Yeah brother,' Oomall answered sliding down one side of the horse and leading him the rest of the way, to where Wolflang now stood. Wolflang recognised the horse immediately.

'You found Abwahnu!' he said happy to see the fine mare again.

'I found her wandering unperturbed not far from the stream where we were abducted. You know I get the feeling she may be deaf,' said Oomall caressing the horse's neck.

'Yes, she is,' said Wolflang feeling ashamed. 'You are the second person to tell me. I never picked up on that fact myself.'

'Well, don't be too hard on yourself,' said Oomall with a grin and then changing the subject added, 'she is one fine mare though.'

Wolflang watched as Oomall rested his head against Abwahnu's and stroked her nose. He seemed to be very fond of the horse, and the horse seemed to enjoy the attention he gave her. She swung her tail, nodded her head and nuzzled him in appreciation. Her nudge was so strong however that she pushed him backwards. As he moved his foot to steady himself he tripped over a large exposed root, falling and landing flat on his back.

'Oof,' Wolflang winced, 'that must have hurt.'

'By all the Gods!' he exclaimed looking up into the sky with a look of amazement on his face.

'What's wrong? Are you hurt?' asked Wolflang with sudden concern.

'No I'm fine,' he answered with a dismissive shake of the head, 'just… look up!'

'What?' asked Wolflang in confusion.

'I said, LOOK… UP!' Oomall repeated pointing up toward the sky.

Oomall's voice resonated in Wolflang's mind as the words the old man in the bar had said flooded back into his mind. "When you find the largest tree… look up." Wolflang looked up to the sky, wondering just what he was going to see. He was, however, unprepared for what his eyes beheld. 'What in Titania?' he exclaimed as he lifted his chin to the sky.

Towering above the trees that immediately surrounded Wolflang and Oomall was the tallest most gigantic tree that the elf had ever seen. It rose far and beyond any of the other trees in the forest and soared amongst the clouds in the sky. Its limbs spanned across the treetops blanketing the sky with foliage.

Wolflang pushed through the shorter, crowded trees that he had slept under during the night keeping his eyes fixed on the enormous tree beyond.

Stepping out of the scrubland, Wolflang entered a small clearing that housed the phenomenal timber.

The shorter trees seemed to surround its base making a thick wall or fence, like soldiers guarding a treasure.

The tree appeared to be taller than that of the palace in Tebelligan and its base, larger than the town square where the elves celebrated every New Moon. His eyes followed the large trunk up into the sky. What was at the very top was more amazing still, for nestled in between the huge boughs of the tree appeared to be a city of sorts.

Wolflang's mouth fell agape as he stood under the humongous tree and looked at the city in awe.

From where he stood he could see buildings going further up into the sky, roads that weaved here, there and everywhere, in and out of branches and little houses that dotted the branches higher up.

Oomall did likewise, squeezing through the army of trees. He entered the clearing with Abwahnu in tow and approached Wolflang, his eyes fixed on the wondrous city above.

'I wonder how one gets up there,' said Oomall.

Leaving Abwahnu to graze, he started to wander around the tree looking for some kind of means of ascending to the top. Wolflang followed close behind.

They walked the perimeter of the tree base and found no clue as to how one made it up to the city in the clouds.

'There must be some way up,' said Wolflang when they had made it back to Abwahnu. 'I mean surely not everyone was just born up there.'

Oomall shrugged his muscular shoulders. 'Maybe visitors are not welcome.'

'Well that can't be true. I mean, the old man at the bar directed me to this location, telling me that I would be able to find Tay Flaigon here,' Wolflang said as he scratched at the dry blood on his neck. 'Surely he meant... up there.'

At that moment the lawfabex pushed out of the scrub and entered the clearing with a stretch and a yawn. Wolflang and an awkward Oomall, who was still less than comfortable with the beast, watched as he shook his massive body and then began to scratch. It seemed the animal was having trouble reaching the itch that was bothering him.

'Maybe you should give him a scratch,' suggested Oomall with a laugh.

Wolflang stood watching the beast wondering whether he should give the lawfabex a hand. Before he could make a move, however, the beast moved to the massive tree and started rubbing his soft body against it. He kept moving and scratching against the tree trying to find the best spot to get the greatest scratch. He found himself a little knot in the wood that he could rub his body against. Moving up and down, wriggling his mass, he seemed to be enjoying his early morning scratch when with great surprise a concealed door in the tree opened all of a sudden. The lawfabex fell backward in shock and bolted behind Wolflang. The elf smiled in amusement and delight.

'There's our way in,' he said looking at Oomall. 'Shall we go and visit this city?'

Oomall thought for a moment and then nodded. 'I am curious to see this place.'

Wolflang was about to walk in through the tree's entry when Oomall called him back.

'Would yer be wanting these brother?' he said heading to Abwahnu and grabbing Wolflang's bag, cloak, bow and quiver.

'What?' he said looking back at his belongings that he had figured were long lost. 'I can't believe all my things were still with Abwahnu. I thought they would have fallen off or something.'

'Actually everything did stay with her except the arrow case, which I found nearby on the ground. I figured it must have been yours, since there was a bow hanging on the saddle. Then there was your cloak which had been laying on the ground where you had been resting on it before we were attacked.'

'Thank you my friend,' Wolflang said as he placed the quiver straps over his shoulders and the bow over his body. He then grabbed his pouch and cloak.

The two walked in the little entrance to the tree, overflowing with curiosity. Through the arched entrance was a small round room with a spiralling wooden staircase carved into the wood of the tree that went up and up as far as the eye could see.

The staircase was interesting in itself as it was carved with all manner of mythical creatures entwined in ivy, that had the look of being wrapped around the banisters. It was a real work of art and craftsmanship. As Wolflang and Oomall ascended the stairs, leading up into the heart of the tree, they were impressed by the sheer work that must have gone into creating the beautiful staircase. It almost felt like a crime to climb them and defile them with their touch. The staircase was lit by the odd hole drilled into the trunk allowing a stream of light to enter in at certain points.

Halfway up Wolflang turned around and looked down. They had come a long way and they were still far from the top. It was a hard and tiring climb.

The lawfabex who had been moaning and growling and pacing at the foot of the staircase had decided that for whatever reason, he and Abwahnu should not be left at the bottom of the tree. After frightening the mare into bolting up the steps of the staircase, he now started to climb the wooden stairs himself, giving Abwahnu the odd pinch with his teeth to encourage her to continue on up to the top.

Wolflang grinned at the strange occurrence as he puffed, trying to catch his breath.

After what felt like an eternity they made it to the final step, which found them inside what appeared to be a small cottage sitting room. The room was rather bare apart from some sparse furniture that looked as if it were designed for nothing more than the purpose of resting one's legs after the long climb.

They opened the door to the cottage and blinked hard as they walked out into the bright sunlight. They stood without speaking, taking it all in as they attempted to catch their breath and recover from the climb. It was like no city either of them had ever seen before.

The large tree limbs had been carved and sanded back to create a smooth road surface that wound its way up, down and around the city. Little shops sat in amongst the boughs, supported by the larger limbs, as did the little houses. Most of the buildings were not all that big but there were a few buildings with two levels nestled in the larger, stronger boughs. The whole city was an engineering masterpiece, each building constructed in such a way and at such a position as to maximise stability.

There was row upon row of houses going as far up the tree as was possible. Rope ladders with little wooden footings were hung where houses were higher or where there were no roads leading to the house's veranda. Little wooden bridges with roped railings were stretched from here to there joining some parts of the tree to others, in some cases linking one house to another.

The houses themselves seemed to be wooden with thatched rooves made from twigs and clay. Some had potted plants and flowers hanging off the windowsills; others were painted with pictures of flowers and trees or artistic symbols. One house, Wolflang noted, had stick figures of each member of the family who lived there, painted on it.

There were people everywhere, out and about, each involved in their business and day-to-day chores. There were people shopping, carrying little baskets with food and groceries. There were neighbours that chatted from the verandas or windows of their houses. There were children who ran about here and there, climbing up ladders playing chasing games with each other. One plump lady swept out her house angering the neighbour below who was being showered in dust.

There was a nice feeling in the city. It was one of peace and tranquillity, of a people living content, enjoying life and not bothered by the turmoil of the world below. In this way he was reminded of Tebelligan.

The door behind Wolflang burst open, hitting him in the back and Abwahnu trotted out onto the road, shaking her mane and whinnying with relief. The lawfabex then strode out of the door in a very casual manner.

There were shrill screams of fear all of a sudden as many of the local people either ran and hid or stood cowering before the strangers.

'He's okay, he won't hurt you,' Wolflang called out to the people after realising what the threat was, 'I promise you... he is with me.'

Wolflang hoped he was right in what he was saying about the creature. He had grown comfortable with the beast and he hoped that he was not putting any of the people at risk by allowing him to stay with them.

For the safety of others and to put his own mind at ease, Wolflang walked with his arm around the beast's hefty neck, keeping himself between others and the lawfabex. He did realise, however, that this was futile and offered no protection if the animal did decide to attack but he noticed that it did seem to make the people more comfortable.

They came to a large post with many arrows pointing different directions. Names or places were scrawled in crude markings on each arrow.

'Fruit and Vegetables, Fresh Fish, Mally Blanc - Seamstress,' Oomall said reading some of the many signs, 'Chezport Inn, Broncos Bar, The Egg Place. Oh look, Recruitment Office... could that be what you are after?'

Wolflang read the sign himself and nodded. 'It would certainly be the best place to start.'

Following the direction of the arrow they walked further down the wooden road. When they came to the end of the road there was another signpost pointing to the right, leading down another limb, or road as it was.

They came to a little grey building with the emblem of a scorpion painted on it.

'Let's try here,' Wolflang said, then leaving Abwahnu standing outside, he opened the door and he, Oomall and the lawfabex entered the building.

The door opened into a small room. As he walked in he noticed a large desk cluttered with many piles of papers and books. There was an empty seat behind the desk and there were a couple of empty seats in front. There were also a few other chairs seated around the room and a smaller table with a jug that had a number of mugs placed in a haphazard fashion around it. The room had a messy look about it as if only a little time earlier there had been many bodies in the space, sitting in the seats and drinking from the mugs. Now it was unoccupied and quiet.

Wolflang looked at Oomall with a baffled expression on his face.

'Maybe we are not in the right place,' suggested Oomall.

'Where were you hoping to be?' came an official voice as a short, stout woman with large, thick spectacles walked out from another room.

She spied the lawfabex and let out a squeal. 'Is he safe?'

'Of course,' said Wolflang with assurance. 'You have nothing to fear.'

The woman seemed less than convinced but carried on despite the presence of the beast.

'Where did you want to be?' she asked again.

'Well, I don't exactly know,' said Wolflang scratching his head, 'but I was looking for a man by the name of Tay Flaigon.'

'Oh, well you do have the right place,' the woman said keeping an official note to her voice. 'Only he isn't here now, he finished up the recruitments earlier and last I saw he was headed for Bronco's Bar. Were you planning on recruiting?'

'Yes, I was… '

'Well, you are a bit late,' she said, her voice devoid of emotion. 'The General conducted his last interviews earlier this morning. You do realise the troops are leaving on the barge later this afternoon?'

'No, I didn't,' Wolflang answered, 'where did you say he had gone? …Bronco's Bar?'

'Yes, but… '

Before she could continue Wolflang ran out of the door, followed by Oomall and the lawfabex.

'We have to hurry. I don't want to miss that barge. Do you remember which way the Bronco's Bar sign directed?'

Oomall thought for a moment.

'This way brother,' Oomall said taking the lead. 'I am sure the sign pointed this way.'

In no time, they came to an open building with what appeared to be a bar inside. A large wooden sign hung on a tree limb above the building with the words Bronco's Bar painted in green and blue script.

'This is it,' said Wolflang pointing at the sign.

There were a couple of wooden steps leading up onto an outside deck that had a roped railing around it. Tables with wooden benches were arranged on the platform.

Wolflang hurried up the steps and then paused to look around. Inside the bar area there were more of the same tables and benches surrounding a semicircular bar which was situated in the middle of the large room. The room and bar was decorated with a nautical theme that seemed out of place high up in a treetop far from the water. Artifacts from shipwrecks were placed around the room; fish netting hung from the ceiling and several small sharks with large, open mouths full of teeth were hung on the walls.

The bar appeared to be deserted apart from a rotund barman standing behind the bar spitting in and wiping some brass tankards.

Oh no I've missed him, thought Wolflang as his heart sank. *He's already gone.*

Just then a man entered the bar from another room in the back with a book in his hand and a cigar hanging out of his mouth. As he hurried past the bar, the barman called out to him.

'Your drink is on the table out there, General.'

The man nodded keeping his steady course. It was then that Wolflang noticed a tankard sitting on the table next to him and the man heading for it.

On reaching the table, the man sat down, placed his cigar in a small stone bowl in the middle of the table and opened up his book, burying his nose in the pages and keeping to himself.

'Excuse me,' said Wolflang coughing to gain attention from the older man. 'Do you happen to know where I can find a man by the name of Tay Flaigon?'

'Who's asking?' was the disinterested reply from the man as he turned a page of his book and continued reading, not bothering to look up at all.

'Well... I am,' answered the elf in a sheepish manner.

The man cast his dark eyes over the top of his book and looked Wolflang up and down.

'Recruitments are over,' he said with a strong, sharp voice and then returned to his book. 'Come back next year.'

The man who was tall, even for a human, sat with his long legs stretched out under the table. He had a mop of dark hair on his head and he twitched his long black moustache on his weathered and scarred face.

He's a giant! the elf thought, feeling a little intimidated.

At that moment the lawfabex began to make a growling sound and rock from side to side on the spot.

'Shhhh!' he hushed the beast sensing that the animal was perhaps hungry again. They had not eaten that morning and Wolflang was feeling hungry also. 'Not much longer now, then we will get something to eat.'

Wolflang turned his attention back to the man. This time the man was looking up at Wolflang with interest.

'I have never seen a bear in the city, let alone a lawfabex of all creatures. Is he your pet?' the man asked concealing a laugh.

'You could say he is my... travel companion,' said Wolflang ignoring the insult. 'He has helped me make it here to find... you. You are Tay Flaigon aren't you?'

'That depends on who is asking. To my friends... yes, I am he but to most I am known as General.'

'Oh...' uttered Wolflang with embarrassment.

Although he had the air and poise of someone of importance, the General looked nothing more than a commoner. Clad in grey slops, similar to that any serf or peasant may be seen in he looked very unassuming.

'I haven't seen an elf since The Great War. Who are you and what are you doing so far from the Tebelligan border?' the General asked as he raised an eyebrow.

'My name is Wolflang O'Mahnus and I have come to join the legion.'

'You wish to become a Scorpion, elf?'

'Yes I do.'

The General leaned forward, slamming the book down on the table as he said in a stern voice. 'Then you need to come back next year because as I said the recruitments are over. Next year you will want to get here on time! Good day.'

The General threw the cigar back into his mouth and puffed away as he picked his book back off the table and thumbed through the pages to find his place again.

'Please General,' Wolflang begged, 'had I known earlier and had I been able to get here any faster... I would have. But it isn't like I have been staying in town and just slept in. I mean we only discovered this place this morning and the first thing we did was look for you. Also, I only met Old Ursidaen yesterday...'

'Old... who?' asked the General with sudden curiosity.

'Ursidaen, he was an old man I met in the bar... didn't I mention that?'

'Ursidaen,' repeated the General shaking his head as he appeared lost in thought, 'that old coot still around?'

'Yes, and he directed me to come here, to find you.'

The General eyed Wolflang with an intense interest. He looked him up and down again, twirling his moustache in contemplation as he sucked on his cigar.

'For him to put you on the path to find me is... interesting to say the least. He wouldn't have done that unless he had seen something... extraordinary in you,' the General stated.

'Well, I don't know about that. I only met him yesterday.'

'Indeed,' the General uttered with a smirk and then asked, pointing with his cigar, 'are you any good with that bow?'

'Yes, excellent,' Wolflang stated with simplicity.

Oomall let out a little snigger at Wolflang's no-nonsense approach.

Wolflang turning to Oomall was unperturbed and added with honesty, 'Well I am.'

'No, no... I like it,' said the General as if settling some dispute. 'He knows what he is and where his strengths lie. Confidence is a key element to a Scorpion's success. We teach it adamantly.'

The General then set his eyes on Oomall as if seeing him for the first time.

'What about you?' he questioned eyeing the half naked, dark man intently. 'Have you come to join too?'

'...Yes...' he answered, 'yes I have.'

Wolflang shot a look at Oomall and smiled, nodding his head. Oomall smiled back.

'What is your experience?' asked the General with a shrewd look.

'I am, by trade, a hunter,' Oomall replied with unease. 'I am able to spear moving targets from a distance...'

'He was also a warrior of his tribe!' Wolflang added giving Oomall a wink.

The General leaned back. Stretching out his legs again, he chewed on the end of the cigar and appeared to look at the sky. He drew a deep puff as Wolflang stood anxiously awaiting an answer.

'Alright,' the General said, 'I will overlook your tardiness this time but I warn you, if either of you breathe a word of this to anyone...'

'There's no reason anyone needs to know about this, General,' Oomall interrupted, sensing the General's concern.

'Good, then that's that,' said the General thumbing the pages of his book. 'We meet, 1900 hours at the pier. Make sure you are packed and ready to leave, we won't be coming back. Bring your horses with you... you both have horses, don't you?'

The General's eyes fell on the chestnut mare standing at the bottom of the steps.

'Well... actually...' Oomall started.

'Well actually,' Wolflang interjected as an idea sprang into his mind, 'the horse belongs to Oomall. I myself have a lawfabex.'

Wolflang pointed at the beast as if presenting him for the first time.

The General puffed hard on his cigar and nodded.

'You know, it's not the craziest idea I've ever heard,' the General said with a laugh. 'The fact is one of the biggest legends and greatest freedom fighters we ever had in the Scorpius legion was Attandu. Of course I was just a boy back then, but I remember hearing all the gossip on the street as word got around about his heroism and bravery. Back then the artist representations showed him riding a bear into battle and that became part of the legend... Attandu and his bear. But once I joined the legion as a young man, I finally got the real story; he was not riding a bear at all but a more superior animal... a lawfabex, much like your friend there.

You will have big shoes to fill, elf. Riding the beast will cause many to judge you at Attandu's level. Unfairly so but on the other hand a lawfabex is quite a deadly weapon in itself and will, I've no doubt, help protect you.'

Wolflang looked to the lawfabex hoping that he was making the right decision in taking him on as a companion. The thing was, every time he looked into the beast's eyes, he felt safe and secure. Why he should feel that way about such a ferocious animal, he couldn't understand but this time was no different. When he looked into the lawfabex's eyes, they seemed to talk back to him. 'Don't worry... I won't let you down,' they seemed to say.

'Well then,' the General said after gulping down the last of his brew, 'I have things to prepare myself before we leave.'

'Of course General,' said Wolflang.

Rising to his feet, the General picked up his book and placed it under one arm, he then stubbed his cigar into the small stone bowl after taking one last, long and harmonious puff.

'I'll see to it that you get some uniforms. We can't have you drifting about the ship... undressed,' the General said taking a step toward the two, his eyes fixed on Oomall.

Oomall nodded looking a little concerned as to what a uniform would entail.

'We will get ourselves ready,' said Wolflang feeling very small standing between Oomall and the General who both towered over him, 'but do you think you might be able to point us in the direction of the pier where we are supposed to be meeting?'

The General looked at the two with a wry smile.

'Straight down this road, behind us,' he said motioning toward a tree branch road that wound behind the bar, 'and I would get cleaned up while you are at it, you look like you have already been in a war.'

With that the General walked down the steps. Wolflang scratched at the crusted blood on his face as he watched the General pass the lawfabex with caution and wander off down the road in the direction Wolflang and Oomall had come from.

'I'm glad you decided to join up with me,' said Wolflang with a smile as they watched the lanky, broad-shouldered man walking away.

'After what happened last evening, I decided that it would better to fight the demons of this world than ignore them and pretend it has nothing to do with me. The truth that I realised was that I add no value to this world in any way, shape or form by wandering the lands like a lost sheep. The past is in the past. It is now time to create a destiny for ourselves brother, and one that serves the country for good has much value.'

Oomall looked down at what he was wearing. Wolflang laughed as he watched the dark man tug at his loincloth.

'I'm not sure how I will go wearing material on my skin though. I have never worn anything much more than this cloth before.'

'Oh, you'll learn to like it,' Wolflang said amused at the thought of the dark man wearing a uniform that was as different to him in a cultural and significant way as his tribal upbringing was to Wolflang. 'After all, you are a part of this world now, you can't go back to your tribe.'

'You're right brother,' Oomall said clasping Wolflang's shoulder in friendship. 'Shall we go and sort out these uniforms then?'

Wolflang nodded, 'Yes, we must, but first let us get ourselves something to eat while we're here, I'm famished.'

As they started to walk back up the steps of Bronco's Bar, Wolflang hesitated, 'I hope you understood that when I said the horse was yours, I meant it. I make a gift of her to you, I know you will take care of her.'

Oomall looked taken aback.

'I can't take her from you.'

'Yes you can and you will. I feel she is better off with you anyway.'

'I don't see that I deserve it but if you insist, brother,' Oomall conceded.

Chapter

XLIX

After a brief stop in Bronco's Bar for a bite to eat, Wolflang and Oomall had been met at the door of the recruitment office by a soldier who had been requested to fit the newcomers with uniforms.

While he wriggled a bit during the fitting, Oomall was the easiest of the two to fit. Wolflang on the other hand caused much difficulty to the helpers, as his elvin frame was just too small to fit even the smallest size uniform they had available.

With one soldier measuring the elf and cutting pieces of material from a small sized uniform, another soldier on hand at the office stitched the pieces back together with much haste. The results were a custom made uniform that fit the elf to perfection. The two had left the office fully uniformed, looking and feeling somewhat like soldiers.

The uniform was a little uncomfortable at first. It wasn't all that different from what Wolflang was used to wearing but there was more material to it. His brown leather vest was replaced with a dark blue vest made of walrus hide, which was known for its thickness. The vest was tied together at the front with cord in a very similar fashion as his own. The biggest difference apart from the weight of the new vest was that he now was required to wear a white, long-sleeved shirt under it. He had never worn sleeves before. Tebelligan was in the North where it was warm to hot for most of the year. In the cooler months Wolflang would wear his cloak when he felt the need for warmth, therefore there had never been any need or want for too many clothes. He felt restricted and he pulled at the shirtsleeves in irritation.

The rest of the uniform was comfortable enough. Black pants that went to his calves with a red scorpion stitched into the fabric on the leg and black leather boots were strange for the elf but not uncomfortable. The boots like the shirt were a lot more confining than his usual cloth shoes. He also wore a long red sash, symbolic of the red scorpion, around his waist.

Over all of this they wore a short, dark blue, leather hooded cape that wrapped around their shoulders and covered their arms. On the inside of the hood a black mask was sewn onto the fabric so that when the hood was covering one's head, a mask was also covering the eyes and nose. The red scorpion was also sewn into the front of the hood above the temple.

Wolflang sympathised with Oomall. If Wolflang could feel a little uncomfortable with the few changes he had to make then Oomall must have felt like a fish out of water in the entire getup.

Oomall did pull at the clothes and adjust them a fair bit but he never complained about feeling uncomfortable or strange, though it was evident he felt it.

Now they walked toward the pier in the direction the General had pointed to them.

The only piers that Wolflang had ever seen went out over water and allowed one to walk from dry land to a boat without getting wet. As they were far from any water and many kitra above the ground, Wolflang couldn't imagine what kind of pier they were headed for.

The little road behind Bronco's Bar wound around through what looked like a row of trees but was in actual fact a lot of smaller branches growing upward off the main tree's branch. The road, or branch, then went out straight, passing the rest of the tree branches. It didn't look like much. While it did have the straight look of a pier, it didn't appear to go anywhere of interest just further into sky.

Further up the road and past the row of trees to one side, the huge branch forked. There, a large platform where many men and a few women all in the same uniform stood around waiting. There were also a number of horses standing by and in one corner a sizeable collection of crates were piled up.

'I wonder what we are waiting for?' said Oomall as they walked up the couple of steps leading onto the platform.

'I don't know,' whispered Wolflang looking around at the crowd who had been preoccupied with each other but now all stared at them, the newcomers. 'They said we would be taking a boat. Perhaps there is somewhere down from here to the ground, where a boat lies waiting on the coast?'

As usual the lawfabex caused much commotion amongst the people waiting. Worried looks and pointing directed at the beast was nothing this time, compared to those soldiers that drew their weapons as a precaution.

'There's nothing to fear,' said Wolflang addressing the crowd, 'he's with me and he will not try to hurt you.'

'Don't talk to us, elf, as if we're scared of that animal,' said one oversized human with hulking muscles. 'I could kill that lawfabex with my bare hands, just let him try something.'

'Hey, brother, there's no need to hurt anyone,' said Oomall trying to calm the enormous man, 'the lawfabex is no threat.'

'I ain't your brother, darky,' the man growled in anger. 'You'll keep out of this if you know what's good for you.'

'Look I wasn't trying to insinuate that you were afraid of the lawfabex. I mean it's quite reasonable for one to fear such an animal but I wasn't trying to suggest that you would be one of those... people,' said Wolflang, feeling like he was digging a hole for himself the more he spoke.

The man, who was now looking down at the elf, sniffed the air indignantly.

'I can't believe the kinds of soldiers they take nowadays... a pea-sized elf and a lanky black man,' he said then added with sarcasm, 'just what the legion needs. They really scraped the bottom of the ocean this year.'

The man let out an obnoxious snigger as he looked around at the crowd in search of support.

'Did you come off the bottom of that same ocean?' questioned Wolflang with cheek, unable to resist retaliation.

The comment enraged the man.

'You'll pay for talking to me that way!' he growled swinging a fist in Wolflang's direction.

Wolflang ducked, the strike missing him with ease.

The man looked down at Wolflang with enormous ire.

'Just leave him be, Borrandi,' came a voice of another large man from behind. 'He is just an elf, after all. He's not worth the trouble.'

Borrandi glared at Wolflang with disdain. 'Yeah, you're right Moranton, he isn't worth my trouble. But I will be watching you elf... you and your pet will keep away from me, if you know what's good for ya!'

Wolflang stood watching the two men laugh and joke amongst themselves, infuriating him.

Oomall put a hand on Wolflang's shoulder, 'Don't worry about it, brother.'

'I don't know how you can ignore them,' said Wolflang with annoyance, 'they were just as insulting to you!'

'How is it insulting to call me darky?' asked Oomall in a passive voice. 'I am dark. There's no way around it. I just don't find it very clever to point out the obvious. I put that down to one's intelligence.'

Wolflang turned away from the mocking men and patted the lawfabex.

'We'll just ignore those two buffoons, won't we Bear?'

'Bear?' questioned Oomall. 'You named the lawfabex... Bear?'

'Well, it's not very original I'll grant you but it suits and it's better than no name at all,' said Wolflang in defence. 'I didn't even get around to naming your horse, someone else had to, I kind of forgot all about the naming thing and it never got done.'

'Well it is easy to remember,' Oomall replied with a smile. 'Whoa! What in the name of the gods is that?'

Wolflang watched as Oomall's jaw dropped then turned to see what the fuss was about.

A large ship materialised from the clouds and was sailing on the white tufts that blanketed the sky. It drifted in slow motion toward the pier much to Wolflang and Oomall's surprise and amazement.

It was an interesting craft, a large wooden vessel with ornate carvings on the hull. No finer ship had he ever witnessed on the sea, however, it was not without its differences. For a start, it did not have great masts that held majestic sails for gathering the wind and pushing the ship forward. This ship had four short masts that had long rounded flat tops that held and supported an enormous balloon. Large belt straps that came up from the masts held the balloon in place. The balloon was the shape of a long fat sausage and seemed to be made of a very strong material.

From where Wolflang stood watching the colossal ship manoeuvring around the tree, he could see that there was a fire lit in a pit under the middle of the balloon. Heat from the fire coursed up into the massive balloon via a hole in its lining above the fire pit. A crewman seemed to be manipulating the fire's heat, which made the vessel drift higher or lower depending on the amount of hot air allowed to enter the balloon.

On the side of the ship was scripted the name, Seadove in large, black lettering and high up on the balloon, a large colourful bird was depicted.

Protruding from the back and sides of the ship were large propellers that spun rapidly. As the vessel approached the pier, the propellers started to slow down almost to a stop and large ropes were thrown down to those waiting on the pier to catch them.

Those on the pier held the craft in place as the ship came to a complete stop with a loud thud as the vessel knocked against the tree. They then tied the thick ropes to short, broad branches that came off the side of the pier.

The pier became busy with preparations for the ship to leave. A loud blast from a horn was heard, filling the air and vibrating the tree. There were calls from people everywhere on and off the boat giving orders.

'LOWER THE PLATFORM!', 'CHECK THE PROPELLER BLADES!', 'UNLOAD THE CARGO!', 'STAND CLEAR, STAND CLEAR!', 'LOAD 'ER UP!' were just some of the many orders flying about. It was a wonder that anyone could follow them but sure enough the crew worked with diligence and followed the demands without question.

Watching over them from on top of the deck was the captain of the sterling craft. He stood silent, not hollering any demands, just overseeing the crew's work. Wearing a magnificent emerald green uniform he stood straight with his arms bent behind his back and his nose in the air with great pride.

'WHAT ARE YOU DIMWITS STANDING AROUND FER? HELP LOAD 'EM UP!' hollered a small plump man directed at a horrified Borrandi and Moranton who happened to be standing in front of the large crates waiting to be loaded onto the ship.

The two men obeyed with obvious resent. Picking up one of the large crates and hoisting it onto their shoulders they grumbled as they walked the heavy box onto the ship. Wolflang couldn't help but laugh.

Once the ship was loaded a tuneful trumpet sounded causing everyone to stop still and look to the vessel. Most people stood with their heads bowed and a hand over their heart as three coffins were brought down off the ship by uniformed crew members.

Family members of the deceased persons rushed to the caskets in tears and sadness. They followed the crew carrying their loved ones down the road.

'That could be us,' Wolflang observed feeling a heavy knot in his throat.

'Nahh!' said Oomall, 'not us brother.'

'BROTHERS, SISTERS, COUNTRYMEN!' came a loud voice from the top of the gangplank. Wolflang and Oomall turned to see General Flaigon, now uniformed in the familiar black ensemble with red trimmings. This time he looked every bit the part of a General with the noticeable differences in his uniform that set him apart from the troops. He wore a black jacket with red cuffs and thick, red bands on the sleeves, a large, dark blue tricorne hat that was adorned with silver ribbing, ostrich plumes and the red scorpion embroidered on one side. Around his waist a thick red sash decorated with many black stripes gave the General a look of great importance and worthiness.

A roaring cheer exploded from the crowd. The General nodded in humble appreciation, then raised a hand to hush the troops as he attempted to address them.

'Today we become united in a common cause. We no longer belong to different races, titles or creeds. We are brothers in arms, or sisters as the case may be. We work together to build up the Scorpius Legion to become a strong, infallible family. Yes, I said family! Look about you, all of you here are a family and as such must look out for each other... remember the Scorpius code of honour, our Vahdeo in the ancient language, the code we live by... we never leave a man behind. One in, all in. We arrive together and we leave together. We die by our code if it comes to that but we never forsake our brothers unto the enemy.' The General paused and the crowd cheered.

Wolflang looked out the corner of his eyes and saw Borrandi glaring at him.

'I think my brother doesn't like me very much,' commented Wolflang with a hushed voice.

'When you get on board this ship you are to consider yourselves Scorpions and uphold that name with pride,' the General continued after the noise from the crowd subsided. 'Many a good man has gone before you in that same uniform and defended this country and defended the people or died trying. You have a legacy to uphold and continue.

If there is any fighting amongst any of you, you're out! If you set out to ridicule or defame any of your brothers, you're out! If you're not up to the training and fail to get any of your stripes, which will be added to your sash… you are out! Do I make myself clear?' The General stood in silence for a moment as a hum of agreeable sound filled the air. 'Good, now you should all say goodbye to your loved ones who you won't be seeing for another three years and you can come aboard.'

Another great cheer went up for the General who waved at the crowd before retreating into the ship. It seemed he was popular with the people.

Wolflang looked around at the many wives and children now gathered around saying their tearful goodbyes. How he wished Lenna could have been there to say a proper farewell to him. He shook his head and walked toward the ship. His heart raced with excitement for what lay ahead.

When everyone was safe on board the unusual ship, the horn sounded and the ropes holding her to the pier were released. The massive vessel moved away with great ease and, catching a breeze, floated toward the North Island.

As Wolflang looked back he could still see the great crowd of friends and family waving and blowing tearful kisses.

From this angle the great city appeared to hover on top of the clouds as if it were a city in the sky. It soon became covered in clouds and disappeared from view as the ship descended out of the bright azure sky.

After about an hour of slow decline, Wolflang watched as the waters of the Northern Sea inched closer to the vessel. Their course became so fast and steady that he thought they were going to crash right into the rushing current. Wolflang gripped the railings unable to take his eyes off the nearing waters below. The ship landed with a soft splash on the sea and with little disturbance began to sail over the Northern waters. The crew worked tirelessly as the balloon was deflated and folded away. Taller masts rose up out of the shorter ones and fine sails were hoisted into the sky. Catching the breeze the ship surged forward and picked up speed.

Looking back, Wolflang could see the main island coast of Titania. He could make out what appeared to be the Dewby Forest but he could not tell where the tree city stood, as that area of the woods was now blanketed in cloud. His eyes searched the coast wishing he could see some sign of Tebelligan but they were too far south from the elvin land. As they sailed the sun set behind them, lighting the sky with an array of warm red colour. Wolflang let out a little sigh and in silence bid his homeland goodbye. Then he turned to face the direction they were headed in and with his heart full of hope and his mind racing with anticipation he focused his attention on the future that lay ahead, one that was at long last, beginning.

Chapter

£

Sleeping in peace after her first full day as a slave, Lenna had melted into the soft mattress of her bed. While the work was tiring and she felt she had to keep constantly occupied in her tasks, she was ever grateful to be no longer travelling in the wagon, away from the trolls and out of Nagrin's clutches. While her new situation was not the most ideal and she was far away from Tebelligan's borders, she had seen first hand how much worse it could be and was, ever thankful that she was safe in Zurrid. The thought of being a slave sickened her to the stomach however, so she did not look at herself in that way... *I am simply an elf who works in an inn. There is nothing wrong with that... it is my choice.* The more she tried to convince herself of it however, the harder time she had believing it. *I am just not free to leave, that's all.*

The evening service had gone better than the previous night where she had muddled up orders and ruffled the cook's feathers. This night she had felt more comfortable as she served food and drinks to the paying customers, some who were lodging for the night and others who were only there for a meal.

Just as Briale had predicted, Lenna was very popular. The humans were fascinated by her, the men ogled her and the ladies asked her all sorts of strange questions. Lenna found herself being very chatty with some of the nicer people. However, she had to be careful not to be caught talking, as every now and then she would get an earful from Madam, reminding her of the fact that she was nothing more than a slave who had work to do.

She had also found being an elf very useful. Early in the evening she had tripped carrying two large pitchers of ale. The brew had spilled and soaked a little balding man who had been most irate and had yelled at her in a language that she could not understand. As Lenna attempted to pardon herself and clean up, the man had noticed her elvin features. Within an instant he was apologising to her for his brazen outburst and helped her clean up the mess.

While the night had been tiresome and busy with the inn's lounge and dining area packed with guests of differing races, Lenna had managed to work the room with very few incidents considering she had never done such work before. Sarvina however, looked to be in her element. She seemed very comfortable serving people. She even showed Lenna how to hold her tray the correct way, take drinks on and off the tray and move through the crowded inn without spilling anything. For the first time since she had met the girl, Sarvina did not seem afraid.

The last thing they were required to do before retiring for the night was to collect the guests' bedpans and empty the contents, cleaning them and returning them to each room. Lenna found it to be an unsavoury job she had been quite disgusted by.

She had been pleased to fall into the bed at the end of the day.

Now, in the early midnight hours there came a rapping at the door and Lenna was all of a sudden startled awake. Sitting up in a daze she tried to make sense of what was going on.

As her eyes adjusted to being awake, she shook the grogginess from her head. Lenna then glanced over to Sarvina's bed.

In the blue-green glow through the little window of their chamber, Lenna could see that the covers had been pulled back and where Sarvina had lain when the two had retired for the evening, there was nothing more than crumpled sheets.

'Sarvina?' Lenna said shaking her head again and rubbing her eyes to see if it made any difference to the situation.

The knock came again, only a little louder this time and was followed by a whispering through the door.

'Lenna, Lenna… can I come in?'

Lenna recognised the voice to be Briale's and ran to the door to open it.

Briale was dressed in a robe and night hat and she held a small candlestick that she waved in front of Lenna.

'Sarvina's missing,' Briale announced in a whisper.

Lenna stared at her in confusion.

'Yeah, she's not in her bed but how did you know?' Lenna asked with fear rising in her throat.

Briale grabbed Lenna's hand and started pulling her out of the room.

'I will explain on the way,' she whispered, bringing a finger up to her mouth to signal silence as they made their way past Madam's bedchamber.

Lenna nodded gathering up her oversized nightshirt, to prevent her tripping.

Once they had snuck around the balcony and slunk down the stairs Briale opened the front door and Lenna could feel a biting wind hiss through the entrance.

Briale's candle, their light source perished and they were left with only the pale light from the moons to guide their path.

'Sarvina came down the stairs and entered the kitchen, frightening the life out of Tesletta, who was finishing up for the night. Tesletta, while not fond of people in her kitchen at the best of times, hates to be surprised and screamed at the poor girl who then ran away,' Briale explained in a rush of words.

'Oh my goodness, I hope she is alright,' said Lenna with growing unease. 'She does frighten easily. What on Titania could have possessed her to go down there in the first place?'

'Tesletta felt, as an afterthought, that she may have been sleepwalking. Is that possible?' Briale said as the two wandered down a stone walkway that took them to the back side of the inn.

'I have not known her all that long and I have never seen her do that before but I suppose it is possible and would make more sense to me than her just up and leaving the room for the sake of it,' answered Lenna with thought.

'I just hope we can track her down before Madam finds out,' said Briale with evident concern for Sarvina.

Lenna appreciated Briale's kindness but wondered why she cared at all.

'Why do you care Briale? I mean, no one else has shown us lowly slaves anything but disregard. What does it matter to you,' Lenna asked with scepticism.

Briale stopped dead in her tracks. 'Slaves!' she cursed with irritation. 'It's all so archaic. It was archaic when my grandparents fled their homeland to be freed from slavery and it's archaic now!'

Lenna was taken aback by Briale's outburst but was reassured by her passion.

'No woman, man, child, elf or whatever should ever be a slave,' Briale continued her rant, 'but while I do not agree with having slaves work under me, I don't have a choice in the matter. When we are alone I will treat you like equals and when Madam is around I will have to treat you otherwise... but I don't like it.'

Lenna appreciated having Briale on side, even if it was only behind closed doors; just knowing she was someone that would watch out for them and help when she could, made Lenna feel like she and Sarvina were not alone.

They walked further down the dark path that took them up a small incline and over a little hill. On the other side of the hill was a park with trees surrounding a lush open area. A narrow tapered entryway provided a walkway through the trees to where wooden benches were placed around about the space creating a relaxing reserve to sit in.

The two wandered through the dusky trees, their bare feet squelching in the dewy grass. Lenna held her arms tight fighting the wind that whistled through the grove and drifted up her nightshirt.

As they neared the first carved bench, Lenna spotted something white, laying beside another bench to the right of them.

Lenna ran toward it without hesitation.

'Lenna, wait!' Briale called after her with fear in her voice. 'Be careful!'

She fell to her knees as she approached the bench but then reeled back in horror as she realised what it was that lay there.

'Urggg!' she groaned as she pulled away from a tuft of soft fur.

Lying in the grass with its back against the wood, stomach ripped open and bits of innards splayed out all over its body was an animal that looked as if it had a large bite taken out of it.

'What is it?' questioned Lenna as she covered her mouth in shock, feeling a queasiness rise through her body.

Holding her robes in one hand and her windswept hair in another, Briale stepped closer to the animal and while leaning over it, attempted to examine it under the low light of the moons.

'It's a Hawazi llama. They inhabit the prairies in Western Marrapassa,' Briale answered, her voice lacking any emotion. 'It looks like something has tried to eat it.'

'Yes it does,' Lenna ventured, keeping back behind Briale, 'but whatever it was that took the bite, didn't seem to like it and spat it right back out again. What could have done such a thing?'

'I don't know, but it was something big judging by the size of the hole,' Briale stated pointing to the llama's open belly.

'Do you think it is still in the vicinity?' Lenna's voice quivered as a cold chill shot down her spine.

Briale stood up and took a few uneasy steps backward. 'I don't know but I don't think we should wait around to find out either.'

The taller woman turned around and started to flee from the reserve in fear.

Lenna stood watching Briale run back through the trees as her own fear paralysed her to the point that she could not move.

Now Lenna could hear all sorts of strange and unholy sounds in the dark that chilled her to the bone.

Briale stopped and looked back at the frightened elf then called back to her in a loud whisper.

'Come on Lenna! We don't want to stay here if there is a wild beast on the prowl tonight.'

'W... w... what ab... b... bout Sssarvina?' Lenna asked with the stillness of a statue, only her eyes seemed to be able to function. Moving them wildly from left to right, she kept checking her surroundings.

A sudden shriek in the distance awoke Lenna's senses further and in an instant she was hearing everything in that small section of woods, loud and sharp.

The wind moving the grass, crickets chirping, a disgruntled screech of a night bird and another howling shriek that sounded closer than before resonated in Lenna's pointy ears. Even the sound of her heart beating in her chest seemed loud and overbearing.

Briale, having seen Lenna's trauma, trundled back and grabbed her by the hand, pulling her back towards the inn.

'I sure hope nothing's happened to her but, we can't stay here and keep searching. Who knows what's out there.'

The sudden sharp pull from Briale was just what Lenna needed to spur her legs forward, and the two ran as fast as they could back up the hill and down the walkway to the gloomy inn.

When the two made it back inside, they each breathed a sigh of relief and attempted to catch their breath.

They crept back up the stairs and said a brief goodnight at Briale's room.

'Good luck, I hope Madam is not too cruel to you tomorrow,' Briale said with sadness as she closed the door.

Lenna had forgotten all about what Madam had said the day before, but she was not worried about what would happen to her if Sarvina was not found. She was not even concerned about what Nagrin would do to her when he discovered that Lenna had not looked after his precious Sarvina. Her only thought was for her friend. She feared what may have become of her.

The dead llama had only just been killed. Therefore whatever beast did bite into it may have been still lurking around, *or maybe it had been startled by Sarvina when she ran out there and...*

She inhaled in fear, then shook her head vigorously, dispelling the awful thoughts she did not want to entertain.

Lenna walked into the room with a dismal sigh, not knowing what more she could do for her friend.

As she closed the door behind her and walked toward her bed by the far wall, she caught movement out of the corner of her eye.

The movement had come from Sarvina's mattress. Lenna's heart skipped a beat as she moved in closer to the bed to take a look.

There laying under the covers was a very bloodied Sarvina, sound asleep.

'Oh my, Sarvina, what happened to you?' Lenna whispered to the girl who did not stir from her slumber. 'I will get something to clean and dress your wounds.'

Lenna ran to the tub room across the way. Taking some cloth and a bar of soap, she hurried back to the room with a bucket, half full of water.

As Lenna cleaned all the blood off Sarvina and examined her for wounds, the blonde woman slept without stirring.

Sarvina had blood on her face, through her hair, on her fingers and smeared all over her gown but none of it seemed to be oozing from her body. She had no cuts or grazes let alone open wounds. The blood that was covering her was not her own.

Lenna pulled away from Sarvina's bed and stared at the sleeping girl with incomprehension.

'Whatever happened to you?' she asked in a soft inaudible voice.

At that moment Sarvina turned onto her side and huddled into the feather pillow. As she did her mouth dropped open and as she began to breathe deeply, a trickle of blood dripped from her mouth, staining the pillow.

Lenna sat closer for a better look and was shocked by the amount of blood that flooded Sarvina's gums. Even stranger, were the sight of her teeth, which were longer and pointier than they had been before. It was like she had two sets of bloodied fangs.

Lenna sat back onto her own bed with her head in her hands staring in bewilderment, trying to wrap her mind around what had gone on that evening.

'Oh Sarvina,' Lenna said in a mournful but controlled voice, 'what are you?'

❧ ❧ ❧

Lenna had a hard time going back to sleep after her ordeal with Sarvina. She tossed and turned, trying not to think about the strange bloodied fangs the girl possessed, where the blood had come from that she had been draped in, or about the llama that had been bitten by some fearsome creature.

Panic overwhelmed and paralysed her. It dragged up all the fear she had felt since she left Tebelligan until she was overcome by terror.

She had managed to keep herself strong throughout the journey to Zurrid. She had been able to restrict her thoughts to things that would not upset her and she had been able to stick her chin out with pride to fool others into believing she was much stronger than she felt. She had refused to be beaten.

Now that strength she had fought so hard to control was waning. She found herself weeping venerably under her covers thinking about Wolflang and Afeclin and missing them to the point that it hurt.

She surprised herself a little by how much she missed her friend Afeclin, in some ways more than Wolflang.

They had a special kinship and there was a certain safety she felt in his presence. He had always been there for Lenna throughout her entire life. When she had been sad, he had cheered her. When she had been sick, he had comforted her and when she had felt alone or had needed a little understanding, Afeclin was the one who listened and reassured her.

Now when she needed him the most, he was not there… it left her feeling empty, desolate and numb.

Sheer exhaustion caused her to drift off to sleep but her dreams were a mere continuation of her distress and longing.

She dreamed of being back in the wagon among the rest of the slaves. She was robed in the same red, bloodstained silk dress that she had seen the woman in the woods wearing.

Journey of Destiny

She was afraid and in desperate need of her friend Afeclin. She searched for him and called to him through her bitter tears.

'Afeclin! Afeclin! Please come… please help me… I am afraid, I need you! Afeclin! Afeclin!' she called over and over again as loud as her choked voice would carry.

All of a sudden, as if by a miracle, Afeclin materialised from nowhere grabbing her and startling her from her cries. She saw his piercing blue eyes looking into hers with concern and affection.

The disturbed dream shook her and roused her. In her sleepy state she looked around for Afeclin expecting to see him before her; disheartened she realised he was not there at all. It took her a moment or two of confusion to comprehend where she was and that it had all been just a dream. She lay back onto the soft pillow, the tears beginning to fall again. It had all seemed so real… she had seen Afeclin's face and she had reached out for him. But there was no Afeclin this time. He had been nothing more than a shadow who could not be reached.

Chapter

LI

Afeclin tossed and turned in his bed after his first full day of training. His mind ached and his body felt tired and sore.

Zallucien had taken him through exercises that worked on his mental focus. He sharpened his mind-probing ability by talking to the old wizard mentally. He practised inciting energy through his body to create a charge in his finger tips that at first was no more than a spark of electricity. Later on in the day he found he could mould that energy force into a small ball within his hands, if only for the briefest moment.

Being able to relax at the end of a long gruelling day of training, Afeclin found himself restless.

He lay still in the early hours of the morning and managed to drift off into a light sleep only.

His journey to Lawry Castle filled his dreams and haunted his soul. He found himself dreaming about the wagon full of slave girls who they watched pass by them in the Woods of Devan. He saw the face of the scarred man in black and heard a laugh that echoed in the quiet still of the night.

Then he heard something that disturbed him even more, a voice calling out to him in a teary, helpless tone. He felt the sadness that accompanied the soft cry and the fear that made the voice quiver. He found himself searching for the source of the cry. He found himself running through woodland in the dead of the night following the sound of his name and chasing the procession of wagons.

The voice was somehow familiar but distorted through the tears. His heart raced as he tried in vain to reach out to it.

At last, the wagons stopped dead in their tracks and Afeclin was able to catch up to the cavalcade. He ran to the wagon full of girls and searched for the one that called for him by name. In amongst the middle of the slaves knelt the woman in the red dress with her face in her hands and long red locks draping over her.

He went to her with urgency and held out his arms to lift her up. She looked up at him with her big brown eyes…

Afeclin startled awake, heaving his body up in the bed, he called out in shock and surprise.

'LENNA!'

Epilogue

Two large heavy metal framed doors opened and a man dressed in black sauntered into a spacious room with high ceilings and chandeliers that hung down on chains of gold.

He walked with slow and reverent steps along the red-carpeted path that led to a platform which held a gold, jewel encrusted throne. There were three wide steps leading up to the throne and the man in black stopped just shy of the last of these stairs and knelt down on one knee, bowing his head before a stout man who sat on the throne in robes of crimson.

'My Lord,' he uttered, taking his wide rimmed hat off and waiting in that position to be excused.

'Arise and report Nagrin,' came the voice of the one seated. 'What say you of your journey into Marrapassa?'

Nagrin stood before the man and clasping his hat in one hand, he began to present his report.

'I have managed to secure the trolls from the north and south of Grath to fight in your Lordship's army. I have acquired local taverns and inn establishments from Fraida in your old kingdom to Desprade in the high north, to Zurrid in the far west. As requested they are being worked by slave girls collected from all over Marrapassa and overseen by loyal subjects to you.'

'You have done well Nagrin. I trust you were not given too much trouble,' the Lord said with a smile, clasping his ringed fingers together in front of him.

'Nothing that I couldn't handle with a little persuasion,' Nagrin hissed through his teeth with a smirk.

The Lord nodded with a grin, indicating he was pleased.

There was a sudden trumpet sound and a young man in formal courtly apparel of red and blue satin ran up to the Lordship's throne and whispered something into his ear.

The Lord let out a spirited holler, 'Well let him in!'

The large doors opened again and this time a mage in black robes donning a hooded cloak that covered his head and shadowed his eyes marched up the carpeted path with directness.

Behind him walked two taller men clad in metal armour that covered them from their heads to their feet. Between them they carried a large wooden box bound in a hefty iron chain and padlock.

'Lord Moorlan,' the mage said lowering his head in respect without pulling back his hood.

'Alkarrien, you bring me good news I trust?' Moorlan said in a casual and gregarious tone.

'I did your bidding,' the mage responded with a dark raspy voice. 'We traveled to the North Island and made our way to the Swamps of Basca. It was not difficult to find our way into Crymonthon's fort. We managed to catch him off guard, the old fool put up a courageous fight but he was no match for my power...'

'I expected nothing less,' interrupted Moorlan with a deep laugh.

'The old wizard is dead. Zallucien's twin brother Zarome died a few years ago and I am now the only wizard left in the whole of Titania,' the dark mage stated with pride.

'HA! Great news. Things are falling into place very nicely. We have reason to celebrate,' Moorlan said with rapture.

'Yes indeed,' responded the mage without emotion.

'But what of that young wizard you saw in a vision, is he no longer a threat?'

'I sent out Shemalks to pick up on his trail, to find him and bring him back to me so that I may deal with him personally. As yet, they have not managed to find him for they were attacked by a lawfabex and only one of them survived to bring me word. However he was able to obtain some useful information before the attack.'

'Oh?'

'The young wizard was headed for Lawry Castle. He is looking to be trained...'

Moorlan let out a wicked laugh. 'Little good that will do him. He shall be easy to find!'

'Yes, he will; once he finds out about Zallucien, he will no doubt seek out Crymonthon. I have sent out more weasels to wait for him in the Swamps of Basca. It is only a matter of time... but he is no threat, my Lord, to our plans.'

'Good... So what is in the box then?' Moorlan asked as he tussled his long black locks behind his ears..

'It is a gift from Crymonthon himself,' the mage said with a slight smirk on his darkened face as he turned toward the armed men and motioned for them to present the box to Lord Moorlan.

They walked forward and placed the box at the foot of the steps in absolute obedience.

'Crymonthon was given charge to protect this item with his life, which of course he did... no one can take that away from the fool but now it is all ours,' the mage said as he caressed the box with a scarred, weathered hand.

'Well, do not keep me in suspense. Let us see what treasure was so great that Crymonthon should die to protect it,' said Moorlan his impatience brewing.

'Patience my Lord, this will take a moment,' said the mage as he closed his eyes and bowed his head. He then stood focusing his energy with his arms stretched wide. He started to shake but then gripping his hands and tightening his knuckles he regained his control. The pupils of his eyes went fire red and he seemed to be whispering certain words over and over, almost chanting. Then the mage stood straight and shouted the words as he directed all his energy toward the locked box, placing a single hand over it.

'ARUGAAS HARAANA'

The sound of wind and storm filled the interior of the large chamber, the chandeliers rattled and swayed, the edge of the carpet lifted and flapped about and Moorlan and Nagrin's hair waved as if on a breeze, yet there was no breeze to be felt.

Then a whirlwind of air spun on top of the mage's hand and as he let it fall it grew bigger and wider, enveloping the heavy box. Sparks flew as the torrent of air spun the box rapidly as if it were as light as a feather. After a few minutes of twisting and turning, the chest stopped and dropped with gentleness to the floor guided by the wizard's careful hand. When it landed the chain and padlock, no longer attached, simply fell to the ground.

'Now, we may open the box,' rasped the mage inviting with a steady hand.

'Did we really need all of your theatrics to unlock the chest Alkarrien?' Moorlan asked with amusement.

'My Lord this box was not only locked with a chain but it was sealed with spell of death. The spell has not only kept intruders from opening it but has also preserved what is inside.'

'Well, let's open it and see,' said Moorlan as his dark thick eyebrows furrowed.

The mage nodded his head and then moved in front of the box and squatted down before it. Heaving the lid of the chest open, he sat looking at it in awe for a moment before getting up and stepping aside for the Lord to see.

'That's it? An egg?' Moorlan spat looking at the large bluish, silver speckled egg in disappointment.

'This egg has been in a state of sleep due to the spell it was under, now that it has been released from the charm it is free to hatch,' the mage stated.

Moorlan and Nagrin looked at each other with confusion.

'What do I care about a hundred year old egg for? How does that help me plan my war?'

The mage looked at him with subtle arrogance and gave a little smirk under his darkened hood.

'Because my Lord, this is the egg of a golden dragon... the last one of its kind.'

𝔊lossary

Afeclin - Human, raised by Endorf the Elvin King of Tebelligan after his parents were killed at the end of the Human War.

Afeclinella - Goddess of daybreak, purity and innocence. Daughter of Ambroza.

Alga - The Eldest of Endorf's biological sons.

Ambroza - The almighty God, ruler over all and father to the other three Gods of Titania.

Armatto - Elvin word meaning 'greatest friend.'

Astoth - The Green moon that has four rings encircling it, forming an X in the sky.

Attandu - Legend of the Scorpius Legion. Attandu rode into battle on a lawfabex.

Bankoi - Trees with strong trunks and feathered leaves of greens, reds and golds.

Bargran - Wolflang's father.

Blighter rabbit - Rabbits with round plump bodies and long floppy ears.

Blue-Stone Creek - A small creek near Lawry Castle. The rich blue water turns anything that touches it blue.

Bragabell - Enormous trees with huge leaves the shape of watermelons and fat potbelly trunks like large bells.

Bristle bushes - Small leafy bushes with prickly branches that stick out all over it.

Caril - Adopted daughter of Devall and Queen over both Avanleah and Rixsus.

Cuthbire - An evil sorcerer that lived four-five hundred years earlier. One of his hands, having been badly deformed in an accident, was replaced by the talons of a mammoth golden eagle.

Cuthbire's Claw - (Also known as death dreams) a gift from the God Ambroza, a premonition in the form of a dream about a magic users death.

Diroriam - large, dark-green feathered leaves with trunks that twist in and out of each other. Small yellow flowers with a sweet fragrance bloom from the trees in the summer.

Doucla - Titanian currency. Made from gold, silver or bronze and on occasion iron ore which is considered serf's gold. They are medium sized flat coins that are stamped on one or both sides indicating the city they were moulded in by the blacksmith who forged them.

Dracasia - (more commonly known as desert dragon-lizard) - Small, spiky scaled lizards that have tiny wings and can propel themselves into the air to fly short distances.

Eliah - Innkeepers daughter and barmaid in Desprade.

Fleurmire - Large, white, royal looking bird with a rotund body, long neck and a series of dark red and maroon feathers that stick out and up the back of its neck and around its head like a collar.

Fynn - Lenna's father.

Gaandi forest mice - Mice with short round ears and stubby little tails on their round bodies.

Garboa cloth - Strong cloth made from woven goats hair.

Garrad - The youngest of Endorf's biological sons.

Glendell - The blue moon of Titania and largest of the three moons.

Habatchiees - (more commonly known as skunks) A dirty, stinky race of dwarf who inhabit the island Boanga.

Haywood birds - Large scarlet feathered birds with long curved beaks.

Hawazii llama - Mainly found wandering the prairies in Western Marrapassa, the wild hawazii llama is highly prized for its valuable white, black or grey wool, which is luxuriously soft and warm.

Hazifa - God of darkness, evil, loathsomeness and disease. Twin to the God Islaraan.

Hervit leech - A flat-headed, blood sucking sea creature with large teeth and a long tubular tail that it uses to attached itself to its prey.

Islaraan - God of goodness and wholesomeness and twin to the God Hazifa.

Jebinna - Lenna's Mother.

Hoashan - A renowned and respected general who is known to be strict and merciless.

Joba leaf - The thick fragrant leaves from a Joba plant used for smoking in a pipe.

Karalee - Wolflang's departed mother.

King Ravash - The King of Rixsus, before the Human War.

King Devall - The King of Avanleah, before the Human War.

Krus - Raan's small red horse.

Lawfabex - Dark brown, half bear/ half wolf animal. It has a bear's head and front legs with a white/grey hump behind its head. Beyond the hump their body becomes slender with its back and hind more like a wolf. It has a short thick horn in the middle of its forehead and black eyes that turn red when angry.

Lawry Castle - Once the place wizards from all over Titania would come to study and master the art of sorcery under The Great Zallucien's tutelage.

Lenna - Elf maiden and childhood friend to Afeclin. In love with Wolflang.

Lumirths - (more commonly known as spider-flies) Eight legged flies with black and red bodies and tubular mouthes.

Malveen - Code word to wizards, meaning 'place of rest'.

Mammoth golden eagle - The greatest and largest bird of Titania. Its bronze feathers are said to shine like gold in the sun, hence its name. It has sharp black claws and is a most noble looking bird with a black beak, green eyes and massive wingspan.

Matia - Lenna's younger sister.

Miicot spider - Large spider with a blue-green shell-like square back and spindly legs.

Monkey leaf - A black wood tree with dark red heart-shaped leaves. Its root system goes deep into the ground to collect nutrients from far below in the richest part of the soil.

Monkey leaf root - Roots of the monkey leaf tree make their way to the surface once the tree has died. These rotten pieces of root are full of nutrients and are extremely good for the body but have a foul after-taste.

Nali-birds - Black birds with long red tufts of plumage on top of their heads that stick up in the air when singing. They have salmon striped breasts and tiny black beaks.

Oomall - A tribesman warrior and hunter from the west of the Graandis Mountain Range.

Orcal ants - Medium sized, dark green tree ants that have a large sac on their rear containing deadly venom.

Peepinco berries - Long plump black berries with three round segments.

Pitangus - (Pit) Lanky goblin. Companion to Typhin and Raan.

Qwiaquet bugs - Red hopping bugs that have long slender legs and a shrill chirp.

Raabarak - Eliah's father.

Raan - Headstrong dwarf. Companion to Typhin and Pit.

Rausmoth flies - Tiny black flies with red wings that live in the desert sand.

Sataya - Silver moon and smallest of the three moons, where the Gods are said to reside.

Sazamel - Endorf's departed Queen.

Scorpius Legion - Specialised and elite army with codes of honour.

Shemalk - (more commonly known as Weasels) A race of people that live underground. Their faces are long, pointy and hairy. They have small noses with unsightly whiskers that poke out from each side of their faces. Their hands are long and slender with sharp claw-like nails. They move more like animals than people.

Sorcerer vinderha - Sorcery room, a private place a wizard uses to work and create magic.

Spiral muse - Violet and lemon coloured flower with a spiral shaped petal that bounces like a spring and pale green, claw shaped, leaves.

Tay Flaigon - Respected general of the Scorpius Legion.

Traffita - Tall, white, willowy trees with long slender leaves that drape from their trunks.

Tula blossom - Tall, majestic trees that have red and green striped foliage and large, spectacular blooms in the spring.

Typhin - Astute human and leader to companions Pit and Raan.

Vahdeo - Code of honour in the ancient language.

White Ghost Owl - Large white owl with deep blue eyes. Its presence is often heard but rarely seen.

X-zaivacress vine - Vines that wind their way around other trees in the vicinity, filling in the empty spaces between the trees. They have rich green leaves and large deep violet flowers at the end of each arm.

Yaaka horn - Short, fat instrument made from the horn of a yaakum bull.

Zarome - Zallucien's evil twin brother.

Zallucien - Great and renowned sorcerer residing over Lawry Castle.

About the Author

'I was never going to be a writer… seriously.'
Somehow despite Leisl's lifelong love for making up and telling
stories, she had no desire to become an author. However, after a creative
urge spurred her on to write an idea for a scene, the world of Titania was
born and she hasn't looked back since.
Born and raised in Australia she has lived in a variety places,
including the Australian outback and Montreal, Canada. She currently
resides in Kitimat, Northern British Columbia with her husband and four
children; she is studying a degree in Criminology and Criminal Justice,
is an amateur theatre actor and enjoys snowboarding during the winter.

Made in the USA
Monee, IL
09 May 2023